Praise for *All Our Shimmering Skies*

"A work of shimmering originality and energy, with extraordinary characters and a clever, thrilling plot. . . . Unputdownable."

—*Sydney Morning Herald*

"A spellbinding saga of survival and transformation in WWII Australia. . . . This is a wonder." —*Publishers Weekly* (starred review)

"Achingly beautiful and poetic in its melancholy, *All Our Shimmering Skies* is a majestic and riveting tale of curses and the true meaning of treasure."

—*Booklist* (starred review)

"Magical. . . . Goodness, hope, and a bit of magic are pitted against gritty realities. The result is unquestionably appealing."

—*Library Journal*

"Dalton is an author of nineteenth-century expansiveness, one with a sense that intelligence, talent for characterization, and sheer narrative brio can still be the whole cloth of the writer's ambition. . . . It is storytelling manna, fallen straight from the Territorian skies."

—*The Australian*

"The follow-up to *Boy Swallows Universe* we could have never imagined, but the one Dalton was destined to gift us. I⸺ of the Australian Gothic crossed ⸺ ⸺ t's a story of heroes and villains, ⸺ ⸺ ⸺ s and birds of prey, real magic ⸺ ⸺ lost treasure and lost life. It's ⸺ favorite childhood adventure ⸺ ⸺ ⸺ Emily Dickinson, Walt Whitmanm and William Shakespeare, with a score by Franz Liszt. It's dead serious. It's completely ridiculous. It's all of these things and more."

—*Booktopia* (Australia)

Praise for *Boy Swallows Universe*

"Hypnotizes you with wonder, and then hammers you with heartbreak. . . . Eli's remarkably poetic voice and his astonishingly open heart take the day. They enable him to carve out the best of what's possible from the worst of what is, which is the miracle that makes this novel marvelous." —*Washington Post*

"Compelling. . . . In this thrilling novel, Trent Dalton takes us along for the ride." —*New York Times Book Review*

"A splashy, profane, and witty debut." —*USA Today*

"At times *Boy Swallows Universe* will grip your attention and then break your heart. It is a story of love, crime, and hope. It is written with love and told with joy. Trent Dalton is a powerful new voice in fiction." —*Washington Book Review*

"Dalton's splashy, stellar debut makes the typical coming-of-age novel look bland by comparison. . . . In less adept hands, these antics might descend into whimsy, but Dalton's broadly observant eye, ability to temper pathos with humor, and thorough understanding of the mechanics of plot prevent the novel from breaking into sparkling pieces. . . . This is an outstanding debut." —*Publishers Weekly* (starred review)

"A marvelously plot-rich novel, which . . . is filled with beautifully lyric prose. . . . Exceptional." —*Booklist* (starred review)

"A captivating and quirky life story that leads the reader on an intense and rewarding journey; highly recommended." —*Library Journal* (starred review)

"An insightful coming-of-age novel."

—*Book Riot*

"Joyous. Simply joyous. I hugged myself as I read it. My heart raced, swelled, burst; my eyes leaked tears; my stomach ached from laughter. . . . This vibrant, vital, altogether miraculous coming-of-age novel marks the debut of an exquisitely gifted storyteller . . . After reading Trent Dalton's book, you won't be the same."

—A. J. Finn, author of *The Woman in the Window*

"Welcome to the weird and wonderful universe of Trent Dalton, whose first work of fiction is, without exaggeration, the best Australian novel I have read in more than a decade. . . . The last hundred pages of *Boy Swallows Universe* propel you like an express train to a conclusion that is profound and complex and unashamedly commercial. . . . The book is jam-packed with such witty and profound insights into what's wrong and what's right with Australia and the world. . . . I read it in two sittings and immediately want to read it again. . . . A rollicking ride, rich in philosophy, wit, truth, and pathos."

—*Sydney Morning Herald* (Australia)

"A wonderful surprise: sharp as a drawer full of knives in terms of subject matter; unrepentantly joyous in its child's-eye view of the world; the best literary debut in a month of Sundays."

—*The Weekend Australian*

"It is such a pleasant shock to encounter a new Australian novel in which joy is shamelessly deployed. . . . It is a story in thrall to the potential the world holds for lightness, laughter, beauty, forgiveness, redemption, and love. . . . [Dalton] invests this unlikely cast and milieu with considerable energy, wit, and charm. He delights in the play of language and imagination that a child can summon: the sense in which the clear moral eye of youth can critique and adore simultaneously without judgment or adult moral finessing." —*The Australian*

LOLA
IN THE
MIRROR

LOLA
IN THE
MIRROR

TRENT
DALTON

ILLUSTRATIONS BY PAUL HEPPELL

HARPER PERENNIAL

NEW YORK • LONDON • TORONTO • SYDNEY • NEW DELHI • AUCKLAND

HARPER ● PERENNIAL

Originally published in 2023 in Australia by Fourth Estate/HarperCollins.

HarperCollins books may be purchased for educational, business, or sales promotional use. For information, please email the Special Markets Department at SPsales@harpercollins.com.

FIRST HARPER PERENNIAL EDITION PUBLISHED 2024.

Illustrations by Paul Heppell

Library of Congress Cataloging-in-Publication Data has been applied for.

ISBN 978-0-06-341474-7 (pbk.)

24 25 26 27 28 LBC 5 4 3 2 1

For anyone who didn't jump in the river.

And for anyone who did.

Author's note

Many of the events in this novel were inspired by stories told to me by people I met in the streets of my city across seventeen years of social affairs journalism. Some of these events involve violence, addiction and self-harm, which some readers may find distressing. Those same people I met in the street also spoke of community, hope and love, and that's why I wrote this book.

LOLA
IN THE
MIRROR

The Tyrannosaurus Waltz

The Tyrannosaurus Waltz

April 2022

Pen and ink on paper

One of the artist's earliest sketches and also one of her most celebrated, drawn on the night of her seventeenth birthday. The artist was still living with her mother in an orange 1987 Toyota HiAce van with four flat tyres. Note the dinosaur head the artist has placed upon the suited man's body. Little is known of his identity, but common opinion suggests he represents the artist's father. Quite possibly the earliest example of the artist's wildly popular and globally acclaimed Girls on the Lam Period. Completed less than two years before she was shot by the banks of the Brisbane River.

My mother danced the Tyrannosaurus Waltz. It is the dance of mothers and their monsters. The Tyrannosaurus Waltz is traditionally performed in the kitchen of any ordinary home, anywhere in Australia. The dance requires a young mother to hold her baby to her chest and stand before the monster who pretends to love them.

'Please let me go,' says the mother.

'Not with my daughter,' says the monster. 'I will kill you first.'

And then the waltz can begin. Mother leads, monster follows. She takes one step to her left and the monster takes one step to his right to block her. The mother then takes one step to her right and the monster takes one step to his left. And now they are dancing.

Mum says I will never dance the Tyrannosaurus Waltz. 'You will not dance with monsters,' she says. 'But one day you will dance with a prince.'

The Tyrannosaurus Waltz can end in any number of ways, but the most shocking and spectacular way to end the dance requires the mother to take a paring knife from the dish rack beside the kitchen sink and thrust it into the soft flesh beneath the monster's Adam's apple. Mother and baby must then run for their lives. And never stop running.

This is how you dance the Tyrannosaurus Waltz.

Temple + Webster
Mirror propped Against
a Brick Wall in
a West End

Panel Beater's
Scrapyard

Temple & Webster Mirror Propped Against a Brick Wall in a West End Panel Beater's Scrapyard

September 2022

Pen and ink on paper

A haunting, dream-like image and the first illustrated appearance of the artist's famed full-length mirror. The titular 'West End panel beater's scrapyard' refers to the home the artist shared with her mother, an orphaned boy who was her best friend, a former military tank driver, a nurse, the nurse's mute son, and a toothless woman managing an addiction to Pascall Clinkers. Sketched some eighteen months before the artist met her one true love, Danny Collins.

'Mirror, mirror, on the grass, what's my future? What's my past?'

People think magic mirrors are found only in fairytales. I found mine last summer on Lime Street, Highgate Hill, in a Brisbane City Council kerbside collection.

'Mirror, mirror, please don't lie. Tell me who you are. Tell me, who am I?'

My magic mirror was resting on a mouldy ping-pong table beside a Cavendish banana box full of baby dolls with limbs and eyeballs missing. My mirror has a matte-gold frame, arched at the top like the entrance to an Arabian princess's bedroom. The family at 36 Lime dumped the mirror because there was a thick diagonal crack across the middle of it. There was a sales sticker on the back: *Temple & Webster: Amina Arched Mirror, $299*. At first I thought that was a bit much, dropping three avocadoes on some place to look when you're brushing your mop, but now, in the thick of this lilac jacaranda spring of my seventeenth year on earth, I consider this mirror that I stare at in the dawn light – the best light for staring into a magic mirror – the second most valuable thing in my life.

It's all the places I've seen inside it. The pyramids of Egypt. Ornamental gardens in Shanghai. That little bar three blocks from Alexanderplatz in Berlin. That Hindu prayer spot by the banks of the Ganges River. And now this cream pink-sky place

I see in there this morning. Darned if that ain't Paris, France. Round green metal coffee table in a public square at the base of the Eiffel Tower. The square is empty because magic mirrors pay no mind to time zones and it's dawn there, too. And there she sits. The girl in the red dress, at the coffee table. Same woman who turns up in all those exotic places in my mirror. Back turned away from me like always. Sipping coffee. Impossibly poised. Effortlessly cool. My faceless friend. My muse.

I get how screwy it all sounds. But this here is the truth of my youth. And if I am to properly document these difficult early years of what is sure to be a wild and long and groundbreaking life as an international artist, then I am compelled to document the big screwy in all its shaky wonder and peril. These moments at dawn in the Tinman's scrapyard are as relevant to my art as all the dark, real stuff that presents itself later in the day: the girls on the lam stuff, the hunger stuff, the bad smells, the violence, the fear, the work, Mum's drug slinging for Lady Flo. And these notes on the screwy are just as valid as anything I can tell you about the running. Sometimes it's the screwy that pulls a girl through.

Before I found my magic mirror, I used the side mirrors on the HiAce to see myself. Never needed any reflection bigger than that. Sometimes it's good to settle for the side-mirror view of life. Sometimes we don't want to see the full picture.

It wasn't always a magic mirror. For months it was just another way for me to see all the freckles on my cheeks, my button nose with the small sunburn scab at the tip, and my cracked lips. Plain ol' mirror it was, for the longest time. Then, at 3 p.m. on 23 April 2022 – my seventeenth birthday – Mum finally decided that I was old enough and hard enough to hear all the gory details about why we'd legged it across the country. She told me the whole blood-curdling story while we shared a round green metal coffee table at Starbucks, beneath the Myer Centre on the corner of Albert and Elizabeth streets. She drank iced tea and I guzzled a strawberry frappé so quickly my brain froze.

She said my father was a good man on the outside, but it had taken her too long to see his insides. She said you gotta be married to a man at least five years before you really see his insides. She said sometimes you can find a light inside a feller that burns so bright that it starts to burn inside you, too. But all my mum found inside my dad was black monster blood. That's the shit that bubbles because it's hot and troubled. Acid monster blood. My dad's blood coulda cleaned your oven. You could pour that stuff across the top of your Subaru Forester (best car I ever slept in: ample leg room, good high interior with plenty of space for changing your pants) and it would burn a steaming hole right down to the engine block.

'Do I have the monster blood in me, Mum?' I asked.

'Nah,' she replied.

'But he's my father,' I said. 'You said I got my gentle art side from you. What if I got a monster side from him?'

'Nah,' Mum said, 'you got more Monet blood than monster blood.'

'Do you have any monster blood, Mum?' I asked.

'Yeah, I think I got some,' she said. 'How do you think I did what I did to your father?'

But that's just the thing. I know for certain she hasn't got a trace of monster blood in her. I swear it. So how does a woman with not a drop of monster inside her do something so – what's the word for it? – *monstrous*.

*

Mum never told me where she was born or how, or who her parents were. The past is dangerous for girls on the lam.

I think she was born from a rock fertilised by a rainbow. One half of her is black stone and the other half is pink and purple and yellow and orange tricks of light. Never heard her raise her voice once. Don't mean she's meek or unwilling to go full gorilla mama. The one and only time I ever saw her come close to violence was when we were at the bar of the only pub in Cracow, a gold-mining town almost five hundred clicks north-west of Brisbane. We were eating a bowl of chips and gravy and there was this drunk woman sitting next to us wearing snakeskin boots and skinny blue jeans who kept saying the words 'silly cunt' to her boyfriend as she ate a T-bone steak with jacket potatoes and vegetables. Mum rightly thought such language was inappropriate for me to hear because I was only nine back then and twice she asked Snakeskin Boots to stop swearing and twice she was ignored. Making her third request, Mum tapped Snakeskin Boots on the shoulder to get her attention and an angry Snakeskin pushed Mum away without even looking at her. 'Fuck off,' she spat. This prompted Mum to grip Snakeskin's neck in her fingers and bring her head close to her dinner plate, from beside which Mum took a gravy-stained steak knife and pointed it directly at Snakeskin's wide-open left eye. 'Say that once more,' Mum whispered.

Now I didn't think that was monstrous of Mum. I just thought it was gangster as fuck. Five minutes later, as we sped through the night on the road to Theodore in a red 1989 Holden Camira that had no right to still be operating in the dust of western Queensland, I told Mum that I was proud of her for being so brave but wished she hadn't reacted like that.

'Why?' Mum asked.

'We had to leave half a bowl of chips and gravy on the bar,' I replied.

'I'm sorry,' Mum said. 'That is, indeed, a tragedy. What kind of animal forces a woman to abandon a bowl of chips and gravy?'

*

When Mum told me about the monster blood and how it felt to stick a paring knife in the throat of her husband in order to save her life and mine, the words landed inside my head like breaking glass. I swear I felt a crack running across my brain, just like the crack in my magic mirror. On one side of that brain crack was everything I knew for certain about the world. Bubblegum. Spaghetti bolognese. The songs of Taylor Swift. Bells on bicycles. On the other side was everything that I saw coming for me. Truth. Adulthood. Hurt and pain and art. So much art. And so many questions. Who was my mother before she ran? Where did we live? Who was I? Who am I?

I went home to the scrapyard that afternoon and I stared so close into my broken mirror that I could see the pores in the skin on my nose. Could see the emerald green of my eyes. Felt like I could see to the end of the universe. But nowhere could I find the monster I was trying to see inside myself.

Then I took a step back and that's when I saw her. Below the crack in the mirror were the old cut-off denim shorts I was wearing and my bare, fire-kindling legs sticking out of a pair of green and white Slazenger sneakers I'd got from Big W. But in the space above the crack I saw a woman in a red dress with her back to me. It was like she was right there beyond the glass, moving inside it, as if I was watching her through a bedroom window.

It was a red knee-length cocktail dress she wore, with cross-straps at the back that exposed her well-formed shoulder blades. She was standing in a city street. In a city that looked much bigger than my city. Her hair was thick and brown and high

9

and rolled into curls that seemed as natural and wondrous as seashells. She raised her left arm and I glimpsed a long white cigarette between her forefinger and middle finger. I could see only a flash of her jawline as she turned to take a deep drag on that cigarette, leaving a ring of vivid red lipstick on the end of the butt.

'Mirror, mirror, in this panel beater's place,' I whispered, 'please show me who you are, please show me your face.'

But the woman in the red dress said nothing. And then she walked away from me. I could see where she was going. Up a wide white stone staircase to what looked like a European castle. But then a yellow cab drove across my frame of view and I realised the scene was unfolding in the city of New York and I knew the building from documentaries Mum and me had watched on the telly. It was no castle she was walking into; it was the Metropolitan Museum of Art.

She does things like that, this woman in the red dress. Because she's international. And she's wanted, not unwanted. She's valuable, not worthless.

*

This morning she sits alone in Paris beneath the most famous tower in the world. Sips a black coffee. Pure white cigarette raised to her lips with her left hand. And then a man in a vintage brown suit with a face I cannot see enters the scene from the left side of the mirror frame and kisses the woman in the red dress for twelve long seconds, square on the lips. Romance in it. Passion in it. Art.

But then a voice from beside me says, 'What the hell are you staring at?'

And the woman in the mirror whips her head to the side to find out who has interrupted her private Parisian kiss.

And I whip my head to the same side to see a woman with her arms folded, looking at me like she's trying to figure how deep my screwy goes.

My rock, fertilised by a rainbow. The first most valuable thing in my life.

Mum.

Mum in the Jumper that Covers Her Scars, Walking Silently by the Brisbane River

Mum in the Jumper That Covers Her Scars, Walking Silently by the Brisbane River

February 2023

Pen and ink on paper

A revealing and tender reflection on the most significant day in the artist's highly complex youth. The artist was two months away from celebrating her eighteenth birthday and experimenting, evidently, with anthropomorphic representations of the ones she loved the most. It is almost certainly the artist's mother – the proud lioness – in the foreground of the sketch, but critics and admirers alike have spent decades furiously debating the significance of the creature emerging slowly from the water behind her. Is it 'the hand of fate', as some have called it? Or does the hand, in fact, represent eighteen years of a mother's running and a past that finally caught up with this lion on the lam?

Who am I? In a world of eight billion people, I'm the seventeen-year-old girl with no name lying on a mattress beside her sleeping mum in a van beside the Brisbane River. I'm the girl with two legs, two arms, short brown hair, a rose-coloured birthmark shaped like a picnic basket on her arse, and a sketchbook in her hands. I'm the girl with a sore neck because her pillow is a washing machine delicates bag filled with increasingly indelicate socks and undies. I'm the girl with a circle of morning sunlight shining on her belly. A single ray of sunshine made for me, admitted by a rust hole in the roof of the van. I'm the girl putting her thumb and forefinger to the circle that's fixed like a spotlight on her night shirt. How wide is the circle of light this morning? Wide as a can of Mortein bug spray.

I'm the girl sketching an image of a beautiful woman in a red dress waiting for a train at night in Berlin. The woman's looking up at a full moon. I place the sketch beneath the circle of light and that real-life light lands precisely on the moon in my drawing and the moon over Berlin lights up like a bedside lamp.

Light, the artist remembered, wasn't really drawn on the page. Light came from shade on the page. The light of our lives, she told herself, is formed by the darkness we place around it.

I scribble a title beneath the sketch: *Woman in Red Dress under Yellow Moon in Berlin*. And I think of names to call myself. Potential names for the artist to scribble beneath her sketches.

'Selena?' I whisper. Selena means 'moon'.

'Vera?' I whisper. Vera means 'true'.

'Wendy?' I whisper. Wendy means 'friend'.

Names are dangerous for girls on the lam. Names could get you busted on the run. If Mum ever blabbed my real name to me, and I then blabbed my real name to someone, and then someone blabbed to the wrong someone else, then my mysterious ol' mum could go to jail for what she did to my dad. I try to tell myself I don't need a name. Plenty of things in this world don't get names. Most rocks don't get names and most rocks have been here longer than all of us. Dogs and cats have names, but South Brisbane fruit bats don't. A possum named Merlin comes to our yard at night for a feed on the scraps from my yard neighbour Roslyn's fruit salads, but most creatures round this river couldn't get a passport to save themselves. Cyclones get names but storms don't. Nor do snails or green ants or earthworms or rainbows. The moon is just called 'the moon'. It's not called Andromeda or something cool and galactic like that. It's just known as 'the moon' because people didn't know back in the day that there were other moons in our solar system. Far as they knew, there was only one of those coin-shaped silver things floating in the night.

Only one of me here, too. That's why people just call me 'the girl in the van' or 'the runaway girl' or 'the daughter of the mother who ran away' or 'the kid with no name in the van' or 'the girl with no home' or 'that homeless girl from West End with dirt on her face'. None of those things say anything about who I really am or who I really wanna be. For a start, I ain't homeless, I'm just houseless. Those two things are about as different as resting your head on a silk pillowcase and resting your head on a brick. And if you really wanna call me anything, then I'd love it if you called me 'the artist'. The artist with no name in the van by the river in West End with the dirt on her face and the hope in her heart and the ache in her neck. Or is that the ache in her heart and the hope in her neck?

I'm not the only one down here by the river struggling to prove who she is. I know floaters right across the city who can't get into houses, can't get on the JobSeeker list, can't get out of *the deep black hole in the night* because they got no identification. Got no licence. Got no passport. Got no mum to say, 'Hey, that's my son.' Got no son to say, 'Hey, that's my mum.' Some got no order in the marble bag of their mind; some have just forgotten how to scream across a Centrelink desk, 'I exist, goddammit, just gimme a second!' I know floaters who lost their names when they lost their hope. Know one old bloke who just calls himself Tea Leaf. First name, Tea. Last name, Leaf. He can't remember the name his mother gave him. He drank that name away. Pissed his whole identity off the rocks lining the Brisbane River. Been two decades since he's even needed it. Not a single identifying factor on his person outside of a tattoo hand-scrawled on the inside of his left forearm: *Marilyn*. You ever tried to get some identification without some identification? It's like trying to go to sleep with your eyes open.

In truth, I've got a dozen names and none. 'Sweetie' and 'love' and 'hon' and 'you' are what Mum calls me. My neighbour Roslyn calls me 'kid'. I have a friend named Esther Inthehole, she of the Kangaroo Point Intheholes. I've never seen Esther's face because she's a recluse who lives in a hole under the St Peter the Apostle Church in Canoe Street. Esther Inthehole calls me 'Liv Bytheriver' because I live in an orange van with no wheels beside the Brisbane River. My best friend, Charlie Mould, aka Prince Charles, calls me 'Princess Diana', aka 'Di Bytheriver', and I always remind Charlie that I'd rather live by the river than

17

die by the river. The Nigerian priest at the St Peter the Apostle Church, Father Joseph Kikelomo, calls me 'Sputnik' because he says I'm always shooting for stars that are too high in my sky. My friend Evelyn Bragg – she's the manager at The Well drop-in centre on Moon Street, the same street where you can find me and mum in our van – always calls me 'Patsy' because I sang one night at a fundraising karaoke event in the drop-in centre rec room and she said I sounded sad but pretty, just like Patsy Cline. Mum's boss, Flora Box, calls me 'Brooke' because I used to let my hair grow out long so that it hung like curtains over my shoulders and that reminded Flo of some actress she loved who starred in some old movie about two kids who got stuck on a tropical island and ate coconuts and bumped uglies all day. Mum's most loyal day-job customer, an old man named George Stringer, calls me 'Laura' because Mum told him my name is Laura Branigan, which is the name of the singer of Mum's all-time favourite name song, 'Gloria'. Mum loves a good name song: 'Jolene', 'Layla', 'Angie', 'Cecilia', 'Beth', 'Rhiannon'. I did a sketch once for Mum that featured all the subjects of her favourite name songs gathered for a reunion in the function room of the Story Bridge Hotel. Runaround Sue and Barbara Ann sipping punch in the corner with Jack and Diane. Billie Jean makin' out with Bobbie McGee. Poor Eleanor Rigby on clean-up duties.

Yeah, I try to tell myself that I don't need a real name. But I reckon I do. I think it's important to know who you really are and who you really want to be. I guess what I'm trying to tell you is that I'm not a rock. And I sure as hell ain't no rainbow.

*

I'm the girl with too many things to draw and too little ink in her pen. Drawings everywhere I look. Images in matte-gold frames. A dozen potential sketches right here in this cramped van this morning. Dirt on my toes at the end of the mattress. Mum's curtains pulled across the van's rear window. *The Artist's Feet with Purple Curtains.*

Mum gets the right wall of the van, the one covered in all the pictures of me growing up that she printed out in the Milton Officeworks. The left wall is mine. A Harry Styles *Rolling Stone* cover pinned there and next to it three pencil sketches that turned out how I wanted. *Portrait of the Artist with Exploding Watermelon Head.* That's me in a sundress with my seeded watermelon head exploding into chunks of mushy pink flesh. *Dom's Dad Died.* I play nine-ball down at The Well with a fifty-six-year-old floater named Dominique Ferrera. This is the moment when Dom dropped the seven-ball on a jump shot then told me her father, Rhyl, died choking on a piece of steak gristle in the Kedron Park Hotel. Dom shrugged her shoulders and sank the eight-ball with a cushion shot that rolled so cleanly along the rail that I suspected witchcraft. *Our Home in Monte Carlo.* A sketch of Mum and me standing beside a 'For Sale' sign in front of a two-storey house made entirely of Arnott's Monte Carlo biscuits.

Footsteps beyond the sliding van door. Roslyn rustling around the yard, fixing breakfast. 'Scram, Justice Cavanagh,' she barks. A stubborn one-legged West End ibis has been joining us for breakfast. Roslyn says the bird acts all superior, like a judge she once encountered in the Brisbane Mags Court. 'No grub for you this mornin', your honour.'

Roslyn means 'gentle horse'. Her voice stirs Mum, who is lying beside me with her belly down on the mattress and her head turned sideways on the pillow towards me.

'Sleep all right?' she asks, eyes still closed.

'I dreamed Pablo Picasso was painting a mural beneath the William Jolly Bridge.'

'You say hi?'

'I did. And he said *hola*. He was painting a great big red blob on the wall beneath the bridge. The blob was scary, like it was alive somehow, throbbing, with all these drippy dark red lines coming from it, like tendrils made of old black blood.'

'Did you ask him what it was?'

'I did. He said, "This is Maria. This is my heart."'

'Who's Maria?'

'I don't know. Then I asked him why he had come all the way to Brisbane, Australia, just to paint beneath the William Jolly Bridge, and he said he had come to tell me my sketches weren't good enough to turn into paintings yet. And then I told him that one day my sketches are gonna hang in New York's Metropolitan Museum of Art and he said that was a dangerous dream and then I asked him how a young artist from Brisbane, Australia, might make it all the way to the Met in New York and he said there's only one way to make it that far. And then he threw a tub of red paint in my face and said, "You must weep."'

'Then what happened?'

'I started sobbin' like an idiot.'

Mum sits up and yawns, rubs her eyes. 'That's an awful dream.'

'No way, Mum,' I say, turning the page of my sketchbook to another blank white page filled with nothing but the whole world. 'It was beautiful.'

*

Home is where the throbbing red blob is. The size of a tennis court, our scrapyard is bordered by a high barbed-wire fence and backs onto the Riverside Drive walking and cycling track that twists along the smelly mangroves lining the Brisbane River behind the West End industrial precinct.

Mum's standing on the dewy scrapyard grass by the van's open door. Right arm down the front of her pyjama bottoms, cleaning her minky with a Huggies baby wipe. In full view of Roslyn by the breakfast campfire two or three metres from us and the early morning riverside joggers running by the fence. She scrunches up the wipe and tosses it into the campfire. Reaches for another wipe from the pack resting on the van's passenger-door sill. Cleans her face with this one then her underarms. Nods at me. Nods at the wipes. 'C'mon, clean up,' she says.

'I'll shower this afternoon at The Well,' I say.

Mum leans in, sniffs my night shirt. 'You sweated last night,' she says. 'You fancy another infection down there?'

I roll my eyes. Roslyn has heard our conversation from the fire. She's seventy-two years old and lives two vehicles along from us in a blue 2002 Honda Jazz. 'She's a bit of a fixer-upper,' Ros always says when she's giving new friends a tour of her four-wheeled home. She has six shirts in the back of her car, two headlamps in her glovebox, eight teeth in her mouth and one forty-seven-year-old daughter in Manly, Sydney. Ros is scribbling notes this morning in a book she calls *The Battle of Good 'n' Bad Shit*. It's a lifelong ledger in which she documents the ups and downs of her days, attempting to establish, before she dies, the ultimate value of human life:

The Good Shit
Harvested strawberries
Rescued a rosella crossing
*   Montague Road with a crook*
*   wing*
Back rub from Kasey D
Hokey pokey ice cream before bed
Ben H returned my nail clippers
Daryl Braithwaite in the hot-tub
*   dream*

The Bad Shit
Poss carcinoma getting bigger on
*   scalp*
Road rage incident on Peel Street
Earthquake in Peru killed 1,100
Left boob still vastly bigger than
*   right*
Bananas won't ripen
Still no letter back from Zoey

'It's the vulva ya gotta worry about,' Ros calls across the yard, no suggestion of modulating her voice for the nature of the conversation. 'The vaginal canal is a self-cleaning miracle of hygiene, but you should always be aware of germs and foreign bodies around the clitoral hood.'

Mum nods knowingly. 'Best listen to Ros – she's had her share of foreign bodies around her clitoral hood.'

Ros howls like a goat impaled on a fence post. Mum snatches another wipe from the pack. 'Or maybe you want Mum to clean it for you, like old times?' Ros suggests.

Mum turns to Ros. 'Hey, you remember cleaning up your girl's bits when she was a bub?'

'Loved it,' Ros says, turning a metal toast rack over the fire. 'Miss it. Wiping my little Zoey's noo noo. Her dumps always looked like chickpea dip.'

Mum nods her head in earnest. 'I never once regretted changing a nappy for you,' she says.

I look at her eyes. I shall call such eyes 'the memory eyes'.

'Mum, are you crying?'

'That was the deal,' she says, fighting a tear before breakfast. 'I did the nursin', the bathin', the mashin', the huggin'. And all you had to do was the shittin'. Every time you shat yourself in those early days was a sigh of relief for me. It meant all your parts were workin' right.'

'Crapple a day keeps the doctor away,' Ros confirms from afar.

I turn to Mum. 'Please stop,' I whisper, reluctantly taking two baby wipes from the pack.

*

Our neighbours June and her son, Sully, pad across the grass to join me, Mum and Ros for breakfast around the yard's corner fire. June and Sully live next to Ros in a ten-foot 1972 red and white Newlands Campmaster caravan.

'What's on the menu, Ros?' June asks.

'Sardines on toast,' Ros replies. 'One or two slices, Sully?'

Sully whispers in his mum's ear. Sully's twenty-two and he's never spoken to me in the two years he's shared our yard. I've never seen him speak to anyone but his mum. People say he's got some kind of disability, but June says her son is nothing but gentle and only in a place as hard as Queensland would gentleness be considered a disability.

June listens to Sully then asks Ros another question. 'Are they the Seacrown sardines from Coles or the Northern Catch sardines from Aldi?'

Ros inspects a can resting on a white tin plate down by her purple Crocs.

'Woolworths Essentials, I'm afraid, Sully,' Ros says.

Sully nods, whispers to his mum again.

'He'll just have toast, and I'll take two slices with the sardines, thanks, Ros,' June says, sitting on an upturned blue milk crate that I found two months ago behind the Parmalat milk factory on Boundary Street.

'Serge gone to work already?' I ask June.

Our neighbour Serge Martin lives next to June and Sully in a 2000 Holden Jackaroo 4x4 and works four shifts a week in a Cannon Hill butcher. Serge means 'servant'.

'I think he's still here,' June says, turning her head towards Serge's truck. Seats folded down in the back. Black sheets blocking out the windows. 'Heard someone shifting about in there this morning.'

The back door of Serge's car opens and a woman with straw-coloured hair past her shoulders steps barefoot onto the grass. She wears red and blue surf shorts and a T-shirt that I like immediately, showing four large birds soaring past a full moon.

A fifth flying bird has crashed headfirst into the side of the moon.

She steps tentatively across the grass and I smile at her when she looks at me. I want her to know that we don't at all mind seeing a stranger emerge from Serge's car, because Serge has always been a socially hopeless case and we're always urging him to get out and meet more people. He struggles in the dating department because he always talks about his butchering work and women just aren't that interested in the long-undervalued art of deboning chickens.

'Mornin', sunshine,' Ros says.

'Good morning,' the woman says, standing on the edge of our breakfast circle.

'Serge still here?' Ros asks.

'He went to work,' the woman replies.

'What's your name?' Ros asks.

'Samantha,' she says. 'Sam.'

'That's a beautiful name,' I say. 'Samantha means "listener".'

Samantha smiles at me, nodding her head. Mid-twenties, I guess. Younger than she looks, like most of us who live here by the river.

'I'm Roslyn. How d'ya know our Serge?'

'We had drinks last night outside the Maritime Museum,' Samantha explains.

'You sleepin' rough?' Ros asks.

'Yeah,' Samantha says. 'Had my name on the wait list for eight months.'

'You got any kids?'

She shakes her head.

'You got any disabilities?'

Shakes her head.

'You might be waitin' for a bit, love,' Ros says, turning to June. 'How long you up to now, Juney?'

'One year, thirty-seven days and round about eight hours, Ros,' June calculates.

'Serge said I could drop here for a bit,' Samantha says.

'Oh, did Serge say that?' replies Ros. 'Well, maybe Serge should have run it past the Wizard before he started talkin' 'bout vacancies in Oz.'

'Ease up, Ros,' Mum says. 'Poor girl just woke up.'

'You usin'?' Ros asks Samantha.

'I was. Not no more.'

'What's your poison?'

'Ice. Brown. But not no more.'

'You like our Serge?' Ros asks.

'Yeah, a bit. He's real sweet. Knows a lot about meat cuts.'

Mum laughs at this.

'You gonna stay true to him?' Ros asks.

'I don't know,' Samantha replies. 'Only just met him.'

Ros points a rusting butter knife at Samantha. 'You get him back on that gear and I'll show you everything *I* know about meat cuts, you understand?'

Samantha nods earnestly. 'I understand.'

'Who's your favourite rugby league team?'

'Canberra Raiders,' Samantha says.

Ros takes a breath. Tilts her head from side to side. 'That's not the right answer,' she says. 'But that's not the wrong answer, neither.' She nods at an empty white plastic chair beside Sully. 'Take a seat. Fancy some sardines on toast?'

'That would be wonderful, thank you, Roslyn,' Samantha says.

Ros hands Samantha a plate of sardines then opens her ledger, and I lean over to see her scribble a new line in 'The Good Shit' column: *Serge pulled a root last night!* And, just like that, we have a new neighbour in Oz.

June nods and smiles, turns her head to the 1989 white Ford panel van parked next to our Toyota. That's where my best friend, Charlie Mould, lives.

'Charlie still getting his beauty sleep?' June asks me.

I shake my head, swallowing a mouthful of sardines and burnt toast. 'Didn't hear him come home last night,' I say.

Ros scoffs. 'I trust he's currently passed out in some cosy spot on the Riverside Expressway.'

Mum's now washing and rinsing her breakfast plate in two army-green dish tubs at a round white plastic garden table beside the fire. She dries the plate and slots it into a dish rack beneath a sign that reads *Wash. Rinse. Dry. Or Ros Will Stab You in Your Sleep.*

Mum taps my shoulder. 'We're off,' she says.

*

In a world of eight billion people, I'm the seventeen-year-old girl with no name sitting in a cold room with a dangerous idiot. This is the packing room of the Ebb 'n' Flo seafood wholesalers shed at 6 Moon Street, which is only a two-minute walk from our abandoned panel beater's scrapyard at 38 Moon Street. I'm the girl sitting with Brandon Box at a long white plastic packing table bearing six Styrofoam boxes containing fresh blue swimmer crabs, Moreton Bay prawns, Endeavour prawns, tiger prawns, king prawns, oysters and whole fish, all waiting to be transferred to the U-shaped glass display cabinet in the sales wet area, which is beyond the white swing doors behind me.

Brandon Box is the only child of Mum's boss, Flora Box, aka 'Lady Flo', the fifty-seven-year-old owner-operator of Ebb 'n' Flo, the best seafood shop in South East Queensland. Flo didn't ask no questions about where we came from and has helped us get by since we came to West End. Brandon Box is an eighteen-year-old lunkhead whose brains are made from the shit-strings people pull from king prawns on Boxing Day. He sits opposite me with his head in an iPad, watching the NBA while he sips a breakfast protein shake. We have history, Brandon and me. All of it gross. Despite the arctic room temperature, he's not even cold in that muscle shirt I know he wears to intentionally expose flashes of side man-boob. Brandon lifts. Weights to his chin, protein shakes to his mouth, petrified junkies into the backs of cars. He's not cold because his monster acid blood keeps him warm.

Over Brandon's shoulder is a wide blue door with a window in its centre, through which I can see the shed's cold concrete receiving and distribution room, where Mum is holding a notepad and scribbling instructions from Flora Box. Flo wears a peach-coloured fleece – she always wears fleeces in the cold packing rooms – white capri pants and white sneakers. Her hair is grey and curled and her terrible vision is aided by clear-framed, thick-lens plastic spectacles that always make her blue eyeballs look milky. Big legs and a big arse.

She hands Mum a stack of Indonesian pirated pop CDs that Flo imported three years ago from Jakarta. Mum says Flo's dangerous. Mum says I should be careful how close I get to Flora Box. But Flo looks to me to be about as dangerous as the women I see holding the money baskets in Father Joe Kikelomo's church on Sunday mornings.

I lift the lid on the Styrofoam box to my right. Fresh Moreton Bay prawns by the thousands. So new they don't even smell. No sweeter prawn in the world. Half the size and twice the peel time of kings and tigers, but twice the taste, too. Brandon raises his head from the iPad.

'One kilo for a flash of your tits,' he whispers.

'One kilo and I won't tell your mum what a creep her son is.'

'All right, half a kilo of prawns, one tit?'

I close the lid on the prawns. 'Do you know who you are, Brandon?'

'No, who am I?'

'No, Brandon, I can't tell you who you are. That's why I'm asking you the question. Do *you* know who you are? And, furthermore' – I sweep my right hand in a circle to indicate the current space he occupies in the universe – 'is *this* the version of you that you always wanted to be?'

Brandon studies my face across the packing table for a moment. For half a second I think he's going to say something meaningful. Saturn's rings will spin in reverse. Gargantuan chunks of ice will miraculously reconnect themselves to polar ice caps. And Brandon Box will say something profound.

Then he laughs. 'The fuck you talkin' 'bout?' Shakes his head, returning to the NBA. Mutters under his breath, 'Loopy bitch.'

I lift the lid on the box to my left. A dozen iced silver-red saddletail snapper.

'When's the Malaysian yellowtail get in?' I ask.

Brandon chuckles, looks up reluctantly from his screen. 'What do you know about the Malaysian yellowtail?'

'Oh, you'd be very surprised to hear the things your mum has told me about the Malaysian yellowtail that comes in here.'

'Bullshit,' Brandon says.

And then our conversation is interrupted by Flora opening the blue door. Mum behind her, slipping the pirated CDs inside a black Adidas backpack slung over her shoulder.

Flora opens her arms wide in my direction. 'Who's got a hug for her Aunty Flo!' she sings.

Mum nods discreetly and I move around the table, flop my head onto Flora's soft waterbed chest and wrap my arms around her stonewall frame.

She rubs my scalp with a palm. 'When's this one gonna start slingin' for me?' she asks. 'How well do you know this city, young lady?'

'Better than the front o' my foot and the back o' my hand, Flo,' I reply.

'I don't doubt it!' she says, patting my shoulder.

'She's not interested,' Mum interjects. Stern. Direct.

Flo looks at Mum. Flo looks at me. 'You're not interested in a bit of real money, honey?' she asks me.

I look at Mum. A small shake of her head, which Flo doesn't miss, because Flo misses nothing.

'Well, I'd love to make those deliveries for you, Flo,' I say. 'But I'm putting all my spare time and energy into becoming a world-famous artist.'

'And who am I to stand in the way of destiny,' Flo says. 'Speaking of which, didn't you promise me a new drawing to go above our price board?'

I pull a rolled sketch from the back pocket of my denim cut-offs, hand it to Flo. 'It's called *Flora Eating a Prawn Sandwich inside a Sperm Whale.*'

I've drawn a picture of Flo in a domestic kitchen, where she's eating a prawn sandwich with seafood sauce and avocado at a table while she reads *Moby Dick*. This whole scene takes place in the belly of Moby Dick the whale.

Flo laughs from her own spacious belly. 'Look at the shoes on me,' she says, pointing at the sketch.

'ASICS Gel-Quantums,' I say, bouncing on my heels, nodding down at Flo's runners.

'You see it all, don't you, pet?' Flo says.

I shrug. 'The artist sees nothing more or less than what she needs to see, Flo.'

Mum taps my shoulder. 'Hey, Picasso,' she says. 'Can you see it's time for us to go?'

*

The artist let her mother walk ahead of her along Riverside Drive that morning. Her mother wore black rubber sandals with blue jeans. She walked with the air of the burdened, the beleaguered: chin tucked to her chest, her hands in the pockets of a hooded black jumper emblazoned with the brand of a popular Australian surfing company. The artist's mother always wore long sleeves when she was working, even in the stickiest Brisbane heat. Any art scholar with the vaguest knowledge of the artist's dark history will be familiar with her mother's lifelong attempts to hide the burn scars across her forearms. The artist's mother said the scars unsettled her clients. The scars stretched up her mother's forearms and looked to the artist like the worst pair of opera gloves ever sewn. The colour of the scars turned from red to pink to brown as the artist turned from toddler to teen. On this particular morning, it looked to the artist like her mother had dipped her arms in two large buckets of peanut butter. The artist's mother knew that the artist knew that the scars were the work of her monster. But this did not stop the artist's mother from telling the artist a series of increasingly outlandish lies concerning their origin. Hot-air balloon mishap, she claimed. Pulled a ten-year-old boy out of a burning fireworks factory, she said. 'Rule number one,' the artist's mother once warned her, laughing, 'never set your farts on fire while wearing silk.'

The artist saw her mother as short and skinny but pretty like a pop star. The artist once thought her mother might have been the tough older sister Kylie Minogue never had. Her mother liked the big bright flower paintings of Georgia O'Keeffe, but she also liked Edvard Munch's Evening on Karl Johan Street, which depicts a number of snobby pedestrians in fancy black dress with faces like ghosts as they stare at the viewer from a nighttime street in Oslo. The pedestrians looked creepy and distant to the artist. She read that Munch painted Evening on Karl Johan Street after he'd waited excitedly for a lover and when she turned up she gave him only a weak smile before scurrying on up the street. 'She totally ghosted him, Mum!' the artist said. 'She made him feel invisible.'

'That's right,' the artist's mother agreed. 'He felt like he didn't exist. That's why he turned that street into a ghost street.'

The artist thought in that moment how intriguing it was to be raised by a woman who appreciated Edvard Munch as much as she appreciated the Spice Girls. Then the artist thought for a moment about what spice her mum would have been if she was a Spice Girl. She thought of Nutmeg Spice initially. Then she settled on Ground Pepper Spice.

See what I did there? Force of habit. Some people bite their fingernails. Some people piss in swimming pools. Me, I have a habit of thinking of my life as the subject of a guided tour in New York's Metropolitan Museum of Art, circa 2100, conducted by a stuffy English art critic named E.P. (Edward Percival) Buckle, who is describing these early nameless and houseless years of my life to an enraptured group of art lovers. Common phenomenon, I'm sure.

In my head, these art lovers are listening to Buckle's insights into my life as they look at my early Brisbane-era ink sketches spread across several rooms of the gallery, part of a posthumous exhibition entitled something subtle and modest like She Was the Greatest Artist Who Ever Lived and Nobody Even Knew Her Fucking Name. As they walk, they comment on my life and my art.

'She was a peculiar child,' they say.

'Frankly, it's a miracle she even made it out of Brisbane,' they say.

'She stirs me,' they say. 'She penetrates me. She speaks directly and profoundly to my fears and my frailties. She is, quite simply, the greatest artist who ever lived and nobody even knew her fucking name.'

Screwy as all get-out, I know, but, truth be blurted, Mr Buckle has really helped me to stand back and assess with clarity and perspective what has been a deeply unusual and unsettling life on the lam. Sometimes when I'm nervous or scared or something worse than both those things, ol' E.P. Buckle comes into my head and starts yabbering and suddenly I feel like I'm someone else. Then I feel like it's not necessarily me who's living through these things. It's someone smarter, more talented, braver. E.P. Buckle brings meaning to everything. It's like he's telling me all these things are happening to me for a reason. Because all these things have to happen in order for me to get to the places E.P. Buckle knows I'm going to. It's amazing how beneficial it can be looking at your life through the lens of a seventy-year-old Englishman who talks like he's got a fountain pen wedged up his jacksie.

*

'Bronwyn?' I ask. 'Bronwyn means "white crow".'

'No,' Mum says.

Mid-morning, walking along the river. Time enough to play the 'Hey, Mum, What's My Real Name' game. She says I'll never guess it, so I might as well not bother, because my name means something beautiful, but also something rare.

'Vanessa?' I ask. 'Vanessa means "butterfly".'

'No.'

The black Adidas backpack hanging from her shoulders. Stress cracks in her heels. I've got my sketchbook in my left hand and, in my right, a black ink Copic Multiliner sketch pen with a one-millimetre nib. Good for sketching wrinkles and toe hairs and stress cracks in heels. If I was to sketch this scene, I'd start with the stress cracks in Mum's heels. *Houseless Single Mother with Heel Cracks.*

'Beatrix?' I ask. 'Beatrix means "voyager".'

'No,' Mum says.

Heel cracks. That's Mum all over. Heel skin like sandpaper. Soles like sponge coral left for dead in the sun. If she's going anywhere, she's walking, when she's not running. Her feet are so hard on the bottom I picture an Eagle Farm horse trainer nailing a set of U-shaped plates to her heels.

She was a teacher before the running. Relief teacher. One of the great all-rounders of Australian education. Mum says walking into a classroom as a relief teacher is like entering a cave of bears in a suit made of salmon skin. She says the reason kids play up so often with relief teachers is because relief teachers go into classrooms blind. They have no knowledge of a child's prior behaviour, good or bad. The good kids see a welcome chance to be bad for a day. The bad kids sniff a chance to be badder. That's why, at roll call every morning, Mum asked kids to say their name and then describe the last time they'd done something kind for someone. She says a kid's less likely to be bad after they've reminded the world, and themselves, how good they can be.

It was because of Mum that I graduated from home school – or what I called 'Hobo High' – a year early. Unofficially, of course. Mum organised a deeply sad but much appreciated graduation ceremony in the scrapyard. Ros baked a vanilla sponge cake and I gave a valedictory speech recalling all the maths classes I'd attended in the back of hot vans; the countless English classes Mum had taught in air-conditioned public libraries along Australia's east coast; marine biology excursions to Stradbroke Island; science excursions to the Brisbane Planetarium; and, my personal favourite, weekly art classes conducted as we walked through the halls of the Queensland Art Gallery. My home-school graduation certificate was made from the inside of a Corn Flakes box. The graduation cap that I tossed halfheartedly into the air upon the ceremony's conclusion was a sweat-stained thrift-shop golf hat emblazoned with the emblem of the Indooroopilly Golf Club.

After the heel cracks, I'd spend some time sketching Mum's hair. I cut her hair short three nights ago with stationery scissors and she cut mine and now we both look like orphaned gutter boys from 1800s London. After the hair, I'd try to shade in some sense of Mum's intimacy, as a houseless person, with dirt. I'm talking about dirt so deep that it forms part of your skin. I'm talking about dirt that you can taste on your fingertips when you eat a Burger Ring. Dirt in your fingernails and dirt on the backs of your legs so old that people mistake it for birthmarks. Epidermal dirt. Dirt as armour. Dirt as shield. Sounds screwy, I know, but sometimes the intimacy with dirt gets so deep that you start feeling earth intimacy, a soil connection in you, and then you start feeling like you're part of the ground. Like you can sleep on any patch of grass, anywhere on earth, because that's what you are now. You are ground. You are dirt. You are earth. Easy to feel if you're out here long enough. Not so easy to draw.

'Marlene?' I ask. 'Marlene means "star".'

'No,' Mum says.

I must remember to make the most of these walks. The peace and comfort of the here and now, while it lasts with Mum. The two of us, while we last. Mum and me. Truth be spat like a watermelon seed, we're on borrowed time. Mum's called it. Ain't nobody changing her mind.

'Maeve?' I ask. 'Maeve means "she who intoxicates".'

'No,' Mum says.

She's turning herself in to the cops on the day I turn eighteen: 23 April. That's only two months from now. I'll be able to live a normal life then, she says. Be safe then, she says. Look after myself then, she says. Be free to chase my artsy-fartsy dreams. *Happy birthday, kid. Now I best be off to the big house.*

*

Long story, but if I'm gonna tell you where all this E.P.-Buckle-talking-in-the-Met stuff came from then it's probably only right that I tell you when the art kick first struck my tail. No telling when a dream's gonna find you. A dream can reach you like a song on the wind or a jab to the jaw.

A big waking-world epiphany hit me when I was twelve years old and Mum and me were living in a friend's caravan in Far North Queensland. We were watching a documentary on a television the size of a letterbox. It was an SBS documentary about a sprawling Pablo Picasso exhibition that was being held in New York's Metropolitan Museum of Art. Now that I'm at the ripe old age of seventeen and ten months, I'm happy to say I've seen plenty of art exhibitions at the Queensland Art Gallery and its black sheep kid brother, the Gallery of Modern Art. But back then the closest thing I'd ever seen to an art exhibition was the tattooed backs of a couple of Comanchero bikers Mum befriended in the Childers McDonald's, 320 kilometres north of Brisbane.

Watching the telly that night, I told Mum that Pablo Picasso reminded me of her a bit because Pablo, just like Mum, had a way of welcoming into his life tragic figures and troubled souls who would both enrich and destroy his spirit. I told Mum how much I loved Pablo Picasso's paintings, particularly his Blue Period, which the documentary said began with the death of his friend Carles Casagemas. He was such a good friend to Picasso that he would go to Barcelona brothels with him, even though Casagemas couldn't, despite his best efforts, convince his winky to stay full rhino. Loyal Casagemas would patiently wait for Picasso to do his passionate business then the two artists would continue their starlit odysseys, discussing portraiture and paints and pain. Casagemas was in love with an artist's model named Germaine Pichot and, in 1901, he arranged a dinner at a Paris café, to which he invited Germaine and his dearest friends to share mountains of food and rivers of absinthe. Little did Germaine and his friends know, this would be, in fact, a farewell dinner.

Casagemas asked for Germaine's hand in marriage that night. Germaine said no. Casagemas pulled a pistol on Germaine and fired. The bullet missed. Casagemas turned the gun towards his own head and shot. The SBS documentary then showed an image of a painting Picasso had completed soon after. It was called *The Death of Casagemas* and it scared me because it looked so real and sad and honest: an oil-paint image of Casagemas's zombie-green head on what looked like a deathbed next to a candle flame. But the only thing Mum and me were really looking at was the big black bullet hole Picasso had painted on his subject's right temple.

'Wow,' I said to Mum. 'I didn't know we were allowed to do that.'

'What, shoot yourself in the noggin?'

'No,' I said. 'I didn't know we could be so honest.'

'Of course you can be so honest,' Mum said. 'How do we ever understand the truth if no one's willing to show it to us?'

It was while watching that documentary that Mum and I started laughing at the way the curator of the Met exhibition in question always referred to Picasso as 'the artist':

'The artist was traumatised by the death of his sister, Conchita.'

'If the artist has a sense of discipline at all, it is an unyielding dedication to a sense of creative ill-discipline.'

'The artist becomes fixated on acrobats and harlequins, which is to say, at long last, he's laughing again.'

Mum and I were eating chipolata sausages and microwaved McCain Winter Vegetables mix. I looked down at the dinner plate resting on my thin twelve-year-old thighs. 'The artist had well and truly evolved out of her Frozen Broccoli Period,' I said in my best high-end museum-curator voice.

'The artist's mother tried not to think about what was in her chipolatas,' Mum responded in the same pompous tone.

Two days later, Mum bought me a hardback book of Picasso paintings from a secondhand bookshop. I was particularly taken with how all the names of his artworks told the straightforward truth about what he was painting. I fell in love with a painting called *Woman in Green*, which featured a woman dressed in green, just like the label promised. I liked his simple names like *Bottle and Wine Glass on a Table* and *The Blind Man's Meal*, which featured a blind man having a meal. I started sketching the plain truths I saw around me and gave them simple titles of my own: *Petrol Station Attendant with Busted Lip*; *Saxa Salt and Chiko Roll on Table*; *Mum Realises I Ate the Last of the Coco Pops*; *Bunnings Sausage on Bread, No Onion*. Then I told my mum that I had stumbled arse-backwards upon my life's dream: to have my drawings exhibited in New York's Metropolitan Museum of Art.

When I was thirteen years old, I announced that I had decided to live the rest of my life as though it was being documented by E.P. Buckle for a posthumous exhibition of my life's work. Common phenomenon, I'm sure.

'I'm gonna live my life boldly,' I declared to Mum. 'Just like Picasso and Casagemas. All the great artists lived their lives boldly. Almost every time, they made the reckless choice. They threw themselves into wild love triangles, drank too much and got themselves hooked on drugs. They lived in shitholes, just like we do, Mum. They didn't care where they lived as long as they had some paint and a clean brush. Picasso coulda lived in a smelly old shoe and still been happy to paint the walls. And they were always so rash and brave. It's like they knew we'd all be reading about them one day and they wanted their stories to be grand and inspiring. Every single time, they chose danger.'

'Many of them also chose dying before the age of forty,' Mum pointed out.

'But the art lives forever, Mum,' I responded. 'The art never dies.'

It's a good idea to assume that one day your life will be the subject of an exhaustive retrospective exhibition because it makes you attempt to live every moment with a sense of its own significance. In my case, the unexpected benefit of this screwy thinking has been the strange and curious phenomenon of me pausing at certain junctures of the unfolding story of my life to consider alternative outcomes in real time.

For example, two weeks ago I found myself standing at the George Street end of Queen Street Mall with every intention of walking casually down the mall to the H&M store opposite the Wintergarden. But then I thought to myself, What if I chose wonder? What if I chose daring? Wouldn't it make for a better story, would it not be more artful, if I cartwheeled all the way instead? And so I did that. I executed thirty-six consecutive cartwheels all the way down to H&M. I nearly karate-kicked a balloon-blower busking outside the Telstra shop. My backpack slipped off twice. And by the time I made it to H&M I was so dizzy that I had to stagger to the garden bed outside Mecca Maxima and chunder up the three Weet-Bix I'd had for breakfast.

But then a Sudanese woman with Apple AirPods in her ears rested a hand on my left shoulder as I went the big vom and asked if I was feeling okay. And she had one of those plastic orange and black Nike water bottles and she let me use the last of her water to wash my mouth out. We sat down on a bench and she told me she was a mum of three who had come to Brisbane in 2003 to escape a civil war so bloody and violent and loud that she can no longer listen to anything on her AirPods other than birdsong. She asked me my name and I said I didn't have one and I asked her to keep it to herself when I told her how Mum and me had been on the run since I was six months old and the reason I didn't know my name was because it's dangerous for girls on the lam to know their names, because girls on the lam can let those names slip to anyone, and when you're on the lam absolutely anyone can get you busted.

'What's your name?' I asked.

'My name is Amina Osman,' she replied.

'Your name is Amina?'

'Yes.'

'I have a Temple & Webster mirror at home named Amina,' I said.

Amina smiled. She didn't seem to find that news as incredible as I found it.

'Don't you find that incredible?' I asked.

Amina shrugged her shoulders and laughed. 'Amina is a very popular name where I come from,' she said. 'It's a good name for a mirror, too.'

'Why's that?' I asked.

'Amina means "trustworthy",' she said. 'Mirrors never lie. That mirror of yours might be the most trustworthy thing in your life.'

Then I pulled out my sketchbook and asked Amina if I could draw her and she said yes and then thirty minutes later I gave her a portrait I entitled *Amina Sitting in the Queen St Mall Listening to Birdsong on Her AirPods.*

And I thought to myself in that moment that this remarkable interaction had only come about because I'd decided to cartwheel to H&M, because I'd decided to choose wonder. And that's just about as close to the point of it as I can get. Do I want to walk through this life of mine? Or do I want to cartwheel through it?

*

'Hey, Mum,' I say as we meander along the river's edge.

'Yes, sweetheart.'

'I think I know what that Pablo dream was about.'

'You do?'

'Yeah. Think I was subconsciously telling myself that it's going to hurt when you turn yourself in, and I will weep for days.'

'You will,' Mum says. 'And so will I.'

'But there will be benefits,' I say.

'What sort of benefits?' Mum asks.

'It will make me a better artist,' I reply.

'How?'

'I've been reading all these art books in the Gallery of Modern Art bookshop.'

'You'd better not be makin' a nuisance of yourself in that shop again.'

'No, the girls behind the counter love me,' I say. 'They let me read in the corner near the T-shirt stand. One girl, Maeve, even pulled out a stool for me to sit on. It was a big yellow stool shaped like a pineapple with its top cut off. Maeve's an artist like me. She's beautiful and intense and she dresses like Helen Frankenthaler dressed in the 1950s.'

'Who's Helen Frankenthaler?'

'American abstract expressionist. She once saw an exhibition by Jackson Pollock and said, "I want to live in this land."'

'I want to live in this land,' Mum repeats. 'Nice way of putting it.'

'I know, right?' I say. 'She saw Pollock's art like it was a place you could visit. Venezuela. Tahiti. Bundaberg. The Land of Jackson Pollock.'

'Tell me about these benefits?' Mum says.

'Well, most of the great artists had something awful happen to them when they were young, and were driven by the pain of that experience. There are so many beautiful paintings that come from things like love and happiness, but I still reckon the really, really great paintings come from really, really great pain. And that's what I'll have when you turn yourself in.'

'Really, really great pain,' Mum says. A long pause. 'Do we have to talk about this?'

'Sorry.'

I forgot how much it hurts her to talk about the running. And the stopping. Ain't nobody changing her mind. Not much use talking about it. Mum asks me the same absurd question every year. Each time she stares into my eyes and grips my shoulders – the way most garden-variety Australian mums might grip their daughter's shoulders when describing the perils of hair straighteners and car sex with boys named Dylan – and asks, 'Are you tired of living like this? Would you like me to turn myself in this year?'

'I don't want you to turn yourself in this year,' I always reply. 'I never want you to turn yourself in.'

My mum never warns me about boys in cars. My mum only warns me about child protection officers in cars.

*

The riverside path runs behind a series of West End factories to our right. Pauls milk. Visy glass. Hanson concrete. To our left is the Brisbane River itself, currently at high tide. *Runaway Girls of the River*. If I was drawing this moment I'd capture the abandoned and collapsed wood and steel wharf to our left where a guy named Gusto has left his tag three times in spray paint. Water birds searching for breakfast around half-submerged mangrove trees along the riverbank. Towering Moreton Bay figs whose trunks have more nooks and crannies than most suburban Brisbane homes.

We'll pass under five bridges on this walk, all of them crossing the river to the city to my left. I've been a teenager for five years now and I've spent all those years beneath these bridges. First, the Go Between Bridge, named after one of Mum's favourite Brisbane bands. It's got all these panels along the side of it in various shades of blue and I always think they look like piano keys and I hope they are playing 'Spring Rain', which is my favourite Go-Betweens song because it's the only song I know that captures how a November rainstorm in Brisbane makes you feel merry and morbid and totally safe, all at the same time.

Then the Merivale Bridge, the double-track rail bridge crossing Milton Reach. There's a big bronze sculpture beneath it that looks like a prison-cell door. Big keyhole in the door, but not a key in sight to unlock it. Mum said it's a memorial to all the kids about my age who lost the ol' life lottery and had to be raised in government homes by the state of Queensland. I used to wonder how that worked and I'd picture a girl coming home from school and being kissed and hugged in a doorway by the cutout shape of Queensland, with legs and sneakers and an apron, and a tea towel hanging over the Gulf of Carpentaria. 'What's behind the door?' I'd ask Mum. And all she'd say was that what was behind the door was the reason we lived in a van in a scrapyard beside a river that smells like a fish fart.

'Barbara?' I ask. 'Barbara means "stranger".'

'No,' Mum says.

The William Jolly Bridge will come after the Merivale Bridge. The William Jolly has thick parallel arches that rise from the river level and are low enough to the road that anyone with half a set of balls can walk all the way over them. My best friend, Charlie Mould, and me once sang 'You Belong with Me' by Taylor Swift while dancing on the apex of one rainbow arch. The Kurilpa pedestrian and bicycle bridge is next and then we'll reach our destination, the manicured gardens beneath the Victoria Bridge.

'Cecilia?' I ask. 'Cecilia means "blind".'

'No,' Mum says. 'And that's enough for today, 'ey?' It sounds like a request but it isn't. She walks on.

'The artist felt bad about the relentless inquisitions she inflicted upon her long-suffering mother,' I say in my E.P. Buckle voice.

Mum stops. Waits for me to catch up. Wraps her left arm around my shoulders. 'The artist's mother dreamed of a simpler life for her daughter,' Mum says E.P. Buckle–style, 'one in which she wouldn't have to be so inquisitive.'

*

High water splashing riverbank rocks that way-way-back black-fellers used to fish on and not-so-way-back British settlers with pumpkin seeds in their pockets used to piss on. Sprawling riverside poinciana trees that a girl like me can sit under for six hours and never get sunburnt, drawing pictures of my neighbours and rhinoceroses and brave medieval knights in dresses and homeless West End drunks in shining armour.

'Look, Mum. Cool frame.'

Six empty yellow kayaks floating fast down the wide brown river. The river is full and violent and powerful this morning, causing the kayaks to flip and roll over each other like hungry crocodiles fighting over a dead chicken.

'Bitch is pissed this morning,' Mum says. 'She's torn them from the Grammar jetty. All that rain we've had, rushing down from the mountains and stirring up our sleepy brown snake.'

Nearby are three domed yellow and green tents occupied by some floaters I know from The Well. There are yellow and green two-person tents like this dotted right along the river's edge, because six months ago The Well's manager, Evelyn Bragg, organised some donations for South Brisbane's homeless from a tent company called Spinifex.

'Well, look what washed up from the river last night,' Mum says.

It's my best friend, Charlie Mould. Sleeping on his back at his favourite drinking spot, under the lamppost on the grass slope beneath the wall of the Hanson concrete plant on Hockings Street. The wall faces the river, is as high and wide as a drive-in cinema screen, and bears a big sign in blue lettering: *Hanson*.

A silver red-wine sack lies by Charlie's side, its pouring tap strangled to death during the night by his manic fingers. Charlie is a year older than me. An eighteen-year-old drunk with a prune for a liver. Floppy mop of brown hair over his forehead. The fifth Beatle. Wears a grey business shirt with a Westpac bank insignia embroidered above the chest pocket, another random item found by duck-diving into a Salvos' clothing bin. Shorts made from black jeans cut off at the kneecaps. Open and weeping grazes down his shins.

I give him a gentle kick in the ribs. 'Oi, Charlie,' I shout.

Kid doesn't move.

Mum comes over all serious. 'You gotta tell 'im to quit drinkin' so hard,' she says. 'His organs, they haven't developed. Dumb shit ain't strong enough to go that hard.'

'I tell him all the time,' I say, leaning down and gently slapping Charlie's left cheek. 'Oi, Charlie,' I bark. 'You gotta get up. You'll fry in this sun.'

Another slap. Charlie stirs. Eyes open, he struggles to make sense of what he sees, blinded by the sun over my shoulder. 'Is that you, God?' he asks, awe in his voice. 'Is this heaven?'

Mum kicks him in the side. 'Yeah. West End, Brisbane. Now get up, Charlie, ya runny egg.'

Charlie laughs, braces for another kick from Mum.

'You good?' I ask, rubbing his forehead. More compassion for Charlie than Mum can muster.

'Yeah, I'm good,' he says, sitting up, wiping grass from his hands and forearms.

Mum unzips the Adidas backpack, pulls out a Coke bottle filled with water and hands it to Charlie.

'Thanks, God,' he says, guzzling the water like he's been walking for four days through a desert.

Mum and me carry on up the riverside walking track.

'Wait, where ya goin'?' Charlie yells.

'It's called work, Charlie,' I shout back over my shoulder.

*

'What are you drawing?' Mum asks.

'You,' I say, adding three quick pen strokes to her jawline. 'Makin' a mess of it.'

We're sitting at the base of the old sawn-stone Victoria Bridge Abutment, at the southern end of the Victoria Bridge, looking across the river to Brisbane Central Business District (CBD) office towers so tall they leave shadows on the water.

'Why can't I get your face right?'

Mum's looking away from me, her eyes fixed on two pedestrians on the riverside walking track.

'The pen keeps lying for you,' Mum says.

The brown stone abutment behind us reminds me of a chessboard rook and I always picture medieval men in domed helmets up there, pouring boiling oil over Mum and me when we stay too long. West End floaters like to sleep here sometimes when it rains, their sleeping bags on the soft surrounding garden beds, sheltered by the bridge, which leads to the south side of the city. We sit on a blue-grey cobblestone garden edging right under a black council lamppost that has a light fitting shaped like Ned Kelly's helmet.

'How's it lyin' for me?'

'Always hard drawing the people we love the most,' Mum says. 'The pen will lie for you. Even when you don't want it to. Every portrait you do of me, always a little bit off. They never look like me because you can't help being kind to me. You keep seeing things that aren't really there. Same reason you keep giving me a lion's head or an elephant's head instead of the ugly mug that's staring at you every day.'

Just something I've been playing with lately. Humans with animal heads to express their true nature. Blame my old man with the monster blood and the T-Rex head.

'I'm being symbolic,' I say. 'The lion represents your strength. The elephant represents how you can't be toppled. You're unstoppable. You're *untopple-able*.'

Weekday quiet down here this morning. Someone passing us every ten minutes or so. Two joggers. A trio of young skateboarders. Mums pushing prams. Couples walking dogs. Tourists wearing too much sunscreen and tourists with beetroot faces who didn't wear enough. Families turning off the riverside walkway to get to the South Bank cultural forecourt and the Queensland Performing Arts Centre behind us.

'Hey, Mum.'

'Yes, sweetheart.'

'Do you know who you are?'

'What do you mean?'

'I mean, who are you?' I ask. 'What are the things about you that make you who you are? What makes you … *you*?'

Mum puts both her hands to her lips. Ponders my question. 'Well, I'm your mum,' she replies. A long pause. And she says nothing more.

'That's it?' I ask. 'That's all that makes you who you are?'

'That's all I need.'

'What if I need more to know who you are?' I ask.

'Like what?'

'I don't know, maybe a name wouldn't go astray.'

'You already have a name for me,' she says. 'It's "Mum". And "Mum" happens to be the most beautiful name in the world.'

'So all you are is my mum?'

Mum shrugs her shoulders. 'I guess so.'

'You're more than just a mum, Mum.'

'Is that right? What else am I?'

'You're Ros's best friend. I think you might be June's best friend, too. You're a good swimmer. You can throw a frisbee halfway across Musgrave Park. You make a mean pancake. You're resourceful. Somehow you got us both across Australia and kept us from starving and kept all them cops guessing at the same time. You're wise. You're a sage. You're a joke-teller. Storyteller. Fugitive. Protector. Teacher. Bravest person I ever met.'

Mum laughs. 'Well, it's nice to know who I am.'

Pen strokes for Mum's nose on my page. Lines for the lines in the bags under her eyes.

Mum turns away. She watches half a gum tree floating down the river. Must have snapped off in the storms. We can sit here for hours because we're shaded by a fig tree that hangs half over us and half over the river in front of us. About five metres to Mum's left is the place where three sections of the riverside walkway meet at a T-junction directly under the Victoria Bridge. One path runs upwards towards West End, another takes walkers along the South Bank boardwalk and another central path slopes down to the Riverside Drive footpath that Mum and me just walked up.

'Don't make me look so pretty,' Mum says. 'You always make me look prettier than I am. Stronger than I am.'

'What's wrong with that?'

'Nothin' wrong with that. It's just not the truth, that's all.'

'All right, I'm gonna start making you look hideous.'

'No, don't do that,' Mum says. 'You just don't have to lie for me so much.'

'Been lyin' for you all my life.'

She gives me a sharp right eye. 'I know you have,' she says. 'But those lies are okay.'

'Why are those lies okay?'

'Because those lies come from a good place.'

'What place is that?' I ask.

Mum shakes her head, turns back to the river. 'You know the place,' she says.

A man who looks to be in his late twenties saunters up to Mum. He's handsome and well dressed in a white linen shirt with blue jeans and loafers. He removes his black Ray-Ban sunglasses. 'Order for Jordan,' he says.

Mum consults a small, yellow spiral notebook in her hand. 'Two hundred,' she says.

Jordan slips Mum two crisp, green hundred-dollar notes. Mum pockets the money, turns to me. 'Gloria,' she says.

I reach into the black Adidas backpack, pull out a worthless Indonesian pirated CD copy of the 1989 Gloria Estefan album *Cuts Both Ways*. Hand the CD to Jordan.

'Thank you,' he says, half-bowing to Mum, then marches off, taking the concrete path that spirals around and up to the Victoria Bridge pedestrian walkway.

I sketch Mum's nose. A perfect ski-jump. Freckles on the hilltops of her cheeks. Tanned skin. Permanent sun damage. Green eyes like mine. But hers are more tired. Hers have seen more of the light than mine. More of the dark, too.

'Hey, I was thinkin', maybe one day I could ask Lady Flo to buy us a ticket to New York.'

Mum's looking up and down the riverside walkway. Just another street trader on the lookout for another loyal customer.

'What makes you think Flo would do that for us?'

'Because I know how much money you've made for her in the past year alone,' I say. 'I know she's good for it.'

''Course she's good for it,' Mum says. 'That doesn't mean she'd part with it.'

'Because she cares for us,' I say. 'Because she loves us.'

Mum whips a hand around, grips my left thigh, too hard, too serious. 'Flo does not love you,' she says. 'Don't you dare think for a second that she wouldn't tape up your arms and legs, lock you in a fish box and drop you in this drink if she had to.' She nods at the river knowingly, as if that fish box stuff was more than just a notion she plucked from thin air, bony right hand clamping tighter on my thigh. 'Only thing that woman loves is her cut-snake son,' Mum says. 'You got that?'

'Yeah, I got that,' I say, raising my knee to pull away from her grip.

A woman, mid-forties, wearing Ralph Lauren sunglasses and a grey business suit interrupts our conversation. 'Excuse me,' she whispers.

Mum turns to her, agitated. 'What?' she barks, forgetting the manners normally expected of a saleswoman.

'Ummm ... Flo said I could pick up the order for Gail,' she says. Palms to her chest, nervous, unsure of herself. 'Ummm ... I'm Gail ... well, I'm not Gail ... but ... you know ... ummm ... Do you understand?'

'Yes, I understand, Gail,' Mum says, presenting a half-smile mined from some quarry deep inside herself. She consults her notepad. Runs a pen through another name. 'One hundred and fifty.'

Gail hands Mum an envelope and Mum turns to me. 'Alanis,' she says.

I sift through the backpack and find a worthless Indonesian pirated CD copy of *Jagged Little Pill* by Alanis Morissette and hand it to Gail.

'Don't open it here, Gail,' I advise.

Gail nods. 'I understand,' she says. She slips the CD into an olive-coloured handbag and hurries away from us.

Back to my drawing. Eyebrows. Eyelashes. Small old scar above her top lip. Sketch the neck. The torso.

Over Mum's left shoulder, at the top of the path that slopes gently down to the river, I see a mum and dad pushing a toddler in a large black stroller with big tyres that look robust enough to haul the kid up to Everest Base Camp. They're speaking a language that sounds like the one my Filipino friend, Eleanora Reyes, speaks sometimes when she's volunteering as a lunch server on Taco Mondays down at The Well. The toddler's mum holds the pram with her right hand as she talks in English now to Dad about which way they will go. Do they want to see the Queensland Museum first or do they want to see the Gallery of Modern Art?

Their chubby kid appears to be a girl about two years old and is dressed in a red button-up wondersuit covered in pink and purple seashells. She seems perfectly content to stare up at the underside of my favourite bridge in Brisbane. Sometimes I imagine the Victoria Bridge being flipped upside down and the three long, massive slabs of concrete holding it up becoming the walls of two parallel race tracks where riders on neon-lit bicycles sprint across the river. I think that little girl in the red wondersuit sees this, too.

Over Mum's right shoulder a couple hold hands as they mosey blissfully along the river. The feller has a sky-blue sweater tied over his shoulders and he makes me think of one of those handsome models I see in the West End Aldi catalogues. His girl is neat and pretty with a big Colgate smile. Our eyes follow them.

'Reckon they'll last?' I ask.

'Nah, they're in trouble,' Mum says.

'Why?'

'Look at their shoes,' she says.

I lean forward for a sharper view. They're wearing the same navy-blue suede Adidas trainers. 'Oh, they're fucked,' I announce.

'Don't swear,' Mum says. 'But you're right. Matching shoes. That just can't be sustained.'

I return to my sketch. Time for the hands. I find hands the hardest to draw. My drawings of fingers always look the same. Yet fingers and hands are as unique to the subject as the face. Crooked middle knuckles on pinky fingers. Moles on index fingers. Ring fingers bending erratically to the outside. Fingers spaced too close together. Thumbs spaced too far from index fingers. Scars and calluses or smoothness with age or wrinkles with age or cracking with time and labour. These things make us who we are as much as our dreams and our memories and our laughter and our tears do.

Mum's got a goofy smile on her face, staring at me. That's her sentimental smile. That's her memory smile.

'What is it?'

'I just remembered the time you said you were gonna draw God. Do you remember that?'

'No.'

'You were nine years old,' Mum says. 'We'd spent a night sleeping in the carpark in that massive Christ Church Cathedral in Newcastle.'

'That was in the Pulsar?'

'Yep. That useless blue Nissan Pulsar. You'd spent all day marvelling at the ceilings inside the church and then you jumped in the back seat of the Pulsar with your sketchbook and you had that ratty ol' *Bob the Builder* flashlight you used to carry around and then you told me you were gonna draw a portrait of God. And I asked you how on earth you were gonna draw a portrait of God when no one knows what God looks like and you said, "Well, we'll all know what God looks like after I draw Him."'

Mum laughs and a tear forms in her eye. She wipes it away with her forefinger.

'Now, that's who you are,' I say.

'What?' she asks, rubbing her eyes with her shoulder sleeve.

'A woman who likes a good cry.'

'There are worse things to be.'

And I put those wet eyes in my sketch. Soft and warm eyes. Good eyes. The kind of eyes that leave nobody doubting who you are. I remember looking up at those eyes as a girl when Mum would talk me to sleep at night when I was scared. She'd tell me fairytale versions of my future life. All the things I was going to do. All the dragons I would slay. All the princes I would dance with.

'Hey, Mum?'

'Yeah.'

'Can I ask you a what-if question?'

'Of course.'

'What if I never meet a prince who wants to dance with me?'

Mum shrugs. 'Then you'll meet a princess,' she says, smiling. 'Or a pauper who is a prince on the inside. A princely pauper who treats you like a princess.'

'How will I ever meet a prince when I live in a van inside a yard most people are too scared to enter?'

A voice interrupts us. A man's voice. Bit too loud for a place so peaceful. Mum looks back over her shoulder to see who's speaking. It's the dad with the big black pram and the toddler in the red wondersuit. He and the mum seem to be arguing about which way they should go. He's pointing towards the west path heading to the State Library and the Queensland Museum. She's pointing towards South Bank. And now he's speaking in his native tongue and jabbing his index finger at her.

Mum turns back to me and raises her eyebrows the way she might raise her eyebrows at a cheap fireworks display. 'What was your question?'

'How will I ever meet a prince when I live in a van inside a yard most people are too scared to enter?'

Mum nods twice. 'The very fact you live in a van inside a scrapyard is the very reason you will meet your prince. Because the world turns, kiddo. This world is all upside down for you right now. But it will right itself soon.'

'When I turn eighteen?' I ask. 'When we go to the cops?'

Mum nods twice again. 'Yeah,' she says. 'When we go to the cops.' She takes a deep breath of river air, placing some kind of value on it, as though river air was a finite resource.

'The world turns for us all,' she says. 'One day you'll wake up and you'll realise the world has turned back upright for you and every bad thing you didn't deserve on the downside is made up for by every good thing rushing at you on the upside. You'll look up one day and see some face and suddenly it'll all make sense and all that bad downside stuff will seem entirely necessary. It'll just be ordinary life, it'll just be the normal turning of the world, but it'll feel miraculous to you. It'll feel engineered for you. It'll feel designed, drawn up like one of those crazy sketches you do. You'll call it fate. You'll say it was meant to be. And maybe it was. Because that's all the world was ever meant to do. Turn. And you were meant to turn with it.'

'The world turns,' I say. 'I like that, Mum. Because that means it's gonna turn for you as well.'

She shrugs. 'Maybe.'

'Twenty-third of April,' I say. 'Not long now, hey, Mum?'

She drops her head, runs a fingernail along the stone edging. 'No,' she says, 'not long now.'

Then she brightens, taps a knuckle on my knee. 'But what do we gotta be until then?'

'We gotta be invisible.'

'That's right,' Mum says, nodding, 'we gotta be invisible.'

'Okay, Mum,' I say. 'Now I just need you to smile.'

'Why?'

'Because I want to draw you smiling.'

She turns to me and gives a tentative smile.

'I mean a real smile.'

'How do I do a real smile?'

'Think of something that really makes you smile.'

Mum shakes her head and thinks for a moment. She looks out to the river and then something makes her laugh. And she turns back to me with a smile that makes me think of the moon at night when we see it through the hole in the roof of the van.

'Now that's a real smile,' I say. 'Hold that smile, will ya.'

Lines across the paper. Quick and true. No teeth in her smile. Lips closed but a smile as wide as that river behind her.

'You look beautiful,' I say. 'What are you thinking ab—'

And I can't finish my question because my attention is seized suddenly and entirely by the vision of a large black pram with big black tyres rolling too fast towards the river behind my mother's back. It's the pram with the chubby kid inside, dressed in the red wondersuit. Just a brief red flash of that suit as the pram rolls on.

This is a wrong vision. An impossible one. A world-turned-upside-down one. Fig trees don't grow on the moon. Queensland lungfish don't go to church on Sundays. Rainbows don't break through rocks. And prams don't roll into the Brisbane River.

Stay Here,
I Love You.

Stay Here, I Love You

February 2023

Pen and ink on paper

A startling image, more famous for what the artist has omitted from the scene than for what she has so darkly and unsettlingly included. This is a work of disseverment and dislocation. The artist depicts a child lost in the woods, like something from a Brothers Grimm fairytale, but there are pieces to this story that are missing. The viewer is not granted all of the necessary information. Things have fallen through the cracks in the sketch. The image is broken, almost like a mirror cracked. The title would suggest a work of love and devotion, but few would suggest this is anything but a reflection on fear.

A howl from the toddler's mother. Guttural. Primal. Terrible. A single shrieking plea to the world that turns too fast, too often, too soon. '*Nooooooo!*' she wails. Gravity and earth and the sloping of ancient land. The pram can only roll from here and that child's mother is too human to stop time and defy gravity and no matter how much she tries to extend her right arm it will not traverse the six or seven metres between the pram's handle and her right-hand fingers which are as straight as my pen. And my brain can form questions faster than I thought it was able to. A mystery in six parts. Why. Is. It. Rolling. So. Fast? Makes no sense from where we sit.

The mother's scream makes my mum turn instantly, as though the pitch of that '*Nooooooo!*' was manufactured in a place common to every mother's bloodwork. '*Noooooooo!*' the toddler's mother screams again, just as she trips on the sloping path and slams face-first into the concrete. 'Christina!' she shrieks as the pram breaks away from the curving footpath and continues straight across a segment of grey decorative cobblestone that descends to the high and irritated Brisbane River. No border on the river's edge to stop the pram. No fencing down there. Just a clean edge of cobblestone then eighty metres, northside to southside, of angry brown river water.

This moment is a story told by fate and chance and freak occurrence and that story's narrative is brutal. Unrelenting.

Horrifying. The pram has nowhere to go but forward and I say something stupid and useless to the air: 'Stop it!' And I don't know who I'm saying that to and why would anyone or anything want to listen to me, anyway? I'm just the invisible girl with the invisible mum watching the impossible unfold in slow motion and fast-forward – impossibly slow, but unbearably quick, too.

The pram's too robust. Too well made. Those big fat tyres are too efficient, move too fast. *Stop it. Stop it. Stop it.* And I know who I'm talking to, now. It's the thing that brought us here. It's the thing that gave me this life. It's the thing that made us run from the monster. It's cruelty. It's life itself. It's living. It's turning. It's art. And it will not stop.

The pram has only gathered more speed by the time it reaches the river's edge. The fat black front tyres fall first then the pram nose-dives for less than a metre before crashing into the thick and raging water. It flips over on impact and the girl in the red wondersuit, held tight by the pram straps, is now upside down, facing the water inside a pocket of air that starts to shrink as the pram goes under.

Then the pitter-patter of rubber-soled deck shoes on stone. Christina's father sprints to the river and launches himself in feet-first, but in his panic he overshoots and crashes into the water more than an arm's length from the pram. The current is already pushing it away from the river's edge and his desperately reaching hand. He flaps his arms furiously and haphazardly but goes nowhere. 'He can't swim!' the mother wails, now back on her feet.

The upturned and bobbing pram is already three body lengths away from the father, who is swallowing mouthfuls of river water as he thrashes in the crazed brown mess. I turn my head to look for help, but there's nobody on the path. Nobody coming from our left. Nobody coming from our right. Everybody's got to where they needed to go this morning. And then I realise my mum is standing above me. She looks at the toddler's mother, whose face is contorted with fear and anguish. Looks at the toddler's father, splashing hopelessly in the water. My mum is so calm. My mum is so still. The pram drifts further on by the current, deeper into the river, bobbing upside down and sinking gradually but somehow still half-afloat. Mum kicks off her rubber thongs, turns to me. 'Stay here,' she says. Her green eyes. Eyes like mine. That strength in her face.

'No, Mum, don't,' I whisper.

But she is the lion. Always the lion. 'Stay here, I love you,' she says.

And she turns and sprints along the river's edge, eyeing the moving pram and anticipating its trajectory. She tears off her hooded Billabong jumper as she runs. A thin white T-shirt underneath. All those scars on her forearms exposed. She sprints almost twenty metres ahead of the pram and then I suck in a deep breath of air and scream 'Mum!' as she dives headfirst into the river. She looks brilliant and strong and brave, powering through the water like the Australian Olympic swimmers I've seen on the television at The Well. She lifts her head to gauge the angle of the drifting pram then drops her head again, her short arms and short legs churning through the water like the paddles at the back of the old *Kookaburra Queen*.

She said, 'Stay here', but I can't stay here. I have to stand and I have to run. 'Help!' I yell. 'Somebody help!' And then in case someone can't hear that, I simply scream. A howl. A primal scream that rattles my ribs. And now I'm moving to the edge of the river where Mum dived in and I can see that she nailed the trajectory. She's cutting the drifting pram off, like a quick-moving missile angle-striking a slower submarine.

The girl's mother runs to the river's edge and screams again. 'Christina!' The woman's broken now. Hysterical. Weeping and wailing. The horror of the moment turning to physical pain. 'David!' she screams. 'He can't swim!' Her husband's still thrashing in the water and the current is dragging him closer to the more powerful flow in the middle of the river.

Mum lifts her head up and finds the pram again, just in time to reach her right arm out and grab one of its wheels before it passes by and drifts away forever. The river wants to drag that upturned girl all the way to its mouth then swallow her and spit her back out into Moreton Bay. But my mum will not let that happen. Stay here, Mum. Stay here, I love you.

She pulls back hard on the drifting pram and slows its movement, two hands on the pram wheel, swimming on her back as her skinny legs paddle against the flow of the current, the force of that angry river. 'Help us!' I scream, and I turn to my right and see two cyclists approaching from the South Bank end of the riverside walking track.

'Christina!' the father howls in the water. And I know the battle is over for that man now. He can't fight the river the way Mum can. He reaches an arm out helplessly as the current drags him past the pram, four body lengths from its reach, and Mum turns her head in time to see him pass. He's just another log now. Another tree limb ripped apart by storms and lost to the river. He looks at my mum and they share a moment of silent understanding. 'Kick,' Mum screams. 'You must kick your legs.' But the man seems frozen. In shock.

'David,' his wife screams again from the river's edge. He finds her on the shore. 'Bless,' he shouts. And then his body is spun around in the whirling current. He's turned on his side and his head is dunked in the river and he can't right himself again. He swallows mouthfuls of water. And then his head disappears for good. '*Davvvvid*,' his wife wails, falling to her knees.

Mum sucks two more breaths and finds her strength. 'Mum!' I yell. And I want to jump in, but she turns to me and shakes her head. No, stay there, she says with that head shake. *Stay here, I love you.* Then she lets the current carry her forward and, using its momentum, in one great effort leaps upwards like a jumping cod while flipping the pram over. The little girl coughs up two mouthfuls of river water and starts to wail, her arms thrashing in the water. Her cries cut her mother in two. 'Christina,' she shrieks.

By now the two cyclists have reached us, a man and a woman in helmets and blue and white tights. The man unclips his pedals, leaps off his racing bike and lets it crash hard to the ground. Throwing off his helmet, he dashes to the river's edge and dives in. Mum's drifting now, too weak to push against the current, and has only enough strength left to hold the pram up out of the water. The cyclist thrashes through the water with clean freestyle strokes, using the current to quicken his pace. He's moving so fast by the time he collides with the pram that he almost makes Mum lose her grip. He helps her prop up the pram, while also thrashing hard with his legs against the current. And I can't quite hear what Mum just said to him, but I think it was 'Take her' because the man has let go of the rear of the pram now and he's moved to the front, where he's wrestling with the harness release button above the toddler's belly. Finally it opens and the man grabs the child out and hugs her to his chest.

And then I see Mum stop him to tell him something I cannot make out from this distance. And she's crying so hard. Why is she crying like that? Stop crying like that, Mum. Stop crying and start swimming! But she just points at me on the riverbank and the man follows her finger then he turns back to Mum and nods his head. What is she saying?

And suddenly he pushes himself backwards, away from Mum and away from the pram. Mum watches him as he turns to face forward, lifts the toddler onto his left shoulder with his left arm then starts stroking hard with his right arm. She lets go of the pram and her head sinks briefly beneath the water as she drifts away. She bobs up again and floats briefly in place, trying to catch enough breath to cross the twenty or so metres she will need to traverse against the current to make it back to me.

'Mum,' I scream. And she finds my face on the riverbank and she mouths the words 'I love you' all the way to me across the troubled surface of the river, and she uses all of her strength to shout, 'I'm so sorry ...' And I swear there is another word at the end of that sentence, but it's muffled in the wind and by the water and disappears in the distance between us. I shake my head at my mum because she has nothing to be sorry for. 'Just swim,' I scream. 'Just move your arms and swim.'

Then my attention is grabbed momentarily by the man in the water with the toddler on his shoulder. He's already near the riverbank, close to me. But there's no place for him to grip on the rocky edging. 'Pass her to me,' I shout. The man's riding partner is beside me now and I ask her to hold my left hand tight with both of her hands. I lean forward as far as I can towards the river and hook my fingers onto the collar of the little girl's soaking-wet red wondersuit.

'Pull me,' I scream. And the woman yanks me back hard and the moment unfolds slowly enough for me to glance over one more time towards Mum as her head slips briefly beneath the water then pops back out again. The child is safe now. I hug her to my chest as the rider pulls me in and I fall hard on a patch of manicured South Bank grass and feel the kid's wet hair against the bottom of my chin as she begins wailing. She's heavier than I expected. She's in shock. Her soft and cold blue cheeks make me cry. The fragility of it all. Breathing too fast.

'Sshhhh,' I whisper. 'I've got you now. I've got you.' And suddenly I want to be a mum. It's the strangest thing. I wish for motherhood. Right now. Right this very second. Something primal in me. Something instinctive. I will raise you by myself, child of the river. You can live with me and Mum in the van with four flat tyres. You'll be so happy. I will keep you safe. I will love you forever.

But then the girl's mother falls on me. 'My baby!' she wails. And I let her go. 'Christina,' the mother howls, clutching the child to her chest as she rocks back and forth. 'Sshhhhh, sshhhhhhhh.'

I look up to see that the female cyclist has got a grip on her partner's wrist and is hauling him to the water's edge. There's only one person left in the water and my eyes try to find that person, but she's not where I last saw her. I can't see her or the pram anywhere.

'Mum!' I scream. And I can't breathe now. I can barely stand up by the river's edge. 'Mum!' But she's gone. I sprint fifty metres along the riverbank, scanning the water. And that's when I see her. Her chest and her head up out of the water, floating on her back in the current. Way, way out in the middle of the river. 'Muuuuum!'

But she doesn't hear me. She's just floating there on her back, looking up at the sky. So calm and graceful. Looks like an angel dropped in the Brisbane River from heaven, arms and legs spread, waiting for the big golden sunbeam elevator back up to the Pearly Gates.

I'm running along the side of the river now, trying to stay with her. 'Stay here, Mum,' I shout. 'I love you.' And I cry, but I don't want to cry because tears cannot save her. Only the current can save her. Only the river can spare her.

All at once I lose my footing on a dip in the ground where a sewerage pipe runs into the river, and I fall hard into the earth, eating dirt and grass as I roll arse over nose. I get to my feet and shake myself off, bleeding at my elbows and kneecaps, and try to find my mum again. But she's not floating or drifting. She has disappeared. She has gone.

'Mum,' I whisper. And I collapse on the mown grass by the river's edge and weep like Pablo Picasso told me to weep.

Drop my head and weep into my hands and weep into my crossed legs and weep into the earth. Then lie flat on my back with my arms out, splayed beneath the blinding sun. Stay like this for minutes and think I'll stay like this forever. But then I feel a gentle hand on my thigh and a voice asks, 'Are you all right?'

The female cyclist kneels beside me. She hasn't taken her sunglasses off, and she's still wearing her helmet. The blinding sun behind her head. 'Just breathe,' she says. 'It's all over now. You are so brave.'

I sit up and stare out at the river as she pats my right shoulder. 'Your mum just did something extraordinary,' she says. 'Your mother is a hero.'

I can't stop crying.

'The police will be here soon,' the woman says. 'Everything's going to be all right. We'll just stay right here.'

Stay here, I love you. Stay right here. The police are coming. Everything is going to be all right. Just stay right here.

'The police will be here soon,' I repeat, nodding. 'The police will be here soon.'

I drop my head and the woman asks me a question, but I don't hear what it is.

She shakes my shoulder gently. 'Hey, darlin',' she says, 'did you hear me? What's your name?'

I lift my head and turn to her, wiping tears and dirt from my eyes with the backs of my hands. 'What's my name?'

'Yeah, honey. What's your name?'

Deep breath. Rub more tears from my eyes. 'I can't tell you what my name is,' I say.

'Why's that darlin'?' the woman asks. She's gentle, soft with her questions.

I manage to stand up, point to the river Mum will call home from now on. 'Because she never told me what it was.'

And then I run. I sprint back along the riverside walking track. Past the man in the cycling tights who is gathering his breath by a stone wall off the walking track, hands on his knees. 'Hey, wait,' he shouts.

But I keep on running.

'Stop!' he yells, standing upright now. 'She gave me a message to give to you.'

I stop so abruptly that I almost pull a muscle in my right thigh. Too much adrenaline inside me to feel any pain. Too much feeling in me to feel anything at all. I turn around and face the man in blue and white cycling tights.

'What did she say?' I ask.

He takes three more steps and stops within arm's reach, wipes river water and sweat from his face. Heaves a deep breath and slows his brain in order to deliver the message exactly as my mum intended. It makes no sense, but he gives every word the time that it deserves.

'She said, "Roslyn will give you the world."'

I don't understand. 'I'm sorry,' I say. 'Can you please repeat that?'

'"Roslyn will give you the world,"' the man says. 'That's what she told me to tell you. Just before I swam away. Those exact words: "Roslyn will give you the world."'

'That's all she said?' I ask.

'That's all she said,' he replies through broken breaths.

I don't know how to respond. Then two words land louder than the rest. 'Thank you,' I say.

And I turn and run.

And the budding artist sprinted hard along that cruel river, stopping for nothing. Breathless. Heedless. Motherless. Just keep running, she told herself. Run for your lonely life. Don't stop until it's safe to stop. Run. Don't stop until you turn eighteen. Until you're an adult. She sprinted through a small crowd of people who had gathered around the other mother and her child, Christina. The mother's eyes found the artist's eyes as she passed. Bless, the man in the water had called her. Bless, he'd said, as though that was her name.

Bless. Now that's what I call a fucking name, the artist told herself in her scrapyard tongue. If her name was to be Bless, then it seemed only fitting that the artist's name on this day would be Curse. Curse Smith. Curse Jones. Curse Nobodyinparticular. And the artist slowed her running for a brief moment as she passed but did not stop. Bless this life, the artist told herself. Bless this child. Curse this villainous river. Just keep running. Back to the Adidas backpack. Back to the sketchbook and the ink pen with the one-millimetre nib and the page that was still open at the sketch of her mother who was now resting with the lungfish at the bottom of the Brisbane River. She stuffed the sketchbook in the bag and ran. Along the boardwalk by the Gallery of Modern Art. Along the smelly mangroves that guided the artist home. Behind the factories and warehouses she called her neighbourhood. Into the pitiful panel beater's scrapyard she called her home.

'Ros!' I shout. 'Ros!' But nobody's here. Nobody by the flameless campfire. Nobody emerging from the cars they call their homes. I run to Ros's Honda. Look through the windows. Nobody in there. And I scream louder this time: 'Roslyn!' Just in case she's close by, fishing for catfish again by the river, talking with her floater friends three doors down along Moon Street. But there's no life here in this yard. No noise but my dying heart inside my chest.

I run to the van that I will no longer share with my mother. Slide the side door open and slam it shut behind me. Crawl on my knees across our mattress and run my shaking hands along the wall of paper printouts. Images of Mum and me, arm in arm on picnic rugs. Mum and me, sunbaking on Manly beach. Mum and me in oversized Bargain City Christmas hats. Mum and me on my birthday, holding little chocolate cupcakes speared with lit candles.

Two more months. Only two more months before I turn eighteen. Two more months until she would say goodbye. She jumped the gun. She beat the starter's pistol. I bang my fist against the wall of the van – any harder and I'd crack a bone. Rage in my stomach running to my hands, which swipe viciously across all these cheap-paper memories. Images crunched and torn, memories destroyed. And the rage in my belly turns to sickness. I'm going to vomit. I slide the van door open and stagger onto the thick scrapyard grass. Bending forward, hands on my knees. Stomach muscles contracting. Mouth filling with saliva and something small crawling like a slug up my throat. Spew it out onto the grass: a ball of sardines and stomach gunk and an unkind follow-up mouthful of green bile and water. Wipe my mouth and turn my head to the sky. World spinning. Me spinning. World turned upside down.

'Ros!' I scream again. 'Ros.'

And I close my eyes to block the sun and all I see is Mum floating and then sinking into that deep brown river. 'Mum!' I scream. 'Mum!'

And I turn in useless circles then collapse in the yard and give myself over to weeping. A kind of sobbing that requires the operation of every muscle in my body. Physical grieving. Loss felt in my jawbone. My elbows know now that she's gone. My shoulder blades know that she's not coming back from that river. My ankles know it. My kidneys know it. After two full minutes of this body sobbing – when it hurts too much in my muscles and bones to cry – I wipe my face and realise I am sitting an arm's length from my Amina mirror. I see now how lost and deranged and desperate I look. Amina means 'trustworthy'. Mirrors are trustworthy. Mirrors never lie.

I walk to the mirror and stare at myself. Place one hand on each side of the mirror and watch myself weeping, then put my forehead so close to the mirror that all I can see is my crying eyes. I decide in this moment to ask the mirror a question and if I continue to get no answers from it then I will bash my useless and nameless forehead against it until my whole upside-down world turns red and that colour will paint itself over all the people in this sunshine city – all the rivers, all the lovers, all the mothers, all the fathers, all the monsters.

I stand up. 'Mirror, mirror, in the grass,' I whisper through gritted teeth as my warm breath forms a cloud of condensation on the mirror, 'what's my future? What's my past?'

I whisper it again. 'Mirror, mirror, on the grass, what's my future? What's my past?' And I start to weep while repeating, 'Mirror, mirror, on the grass, what's my future? What's my past?'

I get no answers, so I take a deep breath of hot, salty river air and pull my forehead back far enough that it can snap into red violence, and that's when I see her face for the first time. The woman in the red dress. All of her perfect face. Deep green eyes staring at me. Perfect cheekbones. Artful cheekbones. A black beauty spot above a full top lip. Bright red lipstick. Curled brown hair. Silver screen stuff. MGM Golden Age Hollywood stuff.

She sucks a drag on a long white cigarette. And, right here inside this useless yard, right now inside the worst day of my life, this woman in the mirror speaks to me. 'Why are you crying?' she asks.

Then she stares at me blankly as she waits for my response.

But I fear speech is no longer part of my skill set. 'Excuse me?' is all I can whisper.

'You heard me. Why are you crying?'

'Because my mum just drowned in the Brisbane River,' I say.

The woman in the red dress nods in understanding then turns her head sideways to exhale a plume of cigarette smoke. Beyond her profile I can see the fern-green wall of what looks like an apartment, and on that wall hangs a framed painting by Pablo Picasso. *Girl on the Ball*, the one where Picasso painted a man sitting on a concrete block staring at a girl standing on a ball. Just like the label promises.

'And what are you gonna do about that?' the woman in the red dress asks.

'About what?'

'About your mum drowning in the Brisbane River?'

'I don't know,' I say. 'I was just about to bang my forehead six times against this mirror and then I was seriously considering joining Mum in the drink.'

'That would be a waste,' the woman in the red dress says, taking another long drag on her cigarette.

'A waste of what?' I ask.

'Everything you're gonna be,' she says. 'Everything you're gonna do. Every laugh. Every tear. Every joke. Every pie with mushy peas you're ever gonna eat. Every song you're ever gonna sing. Every box you're ever gonna tick. Every challenge you're ever gonna lick. Every line of black ink you're ever gonna add to another empty white sketch page. Every splash of colour you're ever gonna brush across this cruel black world.'

'Who are you?' I ask.

'Who am I?'

'Yeah, who are you?'

'What does it matter who I am? Who is anyone? Who are you? Are you the butthole-ugly face I see before me or the ill-formed words I hear from your mouth? Are you the legs that ran from that river or are you the heart that kept you breathing? Are you every dream you have at night or are you every wish that terrifies you in the morning? Are you your sins or are you your redemptions or are you your smile or your rage or your longing or your hope or are you all those tear stains I see running through the dirt caked upon your face? Are you everything you see in the mirror every morning at dawn before the birds have even whistled forth the rising of the sun? Are you all those tragic questions rattling through that troubled head or are you all those answers your mother just carried to the bottom of the Brisbane River?'

'Jeez, I just wanted to know your name.'

'My name? Oh, sorry.' Big drag. Big blow. 'My name is Lola.'

'That's a cool name, Lola.'

'I know.'

'Lola means "sorrow".'

'I know. I'm full of sorrow.'

'Why?'

'Because you just told me your mother drowned in the Brisbane River. That's the saddest thing I've ever heard.'

'I know,' I say. 'That's why I'm gonna walk to the middle of the Victoria Bridge and throw myself in with her.'

'What, you're not even gonna wait for Roslyn to get home?'

'What's that gonna change?'

'Maybe she'll know what that message was all about? The words your mum told that man in tights. Maybe that message holds the key to finding all the answers you've been looking for all this time?'

'What if I don't wanna know all the answers?'

Lola takes another drag, nods her head. 'Yeah, I get that. I think it's safe to say the answers will be tragic.'

'What makes you say that?'

'What part of the past eighteen years of your life makes you think the answers will be anything but tragic?'

'Fair point,' I say.

'But that doesn't mean you should just ignore the answers.'

'I guess you're right. Besides, I can't possibly feel worse than I feel right now.'

She drags on the cigarette. 'Nah, you're gonna feel plenty worse than this.'

'I am?'

'Of course. But then you're gonna feel better than this. And then you're gonna feel worse than ever before. And then, just maybe, you're gonna feel better than you thought you could ever feel.'

'Are you talking about true love?' I ask.

'Well, I'm not talking about chips and gravy,' Lola replies.

My heart expands by half a millimetre inside me. I wipe the tears from my eyes. 'But first I gotta get all the answers?'

'Well, right now, you don't need *all* the answers,' Lola says. 'For now, all you need is the answer to just one question.'

'Which question?'

'How do I stop myself from jumping in the river?'

'Good question,' I say. 'How do I stop myself from jumping in the river?'

'You wait for Roslyn to get home.'

I nod.

'What's your last name, Lola?'

'My last name? Can't you tell? Isn't it obvious to you?'

'Why would it be obvious to me?'

'Because it's apt. It's an aptronym. Do you know what an aptronym is?'

'Yeah,' I say, 'I was reading about aptronyms in the Brisbane Square Library. It's where someone has a name peculiarly suited to where they have found themselves in life. Like the world's fastest man being called Usain Bolt. Or the inventor of the loo being called Thomas Crapper. Sara Blizzard growing up to be a brilliant meteorologist.'

'Nominative determinism,' Lola says. 'People gravitating to existences that fit their names.'

'Spare a thought for Penny Hooker,' I say.

'And your friend Esther Inthehole,' Lola adds.

'She just called herself that because she didn't want to keep using her husband's name. Lot of old single ladies doing that round here. They're just being funny. It's a middle finger to marriage. Tabitha Underthebridge. Sandy Overthehill. Melissa Openforbusiness.'

'And they're very determined to keep raising that middle finger, are they not?'

'Lola Inthedream?' I suggest.

She shakes her head, smiling.

'Lola Inthemind?'

'No.'

'Lola Inthekillerdress?'

She laughs. 'Just Lola is fine for now,' she says.

'Mirror, mirror, on the grass,' I whisper, 'what's my future? What's my past?'

Lola nods and smiles. Another long drag and then she stubs out her cigarette in an ashtray I cannot see.

'Well,' she says, 'I'm not gonna lie.'

'Mirrors never lie,' I say. 'Mirrors are trustworthy. Especially mine.'

She nods twice. 'Your past? I'm afraid it's an unimaginable horror show of tragedy and intrigue. Your past will almost be enough to kill you.' Then she waves a finger at me. 'But you'll survive. You'll grow stronger. You will become a great artist. Because of your strength. Because of your past. Because of how you feel right now. Because you want to jump in the river, but won't.'

She smiles. 'And your future? Well, how shall I put it …?' She winks at me through the mirror. 'It's a fucking triumph!'

Roslyn in the Scrapyard, with Elephant

Roslyn in the Scrapyard, with Elephant

February 2023

Pen and ink on paper

One of several portraits the artist sketched of her longtime scrapyard neighbour Roslyn. Here, an ageing Roslyn appears to share a loving, almost maternal relationship with the unlikely elephant sitting casually to her left. Note the elephant's trunk resting warmly, protectively even, upon Roslyn's right shoulder. For reasons that are not always apparent, the artist features elephants regularly in her work. Perhaps the elephant is being used here to imbue her subject with a sense of power and strength. Or, more likely, to speak to the power of a good memory, a key element to any elephant's survival in the wild.

Guess Mum was being artful. Double meanings and all that. *Roslyn will give you the world.* She'll give me everything I need. She'll give me food and shelter. A squeeze. A hand. A tissue to wipe away all them tears that keep streaming down my dirty cheeks. But even more useful than her tissues are *her* tears. Her own feelings about Mum going down to the bottom of that river. When she cries it makes me feel I'm not so dumb spilling all that valuable H_2O from my blinkies.

Just the two of us now sitting in her Honda. Ros with her hands on the steering wheel, though we're not going anywhere but this quiet scrapyard. Me sitting beside her with a black hole of grief burning through my body, from my brain, where I keep my mum's wisdoms, to my heart, where I keep the rest of her.

'I think your mum and me had an unspoken agreement,' Ros says. 'I wouldn't ask her how she ended up in Moon Street, and she wouldn't ask me. We could shut up and pretend to be sinless mothers for as long as we needed. We'd judge each other on the things we did in the now, and the past could go fuck itself. That was the deal, anyway. Then one night we were suckin' on a bottle of Cointreau by the fire. Warm Cointreau by a campfire, kid, that's the closest thing you'll get to a legal heroin nod. Shit makes you glow, inside and out. Equal parts rectified spirit, Caribbean orange peel and Stasi truth serum. Soon enough I'm spillin' the beans on how I lost my teeth and why I'm so fuckin' terrified of Pascall Clinkers.'

I know this story. We all know this story in the yard. And knowing this story makes me think about how Mum and me came to be living here at the back of the Tinman's Smash Repairs shed at 38 Moon Street, West End, and how it was we came to know Ros, the Wizard of Oz.

*

People always walk past Moon Street without stopping because it's so easy to walk past without stopping, but walking past Moon Street without stopping when you visit West End is a bit like visiting The Louvre and walking past the *Mona Lisa* without stopping. Thin dead-end street. Magic in the daylight and kinda dangerous after dark. The one leading off Montague Road, tucked between Beesley Street and Pidgeon Close. It runs right down to the river, and I've sketched a thousand different versions of it in my mind and in my books.

My beloved ink-pen-perfect Moon Street. Those spray-painted words in yellow on the footpath: *Land Back Bitches!* That electrical box painted with a large image of a red horseshoe magnet forming the letter 'U' in the painted message *U R MAGNETIC*. A red vinyl community couch on the footpath that has lived through relentless sun damage and countless afternoon Brisbane summer hailstorms. The black mulberry tree that Charlie Mould and I pick at in August and September when the berries are fat and ripe. Small business workshops and warehouses that all seem out of place in West End. The Uncommon Valour military surplus shop at number 12 beside Christopher Stoikov's Motorcycle Spares shed at number 14. The Arrowheads archery supplies shop at number 18 beside the West End Radiator Service shed at number 20.

Most of my friends live down the end of Moon Street in cheap government housing units and halfway houses. There's the Queensland Department of Housing unit block at number 28 that everybody calls The Peach on account of its colour. Next to it is The Well, the drop-in centre, at number 30. The backyard of The Well connects to the backyard of the St Peter the Apostle Church on Canoe Street, the small but essential church where local floaters go to pray when they want crumbed lamb cutlets returned to the lunch menu in The Well's kitchen. Flora Box's Ebb 'n' Flo seafood wholesalers shed is further up towards Montague Road, at 6 Moon Street. Because she helped us out when we first arrived in 2017, Mum and I used to look at Lady Flo like she was Glinda, the Good Witch in *The Wizard of Oz*. But Ros and my other neighbour, June, will hear none of that. Ros and June don't call Lady Flo 'the Good Witch of Oz'. They call her 'the Wicked Witch of the West End'.

*

'Do you remember how your Mum used to break down cryin' some days?' Ros asks me from the driver's seat of the Honda Jazz.

'Yeah, I remember,' I say.

I remember a lot of things. Mum biting her fingernails until they bled. Her believing every man we met was a cop or the son of a cop or the brother of a cop or the gay lover of a cop. The running. Running for as long as I had memories. Stories transforming along the way. Sometimes she'd tell strangers we were running from Adelaide. Sometimes she'd say we were running from New Zealand. Sometimes Melbourne. Sometimes Alice Springs. The route of the long-distance run changed so much that I could never work out exactly where we had come from or where we were going. I'd find maps of Australia in atlases in public libraries and try to retrace our long and meandering journey. I'd drag my pencil across a map of the country and the lines would end up circling back on themselves as if I was drawing a big ball of steel wool. I remember deserts and then trees and then snow and then sea and then, from the age of seven, I remember Weipa. A red dirt mining town of four thousand people – half of them kind and the other half kinda drunk – on Queensland's far north Cape York Peninsula, where Mum met a bauxite miner who went by the name of Spin and let us sleep in a caravan he kept near the mouth of Mission River. We could never rent a proper place, not even a proper room with proper windows and proper doors, because Mum could never tell anyone her proper name.

Names. I remember all the names. She was using 'Louise Oxford' when she died. Before we came to Brisbane, she was 'Naomi Murphy'. Before Naomi she was 'Carol Malone' and before Carol she was 'Giaan Bridges'. I remember hair dye. Different colours every six months staining bathroom sinks. Piles of hair on the floors of public toilets. I remember her weight gains. Her binge-eating. Slabs of Cadbury chocolate. Tim-Tams dipped in milk. And her weight shedding. Not eating anything for weeks. Sucking on boiled lollies and apple cider vinegar drinks. I remember her waking up in the night, screaming beside me. Terrible nightmares. Fire dreams. She once dreamed I was burning alive in the Toyota HiAce and she couldn't open the sliding door to get me out. I remember fingers shaking. Weeping. Arms around me. My arms around her. And I remember how she was often broken, not by what was happening around us, or by the street or the scrapyard, or the people who would scare us when we were walking home, but by the memories.

'I used to see her sobbin' into her hands by the river,' Ros says. 'And I'd run up and throw my arms around her and I'd tell her everything was gonna be all right, but she couldn't stop cryin' and I always knew there was somethin' more than sadness in those tears.'

*

The Tinman is a friend of ours named Trevor Prendergast, who is seventy-two years old and dying from lung cancer, which is why he hasn't opened his smash repairs shed in two years. Six years ago, on a Monday morning not long after dawn, the Tinman found Mum and me sleeping in the orange 1987 Toyota HiAce van he'd left rusting to death on an overgrown block of land the size of a tennis court behind his shed. It looked out through West End mangroves to the snaking Brisbane River and was bordered by a high wire fence and three higher lines of barbed wire. For the previous four nights, we'd been sneaking into the yard via the neighbouring property, which was owned by a Korean company that made versatile and reliable luggage products and, conveniently for us, hadn't fixed the loose rear left corner of their back fence. With the help of a pair of rusty fourteen-inch bolt cutters she'd been given by a generous and drunk boilermaker she'd befriended in Weipa, Mum quickly created a hole big enough for us to squeeze through, along with a most unreliable brown vinyl suitcase we'd found on the road into Byron Bay.

'Git the fuck outta my vehicle,' the Tinman barked at Mum, while banging a ratchet handle on the van's rear window. Mum was always brilliant in such moments. She'd rush out from wherever we were sleeping – someone's house, someone's garage, someone's boat, someone's rusted van – and apologise profusely before launching, inevitably, into the dark tale of the Tyrannosaurus Waltz and the many dances she'd had to perform with my father the monster, the tyrant lizard. How she'd danced and danced and how she'd run with me in her arms. Never enough detail to identify herself, but just enough to ensure the blue meanies weren't called.

*

'What else is in tears other than sadness, Ros?' I ask from the passenger seat of the Honda Jazz.

'You really wanna know?'

'Ros, my mother just drowned in the Brisbane River,' I say. 'Every possible hope I have of finding something out about my past drowned with her. Yes, I really wanna know.'

'Guilt,' Ros says. 'Plain ol' miserable guilt. Sure, there was sadness in those tears of hers. But I swear there were a good few capfuls of guilt poured into that mix.'

'How do you know it was guilt?'

'Trust me, kid,' Ros says. 'I know a mother's guilt when I see it.'

*

Tinman Trev comes off all grizzly bear on the outside but inside him, I've come to realise, is a puppy dog with its tongue out running in circles around a bag of doggy biscuits. Like almost everybody else who ever heard Mum talk of the Tyrannosaurus Waltz, the Tinman never phoned the cops. He never chased us off, neither. In my experience, humans are mostly good and decent. In my experience, strangers will more often than not choose compassion over fear, protection over caution.

Maybe it didn't hurt that Mum could have been the sister Kylie and Dannii Minogue never had. She was pretty and she was kind. On the day she met Tinman Trev she must have weighed about as much as a watermelon and she came across just as sweet, with no bad seeds. I'm certain Trev felt sorry for her. Or maybe Trev knew something about tyrant lizards, too, like almost every other Australian I've ever met. 'Make yourself scarce by dawn each morning and you're welcome to stay as long as you like,' he said. 'I don't wanna see you. You gotta be invisible, you understand?'

'I understand,' Mum said. 'Invisible.'

Later that morning, at the public gas barbecue beneath the shadow of Kurilpa Bridge, Mum was frying slices from a knob of rolled chicken meat.

'How do we stay invisible?' she asked me, the way a drill sergeant might ask a young soldier how to polish a boot.

'No names,' I said. 'No noise. No past.'

Mum nodded only once. 'I love you,' she said.

'I love you more,' I said.

'I love you more than all the grass there is in Ireland,' she said.

'I love you more than all the sand there is in Egypt,' I said.

Guilt in those tears. I hadn't considered that. I just thought it was sorrow. I remember her crying so much some nights that she'd dehydrate herself and she'd have to slide open the van door and vomit on the grass of the scrapyard. I don't remember guilt. I remember love. I remember moons. I remember the hole in the van roof, about the size of a tennis ball. I still cover it with the tin lid of a large stew pot when it rains. Sometimes late at night Mum and I would lie back and look up through the hole in the roof and see the white moon and the lives we might have led if Mum had never had to dance the Tyrannosaurus Waltz.

'What did you want to be, Mum?' I asked when I was twelve years old. 'What were your dreams when you were my age?'

'I wanted to be a mum and I wanted to spend my days walking through Brisbane art galleries with my gifted daughter,' she replied.

'Wait, that's exactly what you spend your days doing,' I said.

'I know. All my dreams came true.'

*

One night when I was fifteen and we were looking up at a yellow moon, I asked Mum why I couldn't see the man in the moon and she said that some nights he likes to stay invisible, low key. Not always on show. Anonymous.

'Bit like us,' I said.

'A lot like us,' Mum said.

Then I asked Mum how much longer I had to be invisible for.

'Three more years,' she said.

'What happens in three more years?' I asked.

'That's when you'll be an adult,' she said. 'That's when they can't take you to them places you don't want to go.'

'No more runnin',' I said.

'No more runnin'.'

'I wish I was eighteen tomorrow,' I said.

'I wish it would take an eternity for you to reach eighteen.'

'Why?'

'Because this all has to end then.'

I looked around the van. I didn't see much but a hole in the roof and a slice of the moon.

'What is *this*, anyway?' I asked.

'This is you and me,' Mum said. 'This is paradise.'

'Why does it have to end?' I asked.

'Because one day I'm gonna have to go away,' Mum said.

'Why do you have to go away?' I asked.

'You know why,' Mum replied. 'Because I did something very, very bad. Because one day you'll want me to go away.'

I nestled my head into her breast. 'I don't care what you did,' I said. 'I'll never want you to go away. I love you, Mum. More than all the bicycles in Beijing.'

'I love you more than all the tacos in Mexico,' she shot back.

'Don't make me think of tacos,' I cried.

'Taaaacoooos!' she sighed.

One day you'll want me to go away. I always wondered what she meant by that. I thought she meant that one day I'd grow tired of running. One day I'd want to live a normal life. One day I'd want something more than a van with four flat tyres. But maybe what she really meant was *One day you will know the truth.* Or perhaps: *One day you will hate me for what I have done.*

*

After a year in the orange van, Trev let Mum and me stay during the daylight on weekends. After two years, Trev let Mum and me cut the overgrown grass and build a vegetable patch by the van. Not long after that, he gave Mum a key to the padlock that opened the gate to the rear yard. Not long after that, he let a homeless friend I knew from The Well set up a sleeping bag beside our van because I told Trev what a good kid Charlie Mould was and how great he would be at doing odd jobs around the lawn and the shed. Then one night Charlie turned up to find that Trev had given him a whole new home to sleep in: a 1989 white Ford panel van, gutted and rusted from the inside but fitted with a foam mattress and brand-new bedsheets that Trev had bought from the Arana Hills Kmart. 'You don't ever have to find no heart, Tinman,' Mum said. 'You got the biggest heart in Australia. You're the kindest man in Oz.' And that's why we called the place what we call it. That's why we live in Oz.

*

'I think one day the guilt got too much for your mum,' Ros says. 'I remember you and Charlie were down at the cement factory getting into mischief. Your mum comes to me all distressed. Like she'd been thinkin' so much she'd turned her brain into a big ball of silly string. Talkin' all quick like God had tapped fast-forward on her TV remote. Said she couldn't live with herself no more. Couldn't live with what she'd done.'

'You mean, what she done to my father?' I ask.

'Yeah, maybe it was that. But I think it was something else. I think it was something she'd done to you. She said she was going away. And that's when she reached into her pocket and handed me the world.'

*

Roslyn's 2002 Honda Jazz was also donated by the Tinman. I keep telling her she needs a bigger car with more leg room to sleep in – something like a Subaru Outback or a seven-seat Toyota Kluger – but she always says I'm talking smack because I'm jealous that her car is newer than my van and has tyres that are actually inflated.

Roslyn was a forty-three-year-old wife and mother of a fourteen-year-old daughter when she had an anxiety attack inside St Patrick's Cathedral, Parramatta. She'd been working as an accountant for three family-run community supermarkets across Western Sydney. The anxiety attack occurred at the very moment she looked into an open coffin and saw the face of her dead father, an exceedingly strict and pious man who viewed suburban corner-store confectionery in much the same way as most parents view city-corner narcotics. He flogged Roslyn with the leather razor strop that hung in the family kitchen if he ever found his daughter indulging in those notorious gateway temptations manufactured by the devil: jelly babies and Jaffas. 'You got the prettiest smile in your class,' her father yelled. 'You want your smile to rot away, Ros? Is that what you want?'

That first anxiety attack led to several more anxiety attacks and Roslyn sought advice from a long-term work colleague she knew who had suffered similar attacks in the wake of her husband's premature death from bowel cancer. Her colleague said Roslyn would benefit from finding hobbies that were calming, and she herself had found great relaxation in playing the slots at her local Western Sydney leagues club. She invited Roslyn to join her at the slots every Tuesday and Thursday night. Roslyn found an immediate name-based connection to a brightly coloured machine called Cracklin' Rosie, which was adorned with the image of a vibrant red-haired cowgirl tipping her hat and winking at potential gamblers in a way that suggested they might just get a kick out of slipping a coin in her slot.

Roslyn was soon spending every Tuesday and Thursday night enveloped in Cracklin' Rosie's warm glow, with a cupful of coins in her left hand and, always, a three-hundred-gram bag of Pascall Clinkers candy between her legs. Soon enough, she was visiting Cracklin' Rosie on Wednesdays at lunchtime too. And then Saturday afternoons while waiting to pick up her daughter, Zoey, from netball. And then Monday nights. And then Fridays at lunchtime.

After a while, Cracklin' Rosie turned off the gentle cowgirl charm for Roslyn. She got needy. Got evil. She didn't just want Roslyn's time and calm and hope and desire. She wanted the family's life savings and then she wanted the impossible. She wanted Roslyn to cook the accounting books at her work and transfer small amounts of supermarket money into a secret account established only for Cracklin' Rosie. Five hundred dollars. One thousand. Then ten thousand and twenty thousand.

In the meantime, Roslyn had developed a most unexpected addiction to Pascall Clinkers and she laughs today when she thinks about how she met countless prisoners in the Silverwater Women's Correctional Centre who'd spent their first week in prison cold-kicking heroin and methamphetamines. 'I spent my first week kickin' them fuckin' Clinkers,' she says.

*

Ros leans across my legs from the Honda's driver's seat. She pops open the glovebox. Two headlamps there, along with

McDonald's napkins, Kleenex tissues and a small first-aid kit. There's also lip gloss and an old worn tube of pink zinc cream for her nose, which is always being excavated for nasty carcinomas by Dr Jenyns, the GP who visits The Well every second Friday. Ros digs her left hand deep into the glovebox and grips the world in her hands, a plastic globe the size of a squash ball attached to a keychain, which, in turn, is attached to a silver car key. She holds the keychain in her open palm. Bright blue colours for the sea, the continents in vivid reds and greens and yellows. There's Australia, coloured brown. Dirt brown. Sunburnt brown.

'She gave me this,' Ros says. 'She told me to give it to you. She told me to tell you that she had to go away because she didn't want to hurt you any more than she already had. And that's when I grabbed her by the collar of her shirt and I don't remember ever talkin' more cross to her. I told her she was chicken shit if she ran like that, and I told her she could tell you about that running away stuff to your face because I wasn't gonna be the one who broke a little girl's heart, because that particular little girl didn't have no more hearts left to be broke.'

'She never would have left me like that,' I say.

'Well, I'm happy to say you're right, kid,' Ros says. 'She never did. But she told me to keep this safe, all the same. Just in case something ever happened to her. Just in case them cops she was always fussin' about closed in. Or in case somethin' worse happened.'

Ros hangs the world above my lap from her fingertips. 'Looks like somethin' worse just happened,' she says.

I hold my palm open and she places the globe on it.

'Do you remember where you guys were livin' before you landed here in Oz?' Ros asks.

'Yeah, I remember,' I say. 'Bedrock Wrecking Yard, Rocklea.'

'Yabba dabba doo, kid,' Ros says, nodding. 'You remember the car you guys called home?'

'Yeah, I think I remember. Yellow car. All bashed in at the front. 'Bout as big as a letterbox.'

'What was the make of that car, kid?'

My mind runs through an automotive showreel of cramped rear-seat sleeps, awkward back seat scoops of Heinz tinned spaghetti, movie nights on portable DVD players: *Finding Nemo* in a Ford Laser, *Frozen* in a Ford Focus.

'I can't remember,' I say.

'What was your mum's star sign?'

'Gemini.'

Ros nods. 'Yellow Gemini,' she says. 'Bedrock Wrecking Yard.'

'What am I gonna find in that car, Ros?' I ask, wrapping my fist around the keychain, around Mum's world.

'I don't know, kid,' Ros says. 'She never told me. Maybe it's something beautiful. But maybe it's something terrible, too. I don't know.'

Holding the world in my hand, I think about how the renowned art critic and curator E.P. Buckle might speak of this moment to a group of art lovers walking through the posthumous exhibition of my life and work at the New York Met. What would he say about this moment here and now, when the girl with no name chose danger? Chose daring.

I see a girl in Buckle's gallery group, aged about twelve, wearing a three-quarter-length yellow peacoat. She turns from a painting of mine to her mother, who stands by her side. 'She was sad, wasn't she, Mum?' she says.

'She was very sad,' her mother replies. 'But never forget, she was also brave. She was a cartwheeler.'

Roslyn puts a gentle hand on my closed fist. 'The world belongs to you now, kid,' she says. 'Time to decide what you're gonna do with it.'

"Back of Holden
Gemini Car
filled with
Planets,
Stars
and
Interstellar
Dust

Back of Holden Gemini Car Filled with Planets, Stars and Interstellar Dust

February 2023

Pen and ink on paper

The artist was seventeen years old and heartbroken, though evidently moved by something she had seen inside an abandoned and worthless 1978 Holden Gemini automobile. The piece is seen by many as a tribute to discovery, or what the esteemed Metropolitan Museum of Art curator E.P. Buckle once called 'the luminescence of truth'.

It's 9 p.m. when I tap the metal handle of Roslyn's old black Maglite flashlight against the curtained rear windows of Charlie Mould's white Ford panel van. Walking shoes on my feet. Black Adidas backpack over my shoulders.

Charlie opens the left-side rear door of the van just enough for me to see he's wearing his Paddle Pop lion pyjamas. The ones that say *Cool Bananas* amid a galaxy of floating banana Paddle Pop ice creams. He's got a headlamp strapped to his forehead. 'Princess Diana,' he says.

It was six years ago that Charlie decided to call me 'Princess Di' because that would mean he was my Prince Charles. But Charlie ain't no prince. Charlie's just one of those lovable scoundrels with a hidden heart of gold, like Han Solo, Keith Richards and the Artful Dodger. Charlie's the Artful Dodgiest. Total artist, too. Born for it, like me. Burns for it, like me. We're gonna start an art movement out of Brisbane together. *Nouveau Brisbane. Neo Pineapple. Post Banana.* We can't decide.

'You doin' anything right now?' I whisper.

'Why you whisperin'?' Charlie whispers back.

'I don't know,' I whisper, then return to my normal voice. 'You doin' anything right now?'

'I was doing my Sudoku over a glass of Golden Oak Fruity White.'

'You wanna come help me discover who I am?'

'Sure,' Charlie says.

'Meet me by the side gate in five minutes. Bring that headlamp.'

I start to move away.

'Hey, wait,' Charlie says. 'Come 'ere.' He waves me in to him.

'Why?'

'Just come 'ere, will ya.' He opens the rear door wider as I take two steps closer to him. And he pulls me in to his chest for a hug that lasts more than a minute. Then he sinks his head into my shoulder and whispers to me. 'I counted them up. I got to six. There have been six people in this world who ever really gave a shit about me. You're one of them, Princess. Your mum was one of 'em, too.'

He starts to cry. 'I thought she was an angel,' he says.

And now I sink my head into Charlie's shoulder and cry as well. 'I thought she was, too.'

*

Rocklea train station is eight stops from South Brisbane train station. The Bedrock Wrecking Yard is on Hutton Drive, a seven-minute walk from Rocklea station. Not a soul alive on Hutton Drive at 10 p.m.

'Maybe it's a bag full of gold bricks,' Charlie suggests, tapping a stick on the footpath the way an ice-hockey player might tap a hockey stick on the ice. 'Maybe she was a billionairess before she had to run away with you,' he continues. 'You'd have to keep gold bricks like that in the back of a Gemini. Hard to exchange that shit for cash without answering a bunch of questions.'

'She wasn't a billionairess, Charlie. If she was a billionairess I don't think we would have spent the past six years sleeping in a van.'

'Maybe it's a dead body?'

'What the fuck is in that Golden Oak? It's not a dead body.'

'Maybe it's your old man, all curled up and bony? Did you ever find out what happened to his body? Did she ever tell you where he was buried?'

No, come to think of it, Charlie Mould, she never did tell me that.

'It's not a dead body and it's not the bones of my ol' man,' I say. 'And get rid of that stick. The yard's just around this bend.'

The Bedrock Wrecking Yard is tucked into a row of Hutton Drive industrial sheds: a truck repair yard, custom car detailing sheds, a wholesale food and catering warehouse. There's a high and rusting barbed-wire fence at the front. Inside is a small single-level box of a house with a flat roof that appears to be acting as the yard's sales office. Resting upon the flat roof of this box house is a beat-up frog-green Volkswagen Beetle with a sign sticking out of its roof: *Bedrock Wreckers*. Behind the house is a dirt parking lot of wrecked and rusting cars. Old Holdens and Fords and newer Nissans and Hyundais and Kias and Hondas and Toyotas by the dozen. The gates to the yard are locked with a heavy chain.

'So how do we get in?' Charlie asks.

'I don't know. We used to just walk in. Mum used to know the guy who ran this place.'

We had hitchhiked to Brisbane from Bundaberg in 2017. Mum was looking for a car, and someone at the Emmanuel City Mission, where we'd been going for lunch, had put her onto this place because the guy here used to do up cars and donate them to people who needed wheels but couldn't afford them. He didn't have a car that worked for Mum but said that if it was a place to crash we needed then we were welcome to take our pick from the two hundred or so cars that were rusting out back.

'He was a good man,' I tell Charlie. 'He let us sleep in the Gemini after the gates shut. I can't even remember his name. Damn, what was his fucking name?'

What was it that Ros said? *Yabba dabba doo.*

'Did you ever watch that show *The Flintstones*?' I ask Charlie.

'What the fuck is *The Flintstones*?' he shoots back.

'It's an old cartoon people our parents' age used to watch. It was all, like, modern life – parents dealing with spoilt kids and shit – but set in the Stone Age.'

'How'd that work?'

'I don't know, but it works in cartoons. All the characters lived in a town called Bedrock. I think the guy who ran this place had the same name as one of the characters and that's why he called this place Bedrock. But I can't remember his name. I think it was Ernie or somethin'?'

'*Bert* and Ernie?'

'That's *Sesame Street*,' I say, as we scurry towards the industrial space to the right of the wrecking yard, a large warehouse for a company called Latitude Couriers. I clamber easily over the white concrete wall in front of it, and Charlie follows. We slip down the left side of the warehouse, adjacent to the barbed-wire fence of the wrecking yard. At the back of the warehouse are a scattering of pallet stacks and small shipping containers and a large cast-iron J.J. Richards industrial waste bin on wheels next to a row of empty parking spaces. I look across to the wrecking yard and spot a stack of four crushed cars close to the fence. Press my shoulder against the industrial bin and start pushing. When Charlie tucks his shoulder against the bin beside me, the thing starts moving. Once we have it against the fence, I stand, put a hand on Charlie's shoulder and say, 'Boost?' It's all I have to say because Charlie and me have spent the past six years of our lives boosting each other up over fences and up onto ledges and up into windows all over South East Queensland.

He props his legs and cups his hands, forming a platform for my right boot, which he raises up with one great heave of his noodle arms. I pull Charlie up onto the bin with me then unzip my backpack and pull out Mum's fourteen-inch bolt cutters.

'Will ya take a knee for me, Hercules?'

'You just use me for my body, don't ya?' Charlie replies as he drops his left knee and props his right thigh up for me to stand on with both feet. Once balanced, I reach the bolt cutters up to the three lines of old barbed wire and press the long blue cutting arms together using every bit of power in my shoulder and chest muscles. The wires snap easily and I climb over the fence, pushing the loose barbed wires aside as I step onto the stack of four crushed cars. Behind it is a stack of three cars and then a stack of two cars. It's like a staircase of cars running from the fence and Charlie and me bound down like monkeys descending the steps of an Aztec temple. Charlie lands hard on the final step and a red Commodore releases a loud *boink* that echoes across the yard.

'Quiet,' I whisper through gritted teeth.

The artist switched on the Maglite. Rows of disused cars. Hundreds of them, split by gravel walking paths. Hatchbacks and sedans and SUVs and wagons and old bashed-up English and Swedish cars from the 1980s and old dusted-up Australian cars from the 1990s.

'Where do we find the Gemini?' Charlie asked, strapping his headlamp to his forehead.

'This way,' the artist replied, pressing forth on a gravel path that led towards the rear left side of the yard. Her stomach turned. Her fingers were shaking, as much because of the frightening environment created by the stacks of crushed cars that flanked her as for the thought of what was waiting for her inside the worthless Gemini. 'Mum and I used to walk along these paths,' she said. 'I remember going to the back of the yard and there was a big ol'—'

And she saw it just as she said it. 'A big ol' bus.' It was blue and white with red hubcaps on the wheels. Some kind of school bus from the 1970s. She aimed the flashlight at its broken headlights, its shattered windshield. 'I used to sit in the driver's seat and pretend I was driving Mum to school,' she said. 'And that means the Gemini is just over—'

I scurry down another path flanked by rusting wrecks, turn left and right and left again. And then I stop, tracing my light across the crushed front of a bright yellow Holden Gemini.

'Mum let me choose which car we'd call home,' I say. 'I chose this one because I thought it looked small and overlooked, a bit like how I used to feel all the time. And because Gemini was Mum's star sign. And because the car was the colour of sunshine.' I laugh because a memory hits me hard. 'Ray,' I say. Even cars get names sometimes. People call their cars names like Betty and Bella and Susie and Sparky and Queenie. 'We called the car Ray,' I say. 'Little ray o' sunshine.'

Charlie darts his head around the wrecking yard. 'This place gives me the willies,' he says. 'Why do I feel like a giant rottweiler is about to jump out from the darkness and bite the side of my face off?'

I keep looking at the Gemini. 'It was too small for Mum to sleep in after a while. But there used to be a silver Kia Grand Carnival next to it and Mum would jump in that most nights to stretch out.'

Charlie's getting impatient, tapping his foot on the dirt and shifting his head about. 'Yeah, 'twas the bestest times, 'twas the worstest times ... Let's just look inside this thing so we can get the fuck outta here.'

The doors are unlocked. We run our lights through the car. Yellow foam bursting through the cracks in the torn brown vinyl front seats. The smell of dust and sunburnt car plastics. Nothing in the back seats but possum shit and the reek of piss. We move to the back of the car. I shine my light on the lock, pull Mum's globe keychain from my pocket, stick the key in and turn it. Take a deep breath as I turn my head to Charlie.

He fixes his forehead lamp in place and gives me a reassuring nod of his head. 'That boot's not gonna open itself, sweetheart.'

I lift the lid. Rust and dust in the hinges release a banshee metal-on-metal wail.

'Fuck,' I exclaim, whipping my head around the yard for signs of life. Nothing to see. I turn back to the cavity and find something soft and grey resting there. Charlie comes over and shines his light on it.

'What the fuck?' he says.

'What the fuck,' I whisper.

There it sits in the light. Completely useless and worthless. Yet possibly the most intriguing object I've ever laid my eyes upon. I reach into the back of the car and take it in my hands. It's a knitted grey elephant, a child's soft toy. Hand-knitted by someone who could do such things. Big red circle patches for the elephant's rose-coloured cheeks. Mismatched patterns of cloth for the insides of the ears. Emerald-green buttons for the eyes. Knitted black wool eyelashes. Soft and floppy trunk.

I hug it to my chest because I feel like I know this thing. I bring it to my nose and smell it and for some reason the smell is familiar to me too. In my head I see the face of a woman looking at me in a room coloured only white. And the woman's face is only light. And the woman is saying a name. My name. She's saying that name softly, but I can almost hear what it is. If I shut my eyes and listen hard, if I put this toy elephant close enough to my cheek, then I know I will hear it.

But instead of a name I hear something hard punching through glass and that sound forces an unashamedly feminine squeal from deep within Charlie's chest and we both turn on the spot to find a man holding a flashlight in one hand and a large crowbar in the other, which he has just driven through the driver's-side window of a wrecked Nissan Pintara in a wildly successful effort to scare the shit from our bowels.

'What the fuck are you playin' at?' the man barks.

We can't see his face behind the light.

He bangs the crowbar on the roof of the Nissan. 'You fuckin' scavengers!'

My hands still hold the elephant and I raise it up to the light. 'I'm so sorry,' I say. 'We're not scavengers. I used to sleep in this car with my mum. When I was just a little girl.' I take the keychain from my pocket and hold it up. 'She gave me this key. She wanted me to find what was in the back of this car.'

The man steps closer to me. Shines his light on my face. 'Joan?' he asks. 'Little Joanie? Is that you?'

Joan? Yes, *Joanie the runaway*. I remember now. Mum called me 'Joan' for a bit there. Joan like Joan Jett, one of the all-time great Runaways.

'Yeah, it's me,' I reply.

'Joanie?' Charlie asks quizzically.

The man with the crowbar turns the flashlight to his own face. Big guy. Glasses. Blond curly hair. He's wearing blue-and-white-striped pyjamas – lunatic-chic – but it doesn't look like he showered before bed because I can still see black grease on his hands and one side of his face.

'It's me, Barnie,' he says. 'You remember me?'

Barnie? *Barnie*. 'Yeah ... of course I remember you. How've you been, Barnie?'

'Oh, I've seen brighter days, Joanie,' he says.

'Joanie?' Charlie says again.

'Nobody needs secondhand parts anymore,' Barnie continues. 'So nobody needs ol' Barnie anymore.'

Barnie throws his flashlight on Charlie. 'Who's this?' he asks.

'That's Charlie,' I reply. 'Charlie's my best friend.'

'Where's Paula?' Barnie asks.

Paula? *Paula.* I remember now. Mum called herself 'Paula' for a bit there. Paula like Paula Abdul.

'She's gone, Barnie.'

'Gone? Gone where?'

'Gone to the bottom of the ...' I can't even finish that sentence. 'The river swallowed her, Barnie. She drowned saving the life of a kid named Christina.'

'That was Paula?' Barnie asks. 'That's been all over the news. That was your mum?'

'That was my mum.'

'Fuckin' 'ell,' he says. 'That's a very brave thing she did, Joanie.'

'Tell me about it, Barnie.'

'News showed them cop divers in the water searching for her body. Do ya think they'll find her?'

'All depends, Barnie.'

'On what?'

'On whether or not that river wants to cough her back up.'

He slaps his forehead. 'Ahhh, blow!' He looks for a place to sit and take stock of this news. Finds a spot on the edge of the Pintara. 'Ahhh, blow,' he says again, this time with more emphasis on the 'blow'. 'I just saw her a month ago.'

'You saw Mum a month ago?'

'Yeah, she dropped in to say hi and get her crying all done.'

'What's that supposed to mean?' I ask.

He points at the elephant in my hands. 'Well ... I dunno ... 'Bout two years ago she lobs in here sayin' she left that elephant in the back of your little ol' Gemini there. Lucky I still had the key to that shitbox. I opened up the back and she grabbed that bloody elephant and then the Hoover Dam burst and then I just let her sit by herself in the car there for half an hour just thinkin' and cryin'. Then she comes up to the office and drops the key back and she's not holding that bloody elephant and she says she left it there in the car to keep it safe and I tell her she's picked the perfect spot to keep a thing safe in because nobody's ever gonna come looking for parts from a 1978 Holden Gemini. She says her goodbyes and then a month later she's back again, asking for that key. She tells me that all the people she lives with don't like to see her crying no more.' He points a finger at me. 'You,' he says. 'She said you never liked to see her crying.'

I drop my head, look away from Barnie for some reason. Like I'm ashamed or somethin', but I got nothin' to be ashamed of? Do I?

I look back up at Barnie and he shrugs his shoulders. Adjusts his glasses on the bridge of his nose. 'So she came here to get her cryin' done,' he says. He plays with the brightness on his flashlight, turns it down a notch. 'I thought it was a bit funny at first. Fancy comin' to a wrecking yard in Rocklea just to cry yer guts out? But then I thought it was sweet. I even cried with her once. Gave a few howls in that car for my dead mum. Felt good to cry with Paula. She could cry for Australia, couldn't she?'

I feel dizzy. Squint my eyes and dig my feet into the gravel to steady my balance.

'How many times did she come here, Barnie?' I ask.

'Couldn't say for sure,' he replies. ''Bout once a month, I reckon. I gave her the key in the end so she didn't have to bother knockin' on the office door. She could just go straight down and get her cryin' done.'

I shake my head. Breathless. Floating now. What the fuck is Barnie talking about? I bring the toy elephant to my chest once more.

'You've seen her before, haven't you?' Barnie asks.

'Seen who?'

'The elephant. You've seen her before. Do you know anyone called Elizabeth?'

'What? What are you talking about?'

Barnie struggles to pull himself up from the Pintara. Ambles over to me. Trains his flashlight on the hand-knitted elephant in my hands. Grips the right foreleg in his fingers. 'The name on the band,' he whispers. 'The name!'

And he turns the leg in the light and shows me the plastic identification band fixed around the elephant's lower leg. The kind of identification band normally found on a baby's ankle in a hospital maternity ward.

I bring the band closer to my eyes. Read the wording on the band. Details spat out by a computer.

Name: Finlay, Elizabeth R.
DOB: 23.04.2005
Age: 1D Sex: F
Dr S. Yelland

Then Barnie asks a question that it makes no sense for anyone to be asking. 'Do you know who she was?'

'Who she was,' I whisper. And I stare into the green button eyes of the elephant. *DOB: 23.04.2005*. That's my birthday.

I say the name in my head. Elizabeth Finlay. And again. Elizabeth Finlay. And again. *Elizabeth Finlay*. The elephant's ears and the elephant's trunk and the plastic identification band around the elephant's leg. And in my head and in my memory I see a woman without a face leaning over me and she's tucking this elephant into my chest. 'Elizabeth,' I whisper to myself.

Charlie reads the band on the toy elephant's leg. Puts a hand on my shoulder. 'Who's Elizabeth Finlay?' he whispers.

And I turn to him with tears in my eyes. 'I am.'

Mr and Mrs Finlay

Mr and Mrs Finlay

February 2023

Pen and ink on paper

One of the artist's most haunting and macabre works.
The artist is almost inviting the viewer to attend a wedding
between two lovers in hell. It feels like something one would
expect from the mind of Francis Bacon or Hieronymus Bosch.
'Please join us,' the artist seems to be asking. 'Please come
and witness this horrifying union for yourself.'

Who am I? In a world of eight billion people, I'm the daughter of Mr and Mrs Finlay. I'm a seventeen-year-old artist with a name. I'm the girl pacing across the Victoria Bridge on a bright and windless Tuesday morning in Brisbane, city of possibility, city of answers. An elderly couple, hand in hand, amble towards me from the north end of the bridge. I beam a smile at them because living is a long-odds miracle and the payment we must make for the gift of sunshine and breath is to smile at elderly couples walking hand in hand.

'Hello,' I say.

And the old man raises the brown Fedora on his head. 'Good morning,' he says.

I stop now as they pass me. 'What's your name?' I ask.

The old man stops and his wife stops with him. 'My name is Ken,' he replies.

'Kenneth means "handsome one",' I say.

Ken tilts his head to the side. 'I keep telling my wife that,' he says. 'But she refuses to believe it. What's your name?'

'My name's Elizabeth,' I say. 'Elizabeth means "God is my oath."'

'Nice to meet you, Elizabeth,' he says.

'Too right, Ken,' I say. 'It's real bloody nice to meet Elizabeth.'

*

Brisbane Square is a high-rise building climbing thirty-eight floors above George Street at the top end of the CBD. The Brisbane Square Library occupies the first three levels. The wide glass doors open for me and I scurry across the tiled foyer. Slow my movements down to a casual walk as I pass a library staff member who sits at an information desk at the entrance to the library. We've had words before, this staff member and me. She's old and sour like the oranges Ros tries to grow in the corner of Oz. She wears her hair like an old English sheepdog. Glasses on a rope around her neck. I try to pass her desk without making eye contact. No such luck.

'Hold on, you,' she barks.

I stop. Turn to her desk.

'Where do you think you're going?' she asks.

'I just need to make one quick internet search,' I reply.

'Not today, I'm afraid.'

'Why not today?'

'We have three schools coming through. All the public computer spaces are either occupied or booked.'

'Well, no worries. I'll just go up and wait and see if I can make a brief search between bookings.'

'No, you will not.'

'Why will I not?'

'Because last time you came in here, you and your boyfriend made so much noise that we had to ask you to leave.'

'He's not my boyfriend. And that wasn't our fault. That was Will Ferrell's fault. We were watching *Step Brothers* on Netflix.'

'Our security officer saw your not-boyfriend sipping from a hip flask,' she says.

'Yeah, well, he has a drinking problem,' I say. 'If you had his life, you'd wanna get pissed and watch *Step Brothers* sometimes, too.'

The woman shakes her head. Resolute. 'Nup,' she says. 'You're not coming in today.'

I take a deep breath. Clock the name tag pinned to her chest. Time for a new approach. 'Your name's Ruth,' I say. 'Your name means "compassionate friend". You know how I know that? Because I've got this weird thing about looking up the meanings behind names. I come here to this beautiful library that I love so much to learn about all those beautiful meanings behind all those beautiful names. Do you wanna know why I do that?'

Ruth gives no kind of response.

'I do it, Ruth, because I never actually knew my real name,' I say. 'No bullshit. I lived almost eighteen years of my life without knowing my name. But then last night I discovered what it is. Can you believe that? I got the big answer to the question I've asked ever since I knew the concept of asking questions. And all I need from you, Ruth – my compassionate friend – is for you to let me walk past this desk and go up that escalator over there and then I can patiently wait for one of them computers upstairs to free up and then I can plug that name into Google and maybe learn a thing or two about who I am, where I come from, where I'm going.'

Ruth folds her arms and tilts her head to the side. 'You. Are. Not. Getting. In. Today,' she says.

She stares at me. Ruth means 'face of stone'. Ruth means 'front desk meanie'.

'You know what Ruth really means?' I ask.

'What?'

'Daughter of Satan,' I say. And I sprint from Ruth's desk straight into the library, past two walls of seven-day-return laminated paperbacks, then jump on the escalator. Turn my head to see Ruth down below, desperately punching numbers on her desk phone. She'll be phoning Brad, the beefy security guy who walks around these library levels all sense-aware and ninja-like, as though five guys in hockey masks might one day bust into the fiction section with machine guns demanding all the library's copies of *Normal People*.

I pump my legs hard and sprint up the escalator steps to the second level then run past a long rack of magazines and a rack of Manga comics and graphic novels. Turn sharp left and come to a bay of computers, where high school kids in maroon and grey uniforms are tapping away at keyboards.

I take a seat at a spare computer beside a kid with *Jiang Chen* written across his pencil case. Jiang has hair that hangs like curtains over his face. He takes his earphones from his ears and says, 'Ariel's still using that computer.'

'I'll just be a second, Jiang,' I say. 'You have a beautiful name, by the way. What does Jiang mean?'

'It means "river",' he says.

'Because you go with the flow,' I suggest.

Jiang takes a liking to this notion. 'Damn straight,' he says. 'I'm all about the flow.'

'My name is Elizabeth,' I say. 'You know, like Elizabeth Taylor and Elizabeth the First *and* the Second, of course.'

'Of course,' Jiang says. He stares at me for a moment. Turns back to his computer.

I click on the Google Chrome tab at the bottom of the computer screen. Look over my shoulders for signs of Brad the security guy. Fingers shaking. Start to type a name into the Google search bar. My name. *Elizabeth Finlay*. But I'm moving too fast.

Ellizabjth ...

'Fuck.' Backspace, backspace, backspace.

Elizzabeth ...

Backspace, backspace, backspace.

Over my shoulder I see Brad the security guy marching in my direction past a bay of young adult fantasy books.

Quicker now. Just type the fucking name, Elizabeth.

E-l-i-z-a-b-e-t-h F-i-n-l-a-y.

Enter.

'You!' barks Brad when he reaches the public computer bay. 'Stand up and come with me.'

'Just one second, Brad,' I say.

'No, you were told not to come in here today. Out. Now!'

One eye on Brad. One eye on the computer screen as it flashes up search results.

'All right, I asked you nicely,' Brad says. He stomps on three schoolbags to get to my desk then grips my right arm hard and starts to pull me from my chair.

'Stop, please,' I plead. 'Just a minute.' With Brad still trying to haul me away, I read the first result, highlighted in blue. It's a link to an online newspaper story in the *Daily Telegraph*, and the link itself is a tabloid headline: 'The Monster of March Street: Why did Marcus Finlay crack?'

Brad tugs harder on my arm as I grip the chair with my left hand and plant my feet into the library carpet.

'Easy, tiger,' Jiang says to Brad. 'Just give her a second.'

Beside the headline on the web page there's a small, square screenshot of a couple dancing at some kind of ball. The man wears a tuxedo and a bow tie and he's smiling at the camera. The woman has a purple dress. A bright young face. Curled brown hair, big and high and beautiful.

The face of my mother.

'Mum!' I whisper. The tears come without thought. Without consciousness. The tears come from my blood.

As Brad finally separates me from my chair, I'm still staring at that little square image containing a young and happy version of my mother. 'Wait!' I beg Brad through my tears. '*Please*. Just one second. That's my mum. That's my mum.' But he continues to drag me out of the library.

Please, Brad, I tell myself between tears. Please, Brad, I tell myself because I'm too confused to speak out loud. That's my mum. Please, Brad. That's my dad. Please, Brad. That's my mum and dad. Please, Brad. That's Mr and Mrs Finlay.

*

An hour later.

'Mirror, mirror, beneath the sky, please tell me how, please tell me why.'

Lola takes a drag of her cigarette in my magic mirror.

'Why you? Because you're the one who can take it. Because you're the one who can use it.'

'Use it for what?'

'For your art,' Lola says. 'For your future.' She takes a drink from a tall glass. A slice of lemon wedged between the ice cubes. I can see she's standing in the manicured yard of a mansion with tall white columns and a limestone façade.

Lola Inthemansion. Lola Inthesun. Lola Intheglow.

'Did you get all those answers you were looking for about whatsername?' she asks.

'Elizabeth,' I say. 'Elizabeth Finlay.'

'Yeah, her. Did you get all those answers you were looking for?'

'They kicked me outta the library. Then I started asking random people on the street if I could use their phones for a second to look something up on the internet.'

'Anybody throw you a bone?'

'No. Nobody. I think they thought I was trying to steal their phones.'

'Runnin' around the city like a dizzy chicken, searching for all the answers — "*Whooooooo. Ammmmm. I?*" All the answers are staring you right in the face.' Lola runs a forefinger around the rim of her glass. 'You know exactly who you are,' she says. 'And if you don't know, then I can't tell you.'

'Where do I go now, Lola?'

'Go see Evelyn Bragg at The Well. They got a computer, don't they?'

'The Well's shut on Tuesdays.'

'Looks like it's time to go see Lady Flo then. She hasn't seen you since your Mum died. She'll be glad to see you.'

'I don't wanna ask Flo for a favour. Mum told me never to ask Flo for anything. She said I should never be indebted to Flora Box.'

'She's gonna let you use her computer. As far as favours go, that's about as big as passing someone the salt and pepper.'

'What if he's there?'

'Who?'

'Brandon.'

'You're not scared of that pig, are you?'

'No ... a little bit, maybe ... Yes, I'm scared of that pig.'

'You still thinkin' about that business in the cement factory?'

'I'm always thinkin' about that business in the cement factory.'

'I hope you think about how brave you were during that business?'

'No, I don't usually think about that part.'

'You should always think about that part.'

In the mirror, over Lola's shoulder, I can see a group of daytime partygoers in fine suits and expensive dresses.

'Where are you right now, Lola?'

'I'm in the backyard at Graceland.'

'Elvis's Graceland?'

'Well, I didn't mean Justin Bieber's Graceland.'

A man in a vintage brown suit, whose face I cannot see, calls out to Lola, 'Are you coming?'

Lola turns to the man. 'Just a second,' she says, waving a hand.

'Who's that?' I ask.

'That's my guy.'

Lola Intheromance. Lola Inthelonging. Lola Inthelove.

'Who's your guy?'

'Who's my guy?' she responds. 'Good question. Who is my guy? Is he the hand he puts on my thigh when I'm sad? Is he the foot he rubs against mine when we're reading Dickinson in bed? Is he the Twinings English Breakfast tea he makes me in the morning? Is he the joke he tells me about the two muffins sitting in the oven? Is he the softness of his lips when he kisses me goodbye? Is he the arm around my waist when he says hello? Is he the—'

'Jeez, Lola,' I say, 'I just wanted to know his name.'

'Oh, his name,' she says. 'Well, that's a strange thing for you to ask. I thought you knew his name? I thought you'd always known his name? Why don't you know his name?'

*

Who am I? I'm the girl standing beneath a grey Brisbane sky looking at the giant painted face of Brandon Box, aged nine. A decade ago, Flora Box had the Ebb 'n' Flo seafood shop's front wall decorated with a mural based on a photograph she treasures of her only son when he was a boy trapping mud crabs along the mangrove edges of Kauri Creek, in Tin Can Bay, south of K'gari. Brandon means 'prince'. Brandon Box is not a prince.

The mural suggests Brandon was a sweet and gentle boy – there's a tooth missing from his wide smile and he's laughing as he holds a fat-clawed brown muddy to the camera, his youthful hands safely gripping the base of the crab's back legs. But Brandon Box is not a sweet and gentle boy. Brandon lives in a flat owned by Flo that she bought twenty years ago in the old heritage-listed Torbreck high-rise tower on Dornoch Terrace, Highgate Hill. Brandon had it transformed into a space that now resembles a weights room at a 24/7 Snap Fitness health club.

Brandon makes me nervous the way live mud crabs made me nervous when Flo would ask me to pick them up out of the large blue trawler buckets during my first part-time job, working fill-in shifts in the back packing room. Brandon Box is not a prince. Brandon always looks at me funny. He's been looking at me funny since I was twelve, when Mum first got a cash-in-hand-no-questions-asked-about-the-past-job shelling prawns and cleaning crabs for Flora Box.

When I was thirteen, Charlie Mould and Brandon and me were smoking Winfield Blues and messing around on a skateboard behind the Hanson concrete factory along the river at the end of Hockings Street. It was a Sunday, so the factory gate was shut, and Brandon had the idea of boosting ourselves over the front fence. The Hanson factory occupies an area almost as big as a cricket field. There's a vast asphalt loading area, where we used to watch the trucks fill their rotating tanker drums with ready-mix concrete then drive out into the suburbs of Brisbane. At the back of the complex are two towering, blue, crayon-shaped silos, each the size of a rocket ship's central body. These silos are connected to the mixing plant, a huge, fortress-like building on the left side of the complex, which is bigger than some of the unit blocks I see being built in the more expensive corners of West End. In front of this building is a row of transport parking bays numbered 1 to 12.

From high up on the mixing plant, a conveyor belt slopes downwards across the full width of the loading area. The belt is enclosed by a cylindrical corrugated-metal covering that makes it look like an amusement park slide that might end at a splash pool near the water tower on the right side of the loading area. We'd always make bold statements about creeping into the factory and climbing the series of steep metal staircases that lead to the top of the conveyor belt. From there, we claimed, we'd be able to slide down the outside of the conveyor belt tube like we were on potato sacks at a school fête.

After we hauled ourselves over the factory fence and Charlie took off on the skateboard to the other side of the plant, Brandon pulled me into one of the truck bays – lucky number seven – and tried to get lucky with me, shoving his hand up my shirt and feeling around for my barely-there-yet thirteen-year-old pears. He attached his lips to mine with such speed and force that our front teeth collided. His breath tasted like Winfield Blue cigarettes and the concoction he was carrying in a two-litre soft drink bottle: Fanta mixed with 375 ml of Smirnoff Red. As his fingers tugged at my breasts, I slipped my right leg behind his right calf, planted it firmly to the ground, and pushed hard with closed fists against his chest. He tripped backwards, his arse hit the concrete and his open palms skidded across the ground so roughly that he saw blood when he inspected the damage.

'Frigid bitch,' he muttered, pulling himself to his feet.

'Creepy cunt,' I said, tucking my shirt tight into my pants. 'Wait till I tell yer Mum. You're fucked.'

He leapt aggressively into my personal space, nose to nose. 'You tell her and I'll kill ya,' he whispered.

Then he ran. He climbed over a yellow gate behind the parking bays and disappeared into the mixing plant. Charlie and I spent the next half-hour walking around in there screaming Brandon's name, but he wasn't to be found. Charlie and I had resolved to return to the scrapyard and were already back outside when we heard someone calling to us from high up in the plant. We turned to find Brandon standing at the top of the conveyor belt tube, precariously balanced on its convex exterior. He'd done what we'd only dared to dream of.

'Look at me on the water slide,' he shouted, bouncing once and then twice on the flimsy metal. He must have been fifteen metres up. Nothing but air between one careless vodka-sorry shoe slip and the asphalt below. He spun around on the spot, taking in the view. 'Look, I can see the city from here,' he hollered.

'Get the fuck down, Brandon,' I shouted.

'No,' he replied. 'Not until you tell me you won't tell Mum about what I done.'

'I'm not gonna tell yer mum what you done,' I said. 'Just come down now. You're gonna slip and kill yourself.'

'I won't fall,' he said. And he started stomping his feet and rocking his head like he was slam-dancing to heavy metal music. He jumped up high one more time and his feet slipped on landing and his arse slammed hard onto the domed roofing and he screamed, terrified, fear choking the drink courage from his voice. 'Fuck,' he said, then started slowly descending by bracing his feet on either side of the iron and sliding his backside along the belt casing without ever disconnecting from the metal surface. He looked like a big dumb dog wiping shit from his arse on a patch of grass.

We were back by the river ten minutes later when a local drunk named Barton Forrest stumbled past us with a bag of Coolabah white wine tucked under his arm like a rugby league ball.

'What's that smell?' Brandon barked. He turned to Barton. 'You shit yourself again, Bart?'

'Leave him alone, Brandon,' I said. 'He's not bothering anyone.'

Bart was staggering in wrong angles and directions, closing his eyes to the sun, probably trying to remember under which sprawling fig tree he had pitched his tent.

Brandon got behind Barton and wrapped an arm around his neck. 'You're going the wrong way, Barty,' Brandon said.

Brandon was only fourteen years old back then but he was taller and stronger than Barton and he led him straight to the edge of the river.

'What you're lookin' for is a cold bath, Barty,' Brandon said.

I caught up with them both, with Charlie behind me.

'Let 'im go, Brandon,' I said, pulling his arm away from Bart's shoulder.

'Fuck off,' Brandon snapped, punching at my hand with a closed fist. 'This stinky prick needs a bath.'

It was low tide and there was an exposed sewer pipe that jutted out from the bank, the way a cannon extends from a pirate ship. Brandon led Barton onto the pipe. 'Make sure you wash that arse, Barty,' he said, pushing Barton into the river. The poor drunk belly-flopped hard, facedown, and was too pickled and weak to keep himself afloat. His right cheek emerged twice for air then he simply submitted to the water, face in the drink, bubbles rushing from his mouth.

'Are you fuckin' crazy?' I spat at Brandon as I rushed into the water. I cut my shins on the sharp grey rocks and it was only because it was low tide that I was able to find a firm-enough footing to stand and hold Bart's head out of the water until Charlie could help me drag the poor old soak back to the river's edge.

Sucking in breaths on my hands and knees, I looked up to see Brandon Box howling with laughter at us from atop the sewerage pipe. The blinding sun behind him turned him to shadow and he raised his legs to his ribs one by one as he howled and pointed at me. And all I saw was the tyrannosaurus. All I saw was the tyrant lizard, roaring.

Brandon Box is not a prince.

*

Bone-rattling cold inside the Ebb 'n' Flo seafood sales area. Wet concrete floors and green rubber grip mats. The smell of salt water and fish guts. A chrome-coloured sales counter and then a long rectangle of open and iced seafood display cabinets that fills most of the shed. Whole red emperor. Gold-band snapper, my favourite. Flathead fillets. King and tiger prawns. Blue swimmer sand crab. Mud crab. Mullet. Tailor. Summer whiting and – the closest thing to royalty in Queensland – fresh Moreton Bay bugs. France has the *Mona Lisa*. Egypt has the pyramids. Queensland has Moreton Bay bugs.

Trading hours are over and I know sales went well today because it's only 5.35 p.m. and the market manager, Glenn Ash, has already opened a XXXX Gold. Dressed in blue polo shirts, blue aprons and blue gumboots, Glenn and three workers – all hard-faced and silent ex-crim types in their fifties – pack the unsold seafood into iced Styrofoam boxes.

'Flo here?' I ask.

'Gone home,' Glenn says, wiping his sales counter down with a blue towel. There's a tattooed python with diamonds for eyes snaking around his thick and hairy right forearm, and he's wearing his favourite North Sydney Bears hat, which he always wears when he's working in the shop. People who know Glenn well enough call him 'The Priest'. He got that nickname inside the Sir David Longland Correctional Centre, Wacol, after he unsuccessfully tried to hang himself at the age of nineteen on a stretch of razor wire. The wire left jagged pink scars that, at the age of twenty-one, he had a prison tattooist cover with a black band with an empty square at his Adam's apple, which made it look like he was wearing a priest's clerical collar. This was a wry prison gag, based on the widespread knowledge in the jail that Glenn Ash would be the last man on earth to live a life free from sin. I don't know Glenn Ash well enough to call him 'The Priest'.

'What did you want from Flo?' Glenn asks. At that moment, Brandon enters the sales area from the packing rooms through the white swing doors. He's heard half of the question. Looks at me. 'You want something from Mum?' he asks.

'I just wanted to use her computer,' I reply.

'What for?'

'To search a name on Google.'

Brandon scratches his head, confused. 'We just heard about what your mum did in the river,' he says.

'Who told you about that?'

'Ros told Mum.'

'Please don't tell anyone it was Mum, Brandon,' I plead. 'I don't want the cops walking up and down Moon Street looking for me. They'll take me away. They'll put me someplace I don't wanna be.'

Brandon laughs. 'Believe me, sister, the last thing we want is cops walking up and down Moon Street.'

I'm briefly surprised by the small measure of compassion he invested in that last sentence.

Glenn Ash grips a whole coral trout in his fist and takes it through to the packing room. Just me and Brandon now.

'That was pretty fuckin' brave what your mum did,' he says.

'Tell me about it,' I say.

He rubs his lips with a thumb. 'You want to use my iPad?'

'Huh?' I say, because I'm momentarily confused by his generosity.

'I got my iPad out back,' he says, shrugging his shoulders. He points to the swing doors. 'Just sayin'. Whatever answers you're lookin' for. They're just back there if you need 'em.'

Of course, the artist knew it was perilous to follow Brandon Box into anything, but her desire for the answers she required from her past was greater than the caution she required from her present, so she followed him into Flora Box's office in the back of the Ebb 'n' Flo seafood shop. It was Brandon Box who typed the name Elizabeth Finlay into the Google search bar on the iPad. It was Brandon who tapped on the hyperlinked search option that presented itself at the top of a screen that was sticky with soy sauce stains and protein-shake finger marks. A 2006 Daily

Telegraph *article:* '*The Monster of March Street: Why did Marcus Finlay crack?*'

Brandon's right forefinger taps on the link and I see a new fire burn in his eyes as they dart left and right across the iPad.

'Ffffffuuuuuuuuck.'

'Please pass it to me now, Brandon.'

But Brandon continues to read the article, shaking his head at every word, every sentence, every answer, until ...

'Pass me the fucking iPad, Brandon!' I scream, reaching across Flora Box's work desk and snatching the device from his fingers.

And the heart inside her chest seemed to compress into itself as she read the article, something like matter itself being sucked into the vacuum of a celestial hole. Past and present and future folding in on themselves. The feature spoke of the horrors of a morning in October 2005, when the residents of Bomaderry, on the sleepy and idyllic south-east coast of New South Wales, woke to shocking television news reports about a seemingly happy and kind-hearted Bomaderry mortgage broker named Marcus Finlay who had inexplicably burned himself and his six-month-old baby alive inside a 2003 Mitsubishi Outlander parked in the driveway of a three-year-old two-storey brick house at 34 March Street, Bomaderry. The baby's brave and loving mother, Erica Finlay, had tried and failed to rescue her child from the burning vehicle, suffering severe burns to her arms and upper torso in the process.

The shocking and underlying tragedy of the story was the fact that well prior to the tragic murder-suicide, Erica had informed police about multiple acts of violence she had endured at the hands of her rage-filled husband. She was a dedicated and adaptable high school relief teacher, occupying regular placements at Oakham High School, South Bomaderry, where not a single staff member could recall her expressing any concerns about her relationship with Marcus, who had, hitherto, presented himself as nothing less than an ideal husband.

Erica was remembered glowingly by students. Marcus was remembered by the residents of March Street as outgoing, charismatic and renowned for his street barbecues at which he would delight guests with his signature slow-cooked Texas pulled pork. Unbeknown to the residents of March Street, the New South Wales police had twice issued Marcus Finlay with an apprehended violence order, the second of which he broke by visiting the family home on the day he murdered his daughter. 'They say we live in the luckiest country on earth,' the journalist wrote. 'Lucky for some, to be sure. Not so lucky for the one woman who is killed every week in Australia as a result of family and domestic violence.'

But it wasn't the disturbing details explored in the first half of the article that caused the artist to collapse into her chair in a shaking fit of tears and stomach pain. It was the second half, in which the journalist raised several questions relating to the mysterious disappearance of Erica Finlay. Only two months after the baby girl's death, Erica Finlay's silver Toyota Corolla Ascent was found abandoned in a public carpark in Conjola National Park, eleven thousand hectares of dense bushland and natural lake systems off the Princes Highway, south of Nowra, New South Wales. 'After an exhaustive, month-long search, Erica Finlay's name was sadly added to the national missing persons register. Erica Finlay was never seen again.'

The artist was nearly at the point of vomiting upon herself when she reached the journalist's concluding paragraph, in which he indelicately and unnecessarily turned his investigative gaze upon himself: 'As a father of a young daughter, I think often about the fates of Erica Finlay and her baby daughter, that precious little girl who never got to experience the joys of travel or the satisfaction of a career or the wonders of love. When I think of Erica Finlay, I prefer not to imagine her lost to some nameless forest lake. I like to picture her still out there somewhere, living her best life as I write this very sentence, the life she might have lived, were it not for the Monster of March Street.'

I place the iPad on Flora Box's desk and drop my head into my hands and weep. Brandon Box leans over the desk, grabs the device and speeds through the rest of the article, forming thoughts in his head as he reads.

'Ohhhh, my fucking God,' he exclaims. 'The baby.' He looks at me. White shock across his tanned face. 'Elizabeth Finlay?' Then his shock turns inexplicably to laughter. 'You thought she was you,' he says. 'Fuck me! That's so fucking sad.'

And then he giggles again. 'You are one *loooooopy* bitch.' Laughter like a machine gun. Scattershot and scatterbrained. Pointing at me with his finger.

He rereads the article, shaking his head. 'It says Marcus and Erica Finlay only had one kid.' He looks up at me and laughs again. 'So where the fuck did you come from?'

He leans back in his mother's office chair, brings the iPad up to his belly, rests his feet on the desk and turns back to the article. 'This is *soooooo* fucked up!' he says. More laughter.

And I have to stand. And I have to run out of this room.

'Wait, don't go now,' Brandon says. 'This just got interesting!'

I run. A hand to my mouth because I don't want to make another sound for Brandon Box to laugh at. Through the white doors of the cold packing room. Through the entrance to the shop. Down Moon Street. Past the warehouses and the drop-in centres and the cheap and ugly flophouses that form my sorry neighbourhood. Along the path by the Tinman's work shed and across the yard to my magic mirror.

And I grip the mirror's frame tight with both hands and stare at the glass that bounces my staring straight back at me. 'Lola,' I whisper through my tears. 'Lola, are you there?'

And thank God I can see her. Sitting on a single bed with white sheets. A wooden cross on the wall behind her. Her back turned to me. The hand of the man in the vintage brown suit gently patting her thigh.

'Go away,' she says.

'Lola, I need to talk to you.'

'Go away!' she repeats, with her back still turned to me.

'Go away? Why? You told me to go to Flo's. You told me to do that!'

She doesn't speak. Lola Intheturning. Lola Inthedark. Lola Inthehurt.

'Where are you right now, Lola?' I ask. 'What is that place? Please talk to me.'

'I don't want to talk to you right now,' she says over her shoulder. 'Can't you see I'm in hospital?'

'Hospital? Why are you in hospital?'

Lola Inthedeep. Lola Intherage. Lola Inthedespair.

'Oh, you just don't quit, do you?' she says. 'How many times do I have to tell you ...?' And she turns to me and I see the darkness across her face, the teeth that bite together when she spits, 'LEAVE. ME. ALONE!'

'Lola!' I plead, weeping.

And now I see the horror of her right arm. It has been completely severed at the elbow and the upper arm has turned a deep purple colour. The colour of body rot. I see white bone and red flesh at the end of that horrid half-limb. And I see crimson blood dripping onto the bed, a dark and boiling and troubled kind of blood. A blood so hot it burns holes through Lola's pretty red dress.

Santa-Claus with Sore Head

Santa Claus with Sore Head

December 2023

Pen and ink on paper

An extremely rare piece, acquired by the museum through an anonymous donor. Believed to have been sketched when the artist was eighteen years old and riding a train to Nundah, northern Brisbane. It is through this period that we begin to see the inherent optimism in the artist's sketches continually infused – some might say infected – with distinct notes of melancholia and unprecedented late-teen rage.

Who am I? In a world of eight billion people, I'm none of them. I'm nobody. I'm nothing. I'm an eighteen-year-old glitch in space and time. Nameless. Houseless. No identification. No past. No future. No body. No heart. I'm the ghost of Ann Street, sitting here eating a cheese and bacon roll for breakfast on a stone garden edge next to the Central Station ramp that connects commuters to the corner of Ann and Edward streets. You'd need to throw a white bedsheet over my skull just to see me. Because I possess nothing in this bitter world but the power of invisibility.

My eighteenth birthday was a fizzer. Ros and Charlie stuck eighteen candles in a Woolworths banana cake and told me to make a wish. I was overwhelmed with options, including a fast car and a thick wall. I went with world peace.

More than ten months since Erica Finlay died. If you want to know what I've been doing all this time, I'll paint you a picture. Let's call this picture *Houseless Nobody Crying Her Heart Out on Ann Street*. It shows a girl sitting at this very spot, weeping for ten straight months. She cries so hard her lungs and liver and kidneys slip out with her tears and she loses her heart in the salt of the past. So there she sits, with all her vital organs scattered across the ground by her feet.

I stand and walk into a crowd of people in business suits and smart dresses as they make their busy ways to work. Thirty, forty, fifty strangers surrounding me. I'm a tree root in a river of somebodies. This is a test I conduct at least once a week. A simple test to see if I exist.

I stand still in the middle of all these workers as they pass by. Some bump me with their shoulders and some brush their suitcases against my legs, but nobody looks at me. Nobody sees me. Swear to God. It's the screwiest thing. I'm Edvard Munch and this is my own version of *Evening on Karl Johan Street*. Edvard was ghosted by a girl. I've been ghosted by life. Life has stood me up. Life didn't make it to my table on date night.

I turn on my feet now as all these unfamiliar faces pass me and I search their eyes for some sign that says I exist for them, but I see nothing. I raise my arms like I'm Jesus and the people around me make nothing of it. More city workers passing. Dozens of them. People who exist. Visible people. People with things to do. People who can see their futures because they can see their pasts. See new houses. New cars. New children. I stare at their faces and nobody stares back at mine. They just keep moving around me.

And then I speak. 'I am invisible,' I say.

Nobody hears this and nobody sees me say this. Not a single turn of the head, not a glance, not an eyebrow raised in confusion, not a laugh released in bewilderment.

I say it louder. 'I am invisible.'

Nothing. No change at all. Just all these strangers moving through their own existences.

So now I scream with my arms raised in the air. 'I AM INVISIBLE! I. AM. *INVISIIIBLLLLE!*'

Nothing. Not a single acknowledgement. And that makes perfect sense. For I do not exist. For I am nobody. For I am nothing. But then, truth be blurted, there's power in being nobody. When you're nobody, you are free to be anybody. Astronaut. Actress. Archaeologist. Or even a lowdown, dirty, send-her-straight-to-hell, suburban drug-slinger. Because if nobody can see you, then nobody can see your shame. Nobody can see your sorrow. And nobody can catch you crying your heart out.

*

Two hours later, Santa Claus sits opposite me on the train to Shorncliffe. I think he just glanced at my pears.

The two of us sharing a four-seat passenger bay. My bike resting on a rail by the passenger doors. Outside the window of the moving train is a Claude Monet version of the Brisbane suburbs. Backyard clotheslines. Mango trees with green fruit and weak branches. Orange-brick unit complexes. It's Brisbane, but all the colour's been smudged by velocity.

My black Adidas backpack rests on my right thigh, carrying the Philips portable CD player I bought from JB Hi-Fi for $79 and six of Flora Box's pirated CDs imported from Indonesia – albums by Madonna, Belinda Carlisle, Janet Jackson, Paula Abdul, Whitney Houston and Taylor Swift – which are worthless to anybody but me. No one listens to politicians, birdsong, teenagers, men selling solar panels, elders, whales or compact discs anymore.

Santa carries a drawstring Brisbane Broncos duffel bag over his shoulder. His head rests on his right fist as he watches me pen his image in my sketchbook. Santa's not real. He's just a man in a costume passing Buranda railway station with tired blue eyes and piss breath.

'You done?' he asks.

I lick my right fingertip, smudge the lines beneath his eyes. Capture that 9.35-a.m. morning misery. I shall call such eyes 'the misery eyes'.

'Almost.'

I draw quick. Sketching at speed means no time to dwell on my mistakes. Still life, with velocity. The figure's imperfections work because the whole thing is imperfect. Faces are imperfect and bellies are imperfect and life is imperfect. Life should be drawn quick in clear, rough lines and lived quick, too, riddled with mistakes we have no time to dwell on.

Errors are everywhere in this world. Take me, for example. The girl with the black ink pen. Glitch girl. Big secret but no big deal: I'm not supposed to be here on this train. Harsh reality but no real hurt in it anymore: I'm not supposed to be carrying this black bag. It's not supposed to be like this. This moving train. These trees outside the window. The houses. The public parks. All of it one big tragic glitch that seems more obvious to me with every passing day. I'm onto you, clever little world. The charcoal chicken shop outside the window, the mobile phone repair store, I'm onto you. The sky, I'm onto you. The sun, I'm onto you. This has all been a terrible mistake.

'Can I ask you something, Santa?'

'Sure, just don't ask me what you're getting for Christmas.'

'Why are you on the train in your suit?'

'Runnin' late. Sick o' changin' in and out of this idiot garb.'

As I sketch, I speculate. It's what we artists do. We infer. We feel. Santa ate alone last night. He boarded the train at Wynnum North Station in his suit because he tied one on and slept through his alarm.

'You shouldn't be sitting on a train in your Santa suit,' I say.

'Why not?'

'Santa's not supposed to ride the Shorncliffe line. You're spoiling the magic for the kids.'

'What magic?'

We artists sense things. See things others can't see. Santa lives in a flat in Wynnum with a Serbian man named Petar who works nightshift at the Murarrie slaughterhouse. Beneath the suit, across his hairy chest, is a tattoo of a dragon. I draw quick. Put all these mental notes in the sketch even if nobody will see the notes in the sketch. That's what Van Gogh did. Put all the pain in the paint. Put all the drink in the drawings. All the dreaming, too.

'Christmas magic,' I say. 'Stars that show you where to go in the nighttime. Magical plants that give you licence to kiss anyone you want. Kind fat men who give you everything you wish for on Christmas morning. Please don't forget, Santa, that Christmas magic is one of the few forms of magic that still exists for the kids of Brisbane.'

'Fuck the kids of Brisbane,' Santa says. 'You should see the bruising on my thighs. The kids of Brisbane don't stop. They're like fuckin' termites. Hundreds of 'em, naughty as wasps, asking for nothing but iPhones and sour gummies. That's all that exists for the kids of Brisbane. No magic anymore, just fuckin' telephones and sugar.'

The lips hidden in the beard. The red nose of a drunk. Shade and light. Light and shade.

'Can I ask you something, Santa?'

'Sure, just don't ask me for a Sony PlayStation. I'm all out.'

I close my sketchbook for a moment. Santa runs his eyes over its cover collage of Taylor Swift stickers.

'Do kids ever ask for anything meaningful?'

'Whaddya mean by meaningful?'

'Like, anything that touches your heart, anything that reminds you of what Christmas is all about.'

'What do you think it's all about?' Santa asks.

'It's all about family,' I say. 'It's all about being together with the ones we love. All those people around that tree on Christmas morning. That must be the meaning of life right there. Mum. Dad. Brother. Sister. Simple connection. Simple belonging. Husband. Wife. Daughter. Son. Grandm—'

'Yeah, I get it,' Santa says, 'family.' He thinks for a moment. 'Here's a meaningful Christmas wish,' he continues. 'Just yesterday. Ten-year-old boy named Cassius. Cute kid. Real bright. Gets up close to my ear and whispers what he wants for Christmas. He was all about family, like you. Kid warmed the cockles of my heart.'

'What did he ask for?'

'The retraction of his mum and dad's divorce proceedings.'

'That makes me sad,' I say.

'Me too,' Santa says.

The train slows for the next station. 'Park Road,' a man's peaceful and soothing recorded voice echoes through the carriage. 'Park Road Station.'

'Did you know the guy who does that voice is the same guy who does the ads for what's coming up on Channel Nine News each night?' I ask.

'What voice?'

'The train voice. "Park Road. Park Road Station".'

Santa appears not to care about this.

More shading around the ears. I darken Santa's black right boot resting on his left kneecap. Finished.

I scribble the name of the sketch on the bottom of the thick paper sheet, tear the page out. 'That's for you,' I say.

Santa smiles when he takes the sketch. '*Santa Claus with Sore Head*,' he reads. 'How do you know I've got a sore head?'

'You smell like you've got a sore head.'

Santa nods.

'Santa's got a long day ahead of him,' I say.

'Eight hours in a chair in the Myer toy section,' he says. 'Thirty minutes for lunch. Two five-minute piss breaks. A hundred demanding parents. A thousand privileged kids. Three French hens, two turtle doves and a bullet to blow my brains out.' Santa rubs his eyes and sighs.

'You're tired,' I say.

He nods.

'Santa's not gonna make it to Christmas Day.'

He nods again.

'You want something for that?' I ask, my fingers tapping on my backpack.

Santa sits up in his seat. His voice softens. 'What do you mean?'

'I mean, what does Santa want for Christmas?'

'What have you got?'

'I got things that help Santa go down the chimney,' I say. 'I got things that help Santa go up the chimney. I got things that send you gently off to sleep beside the fireplace and I got things that make you dance inside the fire.'

'Jesus Christ,' Santa says. 'How old are you?'

'Eighteen.'

'You don't look it.'

'How old do I look?'

'You look seventeen,' Santa says. 'How much does it cost to go up the chimney?'

'Fifty.'

Santa opens his duffel bag, pulls out a thin and worn black leather wallet. 'I've got thirty-seven dollars,' he says.

'Bloody hell, Santa, what are they paying you up there in the workshop?' A quick sum in my head. Big sigh. 'All right, St Nick,' I say. 'Christmas discount for broke-arse travellers from the north.'

I reach into the backpack. Hand Santa Claus a CD copy of Taylor Swift's *1989* record.

'What's this?' he asks.

'That's a fake Indonesian compact disc version of Taylor Swift's most accomplished and complete pure pop record to date. Note the clear misspelling in the track-listing that reads

"Out of the Woops" instead of Taylor's intended "Out of the Woods". I would normally charge you an extra $2 for that, but, you know, you bein' Santa an' all …'

'But … where's—'

'Little square bag tucked behind the disc.'

Santa opens the CD case, inspects the thin space behind the disc.

I give Santa a knowing wink.

'How do I know you're not fuckin' me?' he asks.

'Ain't nobody fuckin' you this Christmas but Mrs Claus's little sister, Hilda.'

The train takes a bend and speeds on to South Bank Station.

'I get off at Central,' Santa says. He hands me thirty-seven dollars and takes another look at my sketch. 'I look miserable,' he complains.

'I think you look beautiful,' I respond. 'I think you're perfect. You're riddled with mistakes, but you're perfect, too.'

He shrugs. 'It's a good drawing,' he says. 'I'm no expert, but I know good shit when I see it. You go to art school or somethin'?'

The train rocks on a curve and I wobble in my seat as I smile at Santa. I draw every morning and every night and every chance I get in between. That's what artists do. On Saturdays at lunchtime, I join the free art classes down at The Well. I draw on footpaths with chalky rocks. Draw on rocks with chalk. Draw on myself with ballpoint pens. Draw on the forearms of my friends on Moon Street. Draw in my head. Draw in my dreams. 'No, I don't go to art school,' I say.

'Who taught you to draw like that?'

'Erica Finlay,' I say.

'Who's Erica Finlay?'

'You ever heard of the Monster of March Street?'

'The *what*?' Santa asks.

'Never mind,' I reply.

I stare out the window as the train crosses the Brisbane River on the Merivale Bridge, connecting South Brisbane and Roma Street stations. The river is low.

'Hey, Santa,' I say. 'Did you know more than one thousand Australians have died in rivers and creeks in the past decade alone?'

Santa shakes his head.

'Did you know the Brisbane River is the second deadliest river in Australia, just behind the Murray?'

Santa shakes his head again.

'People come to Brisbane and they jump in that twisty brown snake thinkin' it's all calm and slow, a bit like how we all talk. But that river should be renamed Yagonnadie Creek or some shit, because nothing is what it seems with that thing. Drunk idiots jump in there at night thinkin' they'll be able to swim across it. But that bitch is angry down on the inside. She don't let anyone cross her. She saps their strength with her current. She makes people so tired that eventually they wanna be dragged under just to make it all stop. Down they go, into the black. Someone once told me that if you ever find yourself in that thing when it's really high and really movin', Santa, the only thing you can do is lie on your back and relax and float and pray to God you're not invisible.'

It was Erica Finlay who told me that.

Confusion across Santa's face. 'You're a very interesting person, you know that?'

'Not as interesting as you, Santa.'

Industrial sheds outside the window, made of flimsy corrugated iron. A train whips by, heading south.

'I like talking to strangers on trains,' I say.

'Me too,' Santa says.

'You can tell a stranger on a train anything you want because at some point the train will stop and the stranger will hop off and you'll never have to see that person again. No pasts are necessary on moving trains. No life stories. That makes this little world here on this little carriage a safe world. Does that make sense to you, Santa?'

'Makes a lotta sense,' he says.

The train takes a long right curve as it approaches Central. Santa grips the armrest of his seat and pushes himself to his feet. Leans in for one last thought, gentle and direct. 'You should go to art school,' he says.

I dwell on this for a long moment. 'I think you might be right, Santa,' I say. 'I really should go to art school. I really should be doing anything that is not exactly what I am doing now. I'm in the wrong place, Santa. This has all been a terrible mistake. That ever happen to you, Santa? You wake up one day and you know for certain that you're not where you're supposed to be. You're not in the right place. You're not in the right time. You're not even in the right life. You hate the person you see when you look in the mirror and you would do anything just to get away from that person, even if that meant throwing that person you have become into a fast-moving river. You ever feel that way, Santa?'

Santa stares at me. New light in the misery eyes. After some internal thought, which I can tell from his face includes a measure of concern for my welfare, he repeats his earlier diagnosis. 'You should go to art school.'

The train stops and the passenger doors open. 'Central,' the train voice man says, soothingly, like he just swallowed a box of Tramadol. 'Central Station.'

Santa holds my sketch out. 'Quick,' he says. 'Sign your name at the bottom, will ya?'

'Can't, sorry, Santa,' I say.

'Why not?'

'Because I don't know what it is.'

'What?' he says. 'You don't know your own name?'

I nod.

'I don't believe it,' Santa says. 'That's not possible.'

'Big jolly fat fellers climb down chimneys in Chapel Hill,' I say. 'Reindeers fly over Chermside. A girl lives to eighteen without a name. Anything is possible, Santa. You know that better than anyone.'

*

Riding to George Stringer's house in Nundah. My bike is Italian and fast. A Bianchi road bike, canary yellow, with a hard seat the size of a maxipad. With a gentle street slope and a good wind behind my back, I reckon I must nudge fifty kilometres an hour. The bike was a gift from Esther Inthehole. She ran away from her husband long ago and unofficially changed her last name to 'Inthehole' when she fell in with a loose 'family' of Brisbane floaters – Arthur Inthehole, Ezra Inthehole, Gillian Inthehole – who were living in a series of protected and hard-to-find natural sleep holes set into the Kangaroo Point cliffs, which tower over the Brisbane River opposite the CBD.

Esther means 'star'. I've never seen Esther's face properly because she never emerges from her hole in daylight, as she has become convinced her face is hideous and hard for people to look at. I know that's just bullshit that was drummed into her long ago by her monster. Charlie Mould told me he saw Esther's face one night at 2 a.m. when she was sifting through a small mountain of council pickup waste in Spring Hill. It was too dark to see her face clearly, but Charlie swore she looked like that beautiful actress in *Edward Scissorhands*. Some people on Moon Street say Esther's gone mad inside that hole of hers. I say she's just gone artistic.

Not long after Erica Finlay dived in the drink, I found a canary-yellow bike outside Esther's hole, leaning against the brick wall of the church. Esther's voice echoed out of the hole in the wall. 'Your mum always said she wanted to get you a bike,' Esther said.

'*Erica Finlay* always said she wanted to get me a bike,' I corrected.

'Sorry, Erica Finlay.'

'You didn't steal it, did you, Esther?' I asked.

'Nah, found it,' she replied.

'Looks pretty expensive, Esther.'

'Yeah, and it's Italian. I've named it Macaroni.'

'Where'd you find it?'

'Lying on its side on the amphitheatre hill in Roma Street Parklands. Nobody wanted it.'

'How do you know nobody wanted it?'

'I know unwanted when I see it,' Esther said.

'What if some musclebound Italian cyclist stops me in the street, wanting his bike back?'

Esther thought on this for a moment. 'Tell him if he knows the name of the bike then he can have it back,' she said.

The artist rode with a backpack over her shoulders. Inside that bag was a sketchbook with a page listing the essential items required when your mysterious and troubled guardian is abruptly taken from you when you are seventeen years and ten months old and you are left here on earth to live alone in a rusted van inside an industrial scrapyard bordered by a tall barbed-wire fence.

- *One canary-yellow bicycle, preferably not stolen*
- *One Copic Multiliner drawing pen, 1.0-mm nib, black*
- *One RENDR Hardbound Sketchbook, 5.5 x 8.5 inches, black*
- *One copy of* The Penguin Dictionary of Jokes
- *Six trustworthy neighbours*

- *One box of Redheads Foil-sealed Firelighters*
- *One box of baking soda, to mix with water to make soap, shampoo, deodorant and toothpaste*
- *One thick blanket with a Ken Done cover depicting the Great Barrier Reef*
- *One A3-sized poster of Timothée Chalamet*
- *A steady supply of Heinz tinned spaghetti, to make grilled spaghetti and cheese sandwiches by the campfire*
- *A steady supply of Cottee's Lime Coola cordial*
- *One shared membership keytag to access twenty-four-hour shower and toilet facilities at the Good Life Health Club*
- *A well-paid job that will ensure someone with no identification and no registered government details of any kind can avoid starvation or, far worse for those aged under the age of eighteen, being placed on the looping ghost train ride that is the Queensland state ward system. Ideal jobs include: West End Aldi shelf filler, Queen Street Mall City Beach shop assistant, Queensland Art Gallery tour guide, delivering small packets of heroin to desperate and lonely old people across the suburbs of Brisbane*
- *An ability to resolve unexpected conflicts*
- *An ability to protect oneself during unexpected conflicts*
- *One Baccarat Damashiro fifteen-centimetre stainless-steel filleting knife, sharpened every night before bed.*

Speeding down Buckland Road, past the sporting oval at Nundah State School. Boys playing force-'em-backs with a dirty Steeden ball. A yellow-brick block of units. A man weeding his garden in blue overalls with a black cavoodle by his feet. Sometimes I can see the blazing hot summer suburbs of Brisbane in sketch lines, and for some reason life makes more sense to me that way. It's what we artists do. We translate. We transform. The whole world around me rendered in clean lines of black ink, and when it's drawn it feels like it has a reason to be, like it's not all one big mistake. A picket fence and a letterbox and a front-yard fallen palm frond beside a kid's rip-stick scooter, all pen lines in my head. Stop sign. Footpath. Gutter drain. Cane toad flattened like a pancake. There's beauty in the still and stultifying dullness of it all. The Beauty and Boost waxing clinic on the corner of Buckland Road and Hamson Terrace. Old Queenslander houses on stumps. A satellite dish on a terracotta-tile roof. Solar panels. A parked Triton truck. A bus stop.

And in the middle of this mental sketch rode the young and tortured artist — well before she became a household name — pedalling on the yellow Italian bicycle in big brown combat boots that reached up to her shins. She wore a pair of black denim Bermuda shorts she had found in the Spring Hill St Vincent de Paul thrift shop for fifty cents and, tucked into those shorts, a T-shirt with KYLIE SAYS RELAX in black block lettering across the front.

The artist had, somewhat curiously, temporarily abandoned her quest to uncover her identity. She told herself she did not need to know who she really was. She told herself she wasn't afraid of being hurt again by the truth. She told herself she wasn't fearful of the facts about Erica Finlay and the real reasons she had legged it across the country. She told herself she was too old to be scared of monsters.

Of course, what couldn't be seen in any surface-level self-portrait of the artist was her confusion. Her loss. The longing. The mistake of her. The growing rage inside her. Or the fifteen-centimetre fish-filleting knife hidden down the side of her right boot. What also couldn't be seen was her swollen big toe inside her right boot. At this particular juncture in her life, the artist had grown fond of kicking things. Cans in the street. Windows in unseen corners of abandoned warehouses. Rusted and empty oil drums. Empty bottles of beer and cheap wine. She recalled walking alone one night at 3 a.m. along Montague Road, West End, and unexpectedly and impulsively driving her foot through the left-

side headlight of a parked Maserati. It took her five furious stomps of escalating power and rage to penetrate the casing. This peculiar want to destroy. She had never carried this before.

The artist had also grown fond of stabbing things. The vinyl base of an abandoned two-seat couch left on the footpath of Bristol Street. A basketball left in the gutter on Spring Street. One afternoon, the artist found herself sauntering along the meat cabinet aisle in the Coles supermarket in Merthyr Village, New Farm. The artist looked over her shoulders and she realised she was alone for a moment in the aisle and from the right sleeve of an old grey Puma jacket she slid her filleting knife into her right hand and leaned down to a bay of six wrapped and boneless pork leg roasts and drove her knife swiftly and powerfully into the fatty centre of each of them, then scurried into the biscuit aisle where she selected herself a packet of Arnott's Kingstons for afternoon tea.

Hard left into New Street, George Stringer's street. George is the guy who calls me 'Laura Branigan'. He's a kind old man who lets me eat his mango and ice cream Weis bars and stream *Friends* on his telly while he shoots up. George told me his name means 'farmer', or someone who works in the earth. He was a bookkeeper by trade, and he says he farmed numbers all his life instead of spuds.

Sometimes we play Scrabble when he's high and low in the horse glow and he says strange things about arguing with the ghost of his dead wife, Cleo, who apparently resides in the half-crushed 2005 Audi A4 Quattro parked beneath a jacaranda by the backyard fence, the same 2005 Audi A4 Quattro that Cleo rolled twice along the Bruce Highway on the day she died in 2012.

'Cleo's just like you, Laura,' George said the last time we played Scrabble. 'She lives in a car too. Maybe you could move in with her some time? You'd be moving from a Toyota to an Audi, and that's like moving from Woodridge to Wilston. I know Cleo would like the company. Would you like that, Laura?'

'I'm sorry, George,' I said. 'I can't move in with Cleo. I prefer my river views.'

Then George casually laid down seven Scrabble tiles to build a word, 'xanthous', from my word, 'sector'.

'That's not a word, George!' I objected.

'The bastard son of green and yellow, my dear Laura,' George said.

'Put it in a sentence,' I said.

George thought for a moment then cupped his hands together at his chest. 'The lonely and widowed junkie's liver was a worrying shade of xanthous.'

George lives in a cream-coloured but peeling Queenslander with two high gables flanking a rickety front balcony. The frangipanis down each side of the house look as old as George. His letterbox is filled with junk mail this morning – leaflets for local tree loppers, brochures for bad pizza, next year's calendar from a local business called GET Real Estate. I chain-lock Macaroni to the letterbox pole and grab the junk mail for George so his tired old legs don't have to waddle down the L-shaped wooden staircase I scurry up with my black bag on my back. White wooden French doors open onto George's front balcony. Pot plants hang from the balcony ceiling and flank the front door, where I find a note George has left for me, stuck on with a strip of masking tape.

Laura,

Door's unlocked. Please come in but <u>do not enter my bedroom.</u> I have hung myself. Don't fret. Wanted out. Sorry about the mess. Help yourself to all the Weis bars you want. Merry Christmas. Thanks for being so kind to me. You're the only thing I'll miss.

Your friend,
George

Not a sound inside George's house. Old brown carpet in the hallway and living room. Wood-paneled walls and high ceilings. The big dark brown wooden door to George's bedroom is closed. I stare at it for two full minutes. Then move on. Framed landscape paintings on the living room walls. Western Queensland desert shacks. Shallow creeks and sheep that look certain to die of thirst. A painting of Jesus pulling his robe open to reveal a red heart on fire, like he's Superman. Dishes stacked high and unwashed in George's kitchen. Worcestershire sauce stains hardened on every dinner plate. The bin beneath the sink filled with maggots. A kitchen-bench battalion of black ants worshipping at the altar of a piece of Vegemite on toast. Six macadamia and mango Weis bars in the freezer.

I take two bars, walk back to George's bedroom door and open it. Those squeaky hinges need some oil. I leave the door half-open. And from where I stand, all I can see in George's bedroom is an antique dark brown wooden wardrobe with a tall mirror built into the centre of it, and in this mirror I can see George Stringer's bare legs hovering a foot above his queen-size bed. His legs have turned the colour of a blueberry.

I stare at those legs and feel sick in the waterlogged ball that is my belly because the colour of George's legs makes me think of the colours Erica Finlay must have turned at the bottom of the Brisbane River. And I curse myself for thinking such things and I know I need to harden up. It's just me here now on earth. Just me and the great mistake, in it for keeps. I need to be tough. This mistake of my world is brutal and unmerciful, and I can't fall to pieces every time I see a pair of swinging blue legs. And if I can't be tough right now in this doorway, then I'll pretend to be. So I casually tear the top off a Weis bar wrapper and take a bite.

Blue used to be my favourite colour.

I close the bedroom door and walk back out of the house to the front stairs, where I take a seat on the third step from the top and eat my ice cream as I gaze at the houses of New Street. On the opposite side of the road, a man sits in a parked blue Honda CR-V that looks like it's just been bought or washed. He's watching me, staring at me, I guess you could say. I take another bite of my Weis bar and stare back. His right arm rests on his open window frame. It's a muscular and wiry right arm with one of those big, rugged outdoorsman watches on the wrist, the kind that can track the movements of Russian space hardware and sense when your pet iguana is feeling anxious. White button-up business shirt with rolled-up sleeves. Clean and handsome face with jet-black eyebrows and short salt-and-pepper hair. He turns his head to the street in front of him and starts his car then gives me one last look as he drives away. A trickle of ice cream runs across the top of my hand and I lick it up.

*

Watching *Days of Thunder* an hour later in the living room of Ursula Lang's house, on the Flinders Parade waterfront at Sandgate, second last stop on the Shorncliffe line. The tide is out on the Moreton Bay mud flats beyond Ursula's open frontside windows and a sea breeze fills the house with the smell of salt and mud and the battered lunchtime cod that's cooking in old oil at the fish 'n' chips shop three doors down. Nicole Kidman and Tom Cruise fill the wide screen on the Sony Bravia television that Ursula says she'll give me when she dies. Nicole is playing a neurosurgeon who is deeply concerned that Tom's relentlessly egomaniacal and reckless approach to NASCAR racing will result in brain damage or death. Nicole means 'victory of the people'. Tom means 'twin'. Ursula likes to watch Nicole Kidman movies when she shoots teaspoons of Lady Flo's heroin.

We share a four-seat mid-century green velvet lounge that might be seventy years old, which, I figure, could still be ten years younger than Ursula. I'm eating from a saucer of biscuits Ursula gave me for afternoon tea. One Iced VoVo, one Kingston Cream, two Spicy Fruit Rolls and a Venetian that I'm saving for last.

'Why did you open the door, Vicki?' Ursula asks. She tightens and buckles a hot-pink and black studded belt around her left bicep. Ursula calls me 'Vicki' because I told her my name is Vicki Peterson, like the lead guitarist of The Bangles, one of Erica Finlay's favourite bands.

'I wanted to see him one last time,' I say.

'But he asked you not to enter the bedroom.'

'I know.'

'That was foolish.'

Ursula means 'she-bear'. She has put on make-up, even though I'll be her only guest today. She wears a blue MAC lipstick she likes, called Viva Glam; a broad black velvet headband over thick, straight, white ponytailed hair; a purple satin mini shift dress that exposes her kneecaps and her long legs, thin as tent poles; and black velvet heels. A thick blue vein awakens beneath Ursula's white skin and I wonder if her nervous system is just a series of branches stretching from a tree of electric blue light planted in her stomach.

'What did you see in there?' she asks.

'In where?'

'In George's bedroom.'

I turn my face to Tom Cruise on the television. 'Blue,' I say.

'You saw blue?'

'George's body. It was all blue. Blue like one of your lipsticks.'

'Poor ol' bastard,' Ursula says, reaching for the syringe that rests on the velvet arm of the lounge. She punctures her arm and Nicole the neurosurgeon and Tom the racing-car driver make love on the television. Ursula places the used syringe in an empty can of Kirks Ginger Beer, leans back into the lounge and takes a deep, satisfying breath without even opening her blue lips.

'Why would he do that, Ursula?'

Her eyes are closed. 'Do what?' she asks.

'Check out early like that. Why not stick around for a couple more games of Scrabble? He coulda sold his house and flown to Paris. He coulda robbed a bank and given the money to every kid spoonin' soup right now at The Well. He coulda given the money to me and I coulda looked after him. Why would he just book out like that?'

Ursula loosens the belt around her arm. 'He was tired of losing,' she says.

'Losing what?'

Eyes closed again, resting her back on the lounge. 'Losing your strength, losing your sight, losing your hearing, losing your hair, losing the argument because you keep losing the point,' she says. 'And maybe you can bear all that kinda losing for a bit, but then comes the real hard losing, the real nail-in-the-coffin kinda losing.' She opens her eyes and rests a hand on my thigh. 'Losing the ones you love. Losing friends. Losing your wife. Losing your husband. Then, sure enough, comes the time when all you wanna do is lose yourself.'

Ursula points a finger at me. 'That's where you and Lady Flo come in,' she says. 'You drop by our houses like Mister Sandman to help us float away from ourselves for a spell.'

I feel sick in my stomach. Been feelin' sick for a bit now. And it ain't the Weis bars. 'Pretty rotten way to make a buck, 'ey Ursula?' I say.

Ursula shrugs. 'Supply and demand,' she says. 'Make no mistake, angel … you and ol' Lady Flo are in the sorrow business. And, right now, out here in the Australian suburbs, business is a-boomin'!'

Flora Box is using me. I'm using Flora Box. What else was I gonna do? I was lost. I was low. She vowed to pull me through the loss of Erica Finlay. A girl's gotta eat. Of course I fell into the wide open arms of Lady Flo.

She likes it when I do this, spending quality time with her older clients. Flora says elderly users make the best customers. Often wealthy. Always pay up front. Too tired and weak for trouble. Flora says her older customers pay as much for an hour sitting and chatting to a young woman like me as they do for the small bags of powder I deliver to them. Youth, Flora says, is almost as intoxicating to them as dope. Yeah, a pretty fuggin' sick way to make a buck.

Ursula turns her attention to the television and I turn my gaze there as well. Ursula's buzzed and rubbery head is transfixed by an image on the screen. 'I dressed her once,' she says.

'Who?'

Ursula nods at the television. 'Nicole.'

'When?'

'I was just a nobody in Sydney,' she says. 'Styling and dressing a few politicians' wives for gala events; helping a few busty girls look glamorous for trophy night at the Manly Leagues Club. Then the call came through: "Nicole Kidman's just landed back home and she's got nothin' to wear to the 1995 Sydney premiere of *Batman Forever*." Boom. Off I go. InterContinental Hotel, Sydney. She had the Royal Opera Suite. I burst in, all sweaty and breathless, three dresses in my arms. The room had two wide windows, one for staring at the Sydney Harbour Bridge and one for staring at the Opera House. The afternoon sun was blasting through those windows, setting those red curls on fire and all I saw was that hair, that flame around her, and then she smiled at me and I wondered if I wasn't dreaming. And you know what she said to me, Vicki? You know what she said?'

'What did she say?'

Ursula reaches excitedly for the television remote and pauses *Days of Thunder* on a frame filled with Nicole's face, her head resting on a pillow.

'She said, "Thanks for coming, Ursula."'

She pats her thin cheeks with her palms, eyes watering at the memory.

'Not nobody now, 'ey, Ursula!' I say.

'I certainly felt like somebody that day,' Ursula says. 'I started that day as plain ol' Ursula. I ended that day as Ursula, the woman who once dressed Nicole Kidman.' She nods slowly. 'She chose a silver mini dress. Her legs went to Adelaide in it. The dress had all this bedazzling that made her sparkle. She looked like a human bonfire wrapped in a towel made of tiny diamonds. And when she turned around in front of this tall mirror in the suite, the light bounced off the dress and a hundred little rainbows flashed around her. It was like them paparazzi cameras were going off, but there were no cameras in that room, only rainbows. And she turned and smiled at me. A smile as wide as Sydney Harbour. Flawless skin and cherry-red lipstick. And you know what she said?'

'What did she say?'

'She said, "You make me feel like a star, Ursula."'

Ursula leans back against the lounge, closing her eyes like she's trying to take herself back to that hotel suite, back to the star.

'Do you know she walked all the way down to Circular Quay by herself that evening?' Ursula says. 'No minders. No security. I watched her the whole way. The sun was setting over the harbour and there she was in that dress. Legs and heels and hair. Literally stopping passersby in their tracks. Some people were actually stepping away from her as she passed, like she had some kind of force field around her. She kept her head down as she marched on, and I guess all the gawkers would have assumed she was trying not to make a scene. But I knew what she was really doing.'

'What was she doing, Ursula?'

'She was saving their lives,' she whispers. 'She was looking down because just one brief glance from that particular woman on that particular afternoon woulda stopped a person's heart from beating. One look and she coulda killed 'em dead. A hundred human doornails scattered across Circular Quay.'

We laugh. I take a bite of a Spicy Fruit Roll. Ursula plays the movie again.

'Imagine being so pretty you could kill someone with a single look,' I say.

'What do you mean "imagine", angel?' Ursula asks. 'You looked in the mirror lately?'

I think on this question for a moment. 'It's been a while since I looked in a mirror actually, Ursula,' I say.

We watch the movie for five more minutes in silence before a thought comes to me. 'You got any of them pretty dresses left in your wardrobe, Ursula?' I ask.

She taps the fingers of her left hand excitedly on the arm of her lounge. 'You wanna try one on again?' she asks.

I nod.

The tree of electric blue light sends a pulse to Ursula Lang's eyeballs. 'Which one?' she whispers.

'The red one, Ursula,' I say. 'Of course, the pretty red one.'

Big Dumb, Fuckin' Cocaine Meathead Boy Monster Idiot

Big Dumb Fuckin' Cocaine Meathead Boy Monster Idiot

December 2023

Pen and ink on paper

The artist was furious and wondering if she should ask her boss's accountant, Ephraim Wall, to dissolve four wealthy and foolish university students in a bath of potassium hydroxide. Museum visitors who have purchased the audio accompaniment to this exhibition should now tap on the tile marked '"Till Death Do Us Part", Madonna'.

A simple delivery for four university boys sharing a hotel room on Level 11 of the Marriott Hotel on Queen Street. Death-metal music beyond the door. A hard thump against a wall like someone's head just bounced off plasterboard. I untie the shoelace on my right boot as I always do when I make deliveries to rooms filled with boys who bang their heads against walls. Ring the doorbell.

The music stops and a young guy with red hair and blue eyes opens the door. Tall stick of carrot, can't be much older than twenty. Hair pulled into a top knot, shaved on the sides. Three more guys behind him in the room. The two closest to me are shirtless and sweating, covered in red grip marks and bruising. I figure they've either been wrestling on the room's king-size bed or fucking. They're all giggly and soul-young.

With a swift jink of his neck, Red gestures for me to enter. The door closes behind me. Christmas hats. Corona beer bottles across the coffee table and the TV cabinet. A bong in the corner of the room. A sleeping bag beside the bed. No exits for me but the door Red just closed. He pulls a fistful of fifty-dollar notes from his right pants pocket.

'They said two hundred dollars?'

I nod.

He hands the money over and I slip four pineapples into the grey money belt tied around my waist beneath my Kylie

Minogue T-shirt. In exchange, I hand Red an Indonesian pirated CD copy of *Like a Prayer* by Madonna.

'Gear's behind the disc,' I say.

Red looks puzzled, turns the CD over in his hand with the kind of befuddlement that would suggest I just handed him a page from the Egyptian Book of the Dead.

'It's called a CD,' I say. 'It's how your mum and dad used to listen to Nickelback.'

'I know what it is,' Red snorts.

He takes a small, flat plastic bag of cocaine from inside the case and then studies the fake *Like a Prayer* cover art. Blue jeans, close up at the waist, and the greatest exposed belly in the history of popular culture, adorned by colourful jewels.

'She was the Queen of Pop,' I say. 'That album is her masterwork.'

'I know who she is,' he says. Then he casually flings the CD across the room. It splits into two pieces against the mini-bar fridge and part of me dies inside.

'What's your name?' asks the shirtless and muscular blond boy by the bed.

'My name's Pat Benatar,' I reply, not taking my eyes off Red.

'Why'd your mum and dad give you a boy's name?' Blondie asks.

'Pat's short for Patrice,' I say, still facing Red. 'My mum's name was also Patrice. She died saving baby twins from a burning building. She held her breath for three whole minutes while she ran up three flights of stairs in search of those wailing bubs. After somehow making it back down through the inferno to the ground floor, she collapsed, burns across her arms, dead as a doornail, at the feet of a fireman who gathered up the still-breathing babies.'

I turn to address Blondie. 'If you're ever walking through the gardens near Roma Street Fire Station, look for the little gold plaque dedicated to my mother. It reads, "Thanks for everything, Pat Benatar."'

For no apparent reason, the non-blond shirtless wrestler-lovemaker beside Blondie shouts, 'Eight!'

'Fuck off,' says the fourth guy with the Santa hat, who is holding a glass of neat whisky by a corner desk. 'Six.'

Red lifts the bag of powder up. 'Few lines of this and she might jump to a nine,' he says. University-boy head-nods and high-pitched, peas-for-testicles-university-boy cackles and handclaps all round.

'*Booiiiiiiiiiiiiiii,*' yells Blondie, clicking his fingers.

I find myself wondering if Madonna ever found herself alone in a hotel room with four muscle-bound university rich-boy meatheads and a bag of cocaine.

'You wanna stay and party with us?' asks Red.

'No, thanks.'

Red digs into his left pocket. Pulls out two more fifty-dollar notes. 'How much for you to stay and party with us?'

Fucking rich-boy cocaine meatheads.

'That's deeply insulting, and you are now making me feel uncomfortable,' I say. 'Please stop.'

I shuffle to the hotel room door, but Red blocks my path. 'You don't understand,' he says. 'We *really* want you to stay.'

I step left to move around him, but Red steps to his right to block me again. 'It's my birthday,' he says. And he places his right hand on my left shoulder.

Now the waltz can begin.

Meathead. Mother. Fucker. Almost a foot taller than me. He stands so close that I can smell the beer and the bongs on his breath when he whispers, 'It's my party and I'll fuck if I want to.'

I think on these words for a moment then decide to take a close look at my boots. 'These darn shoelaces,' I say.

As I kneel in front of Red, the shirtless blond gangster-rapper wannabe says in a high-pitched voice, '*While uuuu down derrre beeeeetch,*' and the four meatheads laugh. But then they stop laughing because I'm standing again and pushing the tip of a fifteen-centimetre filleting knife against the soft skin below Red's Adam's apple.

'*Phwat ... d ... fuck!*' he spits.

I whip my head around to the shirtless blond behind me. 'Stay the fuck back, you meatheads, because I'm dying to cut this cunt's voice box out.'

Red raises his arms. 'Stay back,' he says to his friends.

His voice softens. He's just a boy. 'I'm sorry, I'm sorry,' he says.

'No, I'm sorry,' I say. 'I'm so sorry for you because I'm gonna have to tell Lady Flo about this and you're gonna have to die now. You're all gonna have to die now.'

'Wh ... wh ... why?' Red stutters. 'Why do we have to die?'

'Because of love,' I say. 'Because of family.' I pull hard on Red's sleeve, which in turn presses his throat harder against the tip of the filleting knife. 'See, my boss, Lady Flora Box, says she loves me in the kind of way she would love me if I was her own flesh and blood. Loves me like a daughter, which is why she is so relentlessly militant about me reporting back to her any unpleasant incidents that occur during my deliveries. Now, I told you, plainly and clearly, that you were making me feel uncomfortable and then you tried to dance the Tyrannosaurus Waltz.'

'What's the Tyrannosaurus Waltz?' Red asks. 'I don't know the Tyrannosaurus Waltz.'

'Erica Finlay danced the Tyrannosaurus Waltz,' I reply.

'Who's Erica Finlay?' Red squeaks.

'It doesn't fuckin' matter who Erica Finlay is. What matters is that she told me how we all have our monsters. She said all of us will be asked to dance the Tyrannosaurus Waltz at some stage in our life. Could be your arsehole boss. Could be your arsehole daughter. Could be your priest. Could be your accountant. Could be you, Red. Do you know that one Australian woman every week is murdered by some monster just like you in some tragic encounter just like this? Gone, just like that.'

I move closer to him. 'Erica Finlay told me once about how she managed to stop dancing with her monster,' I say. 'Do you wanna know what she told me?'

'What did she tell you?'

'She said she stuck a blade in the monster's voice box. The more I thought about her doing that the more questions I had. How could a woman with such kindness and such love inside her possibly do a thing so violent?' I test the blade against Red's throat. 'But then no woman realises the full extent of what she's capable of until she is forced to realise the full extent of what she's capable of.'

And there's a vision in my head of Erica Finlay holding a paring knife up to Marcus Finlay's throat. And Marcus is goading her, begging her to stick that knife in the soft skin beneath his chin. She told police after the incident in March Street, Bomaderry, that she had almost killed him once. Had she done so then, I wouldn't be standing in this fucking room of idiot Neanderthals. But the vision in my head ends with the truth behind the lie she told me when I turned seventeen. Marcus Finlay grabs her wrist and bends it back until it breaks and the paring knife falls from her grip.

And I scream now in Red's face, 'I WILL NOT DANCE WITH YOU, MONSTER.'

Then I whisper, 'I'm so fucking sorry, you silly boy monster. Now I have to tell Flora Box what has taken place here and, unfortunately for you, Flora is going to have to tell her most loyal friend, Ephraim Wall, and then Ephraim is going to have to pay you four boys a visit, and you four boys are going to have to strip naked and slide into a nice boiling bath of potassium hydroxide. And then you will be invisible, Red. Like you were never even here. Like you never even existed.'

'What the fuck, Lyndsay!' screams the boy in the corner. 'I don't wanna fucking die, man!'

'Listen,' Red says, palms in the air. 'I'm so sorry for making you feel uncomfortable. I'm a fuckin' idiot.'

'A big dumb fuckin' cocaine meathead boy monster idiot,' I confirm.

'Please tell me what I can do to make it up to you,' Red says. 'Please don't tell Flora Box.'

Red's cheeks are roses now. Bubbles of perspiration above his lip like little clear dome tents on a campground of trembling skin. A tiny bubble of blood at the tip of my blade, still pressed against his throat.

'Do any of you fuckin' morons know anything about the *Like a Prayer* album?'

No answers. Just head-shakes and grunts.

'Can I tell you a secret?' I ask Red.

'Yeah, you can tell me a secret,' Red says.

'*Like a Prayer* saved me when Erica Finlay died. It wasn't just the music that helped me. It was the pain. Madonna took her pain and turned it into art. Just like Francis Bacon did. Just like Jackson Pollock. She gave the world all her sacred pain in this album, and I gave you that album as a gesture of kindness from one human to another and you just flung it against the wall like it was a frisbee. Why did you do that?'

'I'm so sorry,' Red says. 'I didn't know what I was doing.'

'But I know exactly what you were doing, Red. Because I know who you are. Do you know who you are?'

'No ... no,' he says. 'Who am I?'

'You are so fucking lucky,' I say. 'You are that fucking lucky that you are completely oblivious to how fucking lucky you actually are. Do you, I wonder, ever think about how one single little event can alter the course of someone's entire life? A woman rolls her Audi on the highway. A woman drowns in the Brisbane River for no reason other than the fact she was brave. Some nameless drug-slinger girl stabs a fish-filleting knife through your throat. Just like that! Boom. One little moment in time and then you wake up one day and you realise you're not so lucky after all. Because you're in a different life now. You're no longer living the life you were supposed to be living. Eight billion lucky idiots moving blissfully through the world, not realising we're all just one tiny little event away from living in a van by the river.'

I punch a knuckle into Red's chest. 'Do you know who you are?' I ask again.

'No, who am I?' Red asks.

'You are the Tyrannosaurus,' I say. 'You are the tyrant lizard.'

I close my eyes for a moment, blade still firmly pressed against Red's throat. Grip the filleting knife hard and whisper, 'The whole *Like a Prayer* album is about dancing with monsters. All through the record we find Madonna having to dance with tyrant lizards: fathers, husbands, God. But never has the Tyrannosaurus Waltz been more perfectly distilled into a five-minute pop song than on track four, which the Queen of Pop so aptly entitled "Till Death Do Us Part".'

I slide the blade tip down from Red's throat to his chest. 'It's about a girl who's been waltzing for years with a tyrant lizard. The lizard smashes up the house and bruises the girl and then the girl lies about their secret waltzing. The brutal and torturous dance continues until the girl realises there is only one way to end it.'

I circle Red's chest with the blade tip and settle it on his heart. 'The girl's gotta die.'

I slide the blade tip down from Red's chest to his belly. 'There is a rage in me, Red. Erica Finlay did something terrible to me.

Because someone like *you* did something terrible to Erica Finlay. My rage is born from love and my rage is born from loss. I've been trying to find the art in it, but the art seems so hard to find these days. But the rage, Red, the rage. It's so very easy to find.'

I tap the knife twice on Red's belly. Draw circles. 'Every time I listen to "Till Death Do Us Part", I wish for a happy ending for the girl who's been dancing the Tyrannosaurus Waltz. You wanna know what my happy ending would be for the girl in that song?'

Red nods twice, urgently. 'What? What would be your happy ending?'

'The girl doesn't die,' I say. 'The girl takes a secret fish-filleting knife from her shoe' – I slide the fish-filleting knife down from Red's belly to his tackle box – 'then the girl cuts the tyrant lizard's dick off and the tyrant lizard weeps when he realises lizards' dicks don't grow back.'

Red draws a sharp breath and freezes. Silence in the room.

'Now get the fuck out of my way.'

Red stands aside, hands raised, and I step through the door.

Blue is still my favourite colour.

*

Back across town on Edward Street, Charlie Mould runs towards me on the Central Station exit ramp. Just seeing him makes me smile. It's nice for a deep and often tortured young artist like me to have someone like Charlie in her life. A boy who lifts my mood just by being. All he has to do to make me happy is to stay visible.

When he sees me, he starts pulling his goofball slow-motion run where he's pretending to be the leading man in our own black and white silver-screen romance and I'm his long-lost leading lady and we're running into each other's arms at the climax of a two-hour weepy.

'Lady Diana!' he shouts.

He screams so loud and theatrically, with his arms raised in unearned triumph, that I know he's been drinking. I know that anyway, because he's a nineteen-year-old alcoholic whose sunken chest and Christmas candy cane arms and legs were formed by a strict diet of Ritz crackers, Laughing Cow cheese triangles, Riverstone roll-your-own tobacco and McWilliam's Royal Reserve Dry Sherry – two litres for $15 flat. And he's got a drinker's rash creeping across his forehead and neck.

That head of Charlie's might just have worked for old Hollywood: bouncing and full brown hair, blue eyes and a lawsuit smile. The rest of him is pure Brisbane. His thin cotton University of Queensland T-shirt carries an image of the university's coat of arms over the motto *Scientia ac Labore*. But Charlie's never been to university. His education ended halfway through Year 6, when he was expelled from Ironside State School in St Lucia for painting a fifty-metre-long cock and balls in motor oil on the school oval then setting it alight in the pre-dawn darkness before school sports day. He told the school principal it was a genuine and bold piece of contemporary art, something akin to the early works of Charlie's heroes Doris Salcedo from Colombia and Thomas Hirschhorn from Switzerland.

'Only through the destruction of all that we consider sacred can we find what lies on the other side of enlightenment,' Charlie explained to his school principal and the police officer called to the scene of the crime.

'And what in Christ's name lies on the other side of enlightenment?' the principal asked.

Charlie took a long moment to consider his answer. 'Jennifer Lopez,' he said.

Charlie means 'freedom'. He's wearing his usual black denim shorts and his shoes are impractical and out-of-sync dark tan leather dress shoes, like the ones the young lawyers wear on

George Street, except they don't wear them with shorts and lime-green Canberra Raiders socks.

He lifts me high in his arms and spins me twice like we haven't seen each other in a year, when, in fact, it was me who woke him up this morning before I rode off on my rounds.

'Get off me,' I say. 'You're all wet with sweat.'

Charlie grips the right strap of an old blue Rip Curl backpack.

'Fuckin' Flo sent me for a drop in Bundamba,' Charlie says. 'I shoulda hopped off the train at Bundamba Station, but I got off one station too soon at Ebbw Vale.'

'It's pronounced *Ebboo* Vale,' I say. 'It's Welsh.'

'What did I say?'

'You said *Ebwer* Vale.'

'Yeah, whatever. Fuckin' station comes up and I scoot out and then I have to walk another two kilometres to a house in Bumfuck to drop some wizz fizz to some thick-necked biker wanker who's tattooed a sledgehammer and cracked skull lines across his forehead. Then he says it's a tick drop and he'll fix Flo up after Christmas and I say I was told by Flo that it most assuredly weren't no tick drop and then the veins pop in his shoulders and he asks me if I'd care to see firsthand how he earned the nickname "Hammer", which forced me to ask him in return if he'd care to see firsthand how I earned the nickname "Bad Cunt with a Massive Cock".'

Charlie's an optimist, the most optimistic person I know. His life began at four o'clock in the morning nineteen years ago when he was found by an Ipswich Hospital nurse at the door of the emergency ward, wrapped in a blue blanket. Charlie reckons being jettisoned early is the best thing that can happen to a human. 'No going down from there,' he says. He claims that's the reason shark mums always abandon their kids in the shark nursery. 'The only way is up, kids! Good luck out there. Play nice. Stay away from Mick Fanning.'

Charlie spent his childhood bouncing around South East Queensland foster families but ran from the system for good when he was woken one night in his bedroom in Rochedale South by what he thought was a mosquito biting the inside of his left elbow. He slapped hard at his arm, only to hit the hands of an older foster brother – one possessing an alarming fixation with vampire lore – who was collecting a large sample of blood via the syringe sticking out of Charlie's arm.

Charlie also means 'warrior'. I met Charlie across a table in The Well's cafeteria when I was twelve and he was thirteen. I understood his artistic genius from the moment he showed me a contemporary art installation piece he was working on called *Charlie Said It Was Good*. The piece, destined for an exhibition of Charlie's work that still hasn't happened yet, will see gallery guests walk into an entirely white room to find nothing but a single bed with a firmly fitted blanket and sheets and a bedroom side table. Guests will open the side table's drawer to find a copy of the Bible in which Charlie has liquid-papered over every use of the name 'God' in the book and replaced it with the name 'Charlie'.

> *In the beginning, Charlie created the heavens and the earth.* – *Genesis 1:1*

> *For all have sinned and fall short of the glory of Charlie.* – *Romans 3:23*

> *Man shall not live by bread alone, but by every word that proceeds from the mouth of Charlie.* – *Matthew 4:4*

I point at Charlie's shirt. 'What's that mean?'

'*Scientia ac Labore*,' he says with a flourish. 'It's Latin for "Knowledge via Boredom".'

Charlie taps the Ann Street pedestrian crossing button with the heel of his shoe. 'You headin' to Flo's?' he asks.

'Yeah, I'm done for the day.'

'I'll come with. But I gotta show you somethin' first.'

*

We stroll down Edward Street, past the old backpackers' hostel, and turn right into Adelaide Street. We talk about how global art movements shouldn't always have to come out of New York, London or Paris. Why can't they come from here and now, on Adelaide Street, Brisbane? We don't see why art lovers, a hundred years from today, shouldn't talk about how Charlie and me were romantic and penniless artists who slept in cars by night and walked the streets of Brisbane by day, delivering small packages of hard drugs in order to stay alive, in order to make our art.

Charlie Mould and the artist were not lovers. They were something more. They were friends in art. Volatile. Captivating. Destructive. Tortured. Like Brisbane's own Lucian Freud and Francis Bacon. Warhol and Basquiat. Gauguin and Van Gogh. Every sketch, every installation, was infused and informed with the street grit and the grime, the wondrous invisible, of Brisbane, that famed and celebrated capital of the glorious Sunshine State. Brisbane, Queensland, Australia: the artistic capital of the world.

We pass the Banh Mi Now shop, where we sometimes stop for lunch on Wednesdays and Thursdays. A lot of our best conversations revolve around what we intend to eat or what we have already eaten during the day. That's a Moon Street thing. Everybody's hungry for something there. Drink. Horse. Coke. Escape. Belonging. Friendship. Forgiveness. Love and love and love and love. Me and Charlie are usually just hungry for a pork belly banh mi.

Next to Banh Mi Now is the Ginger & Garlic Indian Cuisine takeaway shop, and Charlie waves at the owner, Ashish Sood, as he passes. 'Asheeeeeesh!' he hollers with his right fist in the air. Behind a steaming bain marie, Ashish smiles and winks at Charlie as he fills the plastic tub in his left hand with the best chickpea curry in all of Queensland. For years now, Ashish has had the same sign stuck to the window of his takeaway shop: *Free meals for the homeless. Every weekday after 10.45 p.m. Saturday & Sunday after 9 p.m.* Six months ago, Lady Flo placed Charlie on a three-month work ban after she discovered he had consumed a small sample of a heroin drop intended for a wealthy Bulimba couple. After such an indiscretion, Charlie was lucky to still have enough fingers to hold a fork. Over those six long months that Charlie lived jobless and penniless it was Ashish Sood who filled his fork with free 10.45-p.m. tubs of lentil curry and butter chicken and vegetarian pakoras.

'Hey, you seen Esther today?' Charlie asks me.

'No.'

'She wants to talk to you.'

'What about?'

Charlie shrugs. 'I think she's having another episode.'

'What's she been doing?'

'She's been giving all her things away because she had another flood dream.'

'Esther and her fuckin' flood dreams.'

'She saw the whole city underwater. She saw bull sharks swimming past the Batman building. She said she saw your mum still holding her breath down there.'

'You mean Erica Finlay,' I say.

Charlie gives me a tender look. 'Yeah, Erica Finlay. She was sipping a tea on one of those circle tables outside Starbucks on Albert Street. It was all underwater, but she was just sitting there sipping tea.'

I flutter my lips like a neighing horse.

'Don't scoff,' Charlie says. 'Fuck with Esther's visions at your peril. She's an oracle.'

'Esther needs to climb out of that hole and get some sun,' I say.

Resting against the black shopfront wall of the TAB on Adelaide Street are two grey-haired men with brown suntans and browner teeth, Dale 'Pot' Potter and Ivan Salhus. Each holds a cardboard sign. The first thing I read on Pot's sign is the word 'MURDER' in large black capital letters. On closer inspection I can now see the sign reads *Need $$$ for urgent penis surgery. Seriously, the size of this thing is MURDER on my posture.*

Ivan's sign reads *Fascinating facts for 50c a pop!*

I toss a dollar coin into an empty Mortein mosquito coil-burner can sitting in front of Ivan's crossed legs. 'That's two fascinating facts, Ivan,' I say. 'Better not be ones I've heard before.'

'Why, thank you,' Ivan says. He looks me up and down. 'Hey, you settled on a name for yourself yet?'

'Not yet, Ivan.'

'I got a good one for ya.'

'I'm listening.'

Ivan blocks the name out with his hands like it's lit up on a Broadway marquee. 'Genevieve ... Sometimes.'

'What, like, "Sometimes" is the last name?'

'Yeah,' Ivan says. 'Thought it could be a cool last name. Sometimes Genevieve is happy. Sometimes she's sad. You're a bit like that all the time. Genevieve Sometimes. Keeps all your options open.'

I frown, shake my head.

'Rebecca Always?' Ivan ponders, optimistically.

I shrug, shake my head again.

'Juliana Never?' Ivan posits.

I laugh. 'Just gimme the facts, Ivan.'

'Okay,' Ivan continues, looking Charlie up and down, 'your first fact relates to those ridiculous and impractical leather shoes Charlie is wearing.'

'Do tell,' I say.

'Did you know that, until biological softeners were invented in 1908, the most common way to soften the leather in shoes was to smear them with dog shit?'

Pot claps his hands.

'Thanks, Ivan,' I say. 'I did not know that fascinating fact. Second fact, please.'

Ivan rubs his hands and then his chin. 'Did you know that one bite from the Brazilian wandering spider has been known to leave male victims with a four-hour erection?'

'I did not know that either, Ivan,' I say. 'Two for two!'

'I've got a question for you, Ivan,' Charlie says.

'Yes,' Ivan says, ready for anything.

'Where might one find a Brazilian wandering spider in Brisbane?'

Ivan howls, slaps his folded knees. 'Young Prince like you don't need no spider bite to keep his sting!' Ivan laughs again, his rattling chest wheezing and sputtering in the mirth.

Pot points to the southern end of Adelaide Street, towards Brisbane City Hall. 'You seen all that up there yet?'

Charlie nods. 'Saw it this morning. Before the gumshoes even got there.' Tips his head at me. 'Takin' her up to see it now.'

'See what?' I ask.

'Dead body,' Charlie says.

'I don't wanna see no dead body,' I spit.

'Body's gone,' Pot says. 'Cops left an hour ago. He was done in his sleep. They're sayin' it had to be a club or somethin'.'

'Who's sayin' that?' Charlie asks.

Pot leans over and tilts his right ear to the ground. 'The only thing worth listenin' to, Chuckles,' he says. 'The street.' Then he shakes his head and pulls a Glad bag of half-smoked and scavenged cigarette dumpers from underneath his left thigh. 'Whole half of his skull was pushed down into his neck,' he continues, sifting through the dumpers to find a fulsome menthol with red lipstick stains on the butt. 'Poor prick laid there all bloody as Mary till 8 a.m. before anybody even noticed.'

'Poor prick?' Ivan exclaims. 'Who you feelin' sorry for, Pot? Fuckin' slimy rock spider shoulda been dragged through town by a fit horse.'

'That's a fact on which I will concur,' says Charlie. 'Three for three, Ivan.'

*

We walk on up Adelaide Street, passing King George Square, with the sun still so hot even this deep into the afternoon that kids are burning their hands trying to stroke the thick manes of the bronze lion sculptures at the entry to Brisbane City Hall. There's a towering Christmas tree in the centre of the square, decorated with red plastic ribbons, blue and gold plastic stars, plastic candy canes and a giant gold star on top. It's encircled by a white security fence and next to the fence is a red Australia Post box: *Santa's Mailbox.*

Dear Santa,

If she really did what I think she done, can you please tell me why she did it?

How could a person do such a thing?

Was she really that kind of person?

Can you please tell me what it takes for an angel to turn into a monster?

Yours sincerely,

Linda Ronstadt

Vivid blue sky and a city hall clock tower with four faces, which is exactly two more faces than the number of faces Charlie says Leon Rooney had before he was bludgeoned to death sometime before dawn this morning.

'He had no face at all by the time I saw him,' Charlie says.

We pass the King George Square bus station. Pass an avenue of shady and manicured gum trees that rise out of circles of earth in the tiled footpath skirting the sandstone west wall of City Hall. Blue and white chequered barricade tape in the corner of my view. Same tape the cops in *Home and Away* use when there's been a murder in Summer Bay.

'Hey, hobro,' says a Maori woman named Kara Rakena, sitting on a purple yoga mattress with her husband, Rangi, who, in front of his crossed legs, has placed a cardboard sign against an empty Blue Ribbon Neapolitan ice-cream container. It reads: *I prefer 'domestically challenged'.*

'Hey, Kara,' Charlie says.

Kara and Rangi sit in their usual weekday coin-rattle spot a metre away from a bronze statue of Dr Clem Jones, former Lord Mayor of Brisbane. Charlie nods towards the stone balustrade running along a manicured and bark-mulched bromeliad garden beyond the statue. The balusters look like sandstone chessboard pawns and beyond them is a wide and deep cavity where a steel protection grate covers a series of air-conditioning units that cool audiences when the Queensland Symphony Orchestra plays Christmas carols in City Hall's main auditorium. The barricade tape is adorned with the word 'POLICE', a 'no humans' stick-figure icon and a contact number for Crime Stoppers. The tape runs halfway along the stone balustrade and across the air-conditioning maintenance cavity.

'Just showin' me sister where they found Leon,' Charlie says.

Kara shudders. 'I can't look behind there,' she says. 'Fuckin' serial killer roaming the streets of little ol' Brisbane. How the fuck am I s'posed to get any sleep at night?'

'Who's sayin' serial killer?' Charlie asks.

'I'm fuckin' sayin',' Kara says, her voice going up an octave like Kate Bush when she hits the chorus in 'Babooshka'. 'Eight days ago. Same shit, different dero.'

'You mean Bill Moffitt?' I ask.

'Shit yeah,' Kara says. 'Got his head clubbed in while he was sleeping.'

Bill Moffitt. Homeless thug drunk, thirty-five years old and built like a bus. Bill never had to panhandle for his drink money on the street; he'd just beat it out of hardworking and sun-damaged gutter punks once the sun went down. Most of the bag ladies and gents of Brisbane quietly rejoiced when word spread eight days ago that Bill had been found dead at dawn, flat out on a foam mattress beside the old stone Walter Hill drinking fountain in the botanic gardens off Alice Street.

'I thought he was king-hit in a blue,' I say.

'Bullshit,' Kara says. 'That was a cold-blooded attack. No doubt by the same random nutter who done Leon.'

We step through the garden and tread on the base of Clem Jones's statue, where I see, for the first time, the words carved in bronze beneath Clem's left dress shoe: *One must care about a world one will never see.*

By the shaded sandstone walls of City Hall, Charlie glances over each of his shoulders then slips under the barricade tape close to the balustrade and walks to a square stone nook, big enough for a washing machine or small refrigerator, built into the City Hall's west wall beside the maintenance cavity. It's a popular sleeping place for Brisbane floaters, as the balustrade forms a protective screen and heat expelled by the air-conditioning units warms the sometimes-cold night air.

We lean over the balustrade and stare into the nook where Leon Rooney slept for the past three months. Charlie points and my eyes follow his right forefinger to a patch of dry blood that's turned almost black in the summer sun. Half-day-old monster blood. The space has the same smell as wheel-flattened cane toads lying in Brisbane gutters.

'One of the first things I learned as a kid when I started sleepin' rough,' Charlie says, 'was stay away from Leon Rooney.'

Two-parts paedo, Charlie says, one-part pimp. Leon was known for getting noob street kids hooked on drink and drugs and then dangling fixes before their eyes that could be swapped for a finger up his arse or a suck on his grimy lollipop. Nothing but a dirty, filthy tyrant lizard.

'Was there ever a bigger cunt to be found dead on these streets than Leon Rooney?' Charlie asks.

I don't need any time to find my answer. 'Bill Moffitt,' I say.

Charlie nods, spitting into the blood-covered space. 'If we ever bump into this feller with the club,' Charlie says, 'remind me to buy him a banana Paddle Pop.'

'Nah, it can't work like that, Charlie,' I say.

'What can't work like that?'

'The world,' I say. 'We can't go givin' Paddle Pops to psychos who bludgeon people in the street. Don't matter who's coppin' the bludgeoning.'

'All right, then,' Charlie says. 'Can I give 'im a Frosty Fruit?'

Kara calls to us from the street. 'Fuzz cuz, fuzz cuz, fuzz cuz!'

We hear a police siren pulse once from Adelaide Street and we leap back from the balustrade and rush through the City Hall side gardens back onto the footpath then hurry on up Adelaide Street towards George. A police car with two officers inside it motors slowly alongside us.

The officer in the passenger seat brings his window down. 'The fuck you doin', sniffin' round that crime scene, Charlie Mould?' the officer asks. We recognise him immediately. Butterfield's always giving city floaters shit. Always waking them up in the middle of the night and moving them on. Always smashing whisky bottles and beer bottles beside them, kicking personal belongings across sleeping spaces.

'Just gathering some information on who might be killing me in my sleep tonight, Officer Butterfield, if you boys don't hurry up and catch this psycho stalkin' the homeless,' Charlie says, looking straight ahead.

I walk, stout and upright, by his side, one hand on the strap of my backpack as I count how many small packets of powder I'm still carrying. Three CDs, intended for the late George Stringer: *Tuesday Night Music Club*, Sheryl Crow; *Pieces of You*, Jewel; *Martika's Kitchen*, Martika.

'You don't have to concern yourself with that,' Butterfield says. 'You just tell your hobo friends to stay the fuck off the streets when they're catchin' a wink.'

Charlie nods.

'You kids found a job yet? Or are you still just sucking on the government's teet, like the dirty little piggies you are?'

I rest a hand on Charlie's arm. 'Don't,' I whisper.

But he does. 'You'll be happy to know, Officer Butterfield, that I am, in fact, currently in the warm embrace of full-time employment.'

'Is that right, Charlie Mould? Doing what?'

'I'm an on-call fuckboy for a lonely cashed-up Brisbane mum,' he says. 'She's got me working every day of the week, 'cep' Tuesdays.'

'Don't,' I whisper.

But he does.

'What's she got against Tuesdays?' Butterfield asks, laughing.

Charlie stops on the spot, turns to Butterfield. 'Well, your Mum goes to bingo on Tuesdays.'

Butterfield takes half a second to register the line. Then a red fury colours his puffing cheeks. 'You cheeky fuck!' he spits. And the police car brakes hard. Butterfield and his fellow officer spill from their patrol car and Charlie and me sprint up Adelaide Street.

'You fucking idiot, Charlie,' I pant. 'I'm still carryin'.'

'Oh, shit, why you still carryin'?' Charlie asks. 'You split left up here and I'll drag 'em with me.'

I glance over my shoulder to see the two cops chasing us along Adelaide Street.

'Run,' Charlie says. 'Don't stop.'

We rush towards the traffic lights on George Street, where a group of city office workers are waiting to cross through afternoon knock-off traffic. Charlie breaks right at the ANZ bank and I break left across the buzzing street, almost getting clipped by a semi-trailer carrying plastic plumbing pipes turning into Adelaide. I run towards the Criterion pub. One quick look over my right shoulder now to observe the two officers following Charlie. And I see Butterfield instructing his younger, leaner colleague to go after me while he continues to chase Charlie.

I put my head down and sprint along the left-side footpath of George Street, dodging between all these strangers shuffling towards me in suits and ties and dresses and jeans and sneakers and loafers and heels. Dash across a driveway entry to Burnett Lane and weave through a group of Kelvin Grove High School students sucking on Slushies. Come upon a gang of builders fitting out a dining space for a new Subway takeaway store.

'Stop right there!' I hear the young officer shout behind me. And this instruction sparks the interest of a large, bearded man in a bright yellow work vest and steel-cap work boots who is eating a lamb and tabouli kebab as he rests his arse on a small electrical box.

I clock the bearded bloke's interest in me as I run and give him the kind of look that might encourage a man who knows nothing of my past to have sympathy for a young woman who has somehow found herself in the uncomfortable position of being aggressively chased along a busy street by a young and ambitious and evidently fit Queensland cop. And the bearded man and I enjoy a moment of connection, something in his eyes suggesting he's been here, done this, and I even flash him a smile – before he stands from his box and shoulder-barges me so hard that I fly a metre through the air and the left side of my head smashes into the glass front of a foreign-currency exchange.

I drop hard onto the pavement, the left side of my pelvis taking most of the impact. My hand reaches instinctively to my bruised skull. I see my fingertips covered in blood. Look up from the ground to the bearded man still holding his kebab and say, more like a question than a statement, *'Arsehole?'*

And then a thick black boot falls from the sky and lands hard on my chest. The young cop standing over me, sucking mouthfuls of air as he points a police taser at my throat. 'Where you runnin', little piggy?'

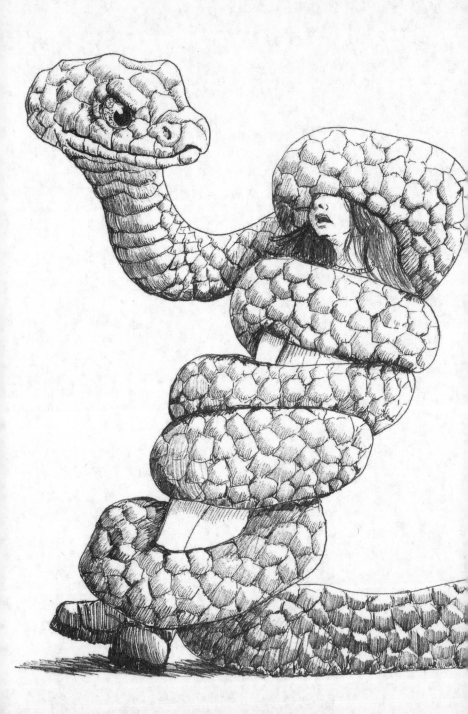

The Long Arm of the Law

The Long Arm of the Law

December 2023

Pen and ink on paper

The figurative long arm of a Queensland police officer wraps, suffocating and inescapable, around the waist, the chest and, finally, the eyes of our beleaguered artist. It appears as though the snake is squeezing something out of the artist, forcing something out of her chest and into her throat. But what exactly? The past? The future? Or maybe just the truth?

Who am I? In a world of eight billion people, I'm the eighteen-year-old lowdown dirty drug-slinger sitting inside a small office on the second floor of the Roma Street Police Station. I'm the girl who's about to get everything she deserves for exploiting human sorrow. For exploiting all those people in the suburbs who can't stand living with who they have become, who purchase Flora Box's powders only to stop themselves from jumping into fast-moving rivers.

They patted me down in the hold room downstairs. They took my backpack. They dragged me into an elevator and that elevator went up one level and then they dragged me down a hall and opened the door of this office and sat me down and suggested I not move a muscle if I knew what was good for me. But I never know what's good for me, so I move my neck muscles and look around the room. Blank white walls. Two entry doors. The one I walked through, behind me. The other one in front of me, beyond a white desk and the black swivel chair that's tucked into it. A desktop computer. A corkboard fixed to the wall to my left. No pictures of criminals on that corkboard. No red strings connecting pictorial clues of unsolved murder cases. Just the drawings of children. Crayon sketches of cities and farmyards and one orange-crayon drawing that shows a man wearing a police officer's cap and shooting a gun from his stick-man right arm. Barely legible words on it: *My ... dad ... is ...*

brayv. On the bottom left corner of the corkboard, a photograph printed out on A4 paper from a cheap colour office printer. Two girls wearing khaki Australia Zoo caps and holding koalas that appear to be on the nod from eucalyptus fixes.

A man carrying a thick folder of papers under his arm enters through the door in front of me. He sits at the white desk. Switches on his computer. Smiles at me. Salt and pepper hair. Black eyebrows. Big fuck-off outdoorsman wristwatch. I know this man.

'You were parked outside George Stringer's house,' I say.

He nods.

'Who are you?' I ask.

'Who am I?' he replies. 'I'm the guy who's been watching you walk in and out of Flora Box's seafood shop twice a day for the past three months. I know you love your prawns, but you can't possibly love them that much.'

He opens his folder of papers and places an A4-size colour photograph in front of me. It's a picture of Flora Box and me walking out of the Ebb 'n' Flo seafood shed. She has her left arm resting gently on my shoulders.

'I'm the guy who's here to ask for your help,' the man says.

'To do what?'

'To put Flora Box behind bars.'

'Why would I help you do that?'

'Because she's everything that is wrong and ugly about this city,' he says. 'Because she's a monster. Because we believe she's been directly responsible for the murder of at least seven individuals in the past five years alone.'

He studies my reaction to this line. I offer nothing.

He offers more. 'Because if you help me put your boss behind bars then my boss is willing to throw you the rope.'

'What rope?'

'The life rope,' he says. 'The one that's gonna pull you from the sea of shit you're currently swimming in. The rope that's gonna save you from all those tired and easily angered men and women in black robes just down the road in the Queensland Magistrates Court, who tend to say all those frank and awkward things to foolish and misguided young women like you.'

'What frank and awkward things?'

'Things like "Unlawful trafficking of a schedule-one drug". Things like "Multiple offences punishable by twenty-five years' imprisonment". Things like, "Eighty per cent non-parole period". Things like, "Goodbye, future. Hello, Wacol Women's."'

Damn. Those things do sound frank and awkward. The man leans forward in his chair.

'You ever think about the future?' he asks.

'That's all I ever think about.'

'Good,' he says. 'You ever see a future for yourself?'

'Yes.'

'What's that future look like to you?'

'I'm gonna be a famous artist,' I say. 'I'm gonna travel the world exhibiting my groundbreaking paintings. I'm gonna fall madly in love with a handsome man who looks like Timothée Chalamet and we're gonna raise five kids in an artist's loft in Manhattan.'

The man does his best not to laugh. 'Have you told Flora these plans?'

'No. Why would I need to tell Flora my plans?'

He shrugs. 'Well, working for Flora Box is usually a job for life, that's all,' he says. 'Especially when said life is somewhat short-lived.'

I fold my arms across my chest. Do my best to play tough. Blue is my favourite colour.

He leans forward, shifts a couple of pens on his desk. 'My name is Detective Sergeant Geoff Topping,' he says. 'I have been—'

'Geoff,' I ponder, 'what does that mean?'

'What does what mean?'

'Your given name,' I say. 'Geoff. What's the meaning behind that name?'

'I don't think it has a meaning.'

'All names have meanings,' I say. 'Caleb means "rage". Callum means "dove". Bridget means "fire". Neil means "fury". Didn't you ever wonder what Geoff means?'

'Not really,' he says. 'I just assumed it meant my dad was quite fond of his brother Geoff.'

I nod enthusiastically, glad the Geoff mystery is almost solved. 'Always comes back to family,' I say.

Officer Topping nods in agreement. 'The question of who I am isn't half as important at this very moment as the question of who the fuck are you and why the fuck did you not tell Constable Peters your name?'

'I don't know my name,' I say.

'So I've been told,' Topping says. 'How could you possibly not know your name?'

'Because Erica Finlay never told me what it was.'

'Who is Erica Finlay?'

'Who *was* Erica Finlay,' I say. 'Erica Finlay died almost a year ago.'

'Who was Erica Finlay?'

'She was the woman who raised me.'

'I'm sorry for your loss,' Geoff says.

'Thank you. You must come across it a bit.'

'What?'

'Loss.'

He thinks on this. 'Yeah,' he says. 'I come across it a bit. How did Erica Finlay die?'

'Well, that's kind of a good story,' I say. 'A good bad story. A really bad good story.'

I turn my eyes to the corkboard to my left. Point at the image of the girls with the koalas. 'They your daughters?'

He nods.

'What are their names?'

'That's Felicia on the left,' he says, 'Celine on the right.'

'Felicia means "lucky",' I say. 'Celine means "moon".' I turn and smile at Geoff Topping. 'Lucky moon.'

Officer Topping switches his desktop computer on.

'They're beautiful,' I say.

'Thank you.'

'That's the meaning of your life right there.'

The computer whirrs into life with air and noise.

'I guess it is.'

'That's all you have to do,' I say. 'Drive up the coast and show those girls a koala. Job well done that day, Officer Topping. People don't realise how easy it is to find the meaning of life. My mu— Erica Finlay told me once that if you want to see the meaning of life then all you have to do is stare directly into the eyes of a child for thirty seconds or more. You ever done that, Detective Geoff?'

'Can't say I have.'

'You should try it some time. Erica said it all comes rushin' at you. Boom. Big bloody waves of it. Pure, uncut meaning of life.'

Officer Topping staring at me now. 'Why didn't Erica Finlay tell you your name before she died?' he asks.

I pause for a moment. Collect my thoughts.

The artist was graceful. The artist was direct.

'Do you remember all those news stories about Baby Christina?' I ask. 'The toddler in the pram in the river, saved by a good Samaritan who was drowned for her efforts?'

I've torn out and kept every newspaper clipping I've ever found on the story. Newspapers I've dug out of public waste bins and snaffled from al-fresco café tables on Albert Street. Endless stories in the *Courier-Mail* across the past ten months charting fruitless attempts to drag Erica Finlay's body from the river and

Baby Christina da Silva's miraculous journey from certain raging river death to giddy suburban Brisbane toddlerhood. Ten months of headlined milestones: 'Baby Christina hops into Easter'; 'Brave Christina learns to swim'; 'Brave Christina's Christmas wish'. Brave? Gimme a fuckin' break. Kid had no choice between living and dying. Erica Finlay, on the other hand …

A couple of stories I keep pinned up on the wall of the van are about Christina's mum, Bless da Silva, and her eternal search to find and thank the mystery daughter of the earthbound angel who died saving brave Christina. I remember seeing her on the rec room television at The Well. She was on Channel Nine News, holding Erica's black Billabong jumper, talking about how a stranger sacrificed everything for her daughter. 'I will never stop searching,' she said. Her eternal search lasted six months. God, Bless.

'I know the story,' Topping says. 'The mother didn't realise she'd released the wheel brake. Pram rolled straight into the river.'

'Yeah, I read that, too,' I say. 'Tragic case of baby brain. Poor Bless had been up all night with a cryin' bub who wasn't eating well. Bless said she was just another new mum, all fogged up in the head. Accidents happen, right?'

Topping shrugs, tilts his head like he's puzzled by my words.

'You cops really swallowed all that?'

'What's that supposed to mean?'

'I know why poor Bless said all that. She knew the truth would be too heavy for Christina to carry through life. Why force someone you love to carry something so heavy?'

'And what's the truth?' Topping asks.

'That pram didn't simply roll down into the river,' I reply.

'What are you talking about?'

'I was there. I saw how fast it was moving. Prams don't roll that fast by themselves. But I'm guessing you don't wanna know why that pram was moving so fast?'

'Why wouldn't I want to know?'

'None of the other cops wanted to know. Where was the truth gonna get anyone? There were only two people under the bridge that day who coulda made that pram go that fast.'

'The father?'

'Or the mother,' I say. 'But what does it matter anyway, right? They've been through enough pain already. What does it matter if one of those people is the reason Erica Finlay is dead?'

'You're telling me this Erica Finlay, the woman who raised you, is the woman who died saving Christina da Silva?'

I nod once.

'That's … extraordinary,' he says.

Nod twice. 'I know,' I say. 'Erica Finlay was often extraordinary.'

'And that means *you* were the mystery girl who pulled Christina up onto the riverbank?'

Nod once.

'That's remarkable.'

Nod twice. 'I know,' I say. 'I am often remarkable.'

Nervously scratch the bottom knuckle of my left thumb.

'I guess you cops will go and tell the world now?'

Topping tilts his head.

'Would you like us to tell the world?'

'No.'

'Why not?'

'Because I want to be known for things I will do in my future, not for things Erica Finlay did in my past.'

Topping smiles and I know that's exactly how he smiles at Felicia and Celine when they surprise him with their spelling. He presses his palms together, takes a deep breath and blows it out over his fingertips, which he has brought to his lips in thought. He pulls a yellow legal pad and a fountain pen from a thin drawer beneath his desk. Scribbles her name at the top of the pad. The name means 'ever powerful'.

'Tell me everything you remember about Erica Finlay,' he says.

And the artist told him everything, a hundred different recollected details of a single woman, spilling forth from the broken levee of her soul. Every lie Erica Finlay ever told her. Every truth the artist found in the endless articles online dedicated to the Monster of March Street, the man who never really was her father. Detective Topping searched online and ran his deep-seeing eyes over the same articles the artist had devoured ten months earlier, word for sorry word. He then asked the artist why she had abandoned her search. Why she'd stopped searching for the answers about her identity. Why she hadn't gone to the police. And the artist said it was because she was still under the age of eighteen back then and feared being taken into care by the state, though those were only half-truths. She told him that she liked her van, her neighbours and her scrapland of Oz. And that was a whole truth.

And then Detective Topping said a series of things that saw the artist having to hold her tears back. He said things that seemed sympathetic to Erica Finlay. He said he knew exactly what Erica meant by the Tyrannosaurus Waltz. He said his own mother had danced the Tyrannosaurus Waltz for twenty years. He said the dancing took its toll. Changed his mother. Changed her heart and changed her brain. Changed who she was. Who she wanted to be. He said that every week of his life now in his day job he saw firsthand the ripple effects of domestic abuse, how the dance could make people do things they never thought they were capable of. Sometimes beautiful things, brave things. But terrible things, too. Sometimes even unforgivable things. And, to be sure, he added, the situation the artist found herself in might be the strangest and saddest ripple he'd seen yet. He asked how much she wondered about her unusual upbringing and how it had come about.

'Every day,' she said. And she told him she'd narrowed it down to just three possibilities. One, Erica had found her somewhere. Two, *somebody somewhere had given her to Erica. Or three … And the artist didn't want to say that third possibility out loud, and she'd never said it aloud, because it already hurt too much just thinking it.*

Detective Topping opens a desk drawer. Slides a smartphone across his desk. The phone has been well used. Glass screen cracked in three places. Black protection case smeared with dirt and finger marks. A mobile phone number on a tattered strip of paper taped to the case.

'What's that?'

'That's a phone,' Topping says. 'Your phone if you want it. That's my number on the back. I want you to go and tell Flora your plans for your future and I want you to look into her eyes when she tells you the truth of the situation you've got yourself into. Then, maybe in a couple of days, I want you to call me on that phone and tell me you're ready to change your fate.'

'Flora Box has helped me through the worst year of my life,' I say. 'She's the closest thing I have to a mum.'

Topping's frustrated now. 'Flora Box is a duplicitous criminal with a talent for exploiting the misfortunes of others for her own financial gain. You are nothing more to her than cheap labour.'

I let the sting of that sentence ease in my gut. 'What makes you think I'm not gonna go straight to Flora's place and tell her every last detail of this meeting, right down to the smiles on the faces of your daughters?'

'Because I saw the look in your eyes when you told me about your future,' he says. 'Because' – he leans closer over his desk – 'if you can help me, then I can help you find the answers to the questions you have always asked yourself. And maybe even help you keep your secret.'

I stare at the phone resting on the desk between us.

'Do you want to know who you are?' Topping asks. 'Are you ready to know who you are?'

*

The artist had spoken to Detective Sergeant Geoff Topping for so long in that office that a full moon had arrived in the night sky by the time she left the police station with her empty black backpack restored to her shoulders. She stared up at the moon from the footpath by the police station steps. Lucky moon, she told herself, because every moon you see is lucky because you are still alive to see it.

The artist thought again about why she had stopped searching for her answers. It was love, of course. She loved Erica Finlay too much. She had loved her like any child loves their mother. She'd loved every night she fell asleep beside her and she'd loved every dawn she woke up beside her with a circle of light glowing on her hungry belly. Every truth, every answer she found in the dark blood story of Erica and Marcus and Elizabeth Finlay tore another strip off the only true love she'd ever known and that felt like her very flesh was being ripped away from her bones. And she knew that the more she lost her love for Erica Finlay, the more she would lose herself. Because answers disintegrate, she told herself. Answers wound. Answers maim. Truth chops your right arm off at the elbow, severs it clean through the bone, leaves it gushing dark red blood across your favourite red dress.

*

'Mirror, mirror, in the lucky moonlight, do you think I'm crazy, or do you think I might be right?'

A silent scrapyard at midnight. I tilt my magic mirror to find the light of the full moon. Just enough to see my reflection. All my neighbours are asleep. It looks like Charlie slipped away from Butterfield the cop, because he's sleeping soundly in his panel van.

I whisper into the mirror, 'Mirror, mirror, in the silvery moon, have you left me too early, Lola? Have you left me too soon?'

'I haven't gone anywhere,' Lola says.

'Lola!'

'Been a while,' she says. Her head is down. She's sitting cross-legged on a single bed with dirty sheets. In a dark room with peeling walls. There's a small television beside her playing a movie. *Far and Away*, starring Tom Cruise and Nicole Kidman. The room looks like one of the flophouse rooms where the elderly stay in The Peach, the state government unit block on Moon Street.

Lola's red dress is stained with blood and torn and frayed at the sides. She takes a long drag on a smoke and her fingers shake. Lines across her face. She seems older than the last time I saw her. Ten years older. Twenty years older.

'It's good to see you, Lola,' I say.

Lola Intheshadow. Lola Intheblack. Lola Inthelow.

She looks up and smiles at me. Teeth missing in her smile. And a blood-stained white cloth bandage holding a medical patch across her right eye.

'Good to see you, too,' she says. And she winks with her left eye.

'What happened to your eye?' I ask.

'Lost it,' she replies.

'How did you lose it?'

'It's the sorrow rot.'

'The sorrow rot? What's the sorrow rot?'

'Ain't you ever heard of the sorrow rot?' Lola asks. 'It's a rare kind of sadness that eats you alive from the inside out. It starts in the heart and then it spreads to your head and then down to your belly and your legs and your toes and back up again to your eyes, where it colours everything you will ever see.'

'Show me your eye.'

'No.'

'Show me, Lola.'

'No. You can't take it. You're not strong enough right now.'

'I can take it, Lola. I've always been able to take it.'

Lola stubs her cigarette out. Exhales a plume of smoke that spreads across her room. She lifts her bloody eye patch up and where her eyeball should be I can see a black hole that appears to have no end to it. It's more a tunnel than a socket. Light catches fine dust particles in it, as if there was air inside that tunnel.

Lola pulls the patch back down. 'Happy now?'

Lola Inthehorror. Lola Inthegore. Lola Inthedread.

'Where's your guy?'

'What guy?'

'Your guy. The sweet guy who looks after you. The guy in the vintage brown suit.'

'Oh, that guy. He went away. He didn't want to be with someone so sad.'

'What's making you so sad?'

'You,' she says. 'It's always you. Don't you get it? Your sorrow is my sorrow. That's how it works for you and me.'

'Are you dying, Lola?'

'I'm not dying,' she says. 'I'm dissolving.'

Lola Intheash. Lola Inthedust. Lola Intheend.

I pull Detective Topping's smartphone from my pocket and tap it against the mirror and for some reason I start to cry.

'You're not gonna leave me, are you, Lola?' I ask. 'Please stay. Please stay with me, Lola.' I wipe a tear from my eye and nod repeatedly as my fist bangs the side of the mirror. 'I'm gonna save you, Lola,' I say. 'I'm gonna make you strong again. I'm gonna get all the answers. I'm gonna find out who I am. And I'm gonna go to art school. And I'm gonna be a famous artist. And I'm gonna fall in love. And I'm gonna make myself happy again and then I'm gonna make you happy again.'

Lola smiles. 'You're gonna find out who you are?'

'Yes, I'm gonna find out who I am!'

'But you already know who you are.'

'No, I don't.'

'You have always known who you are.'

'No, I haven't.'

'Why do you need the world to tell you who you are going to be, when you know exactly who you want to be?'

I drop my head to look away from Lola, but she keeps talking.

'Are you going to let the world tell you who you are, or are you gonna tell the world who you are?'

I don't reply.

'Who are you?' Lola asks.

I say nothing.

'Who are you?' she repeats.

'I get it, Lola,' I say. 'That's enough.'

But she doesn't stop. She puts her face up close to the mirror and I see the anger and the rage and the rot inside her. Purple blotches on her cheeks.

'Why didn't she swim harder?' Lola asks.

'Don't.'

'She couldn't face it, could she? She couldn't bear to tell you the truth.'

Weeping sores across her forehead. Blood in the gaps between her teeth when she spits her words at me. Frightening. Ghostly. Monstrous.

'Who are you?' she asks, louder this time.

'Stop it, Lola.'

'Who are you?' she asks again, screaming this time.

'Stop it. That's enough.'

'WHO ARE YOU? WHO ARE YOU? WHO ARE YOU?'

And I scream back at Lola, 'I said, "Stop it."' And my right fist punches the mirror glass, and two cracks split like forked lightning across her face.

A light goes on in Roslyn's car and I turn to my side to see it. Then I turn back to my magic mirror.

Lola is gone.

The Worst Eating Fish in South East Queensland

The Worst Eating Fish in South East Queensland

December 2023

Pen and ink on paper

It is believed that the artist worked for a time for the Ebb 'n' Flo seafood wholesalers, owned and operated by the notorious 'Lady' Flora Box, a widowed mother with suspected ties to several Australian underworld crime networks. The artist once said that the best eating fish in South East Queensland was white in flesh, flaky on the fork, tasted like the ocean and should be cooked simply with butter, salt and pepper. The artist once said that the worst eating fish in South East Queensland was caught and gutted overseas, its belly lined with concealed quantities of black tar heroin, and imported in iceboxes to the rear entrance of the Ebb 'n' Flo shed at 6 Moon Street, West End.

Wearing a pair of Erica Finlay's shorts this morning, army-green cotton-blend, with Topping's beat-up phone from yesterday bouncing in my pocket. My black T-shirt featuring the four members of The Bangles walking across the Abbey Road pedestrian crossing like The Beatles did, except The Bangles are walking like ancient Egyptians.

Charlie Mould strolling next to me. I stop him at the entry to the Ebb 'n' Flo seafood shop. 'Don't say nothin' 'bout them cops yesterday.'

'I'm not sayin' shit about no cops around Flora Box,' he replies.

Three customers in the seafood sales area this morning. Glenn Ash wrapping four Nile Perch fillets for a woman in a pink tee who rests her right hand on a folding shopping trolley. I walk over to a tall and thin longtime staffer named Nathan Rose, who's shucking fresh Sydney rock oysters on a bench beside two boxes of lemons and limes. Nathan has arctic-blue eyes and blond eyebrows and a long, thick blond goatee that he has tied at the bottom with a rubber band. His head is bald and tanned and there is a solid black tattooed strip running across the centre of his skull, like something a tomahawk-wielding ancient North American might have sported to represent his fifty-plus bear kills. Nathan runs occasional muscle for Flo when he's not shucking fresh oysters. I've heard his shucking technique is not dissimilar to his fingernail-extraction technique.

'Flo in?' I ask.

'She's with someone,' Nathan replies.

'Who's she with?'

'I don't know, some sketchy fuck.'

'Can you ask her if we can go back there and see her.'

'Can't you see I'm busy?' Nathan replies. He's always playing hierarchy shit. My shucker's bigger than yours.

I call across the sales floor to Glenn Ash, who's now reaching for a whole red emperor in the iced display cabinet. 'Glenn, I need Nathan to ask Flo if we can go back there and see her, but he says he's busy.'

Glenn doesn't have to say a word. Just turns his head towards the packing room. Nathan sighs at me, stabs his shucking knife menacingly into a wooden cutting board and holds his gloved hands up as he disappears through the white doors.

'Hey, Glenn, can we have an oyster?' I call.

'Just one each, you scabs,' he replies.

I dig my hand into the box of unshucked Sydney rocks and grip Nathan's shucker. Wrap my left hand in a blue and white tea towel sitting on Nathan's bench. Downward pressure on the left side of the oyster. Tip of the shucking knife into the right-side tip. Pop the top up like I'm opening a tin of paint, then work the knife clockwise until the oyster is revealed, bathing in a pool of fresh sea juice. It takes more than three years to grow one of these little wonders and less than three seconds for one of these little wonders to reach my mouth and slide down my grateful gullet.

I shuck a second oyster for Charlie.

'Oh, you really are a princess,' he says, necking the fat mollusc.

Nathan returns. 'Flo says you can go through.'

Beyond the white doors, staff members are shifting Styrofoam boxes into a large freezer in the packing area on the left. To the right are a high roller-door and a loading bay equipped with pallet trucks and a mini forklift, where seafood transports are delivering the fresh seafood that will be devoured under pergolas and deck shades across the suburbs of Brisbane on Christmas Day. A blue door built into the rear wall of the room opens onto another spacious section of the shed. I knock twice on this door.

'Come in,' Flo calls.

Charlie and I go through the door, both carrying money belts in our hands.

A dog barks as soon as we enter, a terrifying but mercifully obedient German Shepherd, her meat-shredding canine teeth dripping with saliva. She clocks my face and snarls.

'Audrey, sit,' calls the dog's owner from the left side of the room. That's Flo's best friend and business advisor, Ephraim Wall, sitting at his work desk with his reading glasses on, wearing a rust-coloured V-neck jumper, eyes focused on the screen of an Apple Mac desktop computer, tapping his keyboard. Ephraim Wall is tall and thin, late fifties maybe, with the neat haircut of a 1950s Catholic schoolboy. Hard man to read: big believer in the restorative powers of brutal violence but also the joys of watching his favourite actress in *Breakfast at Tiffany's*. He doesn't even turn from his desktop when he addresses Audrey, but the dog relaxes and lies back down on a red square-shaped dog mattress that looks more like a gymnastics fall mat.

The room is cold. Floors made of polished concrete. My eyes are drawn immediately to something not normally found in this space. It's a man, maybe in his thirties. There is a noose around his neck, but I know immediately this man is not dead and blue like George Stringer was because I can see his bare feet slipping and sliding on a large block of dry ice about the size of the cube-shaped IKEA ottomans that Ursula Lang keeps in her living room.

The man is thin and gaunt and wearing navy business slacks with a white business shirt and a burgundy tie. The thick rope around his neck is attached some two metres above him to a load-bearing I-beam running the length of the shed. The man keeps shifting his weight from foot to foot because, I'm guessing, the block of ice is giving him frostbite.

In the centre of the room, my boss, Flora Box, sits on a black folding chair directly in front of the man. She's peering at him through her big, thick, colourless glasses with the kind of curious but unhurried interest with which an art lover might sit and study the headless *Winged Victory* statue in the Louvre. Flo wears a lavender fleece with the collar of a yellow polo shirt sticking out of the neck, and her usual white capri pants and white sneakers. With her powerful hips and broad backside, she surely warrants a bigger chair to sit on when she's watching men squirm in rope nooses.

Charlie always says Flo reminds him of the tuckshop ladies who sold him Chicken Twisties and Strawberry Breakas when he was a kid at Ironside State School. But there's one telling detail in this scene that confirms for me that Flora Box might be a tad more dangerous than the average primary school tuckshop lady: a pair of stainless-steel garden shears resting unremarkably on her right thigh. Not one fucking garden plant in sight, I note, but plenty of fingers and toes.

'The pigeons are home, Ephraim,' Flo says, looking at us over her shoulder and smiling wide. 'Our tireless Christmas couriers.'

We walk straight to Ephraim and hand him our money belts.

'Thank you,' he says.

'How'd you go?' Flo asks.

'Good,' I reply. I turn to Ephraim. 'But George Stringer won't be making any more orders.'

Ephraim looks up at me from his computer, pushing his glasses down to rest on the tip of his nose. I point at the man in the noose. 'He hung himself,' I say.

'Oh, that's a shame.' Flo says that line the way she might say it while standing in front of a supermarket milk cabinet that's all out of Lite White.

Ephraim processes the news without emotion. Then he stands, paces towards Audrey and clicks his tongue, a sign for the dog to quickly vacate the mat she rests on. Ephraim kneels and opens a zip on the side of the mat, revealing two thick white sheets of foam, from between which he retrieves a thin grey laptop computer.

The man on the ice releases a brief pained wail as he loses his footing and temporarily chokes himself on the tightened noose.

'Sshhhhh, petal,' Flo says gently, flexing the shears in her right hand.

The man makes no further sound. A pool of water is slowly forming around the base of the ice.

'Ephraim, bring these two some chairs, will ya?' Flo commands.

Ephraim places the laptop on his work desk then takes two chairs from a stack resting by a beer fridge in the corner of the room. He sets them up for us, one on either side of Flo.

He sits back down at his desk and opens the laptop and I know he's bringing up a page containing coded information on George Stringer, a longtime client whose account is now regrettably closed.

Charlie and I turn our attention to the man in the noose, who's still trying to stand on one freezing-cold foot atop the ice. It's like we're a small audience for a strange vaudeville theatre show.

I shake my head at the sight.

'Don't you go giving me the third degree,' Flo says.

'What?' I say. 'I never said nothin'.'

'You didn't have to,' Flo says. 'I can hear the beat of your bleeding heart.' She gently taps my left kneecap, about a hand's length from where Topping's phone sits in my pocket. 'Don't go giving this bloke a teaspoon of your sugary concern. Little worm deserves worse than this.' Then she leans in close to my ear and whispers behind a cupped hand, 'Don't worry, just spookin' him a bit.'

'Who is he?' I ask.

'He's Bryce,' Flo replies. 'But you two can call him "Fuckhead".'

'G'day, Fuckhead,' Charlie says, not missing a beat.

'What did he do?' I ask.

'Same thing they all do,' Flo says.

'What's that?' I ask.

'He underestimated me.'

'I'm ssss … ss … sssorry, Flo,' the man on the ice stammers.

'Not as ssss … ss … sssorry as you will be, petal,' Flo says. She smiles when she says this and she sounds sweet, like she's running a cake stall for the CWA and she just had to tell someone she's all out of lamingtons.

'Not only did Fuckhead underestimate me,' Flo continues, 'he briefly stole my Christmas spirit. And there's few things I value more this time of year than my Christmas spirit.'

'What's Santa bringing you for Christmas this year, Flo?' Charlie asks.

Flo beams at the question, answers immediately. 'Hair dryer,' she says. 'Remington Hydraluxe Pro. Best dryer in Australia for curly hair. Two-thousand-watt digital motor. Blows at an air speed of a hundred and sixty kilometres an hour. And what do you want for Christmas, young Charles?'

'I want a bottle of 1947 Cheval Blanc, a king-size waterbed and Margot Robbie's phone number, but I'd settle for a NutriBullet.'

'That's one of the things I love most about Christmas,' Flo says. 'The anticipation. Never knowing what you might find under the tree. What about you, Fuckhead?'

'What?' the man on the ice asks, his knuckles making space between the noose and his neck.

'What do you love most about Christmas?'

The man slips on the ice again, recovers. 'I don't know,' he says. 'Carols?'

'Carols, of course,' Flo says. 'What's your favourite Christmas carol, Fuckhead?'

The man raises his head out of the noose. Squeezes three words out of his mouth: '"Little Drummer Boy".'

'Oh, yes,' Flo says. 'That beautiful drummer boy.' She turns to me. 'It's about this boy in the manger with little newborn baby Jesus and everybody's giving gifts to bub, but the poor boy doesn't have a brass razoo. All this kid can do is hit a drum.'

I give Flo a puzzled look. She always does this. Recounts the most universal and ubiquitous stories as if she was the first person to ever encounter them.

She turns to Charlie, continuing her story. 'But then this little boy decides to give little Jesus the best gift of all.' She nods at Charlie, eyes wide. 'Music,' she says. She pats Charlie's thigh, like she's telling him the thrilling plot of a new film she saw only yesterday. 'And this brave little boy steps up and plays his drum like there's no tomorrow.' Then she looks up at the man on the ice. 'Tell 'em what happens next, Fuckhead.'

The man takes a moment to gauge Flo's sanity. 'Baby Jesus smiles at the little drummer boy,' he says.

Flo slaps my thigh. 'Yep,' she says, beaming. 'The kid who had nothing ended up getting the best gift you could ever receive at Christmas: a smile from Jesus.'

She turns to Charlie. 'Now there's a lesson for ya, young Charles. Even when you got nothing, you can still get everything.'

'Thanks, Flo,' Charlie says, deadpan. 'I can't wait for the rest of the world to hear of this remarkable little boy's journey.'

Flo turns back to me. 'What about you, kid?' she asks. 'What do you like most about Christmas?'

'Christmas bonuses,' I say.

She smiles, takes a longer look at me with her glasses pulled down to the tip of her nose. 'You don't say?' she replies, drily. 'Very subtle, kid.'

She winks at Ephraim, who nods in reply then resumes counting the cash from our money belts.

'Those university boys give you any grief?' Flo asks.

Ephraim hears this question and waits on my answer with as much interest as Flo. Red's face in my head. Big dumb fucking cocaine meathead boy monster idiot.

'Nah,' I say. 'All good.'

'You get to Ebbw Vale all right, Charlie?' she asks.

'No worries at all, Flo,' Charlie says. 'And it's pronounced *Ebboo* Vale. Not *Ebwer* Vale. It's Welsh.'

'Mmmmm,' Flo says. 'You wouldn't also happen to know the origins of the term "knuckle sandwich", would you?'

'I believe that one's Irish, Flo,' Charlie says.

Ephraim walks over and hands us sealed envelopes filled with cash, our splits from the delivery earnings. The man on the ice twists his body, swaps his standing foot.

I pocket my cash, turn to Flo. 'Can I ask you a what–if question?'

'A what–if question?'

'Yeah, a what–if question. You know, what if Hitler was dropped on his noggin during birth? What if young Don Bradman preferred to play chess? What if Australia was discovered by James Brown instead of James Cook?'

'You can ask me anything, love.'

'What if I told you I wanted to quit?'

'Quit what?'

'Quit this. Quit delivering drugs for you.'

Flo digests the question for a moment and flexes the shears twice in her right hand.

Charlie leans forward and shakes his head at me across Flo's body. 'What the fuck you talkin' 'bout?' he asks.

'Stay out of it, Chuckles,' I snap back.

Flo turns towards me in her chair and rests an elbow on the seat back. Full attention from Lady Flo herself. 'Well, honey, then I'd have to ask you why you wanted to give up such a promising job opportunity,' she says. 'An opportunity, let it be said, that has kept you afloat in recent months, allowed you to lead somewhat of a stable existence, despite yours and your dear departed mother's unfortunate circumstances.'

'Well, first of all, Erica Finlay wasn't my mother,' I say. 'And, secondly, this is not the life I saw for myself. I am not the person I wanted to be. This life of mine has been one big terrible mistake. It's all wrong. The story's all wrong. I'm all wrong.'

'What's wrong with who you are?' Flo asks. 'You got a decent situation here, don't ya? Sure, that van's a bit of a fixer-upper, but you're makin' your way, aren't ya?'

'I feel like I'm still running,' I say.

'What are you runnin' from now, pet?' Flo asks.

'I'm running from the life I'm supposed to have,' I reply. 'I'm in the wrong life. I wasn't supposed to be doing this for you. I wasn't supposed to be runnin' gear for Lady Flora Box.'

'And what are you supposed to be doing, pet?'

'I think I'm supposed to be doing a three-year visual arts degree at the Queensland College of Art. I think I'm supposed to be learning how to turn my sketches into great paintings. I think I'm supposed to become a world-famous artist. I think there is a beautiful and brilliant version of myself inside me and the longer I stay here with you the more that version of myself grows harder to see. And I think this world of yours, Flora, will kill that person inside me if I continue to let it. And that's why I must stop working for you.'

Flo looks at me with a face full of deep thought and what I read as understanding and compassion. But then she howls with laughter.

'Ya hear that, Ephraim?' Flo says. 'There's a world-famous artist stuck inside our little Moon Street urchin. I wonder who I got stuck inside of me, just dyin' to get out and see the world?'

Ephraim turns to Flo, slides his spectacles to the tip of his nose. 'You've got the Prime Minister of Australia stuck down there, Flo.'

'Is that right?' Flo replies. 'And you, Ephraim, have the Governor of Queensland stuck inside you, and that prissy bastard would appreciate it if you stopped eating all that fuckin' beer-battered flathead!'

Flo falls back in her chair, laughing. But then her face turns serious. 'I'm so sorry, darlin'.' She pats my thigh and her hand lands right on the pocket holding Detective Topping's iPhone. 'I guess that poor headcase of yours, Erica Finlay, never told you everything about what it means to work for Flora Box. Once you start working in this particular industry, you can't just stop. Hate to break it you, sweetie, but you've landed yourself a job for life.'

She moves so close to me that I can see the hairs in her nose when her nostrils flare, as well as a darkness I've not seen before across her eyes and in the trembling of her lips. 'And I honestly don't give a fuck who you got trapped inside your flimsy bag o' bones,' she whispers. Then, turning on a coin, she offers a warm and tender smile. 'We all clear on that now, darlin'?' she adds, her eyelashes flapping behind her glasses.

I feel a shiver down my spine. Fuck this terrible mistake. Fuck this living hell of a life I wasn't supposed to live. I'm momentarily stunned by this change in Flo. Guess I really did just assume I could walk. How fucking stupid am I? And I think of Detective Sergeant Topping and the phone resting in my pocket.

'You could find twenty more kids just like me down at The Well who'd love to take my place,' I say.

'I know I could,' Flo says. 'And none of them could get along with their customers the way you get along with yours. You should hear the things they tell me. "That girl was born to make people smile", they say. "That girl was born to make us happy."'

I shake my head. Feel sick in the stomach. And it ain't no Weis bars. A tear rolls down my cheek.

Flora sees it and reaches a hand out to hold one of mine. 'Oh, pet,' she says. 'I know it's a bitter pill I've asked you to swallow. But I really don't think your life's been a mistake, cherub. I think all the things you call mistakes from your past are actually the things that make you the fine young woman you are. The kind of woman I'd love to call my daughter. The kind of woman I'd be happy to call family.'

She pats my shoulder. 'Time to cheer up now,' she says. 'Because I've got some good news for you.' Her eyebrows spike and her eyes sparkle.

'What good news?'

'You're getting a promotion.'

I turn my eyes to Charlie. He sits up in his seat, concerned. Promotions aren't always welcome when you work for Flora Box.

'What sort of promotion?'

'You're gonna go to work with Brandon,' Flo says.

'Brandon?' I exclaim, a worm turning in my stomach at the sound of the name. 'What doing?'

'Collections.'

'Brandon's doing collections?' Charlie asks.

Flo snaps a sharp look at Charlie, possibly insulted by his dubious tone. 'Yes,' she says firmly. 'He started three months ago and it's the first job he's enjoyed in five years working for the business. Bloody good at it, too.'

Strong-arming debts from feeble and strung-out junkies. Brandon was born for it.

'Why me?' I ask.

'Because I want you to do it,' Flo says.

'Why do you want me to do it?'

'Because Brandon wants you to do it.'

'No,' I say, flatly. 'I don't want to do it.'

'Why not?'

'Because it's fucking dangerous, Flo.'

'Hey, don't swear around our guests,' Flo says, turning towards the man on the ice. 'My apologies, Fuckhead.'

'I don't have the muscle for it,' I say. 'I don't have the mongrel for it.'

'That's exactly why you're perfect for it,' Flo says. 'You're strictly there to talk and smile and keep everybody calm and do what they all say you were born to do: make people happy. Nothing dangerous about it at all.'

I look up at poor Fuckhead struggling to stand still on the ice.

'Can I tell you the truth without you putting my head in a noose?' I ask.

'You can tell me anything, pet.'

'Brandon scares me.'

Flo flexes the shears three times. 'How so?' she wonders.

'He looks at me funny.'

Flo laughs. 'Aw, petal,' she says, waving my thoughts away with a casual palm. 'He likes you. He cares for you. Anyone he cares about, he looks at 'em funny. He's looked at me funny all his life.'

Flo's hand on my thigh again. 'I think it would be nice for you to spend some quality time with Brandon. You might be lucky enough to find the things about Brandon that he keeps hidden from the rest of the world.'

The collection of redback spiders above his cupboard? The box of fingerbones under his bed? The bag of skulls in the back of his car?

'Should I even bother saying no?' I ask.

'Well, as Erica Finlay should have told you, we tend to prefer the word "yes" in this industry.'

I stare ahead in silence.

Flo claps her hands. 'Bonus time!' she announces and winks at Ephraim Wall. He pads to my chair, carrying a small square gift, wrapped neatly in Frosty the Snowman wrapping paper.

'"Pah rumpa pum pum",' Flo sings. I tear off a corner of the wrapping paper, slip a small red cardboard gift box into my right hand. Lift the lid off the box.

Inside is a key. A copper-coloured house key. It sits upon a small square slip of paper with four numbers written on it: *4853*. A pin. A code. A curiosity.

Lady Flo excitedly clasps her hands to her chest. 'Merry Christmas!'

Detective
Sergeant Topping
in a Boat
in a Storm
with a
Life Rope

Detective Sergeant Topping in a Boat in a Storm with a Life Rope

December 2023

Pen and ink on paper

Note the bear's head the artist has placed upon Detective Sergeant Geoff Topping's body. Critics have long maintained the bear was a representation of Officer Topping's deep protective instincts. Or possibly a comment on his reluctance to go outside during winter. The artist was mere weeks away from meeting Danny Collins on the Victoria Bridge.

Eating Tip Top bread with Don Hungarian salami and mayonnaise on the doorstep of my orange Toyota HiAce van, 10.30 a.m. Elizabeth Finlay's toy elephant rests on my mattress. I pull Detective Topping's phone from my pocket. Call the number on the back. Six rings, then: '*You've reached the phone of Detective Sergeant Geoff Topping. Please leave a message.*'

'Hey, Detective Geoff,' I say. 'It's me. The girl with no name. Just callin' to say you were right about *Flor*— ... about my boss. I was thinking about how you're a detective, right? You could probably uncover the truth about anything, right? You could answer any question correctly if you did enough digging? Well, here's my question for you, Detective Geoff. *Do you know who you are?* I assume you have all the information you need to know who you are. I assume you know who your mum and dad were and where they came from and what they believed in and what they were brought up to know as the truth. I assume you have images of yourself as a boy and a sense of how you came to be Detective Sergeant Geoff Topping, loving father of Felicia and Celine. But, honestly, do you know who you are? I'll tell you who I think you are right now, and you can tell me how close I am. I think you're a good father and I think you're a good husband and your wife is pretty, but too often you put crime-fighting before love because your sense of justice is stronger than your sense of devotion. You are a cop. You are a father. You are kind. You are tough. You are fair. You are a good listener. And … you are … ummm … *lonesome*. Yeah, lonesome. That's just a thought that's come to me this minute, and maybe I'm as wrong as an old watch, but I get the feeling that's who you really are. But what do I know? Not who I am, that's for damn sure.'

I end the call. Drop the phone on the mattress by my side. Grip the leg of Elizabeth's elephant. Elizabeth Finlay's identification bracelet still wrapped around its leg. Her birth date beneath her name: *23.04.2005*. Erica said that was my birthday. But that was another lie. I don't even know how old I am.

I pick up Topping's phone again. Tap the number. The same recorded message. 'I'm so fuckin' embarrassed, Geoff,' I say. 'Can you believe I could be so naïve? As if she was just gonna let me go like that. What a prize goof, huh! Well, screw her, right? You know what? I hope you boys bring her down, Geoff. I don't care anymore. I used to think she was family. But you shoulda seen the way she looked at me when she told me she didn't give a fuck about who I got inside me. Flora Box is just another monster. She's just another tyrant lizard.'

I end the call. Slide the van door closed. Pace across the scrapyard. Tap Topping's number again. Wait till the recording ends. 'If you get this message, Detective Geoff, then I'll meet you at the Gallery of Modern Art at three p.m. On the lawn by the river. I'll be sitting beneath that big sculpture of the upside-down elephant. I've got a couple places I gotta be today, but here's some things that can get that big blue meanie brain of yours firin'. Ephraim Wall. He's the guy you really wanna give the ol' interrogation room shakedown to. He's the guy who's really squeezing the juice in all of Flo's operations. You should do yourself a favour and get hold of the laptop he keeps between two sheets of foam in his big ugly dog's mattress. He's got all that fancy cloaking tech on it. Unhackable shit. Untraceable. That's the laptop he uses to reach out to his suppliers. That's the one he uses to get all that Malaysian yellowtail in. You know about the Malaysian yellowtail, don't you? You hook me up with them blood tests that you promised last night, then I'll tell you what days that Malaysian yellowtail comes in. I'll tell you how they used to sew them blocks into the frozen fish bellies but now they sew them into the ice packs surrounding the fish. I'll tell you what truck that yellowtail comes in on. I'll even tell you how the truck driver's name means "mud". How's that for nominative determinism, Detective Geoff? I don't care anymore. If I get the knock for helping you, then maybe that's me getting what I deserve. That's called pointed-pistol determinism. I've aided and abetted a monster. I've lost count of all the bags of powder I've dropped across town for Flora Box. I'm not fuckin' dumb, Detective Geoff. I've always known what those bags do to people. Those bags kill the best versions of ourselves. Those bags killed—'

A beep on Topping's answering system tells me my message time is up, so I call back and finish my sentence. 'Those bags killed my friend George Stringer. Those bags killed all the beautiful and brilliant people who were hiding beneath the skin of all those sad and desperate people across the suburbs who loved seeing me turn up on their doorstep. Sometimes those people could see the best versions of themselves and that's precisely why they needed those bags. Seeing parts of the best versions of themselves was the very thing that was making them sad. You see, Detective Geoff, maybe sometimes you're better off not knowing who you coulda been. Does that make any sense to you at all?'

I end the call. Walk to The Well along Moon Street. Call Topping's number again and leave a message about my neighbourhood. About my neighbours and why they mean something to me. Call again and tell him about Charlie and his drinking issues and Ros and her gambling and Clinkers issues. Call again and tell him about June and Sully and the things June told me about why Sully is as quiet as a mouse. 'It's because his thoughts are all jumbled up inside his noggin and he can't find the right thought to land on, so most of the time he settles on saying nothing,' I explain to Geoff. 'Sully's one of the most thoughtful and generous people I know. He's always taking my dirty clothes to the laundry in The Well for washing. Always carefully hanging my shirts and shorts and smalls for me on the white cord that runs from the Sullivans' caravan roof to the yard's back fence. Always laughing at the butterflies that bob around the clothes. Big, deep foghorn guffaws and howls.'

I tell Detective Geoff how June is a nurse in her late fifties who works nights in the Royal Brisbane Hospital and she sometimes asks Charlie and me to keep an eye out for Sully when we hear him having a turn. And I tell Detective Geoff how Sully will start screaming in the middle of the night and I think it has something to do with his father because June told me once that Sully's father was a tyrant lizard of the worst kind. Cruel and terrifying and often torturous to Sully. June and Sully stopped dancing the Tyrannosaurus Waltz and that meant a mostly miserable but always peaceful life inside a campervan in West End and nursing night shifts whenever June can get them.

'You see, Detective Geoff,' I say, 'June's been on the social housing wait list for the past two years. My friend Evelyn Bragg down at The Well told June that she's unfortunately one of the forty thousand single women over the age of fifty-five living homeless or at risk of homelessness in Queensland. Evelyn says June and Sully have also unfortunately found themselves in a state that grew by 750,000 people over the past decade, and most of those people settled smack-bang in the city they're waiting to find a home in. This is a state with a homelessness rate three times higher than the national average. Then, Evelyn says, you gotta throw in all the bastard floods that keep taking people's homes away, not to mention the 200,000-plus people expected to land in Brisbane from Melbourne and Sydney in the next five years alone. No more room at the inn for anyone out here, Geoff, doesn't matter how fat your wallet is. The apartment blocks are full. The caravan parks are full. The shelters are full. Not enough tents. Not enough places to put them anyway. Not enough scrapyards owned by West End panel beaters with more heart than sense. Sorry, Mary and Joseph, ya gonna have to walk to Adelaide.

'But, like always, Evelyn says, we take hope in the bright smiling faces of our youth. You see, Detective Geoff, the shit's really sprayin' across the fan for them suits up in George Street because now they realise there's working families with young children living on these streets, not just the usual drunks and drug addicts they never lost a wink over. People are gonna start seein' little Joey doin' his Mathletics in Pancake Manor every night and they'll realise he's not ordering no fuckin' pancakes. June says all being well Sully will be housed in a home with electricity and running water just in time for her to take up a welcome residence in the warm soil of the Mount Gravatt Cemetery. "Nice cosy hole in the dirt," she says. "Can't fuckin' wait." Now that's what you call affordable housing, 'ey Detective Geoff.'

And then I breathe and hang up and call back to finish my point. 'See, why I'm telling you all this, Geoff, is because this is the world that Flora Box thrives in. She's been pushing gear on people like June for years. Desperate people who just want a brief break from who they are. They just wanna get away from themselves, ya know, Geoff? Have you ever wanted to just get away from yourself for a bit? Run from who you are? Well, most of the people on Moon Street wanna run away from themselves forever. That's why all of Flora Box's customers are customers for life. And that's why you gotta take her the fuck down, my friend.'

I end the call.

The outside of The Well drop-in centre looks like the headquarters of a German Stasi interrogation unit: two levels of artless grey cement with windows and blinds. But the inside is rainbow-coloured, the walls having been decorated with murals by the centre's art class members. I helped paint the giant loggerhead turtle swimming across the long south wall of the rec room on level one.

Too many single mums in this shelter today. Too many single mums who stopped dancing the Tyrannosaurus Waltz. They and most of the centre regulars are gathered in a talking-circle in the rec room beneath the television that hangs from the ceiling. Evelyn Bragg has summoned them for an urgent update on the scary fucker who's been clubbing homies to death across the city. Charlie and Roslyn stand at the edge of the circle. Roslyn's holding the same A4 sheet of paper the others are holding.

I tap her shoulder. 'What's that?' I ask.

She turns to me and whispers, 'Police got a witness sketch on our friendly neighbourhood psycho killer. He had a chop at Popeye Lawson last night. Ol' Pop was sleepin' beneath the Mahatma Gandhi statue on Wickham Terrace. Woke to a cricket bat cracking his jaw in four places. Woulda been six 'n' out for Pop if two drunk fellers hadn't staggered by the scene.'

She hands me the sheet. A black-and-white sketch of a man with a chin shaped like a spade, doorstop for a nose. He wears a hooded sports jumper, with the hood pulled down over his eyes and forehead.

'Rest assured I am in constant contact with police beats in the valley, the city and Roma Street,' Evelyn says.

Evelyn Bragg is short and thin with red hair and green spectacles. She wears colourful cardigans and green Dunlop KT-26 running shoes with colourful socks. She's fierce and terrifying when she needs to be, but kind, always. Never tolerates drunkenness and thuggery. She's got a big Samoan police officer on speed dial in case of any trouble. His name's Tristan and he's from the West End Police Beat and I once saw him snap the blade off a steak knife held by a wild floater on a coke implosion.

'I could not be more serious when I urge you to consider where you sleep tonight,' Evelyn says. 'It's not the first time we've seen a damaged and dangerous individual bring violence upon our homeless and at-risk communities. Unfortunately for all of us, because of this extremely hostile individual, where you sleep rough this summer has now become a matter of life and death. Please do not sleep alone or in exposed places. No dark spots in parks. No isolated urban spaces. Please catch a nod in the day beds here when you can. If you're gonna sleep out at night, then do it in couples or groups and in the malls near police beats, or find yourself a spot with multiple CCTV surveillance angles. Do not sleep or pass out by the mangroves on the river.'

I elbow Charlie in the ribs. 'That means you, knobhead,' I whisper.

'Don't sleep or pass out in construction sites,' Evelyn continues. 'And, for fuck's sake, do not sleep or pass out in the botanic gardens.' She looks down to a folder in her hands, flips over to a new page of notes. 'Now, moving right along from cold-blooded murder to the Games of the Thirty-fifth Olympiad!' Some in the crowd laugh and clap, others boo and hiss theatrically. 'This place is the only home most of you have got,' she says. 'If you want to see this place survive, you need to sign the petition. These fuckers won't take The Well without a fight.'

Last month, Evelyn was informed of the Queensland Government's plans to transform Moon Street – and almost half of the buildings, unit complexes and orange Toyota HiAce vans that stand upon it – into an athlete's village for members of Italy's Olympic Games team during the 2032 Olympic Games, which, quite remarkably, will be hosted by our very own brown snake river city of Brisbane.

'Please remind your government that you believe basic human shelter is more important than sport,' Evelyn shouts. 'I love a good Olympics as much as the next ginger-haired dyke, but let's not forget our social responsibilities. Let's not forget hunger. Let's not forget desperation—'

'Let's not forget Dulcie's pavlova,' shouts an old centre regular, Jock Sinclair, who many believe survived a recent bout of cancer only because of his unwavering faith in canteen cook Dulcie Prior's rhubarb and pistachio pavlova.

'Good point, Jock,' Evelyn says. 'If you sign the petition for nothing else, please sign it for Dulcie's pavlova.'

Evelyn's the unofficial mayor of Moon Street. Heart bigger than a pineapple, prickly personality like pineapple skin. Evelyn loved Erica Finlay like a sister and Erica loved Evelyn even more than Evelyn loved her. Evelyn means 'wished-for child'. As the manager of The Well for the past ten years, Evelyn's been strangled and spat on and stabbed in the stomach with a fork, but mostly she's been hugged by the thousands of drop-ins who come to access the centre's services six days a week. Hot-shower services. Food services. Counselling services. Drug and alcohol rehabilitation services. Employment services. Some two hundred free lunch and dinner meals a day, served by volunteers, all wrangled by Evelyn, in the centre kitchen. There are about six thousand homeless people in the city of Brisbane on any given day and about three thousand of those people have hugged Evelyn at some stage in their life. Some regulars are addicts who can't kick. Some are lonely and some are lost. Many have paying jobs, but just not the kind that cover the payments on increasingly hard-to-find rental properties across Queensland. Beautiful one day, perfectly fucked by inflation and a housing shortage the next.

'And, finally, ladies and gentlemen,' Evelyn says. She throws a thumb towards my neighbours from Oz, Serge and Samantha, who are holding hands beside Evelyn. They've been a thing ever since Sam lobbed in on the morning Erica Finlay died. 'Serge has got an announcement.'

Serge scratches his cheek, steps reluctantly into the circle. He's wearing his olive-green cardigan, even though it's thirty-five degrees outside. He never takes that cardigan off. 'Yeah, um, thanks Ev,' he says. 'I just wanted to tell you all … um—' And he breaks down in tears, rubbing his eyes with his fingers. 'I'm gonna be a dad!' he exclaims through his crying. He throws an arm around Sam. 'And better than that, Sammy's gonna be a mum!'

Every guest in The Well rejoices. Deafening whistles. Tex Bishop, a sun-damaged drunk with an unlit rolled cigarette in his hand and a wheezy laugh like Keith Richards, crash-tackles Serge, who cushions Tex's impact with a hug. Then Sam's crying into Serge's shoulder and I want to talk into my phone and tell Detective Sergeant Geoff Topping about all the beautiful things that can happen in Moon Street. I want to tell him the story of Serge Martin.

He used to drive tanks for the Australian army, but then he went to an end-of-season celebration for the Mayne Australian Rules football club in Enoggera, north-west Brisbane, where he threw himself at a young and promising local footballer who had just head-butted his own fiancée. Two of the young footballer's friends then threw themselves at Serge and one of them was carrying a Tooheys New beer bottle, which he immediately smashed over Serge's head, slicing and permanently blinding his left eye. The army lost Serge and Serge lost his mind in booze and pills. The parish priest at the St Peter the Apostle Church on Canoe Street, Father Joseph Kikelomo, found Serge unconscious one Saturday morning, five years ago, on the free-throw line of the public basketball half-court in Davies Park. Father Joe got Serge to hospital and visited his recovery bed five times in the following week. During the fifth visit, Serge wept and spoke of his fear of going back out onto the streets because he was certain he was going to intentionally overdose on a fix of something brown and heavy.

All that Father Joe had to offer in response was some words from the Bible. "'The night is far spent, the day is at hand.'"

But then he stood up and slipped off the olive-green cardigan he was wearing. "'Therefore let us cast off the works of darkness, and let us put on the armour of light.'" And he handed his cardigan to Serge. 'I want you to put this cardigan on when you walk out of this hospital.'

'Why?' Serge asked.

'Because this cardigan will be your armour,' Father Joe said. 'Your armour of light. When you wear this armour, you will feel strong. Maybe even strong enough to forget about that final fix.'

Whatever gets you through midnight on Moon Street. Star and moon scenes through rust holes in car roofs. Reliable ink pens and headlamps and blank white paper. Or ugly olive-green cardigans, like the one Serge then wore every day for six months straight, even halfway into a baking Brisbane summer, until he was certain his strange new armour of light had got him clean and sober for the first time in half a decade.

A few weeks after Serge settled into his useless Holden Jackaroo wreck, confirming himself as a permanent resident of Oz, he painted a welcome sign on a piece of broken fence paling that he staked into the soft soil beside his car: 'There's no place like home.'

'It's still early days,' Serge tells his centre friends. 'But Sammy seems all good under the hood.'

I wrap my arms around Sam. Give Serge a long kiss on his cheek.

'Thanks, sis,' he says.

'Now for some sad but good news,' Evelyn says. 'Our transitions chief, Sita, and those angels at Bric Housing were able to leverage Sam's baby news to get these two a one-bedroom unit in Spring-in-my-fuckin'-step Hill. Yes, ladies and gentlemen, I'm talking about an actual home with a roof and running water! Praise the fuckin' Lord!'

The centre guests hoot and holler and Evelyn raises a clenched fist. 'Now, forgive me, Serge and Sam, but I worded a few of your friends up earlier and they'd now like to shower you with riches!'

A series of Well regulars line up in single file and begin presenting Serge and Sam with gifts, the way royal palace guests might present gifts to a king and his queen.

'I want you to have my heater,' says one.

'Here's my electric frying pan,' says another.

'Here's the password to my Netflix account.'

'Take my toaster.'

'It's an iPad. Sorry about the cracks.'

'It's Peter Alexander. Never been used. They call it a "romper".'

*

After the gathering disperses, I walk over to Evelyn's office so I can catch her before she goes back to her desk.

'Hey, you,' Evelyn says. 'Everything fine, Patsy Cline?'

'Fine as can be, Brenda Lee,' I say.

'Whatchu been doin'?'

'Work.'

'Lady Flo–type work?'

Nod twice. Evelyn shakes her head in disappointment. 'You know she's not your friend, right? You know that woman's not capable of loving anyone but her son.'

'Yeah, so I heard,' I say. 'Hey, can I ask you somethin'?'

'Yes, but I'll tell you straight up, I'm all outta Woolies vouchers.'

'I'm not chasing Woolies vouchers.'

'What are you chasing?'

'I'm chasing a spot in art school,' I say. 'I've been looking up courses at the Queensland College of Art.'

Evelyn's eyes light up. She folds her arms across her chest, nodding enthusiastically. 'Well, it's about fuckin' time, Patsy Cline. You're too gifted to be runnin' errands for Flora Box.'

'Well, I'm a slow learner, Tina Turner. You still do that thing here where you hook streeties up to uni courses and all that?'

Evelyn smiles. 'Yeah, we still do that thing. We got a tertiary education officer in here every Wednesday between two and four.'

'Can you please book me in for an appointment?'

'Yeah, I can do that. On one condition.'

Way ahead of her. 'I stop working for Flora?'

Evelyn winks. 'See what I'm talkin' 'bout?' she says. 'Gifted.'

I turn and walk away.

'What about the money?'

I turn back to Evelyn. 'What money?'

'The thirty k or so it's gonna cost you to go to art school for three years.'

'That's how much it costs?'

'Yeah, that's how much it costs. Why? How much you got saved?'

I think on this for a moment. 'Twenty-six dollars and eighty-five cents.'

Evelyn smiles. 'Well, that's a start,' she says. 'And there's something else you're gonna need.'

'Yeah, what's that?'

'A name,' she says.

'I'm workin' on it.'

'About bloody time,' Evelyn says. And she turns and walks back into her office whistling 'Crazy' by Patsy Cline.

*

After lunch, I jump the wire fence between The Well and the back of the St Peter the Apostle Church on Canoe Street. Pad across the grass to Esther's hole in the church's rear wall. Kneel down and stare into the black void beyond the small, triangular opening, which most adults would be too big to squeeze through.

'You there, Esther?' I ask.

A voice from the black. An older woman's voice. 'Yeah, I'm here.'

'Heard you needed to see me?'

'Yeah, I gotta tell you something.'

'What do you need to tell me, Esther?'

'Are you alone?'

'Yeah, I'm alone. What is it?'

'You need to stay away from the river,' she says.

'Why?'

'Because I had a dream about you.'

'Yeah, Charlie told me. You had another flood dream.'

'It wasn't just another flood dream,' she says.

The sound of Esther biting into an apple.

'That a Pink Lady?' I ask.

'Royal Gala,' she says.

'You got any more?'

A soft and ripe, mottled red and orange apple rolls gently onto the grass from within Esther's black hole.

I take two large bites. 'Charlie said you saw Erica Finlay in the dream,' I say, wiping apple juice from the sides of my mouth. 'She was having a cuppa underwater in the Myer Centre Starbucks.'

'She was,' Esther says. 'Just sittin' there underwater. All relaxed. I remember she told me that was her favourite spot. She told me you two would sit and watch people walking past outside through the glass and they'd have no idea you were watching them. She said it was like you were invisible. She'd have a tea and you'd have a strawberry milkshake.'

'Frappé,' I say.

'Whazzat?' Esther calls from inside the hole.

'I'd have a strawberry and cream frappé and Erica would have Earl Grey tea,' I say.

'That's it,' Esther says. 'She was just sippin' her tea in the dream, all these people and all these objects from the city floating in the water around her. Garbage cans. Dogs on leashes. Cars. Scooters. Skateboards. I saw a box of Krispy Kreme doughnuts floating by.'

'So, what's all that supposed to mean?' I ask.

'I think it's safe to say we're gonna get another flood by the end of this summer,' Esther replies. 'Gonna be a big one, too. I think Moon Street is gonna get washed away this time. All the people. You, me, Charlie. Your van. The Tinman's shed. The Well. It's all gonna go under this time. We're on borrowed time, kid.'

Esther sometimes talks like a crazy prepper but, in her defence, it's been feeling a bit doomy and gloomy by the river at this time every year for the past three or four. People used to talk about a hundred-year-flood in this city, but it feels, lately, that the hundred-year-flood rolls around every two or three years.

'Think you might be wrong this time, Esther,' I say.

'I hope I am,' she says. 'But I think you should get your shit ready, just in case.'

'It hasn't even rained in two months,' I say.

'You sound like the Pompeii baker who said, "That volcano hasn't erupted in twenty thousand years."'

'Well, doesn't worry me none, either way,' I say. 'Got no shit to save from the great flood.'

'What about all those beautiful drawings?' she asks.

I shrug, take another bite of the apple. 'Yeah, well, they're not worth much right now, I'm afraid.'

'Not right now,' she says. 'But just wait until you make a name for yourself.'

Esther Inthehole is convinced that I will one day make a name for myself. Esther Inthehole is convinced she can see the future. But Esther Inthehole says we can all see the future, if only just a bit of it. Every day we glimpse things that haven't happened yet, she says. We see children playing on slippery dips and swings and see the men and women they'll become. We read the sky in the morning and plan our afternoon picnics accordingly. We watch new couples kiss and see our personal visions of how it's all going to end. A tennis ball bounces three times onto a road filled with moving cars and a small boy is hellbent on running after it, and we feel certain of what's going to happen next because we've already seen it. We check our bank accounts and we see how our years will soon unravel. We stare into mirrors and see how our faces will crack and sag and crumble, decades from now. A loving mum watches her daughter walk nervously down a church aisle in a wedding dress and she turns her head to the man that perfect girl is about to marry and sees, through windows in the back of her mind and in the pit of her stomach, a future where this fresh white love turns to mud, and she wants to stand up in front of her oldest friends and scream, *'Please don't do what I did!'*, and she wants to take her daughter's hand and run away with her, but when her daughter smiles at her all she can do is smile right back and shed a tear of joy and sorrow.

We have hunches and instincts and twitches and inklings. We prophesise daily. This job will make me happy. This party will make me bored. This love will make me hurt. We walk out of movie theatres because we already know what's going to happen. We read sweeping love stories told by young romantics just like me and we convince ourselves that we can see where these stories are going because we're certain we've seen it all before.

But one day you will dance with a prince, Erica Finlay said. When she said that to me it sounded like she could see the future. It made me feel like Cinderella. Like there was a prince waiting for me on the palace staircase of my destiny. But destiny's just something us arty types like to think about because it makes sense of all the terrifyingly random shit that unravels in a day. *But one day you will dance with a prince*, Erica Finlay said. Like she knew it to be true. Esther says Erica could see the future. But I know Erica only had her eyes on the past.

'You were on the other side of that table with Erica,' Esther continues, returning to her dream.

'I was?' I reply, taking another bite of the apple.

'Yep. But then you finished your drink and you smiled at Erica and made to leave the table, but she gripped your wrist and smiled back at you.' Esther is silent for a moment. 'I miss that beautiful smile, you know.'

'Yeah, I know,' I say.

'But then her smile disappeared,' Esther continues. 'And you looked at the fingers holding your hand and the nails on those fingers had turned into claws. And you looked at her face and her face turned into the face of a monster. And you tried to swim away, but the monster was too strong. It was gripping the shoulder strap on your dress and you couldn't hold your breath any longer, started swallowing water.'

'Then what happened?' I ask.

'Nothing,' Esther says. 'That was it. I woke up after that.'

Two more bites of the apple and I throw the core into a lilly-pilly hedge lining the back fence of the church grounds.

'So, what does all that mean, Esther?'

'It could mean many things.'

'Or nothing whatsoever,' I say. 'Or, like most dreams, it could mean you were cold and you needed to pull the blanket back up over your chest.'

'Or,' Esther says, 'it could mean that I've seen you sitting by the river all them nights down by the Victoria Bridge, just staring at that shifty water. I've seen you there with that sketchbook on your lap in the moonlight. Like you're waiting. Waiting for someone to pop their head out of the river and crawl up those muddy banks to you. All slimy and covered in mud and river muck. Like some sea creature from the black abyss. Like some monster.'

A vision in my head of Esther in the shadows. The woman without a face, standing in the mangroves, watching me sketching by the river under moonlight. The mud-brown river twinkling at night like it could be the cleanest river in the world.

'It's nice to know you're watching out for me, Esther,' I say.

'Watching out for you,' Esther says. 'Watching over you.'

'You must be my guardian angel, Esther.'

'Nah, I'm just some ol' witch in a hole who wants you to stay away from that river.' And just as she says that something wet lands on the bare skin where my hair parts on my scalp. Then something wet lands on the toe of my left boot.

I look to the sky. For the first time in two months, it's raining.

*

By 3 p.m., the rain has chased the usual book readers, daylight dreamers and lovers away from the lawns surrounding the Gallery of Modern Art. I'm sitting with my backpack shielding my head, Topping's phone gripped in my right hand, my damp backside flat on the bark floor of an outdoor sculpture space that features a great big bronze elephant that looks like it's just tumbled off a mountain and landed flush on the top of its huge round head. My elbow rests on its bronze tusk.

A voice behind my back on the other side of the elephant sculpture. 'Please pass on my congratulations to Serge and Sam,' Detective Topping says.

I turn my head to find him sitting with his elbow resting on the elephant's other tusk, facing away from me. Casual T-shirt, blue jeans and rubber thongs. Bright orange umbrella over his head.

Two big bronze ears, two big eyes and a trunk between us.

'What the fuck?' I say. 'How do you know about Serge and Sam?'

He points at the phone in my hand. 'It's not just a phone,' he says.

I look down at it. 'You're an arsehole.'

'I'm sorry.'

'What is this?'

'It's a remotely activated listening device,' he says. 'A roving bug.'

'You've been listening the whole time?'

He nods.

'You're such a fuckin' arsehole.'

He shrugs, nods again. 'I got your messages,' he says. 'Information like that is extremely valuable to our investigation.'

'Valuable enough for you to leave me the fuck alone?'

'Not that valuable,' he says. 'But valuable enough for me to keep my promise.'

He tosses a card over the elephant's trunk between us. There's an address on it.

'That's our pathology unit,' he says. 'They know you're coming. You get those blood tests done, I'll get you your answers.'

'How long's it gonna take you?'

'For what?'

'To find out who I am?'

'Hard to say,' he says. 'It all depends on who you are.'

'So what am I supposed to do in the meantime?'

'You go to work with Brandon Box,' Topping says.

'But I hate Brandon Box. He's a monster.'

'Just get 'im talking. Talking so much he'll talk himself out of your life for good. Do you think you can do that?'

'Do I have a choice?'

'Right now I can offer you about as much choice as Flora Box is offering,' he says. 'The difference is none of my options end with you in a box.'

Topping stands and wipes pieces of bark from his backside.

'Flora gave you something for your Christmas bonus?' he asks.

I nod. Picture the copper-coloured house key. I know the pin code by heart: 4853.

'Tell me what she gave you?' he asks.

I improvise an answer. Keep this card close to my chest. 'A Copic Multiliner pen,' I reply. 'The one with the one-millimetre nib. Best sketch pen in the world.'

Topping nods, puts his hands in the pockets of his jeans.

'I liked your question,' Geoff says.

'What question?'

'Do you know who you are?' he replies.

'Well, I thought if anyone's gonna know the answer to that question it's gonna be you.'

'Well, I have been doing some digging,' he says.

That makes me smile. 'Any solid leads?'

'Plenty,' he says. 'Thought I might get a statement from my mum. My wife, maybe. I'll need some more substantial evidence to build a case. But I think I had a breakthrough just last night.'

'What happened last night?'

'I was tucking my youngest daughter into bed and I did what Erica Finlay said. Stared directly into the eyes of a child for thirty seconds or more. I asked Celine if I could do it with her. And she laughed and grabbed my cheeks and got so close to my face that our noses were almost touching. And we went longer than thirty seconds. I reckon we must have gone for three minutes or more.'

'Three minutes or more?' I exclaim. 'Wow, solid stretch. Did you see it?'

'See what?'

'The meaning of life?'

'Yeah, actually, I think I did.'

'What did you see?'

'I can't tell you that.'

'Why not?'

'Because I don't want to spoil it for you.'

He turns and walks away across the gallery lawn. 'It's something you have to see for yourself,' he says over his shoulder.

'But I can't,' I call after him.

'Why not?' he asks, still walking away.

'Because I don't know any children.'

Christina and the Lion

December 2023

Pen and ink on paper

Swimming in a river of troubles, the artist clings to her sketchbook as though it's a lifebuoy keeping her afloat. She finds a beacon, of a kind, in the unlikely form of a young girl standing on a suburban letterbox. Few subjects have ever been rendered by the artist with such care and devotion, and it is clear she shared some form of profound connection with the young girl. Little is known of the girl's identity, but we can at least assume she is the titular Christina.

The front door is red and the small weatherboard house is white. Number 37 Doyle Street, Oxley. The mother holds her daughter's hand as she turns to lock the front door. The child breaks from her grasp, skips down the brown concrete path to the gate and flips open a black letterbox for no other reason than to look inside it. Then she runs out the gate and performs three star jumps on the grassy nature strip, evidently thrilled by her escape from her house. She's wearing a blue tutu and sparkly silver slippers. Carries a fluffy toy, tucked in her left armpit. Simba from *The Lion King*. She sprints twenty metres down the nature strip.

'Christina,' her mum calls. 'Wait for me.'

Bless da Silva closes the front gate to her house. This is where she stood for the press conferences when she held Erica Finlay's hooded jumper up for the television cameras.

It is so very hard to draw pure light on a white piece of paper. The light is formed by the darkness we place around it. This girl, almost three years old now, is purest light, and she has been formed without darkness around her. Purest joy. Fished from a river and granted this perfect moment in the suburbs.

Mother and daughter stroll to the council park at the end of the street. Paradise is a play gym and a basketball half-court in a park in Oxley, Brisbane, eleven stops from Central along the Ipswich train line. I sketch this moment in my mind. Turn all this life to lines in black ink. The purple jacaranda that she spins in circles beneath. The red and black polka-dot bow clip making the fringe of her hair stand up like a cactus plant. The two rainbow lorikeets she chases then watches fly up into the clouds.

They meet a friend of Bless's, mother to a boy about the same age as Christina. He wears a shirt that reads *Give Peas a Chance*.

A tubed slide, spinners and rockers. A fort made of metal and plastic and white rope. Monkey bars. Wonky wooden bridges. Bless and her friend on a park bench seat, sipping coffee from keep cups. Bags of supplies and brightly coloured plastic water bottles by their feet. And me, leaning on my bike, out of view, by a high black metal fence. Like some crooked stalker girl.

But it's not like that. I just wanna see her again. *It's nice to see you again, Christina. You wouldn't remember me. I reached out and grabbed you that day by the river. Allow me to introduce myself. My name is. My name is. My name is.*

Christina and the lion board a spinning wheel that looks like a teacup from an Alice in Wonderland picnic. She begs her friend to spin her, and who could resist that face? He grips the rim of the teacup and his legs push hard like he's pushing off from a track sprinter's starting block. Around she goes. The river girl. Gravity pushes her head back and she looks at the endless white-cloud sky. 'Wowwwwwww!' she hollers as she spins.

The world turns. The world turns for all of us. Especially Christina. And she makes me laugh. The sound slips from my mouth and makes Bless da Silva turn towards me. We lock eyes for a moment. The stillness of familiarity. Then the creep of it. The past on her face.

And now I've stayed here too long. And now I must ride.

But One Day

You Will

Dance

with a

Prince

But One Day You Will Dance with a Prince

December 2023

Pen and ink on paper

Note the staining on the left edge of the paper. Analysts first believed these stains had been caused by white wine, most likely from a glass held by the notorious young lush Charlie Mould. However, after significant chemical analysis, it has since been established that they were caused by drops of chlorinated water. One of the most optimistic works in the artist's oeuvre and clearly the product of a young woman who was beginning to believe in love, fate and the value of horrific mistakes.

A ll I want for Christmas is a friend.

'Count me,' says Charlie, a skinny, sunbaking nineteen-year-old drunk with a skinny wet dick in red Bonds underpants as he rolls into the swimming pool. Splashes land in his glass of red wine at the pool's edge.

Skinny and weedy eighteen-year-old me on the sun lounge in a two-year-old bra and undies, with a sketchbook and a sketch pen, watching Charlie drop like a log amid bubbles to the bottom of the pool.

'One Burpengary,' I begin. 'Two Burpengary. Three Burpengary. Four Burpengary.'

Charlie plays dead at the bottom of the pool. Counting in my head. Twelve Burpengary. Thirteen Burpengary. If he really was going, of course, I'd be going with him. Best friends should always travel together. Sunshine Coast on the Landsborough line. Gold Coast on the Helensvale line. Ipswich on the Rosewood line. Heaven on the Pearly Gates line. *Knock, knock.*

Thirty-one Burpengary. Thirty-two Burpengary.

Guess they call this place a mansion. Not the Beyoncé, Beverly Hills kind, but the Brisbane, Australia, kind. Two storeys in Gothic sandstone. Steep-pitched shingle roofs. A driveway so long that Charlie sang the entire first half of 'Jesus Walks' by Kanye when we walked down it before dawn.

The high northern side of the city. Hamilton Hill. Views of the twisting brown Brisbane River, but not a neighbour to be seen through side-of-house screens of old jacarandas, dense camphor laurels and Moreton Bay chestnuts. The driveway leads to an oval-shaped rose garden circling a water fountain crowned by a winged and naked male angel. Sandstone pillars flank white marble steps to a grand white front doorway that looked to me at 4.30 a.m. to be the kind of door you'd need to employ three strong manservants to open and fetch the morning paper.

The mansion's backyard swimming pool is at the end of a lawn the size of half a soccer field. The grass, mown in clever crisscrossing strips to resemble the pattern on a chessboard, seems positively ecstatic to be alive.

Forty-two Burpengary. Forty-three Burpengary. Charlie's a watercolour painting at the bottom of the pool. I stuff my sketchbook and pen inside my backpack. Dive in the pool. The water is warm from half a day of high summer sun. Two strong breast strokes and then I'm floating dead-armed underwater above Charlie, who has his eyes closed and his skin-and-bone arms folded across his chest. Dracula sleeping in his coffin. Long, thick brown hair possessing, underwater, all the form and shape of fire. A small pearl-shaped bubble escapes from his left nostril and then he opens his eyes slowly. He smiles when he sees me because he always smiles when he sees me. *Stay in this moment, Charlie. Let's never go up to the surface. Let's never go back. Let's never go back to work. Let's stay down here.* At the bottom of a swimming pool on Hamilton Hill, at the top of the city.

I tap my right ear, asking him to nod if he can hear me.

And Charlie nods, down here in this blue underwater planet.

Then I scream, 'Colourful!'

And he screams the same word back at me. Because when you scream 'colourful' underwater it looks and sounds like you're screaming 'I love you.' Colourful. Colourful. Colourful. *I love you. I love you. I love you.*

'Colourful, Charlie,' I scream again. And my love for my friend turns to bubbles, and maybe bubbles are all it deserves. Charlie laughs. And then he moves closer to me. Fifty-five Burpengary. Fifty-six Burpengary. Close enough to kiss me and close enough for me to worry he might kiss me. Fifty-seven Burpengary. Fifty-eight Burpengary. He doesn't scream his words. He only mouths them.

'I love you,' he says. And then he's out of breath at fifty-nine seconds and he swims to the surface of the pool as I sink to the bottom.

Peaceful down here. Quiet down here. The longest I've ever held my breath underwater is two minutes and sixteen seconds, which is about a full minute longer than most people can hold their breath. I feel like I can stay down here for at least two minutes today. Maybe more because it's Christmas Day and my lungs are filled with the spirit of Christmas.

I spend the two minutes or so thinking about inheritance, like I always do. Where did the colour of my eyes come from? Where did these floating fingers come from? Where did my lungs come from? My breath? My heartbeat? My heart?

*

Inside the mansion now with my hair still wet from the morning swim. Arms and legs still smelling of chlorine. Charlie is down in the cellar selecting a red wine to have with lunch. Stillness. Quiet on Christmas Day. I'm padding barefoot through the mansion's hallway. Oil paintings hanging from the walls.

Draw this scene. Put it in black ink on paper in my head. *The Artist and the House of Her Wildest Dreams.* Six large rooms, three on each side of the corridor. The kitchen looks like something used by a high-class restaurant. The dining room has a table almost as long as the room. Good wood. Is this what mahogany looks like? I run my fingers along the tabletop. No dust. Not a single fleck of dust in the whole joint. I make a mental note to ask Charlie if he wants to play a game of air hockey after Christmas lunch.

A framed oil painting of a family on the wall at the far end of the table. Father, mother, daughter, son. The father in his suit looks so proud. He looks so loving, his left arm around his wife, who wears a violet dress, has flowing brown hair and looks so glamorous, like she wouldn't be out of place in *Days of Our Lives*. Their daughter looks bright and athletic and good and successful and everything her mother and father could possibly want her to be. And the son. He looks younger than the daughter. His smile isn't as wide as everybody else's. It's like he's sending a message to the painter of the portrait. *I'm doing this reluctantly*, he's saying. *The minute you are done, I'm on my canary yellow racing bike and I'm out of here. I shall be released.* Hands by his side in a brown suit. I guess you could say that's almost a vintage brown suit. Brown leather shoes on his feet. Caramel-coloured hair. Muscular. Athletic. Kinda handsome. Like, really kinda totally fuckin' handsome. Something about him makes me think of the painted electrical box on Moon Street: *U R MAGNETIC*. Striking. You know, like a stick of lightning in the sky. You know, like a matchstick. Like fire.

'Who are you?' I say out loud to myself as I stare at the handsome young man in the brown suit, son of the king and the queen of this impossible house. And I remember the words of Erica Finlay. 'But one day you will dance with a prince,' I whisper.

*

'Merry Christmas,' Flo said. The gift was a house key and the address of a luxury home in Hamilton Hill. Plus a four-digit pin for the security pad beside the rear-of-house laundry door.

Not the first time Flo's done this. Standard practice for her. Just another way for a desperate Brisbane junkie to square a debt with Flo and Ephraim, the man that junkie might find standing nearby with a battery-operated Ryobi drill in his hand. Can't make things square with Flo? Then all she'll need from you is a spare key to the house of someone you love. Your parents' house. Your uncle's house. Your ex-wife's parents' house. Easiest thing in the world, stealing a spare key from someone you love. They've already told you where to find it. If there's a security system, Flo's going to need the code. If there's a video surveillance system, she'll kindly ask you to disable it. And then you will be square. No questions asked.

'The family are on their annual summer holiday in Noosa,' Flo said. 'Please be invisible.' The best thieves, Flo says, are the invisible ones. The ones who steal little and steal long. Invisible thieves will leave a home spotless. Like it was never touched in the first place. No forced entries. No apparent signs of robbery. Some people are so lucky, so blessed by time and place and birth, that they can barely stay across what treasures have been gained and what treasures may have rolled haphazardly into the cracks in the old wood beneath the dresser. The invisible thief takes a necklace in April and returns for a diamond earring stud in September. Never both earrings together. It won't be till December that the stud's owner will say to her husband by the bedroom dressing table, 'Fuck, babe, I think the cleaner vacuumed up one of my diamond studs.' Thirty minutes later it will dawn on her: 'Fuck, babe, I think the cleaner is stealing from us.'

*

We're here because of the sweet-faced girl in the family portrait. Flo says her name is Samara Collins. Bright shining star, aged twenty-one. Former school vice-captain of Somerville House. Studies law at the University of Queensland. Bright shining star and a raging meth fuck-up who, in the space of a dizzying nine-month-long group crank binge, helped chalk up debts to Lady Flo to the sum of $15,000 plus change. Samara, Flo says, made the foolish mistake in her first year of university of falling in love with a roguish and penniless twenty-two-year-old UQ English lit scholarship student named P.J. Gleeson, who lived in a three-bedroom Kelvin Grove sharehouse comprised solely of raging meth fuck-ups.

Samara and P.J. lay back, panicked and petrified, on bean bags on the living room floor of the Kelvin Grove house when Ephraim Wall stood over them and detailed the various forms of currency in which Lady Flo was willing to accept the money she was owed. 'She will accept it in dollars,' Ephraim explained, 'by cheque, bank transfer or whatever you prefer. She will also accept what is owed in bones. Toes, fingers, ears – whatever you prefer.'

Then he looked into the eyes of Samara Collins. He knew her entire family history, dating back to her 1840s western Queensland pastoralist ancestors. He knew about her great-great-great-grandfather Henry Collins, part-owner of the state's first bank, a branch of the Bank of New South Wales, which opened on Queen Street in November 1850. He knew about the historic family home on Hamilton Hill, built in 1908 by Samara's great-grandfather the Right Honourable Alfred Talbot Collins, a judge in the Supreme Court of Queensland. He knew Samara's father's name was Conrad Collins and that he was joint head of the Collins Lambert law firm on Eagle Street. He knew Samara's mother's name was Gwynne Collins. He knew Samara's younger brother's name was Danny Collins. He even knew Samara's middle name.

'And she will also accept it in the form of a simple house key from you, Samara Eleanor Collins,' Ephraim said.

I like it here. It's warm here. It feels like family here. French doors everywhere leading out to small balconies. Decorative archways leading to grand living rooms with grand pianos and cabinets filled with expensive wines and whiskies and endless bookshelves lined with expensive and rare hardback books. Rugs as big as squash courts. Cedar wood. So much cedar wood that it smells like the time Erica and me went walking through forests near the Mary River.

'More wine?' calls Charlie. He's sitting at one end of the Collins family's long formal dining table. I'm sitting at the other end. It feels like there's the length of a cricket pitch between us.

'I'm good,' I call.

This is Christmas lunch. Our plates are filled with items that won't be missed from the fridge and the walk-in pantry. Pickled goods. Slices of cheese. Turkish delight. A jar of stuffed olives. Duck liver pâté. Organic orange and chilli chocolate.

There's an old hardback copy of *Moby Dick* beside Charlie's dinner plate. He took it from the library. Wants to give it to Flo as a thank-you gift. From the cellar, he took a bottle of Penfolds Bin 169 Cabernet Sauvignon 2009 that he figures might be worth $500. Mr Collins won't notice it's missing, Charlie says, because there's at least a hundred bottles of red down in that cellar, and six of them are Penfolds Bin 169 Cabernet Sauvignon 2009.

Charlie tops up his drink and raises his glass high. 'There once was a man from Nantucket,' he roars, poetically, 'who tasted his wine by the bucket. He was partial to red, though his taste buds were dead. So nine times a day he said, "Fuck it".' Charlie guzzles the whole glass.

'I wish you'd stop drinkin' so hard, Charlie,' I say.

'Can't, won't, don't want to, ya can't make me, no reason to even try,' he says in quickfire bullet points.

'What if dyin' was a reason?'

'Not afraid of dyin',' he says.

'What if I was a reason?'

He bites his top lip. Smiles. Raises his glass to me. 'Now there's a reason,' he says. More serious than I expected.

'You'd be beautiful off the drink, I reckon,' I say. 'Less spiky. Less ill-mannered. Most people find the world more tolerable on the piss. I think you'd be the opposite. I think you're more patient when you're sober.'

'Fuck no,' Charlie says. 'I'd be a pain in the arse off the drink. Miserable. Cranky. Possibly brilliant, though.'

'This is ridiculous, come sit over here,' I say.

'No, I've always wanted to have a meal like this,' Charlie calls across the long table. 'Makes me feel like Bill Gates. Better yet, Bruce Wayne. Alfred,' he hollers, 'more wine.'

He holds up the bottle, studies the label. 'Two thousand and nine,' he says. 'Good year.'

'Where were you in 2009?' I ask.

'I was living with the Robinsons,' he says. 'They were Mormons. Good people. Huge meals every night. But Mrs Robinson made a vegetarian meatloaf that dead set tasted like manure.'

'How do you make a vegetarian meatloaf?'

'Three cups of lentils, two tablespoons of yeast, one cup of best intentions,' Charlie says. 'Where were you in 2009?'

'I don't know,' I say. 'I was four. I just remember lots of sand and heat when I was four. I think we mighta been near the desert in South Australia. I remember seeing all these holes in the ground. Hundreds of them. Thousands of them. Everywhere we went. Holes that Erica told me to stay away from because I could fall inside one of them and die and never be found.'

'What were they?'

'I never found out.'

'They sound like graves,' Charlie says. 'You were in the land of the dead.'

'Nah, it definitely wasn't Ipswich.'

'Fuck you, I was born in Ipswich,' Charlie roars. He picks up a pickled onion from his lunch plate and throws it at me. I duck the onion, laughing.

'Don't throw shit,' I say. 'We gotta be invisible. Leave this place spotless. Just like we found it.'

I sip my wine. Gaze around the room. 'I want to keep coming back here, Charlie,' I say. 'Reckon this could be our special place. A place to look forward to. Every time the family goes away, in we come. We'll be invisible. Every time. That's how we get to come back. Leave it just like we found it.'

Charlie smiles. Pulls a single earring from his pocket and holds it between his forefinger and thumb. A cross of gold with small diamonds set into each quadrant formed by the cross. He holds the earring up to the light shining through the dining room's floor-to-ceiling stained-glass windows.

'Just like we found it,' he says.

*

When night falls we adjourn to the living room and sit under the Collins family's Christmas tree. All I ever wanted for Christmas was a Christmas tree this big with red and gold baubles and porcelain angels and bells hanging from the branches. And a blinding gold Star of Bethlehem crowning the tree.

I sit with my legs crossed on the rug beneath the tree. Charlie's on his back, with his head on a cushion, his glass of wine tucked by his ribs.

'You're thinking about Erica Finlay,' Charlie guesses.

'I'm always thinkin' about her.'

'You miss her, don't ya?'

'Why would I miss the woman who ruined my life?' I reply.

'Easy,' he says. 'Love's pretty strong, Princess. I've always loved the people who ruined my life. I hate all those people. But I love all those people too. Because love's stronger than hate. And it's way stronger than ruin.'

Charlie takes a deep breath. His big right toe taps a gold bauble hanging at the bottom of the tree. 'Christmas is a bag o' dicks,' he says. 'Always gets people thinkin' too much.'

I nod three times. Reach my left arm out and rest it on Charlie's shoulders. Then I stare at his face and then I lean down and place a gentle kiss on his left cheek. 'Thank you, Charlie.'

'For what?'

'For bein' the brother I never got to sit next to beside a tree on Christmas Day. For bein' family to me.'

Charlie nods. He's silent for a moment. Taps the gold bauble again with his big toe. 'Can I ask you a what-if question?'

'You can ask me anything, Charlie,' I say.

'What if I was more than just a brother to you?' he asks.

I look away. Look down.

'What if I did stop drinkin'?' he asks. 'What if I got my shit together? What if I went out and got a proper job. Became a carpenter or some shit. Accountant. Guy who sells you a television at The Good Guys. I'm a good guy. I could do that shit. What if I signed us up for some nice place to live. What if I got us the fuck outta that scrapyard?'

He sits up now and places his drink by his side. Stretches his right hand out and his palm gently finds a home beneath my chin. 'I meant what I said,' he says. 'Always have. Always will.'

I drop my head and reach for his hand on my chin.

'Colourful,' he whispers.

And his face moves close to mine. His lips move close to mine. Our noses touch. I can feel his breath. And I think about cartwheeling. Do I want to walk through this life or do I want to cartwheel through it? How would E.P. Buckle speak of this moment from my time on earth as he strolled through the halls of the Metropolitan Museum of Art? I want to live like the great artists lived. I want to live boldly. Rashly. I want to make the dangerous choice. I want to kiss him, but I don't want to keep on kissing him. Because he means more to me than passion. I love this boy more than danger and desire. I love this boy more than art. And so I turn my face away from his and bring his body in for the embrace I need on Christmas Day. I hold my family tight. My lips to his ear. 'I'm sorry, Charlie,' I whisper.

*

The prince's bedroom on Christmas night. Silent night, holy night. It's late now and Charlie is still downstairs, passed out with his head resting on the living room's grand piano, down there at the bottom of the huge timber staircase that brought me up to Danny Collins's bedroom. A tidy bedroom. Music posters on the walls. Tour posters for Australian indie bands. Ball Park Music. Camp Cope. King Gizzard and the Lizard Wizard. An image of John Lennon arm-wrestling a shirtless Paul McCartney.

I pull out Detective Geoff's phone. 'Are you still listening, Detective Geoff?' I ask. 'Are you out there somewhere? You're probably cosied up with the kids and your wife, sipping eggnog. I never asked you your wife's name. Lemme guess. Theresa? Mabel? Jessica? Lily? Yeah ... Lily. Lily means "pure".'

A poster on Danny Collins's wall for Alfred Hitchcock's *Vertigo*. A stack of legal textbooks on his work desk. Study papers marked with titles that make no sense to me: *LAWS5172: Advanced Jurisprudence, LAWS5165: Jessup International Law Moot*. Sporting trophies on his bookshelf. Gold medals for swimming. *Age Champion Under 17s Brisbane North*. Freestyle winner. Butterfly winner. A miniature DeLorean time machine from the

Back to the Future films, which I push with my right forefinger along Danny's bookshelf until I come to a corkboard fixed to the wall beside Danny's bed. He's pinned items of interest to the board. A badge that reads *War is Poppycock*.

'How did you and Lily meet?' I ask into the phone. 'Did fate shove you in the back, trip you over on the street? Did you lift your head up from the dust and see her holding a hand out to help you up? Or did you work for it? Did you put your back and your heart into it? Did you gamble everything on it? Pride and trust and everything you are? Did you give it all to her? Was she willing to take every part of you?'

A postcard of a sapphire blue butterfly, like the ones I used to see in Far North Queensland. A folded train timetable for the London Underground. A cutout image of Abraham Lincoln. A small card with a long, tiny-font quote from Walt Whitman about love and time and sitting on the grass with the ones we never have enough time to love. Photographs from Danny's teenage life. Danny arm in arm with his mum and dad. Danny and Samara and a birthday cake with candles that Samara is about to blow out. Danny and Samara in a National Sorry Day march across the Victoria Bridge. Danny and some friends in suits. High school graduation, maybe. His school formal, maybe. He makes me smile. The joy in the boy. The life in the young man. It looks to me like there were no mistakes in the life of Danny Collins. No monsters. It looks to me like he's exactly where he's supposed to be. And I wonder if that's where I would have been if Erica Finlay hadn't had to dance with her monster. If she hadn't had to dance the Tyrannosaurus Waltz. If I didn't have to be invisible.

'How did you know it was her?' I say into the phone. 'Her, out of eight billion people in the world. Awfully lucky you saw her in a crowd that big.'

I sit down on Danny's bed. Queen-size. Crisscrossed blue and grey stripes on a thick, soft quilt cover that's too hot to use on

Christmas night in Brisbane. Two pillows. I rub my bare feet on his carpet and yawn because we were up at 3 a.m. to be at the gates of this house when it was still dark. And I wonder what it's like to sleep in a room like this, just for a night, among family who love you as much as Danny Collins's family clearly love him.

I speak one last time into the phone. 'Goodnight, Detective Geoff,' I say. 'Merry Christmas.' Fold my legs up onto the bed and lie down on my side, facing the corkboard and the photographs of Danny Collins's life. Rest my head on Danny's pillow and let my heavy eyelids close and open and close and open. Let that bright boy's smile be the last thing I see upon this almost perfect Christmas night. And I'm almost out for the count when I feel something solid beneath the soft pillow. Something hard and flat. I slip a hand beneath the pillow. It's a thin book. Black cover. I've seen one of these before. It's a Moleskine hardcover sketchbook. Feels like it's covered in leather. Something classic about it. A4 size. On the first page is a sketch. Black ink on paper. A decent drawing pen. Good thick lines of ink. It's an image of a council park bench. On the top left corner of the bench's backrest sits what looks like a honeyeater bird, probably a noisy miner. On the right side of the bench seat lies an empty and open packet of Burger Rings. Just an ordinary everyday piece of litter, but the artist has somehow captured that exquisite ordinariness with such passion and attention that the image becomes extraordinary. The artist seems to know something of proportion and perspective. Symmetry and balance. Cast shadow and core shadow. Shading in areas around the foot of the park bench suggests the artist knows something about the laws of light.

On the next page there's an ink sketch of a man in a kilt holding a set of bagpipes in a city street. I think it's Piper Joe, who sometimes busks for coins in King George Square. On the page after that is a woman holding an umbrella with her right arm outstretched. She's giving someone directions. There's a speech bubble coming from the woman's mouth and inside the bubble are the words 'Take a right at Hungry Jack's.' I flip through the pages. Endless moments in time. Captured life sketches. A boy holding a balloon animal. A speech bubble coming from his mouth: 'Looks more like a rhino.' An ibis with its long black beak reaching into a student's unzipped schoolbag. A sketch of a floater on a makeshift mattress, sleeping beside the Old Windmill on Wickham Terrace, Spring Hill, one of my favourite landmarks in Brisbane. A mum tightening the straps on her son's bicycle helmet: 'Because Mum doesn't feel like visiting the emergency department today, Connor.' A boy in a Superman cape. 'Flying's more fun now I'm seven,' he says. A man in a suit holding a beer at a bar: 'I honestly thought she was happy.'

And then I flip to a sketch that I dwell on for several minutes. It's an image of a girl. A young woman, maybe around the age of eighteen. She's standing near the Australia Post box on the corner of Ann and Edward streets. A bicycle by her side. Her arms raised to the sky. Palms out. Boots. Black Bermuda shorts. And a shirt that reads, in black block lettering, *KYLIE SAYS RELAX*.

'What … the … fuck?' I whisper to myself.

I sit upright on the edge of the bed. Something right and true that the artist has captured in the girl. The sorrow in the girl. The hope in the girl. The words coming from the girl's mouth. Silly words. Dumb words that never should have been captured in time. 'I am invisible,' the speech bubble reads. 'I AM INVISIBLE!'

'He saw me,' I whisper through tears of something stronger than sorrow. And I see myself as a black ink sketch on white paper inside this very moment on this very bed and I rub the words in my speech bubble out and replace them with stronger ones that I'd be happy to have captured in a speech bubble until the end of time: 'He sees me.'

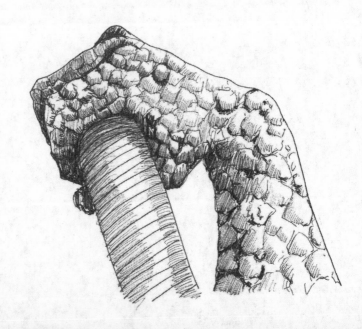

I Don't Need You to Let Me

January 2024

Pen and ink on paper

The artist was eighteen and working in debt collections for the famed Brisbane criminal underworld figure Flora Box. The fear in the work is palpable. The artistic choices on display seem very deliberate, as though the artist invested much time and effort in conveying the obvious menace to be found within her subject. Critics consider this piece to be part of the artist's renowned Beleaguered Girl Balances on the Edge of Good and Evil Period.

The middle of January. New year. New door. *Knock, knock.* *Who's there?* I'm not entirely sure. In a world of eight billion people, it's the artist with no name. *And you must be Brandon Box.*

Is every collection day gonna start like this? We meet at Brandon's place in Highgate Hill at 9 a.m. He opens the orange door of his Torbreck apartment, always shirtless and always tanned. Always ten minutes to go on his morning workout. I asked him last week if it might be better if I just turned up at 9.10.

He bench-presses eight heavy weights hanging on a silver pole then stares at himself in a floor-to-ceiling mirror that stretches across the entire eastern wall of his apartment. 'Not sure you've got enough reflective surface in here, Brandon,' I observed last week. A chin-up pole in the doorway of his bedroom. A punching bag hanging from a ceiling beam. I don't think he ever asks himself anything useful in that long mirror. Who the fuck are you, Brandon Box? What exactly are you hoping those muscles will tell you? You keep looking at those muscles like you want them to tell you something. You keep flexing those biceps as though you're trying to wake them up. What exactly do you need from them?

Across his back is a vivid tattoo of a lion and lioness in some kind of Serengeti sunset scene. The lions stare east and west and between them, safe and sound, is a lion cub. The lioness, Brandon says, is his mum, Flo. The male lion is Brandon's late father, John

Box, who, Brandon says, was executed by shotgun in a brutal and abrupt outlaw motorcycle gang retribution killing. The lion cub, of course, is Brandon, and he says the tattoo is a permanent reminder of family and how he's the chosen one who must now lead their business in his late father's absence. I don't think it's wise for me to tell Brandon that the lion cub on his back does not remind me of family and Brisbane criminal underworld legacies as much as it reminds me of Simba from *The Lion King*.

Same routine in front of the mirror every time. Flex the biceps, then the triceps. Flex those tortoise-shell abdominals. Flex the thighs and calves and then – Brandon's regular full-stop, signature sign-off from the mirror – he somehow bounces his pecs so they look like sock puppets communicating in a cereal box theatre. Then he towels off his sweat as he moves to his kitchen bench. Into a blue and white blender he scoops a concoction of muscle-building powders that he keeps in four separate Woolworths Choc-nilla ice cream containers resting permanently on his kitchen bench. The blender is offensively loud, and he runs it on full for a minute then guzzles his mystery super drink straight from the jar.

I tap Detective Geoff's covert listening phone in the pocket of my jeans. Brandon doesn't suspect a thing. Brandon is a dangerous idiot. Brandon has a new, large tattoo, occupying his left shoulder, of a demon-like creature in a hooded cloak carrying a sawn-off shotgun.

'Who's he?' I ask, pointing at it.

'He's the Grim Reaper,' Brandon replies.

'I thought the Grim Reaper carried a sickle?'

'He used to,' Brandon says. 'These days he prefers to carry a shotgun.'

*

Knock, knock. Who's there? It's just me and Brandon Box and we've come to collect the money you owe Lady Flo.

'But I don't have it yet,' says a mother of three in Deception Bay. Her name is Tracey Loane and her right hand shakes when she brings a Longbeach Mild to her mouth. Too thin. Open sores on her neck and cheeks that she can't stop scratching.

We're sitting at Tracey's kitchen table. Her two eldest kids are at school and I'm glad of that. By her right foot, her baby girl, Asha, sleeps in a bouncinette that has a pattern like the coat of one of the 101 Dalmatians. Brandon stands by the front door.

'Then we gotta find some way for you to get it, Tracey,' I say, softly.

She's made me a lemon cordial. She's put ice in the cup because it's hot outside and I'm sweating from driving across Brisbane in Brandon's silver Nissan Skyline, listening to rap songs about rooting and killing and killing and rooting.

Tracey looks up at Brandon, who is cracking the joints and muscles in his thick neck. 'What's he here for?' she asks. 'I'm good for it. I always have been. Flo didn't need to bring no thug here to shake me down.'

'He's here for me,' I say. 'Just in case anyone gives me a hard time.'

'I'm not gonna give you a hard time,' Tracey says, ashing her cigarette. 'I'll give you a fuckin' cordial. That's about all I'll give ya. Fuck me.'

'Why don't you have the money?'

'My fuckin' boy, Gareth,' she says. 'He got the lead in the school musical. He's playing Danny Zuko in *Grease*. He had to go to a musical camp and I gave him all the money for that. I know I shoulda given that money to Flo, but I guess I just wanted to make him happy, you know, because I haven't seen the kid happy for about five years, and fuck me if I thought it was worth coppin' a floggin' from one of Flo's goons if it meant seein' my kid's teeth for once because he's finally fuckin' smiling.'

'Do you know anyone who could help with the payment?' I ask.

Tracey takes a long drag, stubs her cigarette out.

'Would your mum and dad give you a loan?' I ask.

'Cunts,' Tracey says, shaking her head.

'Who?'

'Mum and Dad,' she says. 'Dead-set cunts.'

'I'm sorry to hear that,' I say. 'You got anyone else who might help out?'

Tracey's baby wakes in the bouncinette and darts her head about, trying to make sense of her surroundings.

'I'll go begging from my grandma again or somethin',' Tracey says. 'I'll square it, don't worry.'

'I'll tell Flo about musical camp,' I say. 'She's pretty good with shit like that. But you really gotta square it, Tracey.' I nod towards Brandon. 'Because it'll be Vin Diesel over there talkin' to ya next time and lemon cordial just won't cut it with him.'

Asha starts crying. Tracey picks her up, holds her to her chest.

'You need to stop using,' I say.

'No shit, Sherlock,' she snaps. She rocks Asha in her arms and takes a deep breath. 'I'm sorry,' she says. 'I've been tryin' to get away from it all, you know. Just can't get off the merry-go-round. Shit just keeps spinnin'.'

I look around the kitchen. Dishes piled up. Empty baby food bottles. A bin full of used nappies tied up in shopping bags.

'You got a pen?' I ask.

Tracey puts Asha on her thigh and points at the drawers next to her kitchen sink. I open the third drawer down and find a blue Kilometrico and scribble a mobile phone number on the back of an overdue Telstra phone bill resting on Tracey's kitchen bench. Then slap the number down on the table in front of Tracey and Asha.

'That's the number of a woman named Evelyn,' I say. 'She works in The Well, a drop-in centre I go to sometimes in West End. Swear to God, Tracey, Evelyn's got more folks off junk than I've had bowls of Corn Flakes. She's the fuckin' junkie whisperer. You should call her. Guarantee she'll know the right person on this side of town who can help you.' I tap my fingers on the phone number. 'Call her,' I say. 'Get the fuck off the merry-go-round.'

Tracey stares at the number for a moment. Baby Asha starts wailing.

'Sshhh,' Tracey says, soft and soothing. 'Sshhh, Asha.'

'It means "hope", you know,' I say.

'What?' Tracey asks.

I nod at Asha. 'The name Asha. It means "hope".'

A smile threatens to invade Tracey's face. 'Fuck me,' she says, shaking her head and staring into Asha's eyes. 'And here I was thinkin' I was all out.'

*

Thump, thump go the wheels of Brandon's Nissan, crossing bumps in the road beneath the grey Lego Technic framework of the Story Bridge. A debt to collect from two men in a unit in Moorooka.

Brandon reverses into a parking space not far from a bus shelter on busy Beaudesert Road. Looks through the driver's-side window to a unit complex consisting of two white-brick, two-storey buildings with brown staircases. Kills the engine, darts his head about, scans the surroundings. 'Now, I'd appreciate it if you didn't try to save these next two fucktards,' he says.

'I was just tryin' to show her some alternatives,' I say.

'Yeah, well, if you're lucky, I won't tell Mum about your welfare work.'

'What's wrong with offering a few alternatives to all that sorrow she had surrounding her back there?'

'Alternatives are bad for business,' Brandon says. 'All that sorrow you're talking about has kept you from going hungry for the past seven years, so don't try an' come over all Mother Teresa on me.'

He leans over my lap, opens the glove compartment. Finds two black pistols. One has a strip of red electrical tape wrapped around the pistol butt. He leans forward and slips this pistol behind his back, hanging the butt end on his belt, lets his loose white Converse shirt drop back over the gun. Hands me the other gun.

I reel back. 'I'm not carrying no gun into no fuckin' Moorooka drug den, Brandon.'

'I don't expect you to,' he says. 'Fuck. It's not even loaded.' He tucks the gun down the front of his pants. 'Come on.'

We pace quietly down the central tiled walkway of the apartment complex. Two blocks. Eight apartments per block. Four on top, four below. Brandon walks to the far end of the complex and takes a sharp right turn down another walkway bordered to his right by a high, old, dark brown timber fence that encloses the backyards of the four ground-floor apartments. Each yard has a small, square concrete barbecue space, a folding clothesline and a sad patch of lawn the size of a ping-pong table.

At the end of the long fence, Brandon kneels down and peers through the cracks between the fence palings of the fourth backyard. He turns to me. 'One or both of these fucktards are gonna try and run back out here,' he whispers. 'And then they're gonna try and scramble over this fence and scurry off to Adelaide or some shit, but that's not gonna happen because you're gonna take this.' He pulls the pistol from the front of his pants. 'All you have to do is stand here and the minute you see some junkie scumbag's head appear over the top of the fence, simply point the gun between the two eyeballs looking at you and encourage the owner of those eyeballs to go back where they came from.'

I shake my head. This has all been a terrible mistake. Have you ever woken up from your sleep inside a life that was not intended for you? Have you ever made the shocking and heartbreaking discovery that you are, in fact, the central figure in the greatest charade ever constructed by time and place and existence?

'What if they have guns themselves?' I ask.

'They don't have guns,' he scoffs. 'These scratchy fucks can't afford toilet paper, let alone illegal weapons.'

He forces the gun into my hand, which remains limp and useless.

'Hold it tight,' he says. His left hand grips my right wrist, hard enough to bruise it. 'Fuckin' hold it,' he spits. My hand grips the gun. He scurries back down the walkway.

I squat behind the fence. Forearms resting on my thighs. Stare up at the grey sky. There was rain this morning. There was rain yesterday. There will be more rain this afternoon and there will be more rain tomorrow. *We're on borrowed time, kid*, Esther said. This has all been a terrible mistake.

But then I think about Danny Collins. Think about the boy in the family portrait in the house on Hamilton Hill. Think about his drawings. All those ways he captured his subjects. So artful. So careful. So clever. So kind. So true. *I am invisible*, the girl said as she smiled. Danny Collins captured her smiling so wide that it was obvious he believed the girl's invisibility was her greatest asset. He believed invisibility was her source of pride. Her finest gift. Danny Collins made her look like she was meant to be. He made her look like she was not at all a terrible mistake. He made her look predestined. A thousand and one mistakes all moving towards one glorious and perfect correction.

My thoughts are interrupted by the sound of a sliding flyscreen door being kicked off its tracks. I turn to see, through the fence palings, a tall, thin, shirtless, spiky-haired man in a loose pair of yellow underpants. With desperation and more than a little athletic flare, he reaches his back fence in just five long strides.

'Stop, cunt,' Brandon calls from inside the apartment.

The tall man does not stop. He grabs hold of the top of the fence, pulls himself up and swings first one leg then the other onto the top rail. Perched there precariously, he looks down to the walkway – and that's exactly when he finds me pointing a black pistol at the space between his throbbing eyeballs.

'Please stop,' I say.

The man with spiky hair sighs. 'Fuck me,' he says, defeated. 'Who are you?'

'Wish I could tell ya,' I reply.

He sighs and allows himself to be pulled down like a stubborn vine by Brandon. I hear his body hit his small patch of backyard grass with a heavy thud.

'You wanna run from me, cunt,' Brandon barks. Through the cracks between the fence palings, I see the butt of Brandon's pistol meet the tall man's nose then I see blood spill across his chest. I turn away from the fence. I'm squatting again. And I'm looking again at the sky, shuddering every time Brandon's right boot finds a shoulder or a rib or a temple to stomp on. This has all been a terrible mistake, I tell myself. Please stop. Please stop. Please stop. I am not invisible, I tell myself. I exist, I tell myself. Allow me to introduce myself. My name is. My name is. My name is.

*

Back inside the Nissan, Brandon finds a McDonald's napkin in the car's central console and wipes blood from his fingers and the butt of his pistol.

'Do you like JK-47?' he asks, casually.

I can't look at his red hands. Can't look at his face. Just stare ahead through the windshield at an old woman pulling her groceries in a shopping trolley.

'What's JK-47?' I ask.

'You mean who's JK-47?' Brandon replies. 'Best rapper in Australia. Blackfeller from Tweed Heads. Quick as a trick, that motherfucker. Sounds like Kendrick on fast-forward.'

'I see.'

'He's playing The Zoo tonight,' Brandon says, squashing the blood-covered napkin into a ball and tossing it over his left shoulder into the Nissan's back seat. 'You wanna come with me?' he asks.

'Can't,' I say.

'Why not?'

'I got plans.'

'Doin' what?'

'I'm seein' someone.'

'Do I know this someone?'

'You don't know him.'

'You found yourself another swamp rat down by the river?'

'He's from Hamilton Hill, in fact.'

Brandon smiles, opens a white plastic bottle of Extra chewing gum, strawberry flavour. Pops two pieces in his mouth. 'I call bullshit,' he scoffs. 'You're gonna be walkin' the streets with that waster Charlie again. That's all you'll be doin' tonight.'

'Charlie's not a waster,' I say. 'He's a brilliant contemporary artist.'

'Charlie's a fuckin' loudmouth drunk waster who'll be dead in five years, max,' Brandon says.

'I always think it's interesting how people choose to see the futures of others,' I say. 'It makes sense that you'd only see bad things in the future for Charlie.'

'Why does that make sense?' Brandon asks.

'Because you're bad at heart,' I say, staring blankly. 'Bad-at-heart people only see bad futures for others because they want bad things to happen to people. Good-at-heart people only see good things for others because they want good things to happen to people.'

'So, what do you see in the future for me, Miss Goody Two-shoes?'

'You don't wanna know.'

'Why don't I wanna know?'

'Because I'm not so good all the time,' I say. 'I don't always see good things for people.'

'Well, I've seen your future,' he says.

'You have?'

'Yeah.' Brandon laughs. 'You got your eyes closed and you're smiling and your pussy's wet and I'm slapping your arse from behind and JK-47's singing on the stereo and I ain't ever been so fuckin' good for you.'

I turn to Brandon. Look him in the eye. 'That's never gonna happen.'

Brandon laughs again.

'I'll kill you first,' I say.

Brandon howls now, shakes his head. 'Nah, I don't think so. Erica couldn't do it and you can't do it either.'

'Monsters don't need to have the monster in them from the start,' I say. 'Monsters can be made, Brandon. And it's monsters like you who make more monsters.'

More laughter.

I hold his gaze. No doubt to be conveyed in what I need to say now. 'I will never, ever let you touch me like that.'

He smiles. Turns the key in the ignition, turns the fans up on the air-conditioning. 'I don't think you quite understand the situation you're in,' he says. He's not laughing anymore. 'You're workin' for me now. I don't need you to let me.'

*

Lunchtime in the scrapyard now and I'm eating a Vegemite and lettuce sandwich in front of my mirror as Lola advises me on what I should do if Brandon Box lays a single unwanted finger on my body.

'You still got that filleting knife?' she grumbles.

I nod once.

'Good,' Lola says, before licking salt from the top of her hand and shooting a small glass of tequila. She's inside what looks like a Mexican cantina and she's wearing a ridiculous pirate's eye patch over her empty right eye socket.

'I suggest you cut off his balls and drop them in his blender,' she says. 'Testicle smoothies work wonders for muscle growth.'

'I think you've been drinkin' too much, Lola.'

'I think you've been thinkin' too much,' she replies.

'To be honest, Lola, I don't think I'd ever have the guts to actually use that knife.'

'No woman realises the full extent of what she's capable of until she is forced to realise the full extent of what she's capable of,' Lola proclaims.

I swallow the last corner of my sandwich. 'You look good today, Lola,' I say.

She scoffs. 'I look like shit,' she says.

'You look better than the last time I saw you. It's your skin. Maybe I'm seein' things, but I think you're glowing.'

She laughs. 'The hell you talkin' 'bout?' She raises her left hand and studies her bare forearm. Sits back on her barstool, momentarily stunned. 'Well, goddam, would you look at that!'

*

Two hours later. Detective Geoff eats a tuna and avocado sushi roll as he sits on the bench at the back of King George Square beside a bronze statue of Emma Miller, the early 1900s shirtmaker and suffragette who stuck a hatpin in a horse during a women's rights march on Parliament House, causing the horse's occupant, Queensland Police Commissioner William Cahill, to be flung from his saddle.

I leave three body widths between us when I sit. Minimal eye contact. Real spy-like shit.

'Classy feller, that Brandon,' Topping says, his left cheek full of rice and seaweed.

I drop my backpack at my feet, shake my head as I wipe sweat from my forehead with the back of my hand. 'Classy as a haemorrhoid.' I sigh.

'You're still moving your legs when he's talking,' Topping says. 'Compromises the audio feed. You got some kinda restless leg syndrome or somethin'?'

I grit my teeth, bite my tongue. 'Well, maybe I'm a bit jumpy thinking he's gonna smell the rat-arsed squealer who's sittin' right beside him with an open party line to Queensland's finest fuzz.' I point at the Brisbane City Hall clocktower that rises above us. 'You say one more word about my spy work, I'll drop your stupid fucking bug phone from up there. Thing doesn't even come with Spotify.'

Topping holds his palms up in surrender. 'I'm sorry,' he says.

'This is bullshit,' I say. 'Is this even allowed? Throwing me to the wolves like this? Aren't there laws around cops forcing people to do this shit?'

'Calm down,' he says.

'Don't tell me to calm down. Did you hear him threaten me? He's attacked me before, this prick.'

'Listen to me,' Topping says. 'We are watching. We will continue to be watching. He lays a hand on you, I'll be there in a flash.'

'How quick is that?'

'What?'

'How quick is a flash?'

'A flash is as quick as ... a flash.'

'I might need you to be quicker than that.'

'Look, you're right. I get it. It's not fair. It's not right at all that one girl should have to shoulder such responsibility. But it's also working. You're doing an outstanding job. We are closer than we've ever been before. We are weeks, days even, from setting this whole stinking operation alight. All because of you.'

'Haven't you got enough now?' I ask. 'Just hit the big red button and get them blue meanie lights flashin'.'

He places the plastic sushi container and three small empty soy sauce containers shaped like fish beside his thigh. He takes one of the fish containers and holds it up in his fingers. 'You know a bit about fish, don't you?'

'Yeah, I know a bit about fish.'

He waves the plastic fish up and down like it's swimming in the sea. 'So, you know, then, that there are little fish and big fish in the sea?'

'I'm aware of this phenomenon,' I say.

'Which means there are always littler fish to catch and there are always bigger fish to catch.'

I nod twice.

'Well, I think it's fair to say that Flora Box is a nice big juicy coral trout,' Topping says.

'Good eating fish,' I remark.

'Great eating,' Topping confirms. 'But we were never fishing for coral trout. We're gonna catch the Great White Shark.'

I nod again. 'Big fish,' I say. 'Not so great to eat.'

'No,' Topping says, 'but real fun to catch.' His eyes light up briefly. 'We're closing in on the international supply lines. Imports. Invisible shipping networks. Points of origin.'

'And what exactly are you doing for me during your little fishing trip?'

'We're finding your answers,' he says. He wipes soy sauce from his lips.

'You found somethin'?' I ask.

He drops the plastic fish in the sushi container. Rubs his hands together. Tenderness when he turns to me. 'We found everything,' he replies.

I look at his face then stare at my boots. Turn around for a moment and see the Brisbane City Hall clockface, the minute hand making its way around the world.

'I need you to come to my office tomorrow,' Topping says.

'You know that's dangerous.'

'We'll get you in through the back. No one's gonna know.'

'Why your office?'

'Someone wants to meet you there.'

'Who?'

'Detective Sergeant Cameron Millar,' Topping says.

'Where's he from?' I ask.

'He's flown all the way from Perth just to meet you,' Topping replies.

'Perth,' I say. 'I've never been to Perth.'

'Yes, you have,' Topping says. 'You were born there.'

A long silence between us.

'Tomorrow morning,' Topping says. 'Ten o'clock.'

I still say nothing. Then I pick up my backpack, turn and walk.

'Wait, where you going?' Topping asks.

'I gotta go see someone,' I reply.

Because he saw me.

Two Lovers
in a Boat,
Floating towards
the Light

Two Lovers in a Boat, Floating Towards the Light

January 2024

Pen and ink on paper

At first glance, one of the most hopeful of the artist's early works. Two young lovers floating on a beam of silver light formed by a full moon shining over the Brisbane River. Look closer and one can't help but notice that their 'vessel' – a rare Queensland lungfish – has no motor and our lovestruck passengers grip no paddles. They are floating inextricably and irreversibly towards their fate. Look closer again and one discovers that the light in this image is not coming from the moon. It is a flashlight that illuminates our lovers. But who is holding the light?

He saw me because he likes to look. He watches things. People, babies, dogs and cats and clouds. He's staring now at a slim silver-grey darter bird gliding alongside our CityCat ferry to the CBD. His hair is caramel-coloured, all messed up by the wind. And I know that thing the river air does to him because it does the same thing to me. It makes me breathe. It makes me alive. It makes me wonder. It makes me draw. Documenting life in black pen to make sense of it all.

He sits at the rear of the ferry, in the corner of the outdoor sitting area. I watch him through the rear windows of the indoor sitting area, where most passengers are sheltering from the baking sun. Sit where I can see him and he can't see me. We passengers are invisible to him, might not even exist for him. But the darter bird exists for Danny Collins. It floats above him, rising and falling on unseen pockets of air. Wings wide, eyes on the water, hunting for fish. The boy from the house on Hamilton Hill, staring. His sketchbook between his right thigh and the base of his right forearm. Protect the sketches at all costs. Take me, that grip suggests, but let the sketches live. Danny Collins is an artist.

This is where he always sits when he rides the ferry. Same seat as yesterday. Same as the two days before that. When he ventures into the city to draw, he always takes the same route. Down Langside Road, right into Crescent Road, left into Kingsford Smith Drive, then along the bicycle path running by the river.

Black jeans and old blue Chuck Taylor gym shoes. Floppy navy-blue shirt with holes in the back. No interest in appearance, but interested in the appearance of things. We artists see things others can't see. We artists infer. We artists intuit. A black drawing pen between his fingers. The boy is made up of a soul and a heart and two lungs and two legs and temples on either side of his forehead and a nose and a set of lips beneath that nose and a smile he reserves for river birds.

He disembarks at the QUT Gardens Point ferry terminal. In the nearby botanic gardens he sketches a boy kicking a soccer ball. In Albert Street, he draws a large man in a Hawaiian shirt busking ukulele songs. In Queens Gardens, he sits on a bench and sketches a pigeon unceremoniously shitting on Queen Victoria's crown. An old drunk staggers from the Irish Murphy's pub on George Street and drops onto the bench beside Danny like a dropped bag of potatoes. He's too drunk to roll his cigarette, so he leans over to Danny. The boy helps him because he's kind. Rolls the cigarette and lights it for him. The old man asks about Danny's sketchbook and Danny lets him take a look at the images inside. Impressed, the old man requests a sketch of his own. I think Danny just said, 'Stay still,' but I can't be sure from so far away. He draws quickly. Fluid strokes. Confidence in the moment. The moment is more important than the mistakes. Mistakes are meant to be made, I tell myself. Mistakes are meant to be.

*

In Queen Street Mall, Danny stops to watch a boy in a suit who can't be older than six tilt his head up and observe a small sky-writing plane spelling out *RISE*.

On Adelaide Street, I'm standing in the entry foyer of David Jones when I watch Danny stop on the footpath and toss a dollar coin to the man with all the facts, Ivan Salhus, who's resting on a yoga mat. Ivan smiles and gives Danny two of his countless facts. It looks like they've met before.

On Charlotte Street, Danny sketches a group of people waiting for their orders outside the A.J. Vietnamese Noodle House. Further up Charlotte Street, someone has graffitied *Desolation Inc!* in lime-green spray paint across the brown brick wall beside Pancake Manor, the twenty-four-hour establishment Charlie and I like to stop at sometimes when making deliveries. No pattern to Danny's wandering. No destination. So much time this far outside of time. And when I watch him, it makes me feel like I've stepped outside with him.

He stops in front of a sushi bar near the 7-Eleven on Albert Street, where two businessmen are having a heated exchange. Bad business deal, maybe. Bad love gone wrong, maybe. Or maybe somebody took the last California roll. Danny's sketching too close to these guys and I want to tell him to keep his distance because I know they won't appreciate the art in the moment. Yep, there they go, turning to Danny with rage on their faces. 'What the fuck do you think you're doing?' screams one man. And Danny closes his sketchbook and walks away from the angry men, who do not chase him because their sushi is worth more to them than punching the lights out of Danny Collins, the prince with the pen from the house on Hamilton Hill.

*

Night comes and Danny eats a Whopper and chips from the Hungry Jack's in the middle of Queen Street Mall. The daytime workers catch their trains and buses home. The cleaners arrive, brushing food scraps and fast-food wrappers into long-handled dustpans. Hulking street-sweeping machines like mini tanks move up and down the gutters of Adelaide Street. Then the first floaters appear, some of whom I know from The Well, securing their sleeping digs early, glad the foot traffic is gone and all that mall concrete and marble belongs to them again.

Danny resting with his back flat on the stone edge of a fountain, his head on his sketchbook, looking up at the stars. Nothing rushing him. Then he rolls off and walks up the mall to George Street. Crosses near a man with dreadlocks playing calypso rhythms on a gleaming steel pan in front of the stone steps rising to the Treasury Casino, which is floodlit in pink like something from a Barbie Goes to Vegas gift box. He crosses William Street and ambles along the pedestrian footpath of the Victoria Bridge, which overlooks a Brisbane River that has shed its dirty daytime appearance and gained a nighttime shimmer, thanks to the lightbulb moon in the sky.

In the middle of the bridge, Danny stops and rests his elbows on the railing. Leans over and studies the water, then seems to be studying something else. Maybe the distance between himself and the water. He leans back then leans forward again. Back and forward. Back and forward. I'm leaning on the railing too, some thirty or so metres to his left, my head angled right to make it look as though I could be staring at the white Wheel of Brisbane turning slowly in the South Bank cultural forecourt when, in fact, all I'm seeing is him.

He takes a deep breath and runs a hand through his hair. Hugs his sketchbook to his chest. And then he cries. Rubs his eyes with the back of his right hand, which still clutches his sketchbook. I instinctively move four sidesteps towards him along the bridge railing. I want to be beside him. I want to tell him what Ursula Lang says about tears, how she considers laughter the second-best way to instantly connect with a stranger, and how she considers crying the first-best way to connect with a stranger. A declaration to the world that you feel. A declaration to the world that you are here, and not afraid to know what here feels like.

He rubs his eyes again and shakes his head. Opens his sketchbook and looks towards three towering cranes lit up atop three office towers. The cranes look like storks pecking for grubs on tree stumps. The glowing light of the city reveals the faint ghost fog of low night clouds creeping across the river. Danny sketches the scene. Draws quick. No dwelling on mistakes. His head darts back and forth between the sketchbook and the cranes. He's lost in the drawing. So lost, in fact, that he doesn't notice the two young men speeding towards him from the southern end of the bridge on orange and black electric scooters.

He takes a step back to better assess the scene and accidentally steps into the path of the first scooter rider, who barks a series of swear words at Danny as he yanks the scooter's steering handle left to avoid hitting him then slams hard into the walkway railing. The second rider brakes, leaps off his scooter and pushes Danny so hard that he falls on his arse, scraping his bare elbows on the asphalt walkway. Rough souls, these two. On the drink. On the wiz, even. Early twenties. Wiry and menacing.

The second scooter rider wears a Lonsdale jacket with the collar zipped up to his chin. Tattoos across his knuckles. 'The fuck ya doin', cunt?' he snaps at Danny.

I start walking towards the scene as Danny pulls himself to his feet. Blood running from a graze on his right elbow. 'I'm sorry,' he says. Well spoken. Gentle. 'I was … drawing.' He points at the north side of the river. 'The cranes … on the … the buildings.'

The first scooter rider reaches around from behind Danny's back and yanks his sketchbook from his grip. 'How the fuck can you draw when you're blind as a bat?' he asks, pushing Danny from behind. 'You nearly killed me, faggot.'

He's wearing an Adidas tank top. Basketball shorts past his kneecaps. Nike running shoes. Looks like he works out. He flips open Danny's sketchbook. 'You got anything to say for yourself, faggot?'

Just a few metres from them now, I stop and bend down to my right boot.

'I apologise,' Danny says. 'Didn't mean to cause any trouble.'

'And I won't mean to throw your drawings into the river, faggot,' the first rider says.

'Please don't do that,' Danny asks.

'Some good drawings here, faggot,' the first rider says, turning the pages. He holds up a sketch of a bird. 'What sorta bird is that?'

'It's a superb fairywren,' Danny says.

'What makes it so superb?'

Danny's answer is longer than the scooter thug expected. 'Superb fairywren mothers sing to their chicks when they're still in their eggs. There's a secret code in their birdsong. A kind of sonic password they share with their chicks in the form of a special incubation call. When the chicks hatch, they already know this special call and so if they sing it, their mum will be able to find them, even in the dark. It's kind of a shared … biological … love song.'

The two scooter riders are temporarily stilled by this information. And I think Danny Collins is fucking with these guys. Meeting their aggression with wonder.

Then the stillness is broken. 'The fuck you talkin' about?' the second rider asks as he thrusts a palm hard against Danny's shoulder.

Danny instinctively responds, shoving the second rider back just as hard. 'Please stop fucking pushing me,' he spits. And he's no longer the sweet boy talking about motherly birds and this scene is about to explode.

'Woah, this faggot's got some spark,' the second rider says, clenching his right fist and rushing straight at Danny.

'Please stop,' I say. And the second rider turns to confront the somewhat unexpected sight of me standing behind his scooter-riding friend with a razor-sharp filleting knife at his throat.

Danny Collins turns now, too, to hear what I have to say next, confusion across his face.

'This cuts through a shark's tail like a hot knife through butter,' I say. 'I could bleed this thug's neck like it's a Moreton Island tailor.'

'Are you fuckin' crazy?' the first rider asks, shifting his feet in my unsettling embrace.

'Not crazy,' I say. 'Just tired. Tired of the tyrant lizards like you, always wanting to destroy someone's art. Always wanting to turn the beautiful stuff into ugly stuff.' I look at the second rider. 'I know you two,' I say. 'I've seen you working out at that outdoor gym beneath the Go Between Bridge.'

'Yeah, I seen you around,' the second rider says. 'You're always sniffing around those homeless bums.'

'Houseless,' I say.

'What?' spits the second rider.

'They are houseless, not homeless. Many of them have homes. Just not houses.'

'Who gives a fuck?'

'Nobody,' I say. 'That's the whole problem. Nobody gives a fuck. But, anyway, the point is, if you work out beneath the Go Between Bridge then there's a good chance you know my work colleague, Brandon Box, who also works out beneath the Go Between Bridge. You boys know Brandon Box?'

'Yeah, I know Brandon,' the second rider says.

'If you know Brandon then I'm guessing you know about Brandon's mum, Flora?'

'Yeah, I know about Flora.'

'How much do you know about Flora?' I ask.

'I know enough,' he replies.

'You know enough,' I repeat. 'Well, did you know that she cares for me like I'm her own flesh and blood?'

'Just jump these cunts,' the first rider snaps, wriggling against my blade.

'Shut the fuck up,' the second rider instructs.

'Yeah, shut the fuck up,' I whisper in his friend's ear. I bring the blade closer to his neck, one centimetre below his Adam's apple. Turn again to the second rider, nod at Danny Collins. 'This man is an artist,' I say. 'He's good at drawing fairywrens. He's not good at fighting thugs on scooters. This would not be a fair fight. Your worlds have temporarily and unfortunately collided on this beautiful bridge tonight, but why don't you just hand him back his sketchbook and he can go on making art and you two can go on making pain for your parents and I don't have to say a word to my friend Flora Box about any of it.' And I stare into the eyes of the monster. The tyrant lizard in the Lonsdale jacket.

He considers my suggestion for almost ten seconds.

'Give 'im his book,' he says, stepping back onto his electric scooter. Then he pulls the throttle and speeds past Danny. 'Watch where yer fuckin' walkin',' he says, zooming north along the bridge.

The first rider drops Danny's sketchbook to the ground. I remove my arms from around his neck but keep the knife raised. He spits on the ground near Danny's shoes. 'You got yourself a guardian angel there, bird boy. She musta heard you singin' in the dark.'

Then he grabs his scooter, mounts and speeds away.

*

Now there's nobody on the bridge but us. Danny Collins from the mansion on Hamilton Hill and me from the orange Toyota

HiAce van on Moon Street. And it feels like there's nobody else on earth. Because it's quiet now. No buses passing. No cars. No people. There's a space between us and Danny's sketchbook is on the ground in the middle of that space. He stares at me. Studies me. Tilts his head like I'm a painting he's trying to understand. I mirror his movements, like I'm some kind of alien trying to make sense of a scruffy caramel-haired boy from Brisbane who likes to draw.

My smile makes him smile. But he cuts his smile off and replaces brief joy with confusion. His mouth opens and I know he's about to say something, so I raise my right forefinger.

'Wait,' I say, and bring my finger to my lips. 'Before you say anything, would you do me a favour and consider the next words that come out of your mouth as though those words will be written about a hundred years from now?'

He squints, pulls his head back, confused.

'Do you think you could do that for me?' I ask.

He scratches his head, offers a dicey smile.

'What if you and I were about to share a remarkable story together?' I continue. 'What if that story lasted for the rest of our lives? And what if people wrote about that story in years to come? Maybe we're only gonna know each other for the next five minutes, or maybe you'll talk to me for half an hour and realise I'm cracked and you hate my guts and you'll sprint off into the city and I'll never see you again. That's fine. But what if this was the very beginning of a beautiful story that will last until I die? And what if we are brilliant? And what if we both become groundbreaking and famous? And what if our story was discussed by great writers and thinkers far into the future? They would write about the very next words that are about to come out of your mouth because those words, for the rest of time, will be remembered as the first words you ever said to me.'

He laughs. Bites his bottom lip.

'I know that sounds screwy,' I say. 'You must think I'm cracked. You don't need half an hour to work that out.'

He shakes his head. He means no without saying no because maybe no is not the first word he wants to say to me. He takes one step closer. Goes to say something but catches himself. Looks down at his shoes, brings a thumb to his mouth in thought then raises his head and smiles briefly, like a flash of wonder has gone through his brain and lit up his life. Moves closer to me and puts his hand to his chest as though he's about to announce something grand and brave and strong. A proclamation. But then he stops, and I'm guessing he must have had second thoughts about what he wants to say because he raises his left forefinger as he turns away from me, meaning 'Wait', though he doesn't want that word to be the first he ever says to me. And he stumbles back to the railing, keeping his hand up. *Almost there. Just a second. Be with you soon.* Then he drops his arm, stares down at the river beneath us, takes a deep breath, turns and looks into my eyes, and his face is so wonderfully serious and true.

'I love you,' he says.

'What?' I recoil.

'I love you,' he says.

I shake my head in disgust. 'You can't say that.'

'Why not?' he asks.

'You totally overshot it,' I reply. 'I'm sorry. You went too far. That's ridiculous.'

'No, I didn't,' he says. 'You don't know what I'm feeling right now. Maybe I didn't go far enough? I thought about saying something else that was bullshit and boring but then I decided that if people were really gonna read about us in a hundred years' time then I wanted them to know I said something brave and beautiful. "Fuck it. I love you." That's gonna go down great a hundred years from now. No matter what happens from here on. Me throwing that out there like that, it's cool as shit.'

'You chose daring,' I say. 'You cartwheeled instead of walking.'

'What? Sorry, I'm confused.'

'Doesn't matter. You don't love me. You can't possibly love me.'

'It happened very quickly,' he says. 'I just decided to fast-forward through six to twelve months of agonising self-doubt. Boom. Here we are.'

A laugh spills from my lips. 'You don't even know me,' I say.

'I know you,' he says. 'I've known you for three long minutes now and I've loved every second of them.'

'You can't say things that big so soon,' I say. 'And that's maybe the biggest thing you can say.'

He raises his hands in the air. Looks around at the night. What could he possibly be looking at?

'Do you feel that?' he asks.

'Feel what?'

'The alive. The alive of this moment.'

'The alive?'

'Yeah, the alive,' he says. 'You gotta say it like it's got a capital *T* and a capital *A*. The Alive. I swear, something you just said made me think about The Alive. Like being alive is a thing that you touch and see and feel. As real a thing as electricity. Do you feel that? It's The Alive.'

I feel it. Though I don't tell him that I feel it, because I'm still not entirely sure what it is.

'Will you marry me?' he asks.

'Stop it,' I say. Serious now.

He laughs and I can't help myself from laughing with him.

'That's not fuckin' funny,' I say.

'I'm not being fuckin' funny,' he says. 'I'm being brave. Fuck it. Will you marry me? That's what I feel like saying. That's the truest thing that came to me. I'm just telling all those people one hundred years from now how I feel right now on this night, on this bridge, in this very moment right here with you. I know you. I actually know you better than you think I know you. I've seen you in the city before. And now you're standing right in front of me. You just saved me from some arseholes who were gonna throw my sketchbook into the river and that's actually incredible to me, in itself, because you're not gonna believe some of the sketches I have in that sketchbook. Yep. Fuck it. That's what I want to say to you first. I love you. I want to marry you. I want those to be my first words to you. You can say whatever you want back to me. But let it be known for the rest of my days, that's what I said first and I'm glad I made those first words count.'

'You can change the words if you want to,' I say.

'Nup, I'm all good,' he says. 'Too late now, anyway. Those words are out. Even if I changed those words, they'd still be out. They're free. They're halfway to the Gabba by now. No getting them back.'

Me smiling now, lips as wide as this empty bridge.

He brings his palms to his forehead. 'Wait till you hear the next words I've got to say to you.'

'Can't wait,' I say. 'You got a general theme in mind other than love and marriage?'

He nods, confidently. 'Wonder,' he says. 'Pure wonder. Miracles, maybe. You ready for my next words?'

'Sure,' I say.

'It's you,' he says, shaking his head. 'I can't believe it's you. It's really you.'

I raise my eyebrows and can't help chuckling at the way he says 'It's you,' the way I might say 'It's you' if Taylor Swift sold me a soft-serve cone in the Milton McDonald's.

'I'm sorry,' I say. 'Have we met?'

'Yes,' Danny says, the word leaping involuntarily from his lips. 'I mean ... no ... but ... yes. I've seen you before.'

He stands still. This awkward space between us. Nobody moving yet to pick up the sketchbook. I'll pick it up soon if he doesn't. Those images don't belong down there. But still he stares.

I want him to pick up the sketchbook. I want him to show me his images. The invisible girl on the corner of Ann and Edward streets.

He raises a hand now to scratch his chin, but the hand stays on his face as though he's checking he's a creation of flesh and blood and not a product of strange moonlit dreams.

I kneel and collect the sketchbook. Wipe the footpath grit and dust from its cover pages. Move closer to Danny and hold out the book.

He takes it only out of instinct, because his thoughts and his gaze are still fixed on me. 'It's you,' he says again.

The boy makes me laugh. 'Yep, it's me,' I say.

He shakes his head and opens his sketchbook. 'I draw stuff,' he says.

'I heard,' I say. 'You draw superb fairywrens.'

Danny still piecing together the jigsaw of fate and more than a little subtle surveillance on my part. 'I don't just draw fairywrens,' he says. 'I come into the city almost every day. I like to walk around and draw all the things I see.'

'What kinds of things?'

'All kinds of things. Unusual things. Strange things. Sad things.' He shifts a clump of hair out of his eyes to see me better. 'Beautiful things.'

He starts flipping through the sketchbook, searching for an image he has in his mind. 'A few weeks back, before Christmas,' he says, 'I was sitting in Ann Street, just across from the ramp that goes up to Central Station, with my back against the wall of the Adina hotel. Just sitting there drawing things that passed by.' He finds the image he's looking for. 'And I looked up and there were all these cars waiting for the traffic lights to turn green and then the cars all moved left and there was nothing in my view but this girl who was sitting across the street from me with a sketchbook, drawing something.'

He doesn't show me the image. Just looks at me and tries to draw a memory with words. 'It was like we were a mirror,' he says.

'A mirror?' I repeat.

'A reflection,' he says. 'Two sides of the same coin. I looked over and it was like I saw myself. Then I watched this girl stand up as all these people were passing her.' He speaks like he's talking about a dream he had. 'And she did the most remarkable thing. It was the eight-to-five business crowd, all heading to the station or some other place. And this girl stood in the middle of all these people who were passing her and raised her arms up in the air and screamed—'

'"I am invisible,"' I say. I like the way he draws things with his words, so I've chosen to finish his drawing for him.

Danny steps closer to me. Nods. '"I am invisible,"' he whispers. And he shows me the sketch he was looking for. It's me and it's the corner of Ann and Edward streets and it's the same image I saw when I was sitting on Danny Collins's bed on Christmas night.

'You saw me,' I say.

'I saw you. I wanted to run across the road and tell you right away that I saw you. I wanted you to know you weren't invisible. I wanted you to know you were seen. But then I saw you hug your friend, and you walked on down Edward Street and I went back to where I was sitting against the wall and decided to draw exactly what I'd seen. It was you.' He taps on my image in the drawing. 'It is you.'

'Yep, it's me,' I say.

He presents the sketchbook to me like it's a chicken roast he's pulled from an oven, and I flip through the pages.

Danny's cheeks are red. The sweet boy from Hamilton Hill is flustered.

'Your drawings are beautiful,' I say. 'They're riddled with errors but they're perfect, too. I like how fast you draw. You have a gift for expression and the energy you give your subjects comes from your speed. Yet the bones are true too. Good sense of light and shade. Solid handle on perspective. Most importantly, you understand that the image is only as good as the story it tells.'

'You draw a lot too?'

'Every chance I get,' I say. 'I'm saving up to study at the Queensland College of Art. I want to learn how to turn my good sketches into great paintings and then I want to move to New York and show my work in the Metropolitan Museum of Art.'

'Take me with you,' he says.

I smile at him. Can't tell if he's serious or not. Can't tell if he's a prince or a rogue or a thief. Only one thing for certain. 'I'm really glad you saw me across that street.'

Silence now. Danny staring at me again. 'So, what do we do now?' he asks.

And I laugh out loud at this. 'What do you mean, "What do we do now?"'

'This moment is remarkable, don't you think?' he replies. 'What are the chances we would meet like this? It's impossible. Some knucklehead is about to throw my sketchbook over the bridge and then my sketchbook is rescued by the real-life girl who features in the sketchbook?'

'That is pretty remarkable, now you mention it,' I say. 'Almost like it happened by design. By fate, maybe.'

It's almost enough to make a girl believe in the power of mistakes. Make her believe in the meaning of misfortune. Make her believe that every sorrow-sucking misbegotten misery of her past had to occur in order for her to be here in the shimmering now. Neck-deep in The Alive.

'So, what *do* we do now?' he asks.

'Why do we have to do anything now?'

'Something this remarkable must be happening for a reason,' he says. 'I think we need to find out what that reason is.'

I move to the railing. Rest my elbows on its black metal surface. 'Well, here's what I'm going to do now,' I say. 'I'm going to stand here and be quiet as I stare at this river for fifteen minutes and think about my past.'

'Another extraordinary twist of fate,' Danny says, eyes alight. 'Another glorious coincidence. That's exactly what I was going to do. Mind if I join you?'

I laugh and shake my head.

Danny rests his elbows on the railing. There's enough room on its flat top to hold his sketchbook there safely.

The river shimmers. We stare down at it in silence. A tourist boat passes under the bridge. I can see a yellow buoy in the water and it's round at the bottom where it bobs on the surface and it has two intersecting metal X-shapes above a flashing orange light. It's about twenty metres out from the riverbank – almost exactly, I suddenly realise, where Erica Finlay reached Christina's drifting pram almost a year ago. I know it's just a safety marker for boats at night, but it feels like a monument to Erica's bravery. Here is where it all took place. Here is where it all started turning for the artist.

What was it she said? *The world turns for us all. One day you'll wake up and you'll realise the world has turned back upright for you and every bad thing you didn't deserve on the downside is made up for by every good thing rushing at you on the upside. You'll look up one day and see some face and suddenly it'll all make sense and all that bad downside stuff will seem entirely necessary. It'll just be ordinary life; it'll just be the normal turning of the world, but it'll feel miraculous to you. It'll feel engineered for you. It'll feel designed, drawn up like one of those crazy sketches you do. You'll call it fate. You'll say it was meant to be.*

And maybe it was. Because that's all the world was ever meant to do.
Turn. And you were meant to turn with it.

Warm summer air. A couple on the bridge pass behind us, arm in arm. Two teens on skateboards coming from the north end of the bridge, fishtailing their way to South Bank. The pink lights of the casino. The white light of the Wheel of Brisbane.

I look up at the moon. Danny's gaze goes nowhere mine hasn't gone before it.

Almost three minutes of silence before he can't help himself from breaking it. 'It's shaped like an M&M, you know,' he says, head tilted to the night sky.

'What is?'

'The moon. People think it's shaped like a golf ball, but it's really shaped like an M&M. People think it's perfectly round, but we're only seeing what's being lit up for us by the sun.'

I nod towards the moon.

'There's a guy who sits on Adelaide Street,' Danny says. 'He told me that. Ivan's his name. You give him a dollar and he gives you two fascinating facts in return.'

'What else has Ivan told you?'

'The average person will spend six months of their life just waiting for red traffic lights to turn green,' Danny says.

'Seems awfully wasteful,' I say. 'Did Ivan tell you anything useful?'

'He told me the meaning of life,' Danny says, shrugging his shoulders.

'He did?'

'He did. I told him I would give him twenty dollars if he could give me a satisfactory answer to the question "What is the meaning of life?"'

'Did he give you an answer?'

'He did.'

'Did you give him the twenty dollars?'

TRENT DALTON

'I did.'

I turn to Danny, rest my right cheek on my closed right fist. Say nothing. Look into his eyes.

'Don't you wanna know what his answer was?' he asks.

I shake my head. 'I already know the answer to that one.'

'You do? Okay, what's the meaning of life?'

'Well, according to Ivan, it's to love as many people as you can before you die. And to let as many people as you can love you back.'

'Holy shit,' Danny says, 'that's exactly what Ivan said!'

'Well, that's what Ivan believes,' I say.

'What do you believe?' Danny asks. 'What's the meaning of life for you?'

'Cartwheels,' I say.

'Cartwheels.' Danny nods. 'Of course.'

I shake my head. 'I don't know,' I say. 'A woman once told me that if you stare directly into the eyes of a child for thirty seconds or more you'll see the meaning of life. She said you can see it in their eyes.'

'You ever done that?'

'Nah,' I say. 'Don't know any children to do it with.'

'What's your name?' Danny asks.

I take a moment to answer. 'My name is Vicki Peterson,' I say.

Danny nods, laughs. 'Cool,' he says. 'You got the same name as the lead guitarist from The Bangles.'

Danny Collins knows The Bangles. Of all the all-girl pop-rock bands in all the world, Danny Collins knows The Bangles.

'What's your name?' I ask.

'Danny,' he says. 'Danny Collins.'

'It's nice to stand on a bridge and stare at a river with you, Danny Collins.'

'Nice to stand on a bridge and stare at a river with you, Vicki Peterson.'

298

I drop my head. I'm making push-up movements against the bridge railing because I'm thinking about saying something important to this boy from Hamilton Hill. Back and forth. Backwards and forwards. 'Can I ask you a what-if question?'

'Sure,' he says. 'I love what-if questions.'

I let go of the railing and turn to face him. 'What if I told you the truth?' I say. 'But what if every truth I told you had to stay right here with us. And what if you told me nothing but the truth as well and all those truths between us had to stay with us here in the night. In the night world.'

Danny looks like he's about to say something, but he's too confused to form a sentence.

I cast my gaze across the city. 'Look at this place,' I say. 'This whole city goes to sleep at nine p.m.'

'Sinatra sang about this city,' Danny observes. 'I want to wake up in the city that never misses eight hours' sleep.'

Danny makes me smile.

'You walk around this place on a weeknight like this and it feels like you're the only person alive,' I say. 'And the only world that exists in this place is the one that you're the centre of. It's a different place after nine p.m. What if this world became our world? Our nighttime world that only exists when Brisbane sleeps. And, inside this world, what if I told you only the truth? If such a world existed, would you want to share it with me?'

'Why me?' Danny asks.

'Because I don't know you,' I reply. 'Because we could walk around this city like we were just two strangers talkin' on a train. Because you don't know me, but, for some reason, you saw me.'

He thinks for a long moment. A 385 bus crosses the bridge behind us, rumbling and moaning as the driver crunches through the gears.

'Yes,' Danny says.

'Yes what?' I ask.

'My answer is yes. I would like to share that world with you.'

I nod three times. Turn back to the river. 'Real nice to hear that, Danny Collins.'

'Real nice to be asked, Vicki Peterson.'

He rests his elbows on the railing again. We stare at the river in silence.

'So, what now?' he asks.

I breathe the warm night air in through my nose. Blow it back out through my mouth. 'Now I tell you the truth,' I say.

*

Half an hour later. Two artists walking south in the night along the Victoria Bridge.

'So, where do you live?' Danny asks.

'Not far from here,' I reply. 'Small place. Nothin' flash.'

'I can see you sketching in some cool townhouse in New Farm.'

'Nah, my place is smaller than that.'

'A cosy little artist's loft?'

'Smaller.'

'An attic. You live in a grungy attic like a Moulin Rouge artist?'

'A van,' I say. 'I live in an orange 1987 Toyota HiAce van.'

Danny slows his walking. 'Where's your van?'

'Not far from here,' I say.

'So … you drive around and stuff … sleep where you park?'

'Nope. The van's got four flat tyres. It's been parked in a scrapyard since I was twelve.'

'Can I see it?'

'No.'

'Why not?'

'Because it's fucking embarrassing taking a boy home to show him your bed beside the handbrake.'

'You're homeless?' he asks.

'Not homeless,' I reply. 'Houseless. You got a problem with that?'

'No,' he says, stopping on the spot. 'I got no problem with that.'

We walk on.

'How old are you?'

'Eighteen,' I say.

'You've been sleeping in a van for six years?'

I nod three times, slowly.

'What's that like?'

'Scary,' I say. 'And demoralising. Tiring. But fun every once in a while. Cold in winter. Too hot in summer – can't wind the front windows down to let the air in 'cuz there's too many mosquitoes. Hole in the roof that leaks when it rains. Running out of room to store my drawings. Some mornings I wake up to find a carpet snake curled up beneath the steering wheel in what is essentially my kitchen. There's no lock on the van, so people sometimes steal stuff. I've had to tape a sign to the sliding door that says, *Take what you think you need but please don't take my drawings. They are all I have in this godforsaken world.*'

'Fuck me,' Danny says, 'that sounds awful.'

'It was fine when Erica Finlay was living with me.'

'Who's Erica Finlay?'

'She's the woman who raised me.'

'She was your mum?'

'No. But she loved me like she was. You can live through anything when you're living with someone you love, who loves you back. I'm not homeless but I've got about thirty homeless friends who sleep way rougher than me and I reckon every one of them would tell you the thing they miss most about home has got nothing to do with running water and IKEA ottomans.

What they miss is love. You can survive almost anything if you know there's someone out there who still gives two or three shits about you.'

'Where's Erica Finlay now?'

I nod ahead. 'I'll show you.'

*

We come to the marble memorial at the end of the bridge, dedicated to an eleven-year-old Greek newspaper boy named Hector Vasyli, who was accidentally hit and killed by a swerving car on this bridge in 1918, just when he was deliriously happy and welcoming home returned World War I soldiers he worshipped. Mistakes have been made. Mistakes will always be made.

The bridge walkway gently curves left and follows a garden path that folds back around to the river, the South Bank cultural forecourt and the three-dimensional *BRISBANE* sign that kids with sticky ice cream fingers crawl on and climb up in the daytime. I take Danny to the riverbank, past the base of the Victoria Bridge Abutment, where Erica Finlay and I used to sit when she was selling Flo's gear to the good citizens of Brisbane.

High tide tonight and the river is full and dangerous. We've had rain all week, but the big wet's eased for a spell. The smell of mangroves and sewage waste and dead fish this close to the water. Danny and me staring out at the brown snake river.

'You remember the story of Baby Christina?' I ask Danny.

Danny raises his head to the sky, rubs his chin. Nothing coming to mind.

'About a year ago now,' I say. 'Pram rolled into the river right here. This good Samaritan jumped in and stopped the pram from sinking. Baby survived. Good Samaritan wasn't so lucky.'

Danny clicks his fingers. 'Yeah, I remember now,' he says. 'They tried to work out who she was. Nobody knew a thing about her.'

I nod twice, tap the heel of my boot nervously on the cobblestone river's edge. 'That was Erica Finlay,' I say, and stare out to the place where I watched her face sink beneath the surface.

'She was a hero,' Danny says.

'She was that day.'

The yellow buoy we saw bobbing in the water from the bridge looks bigger down here. From this perspective. So many different ways of seeing things.

'I'm not supposed to be here, Danny,' I say.

'You're not?'

'No, I'm not. My life wasn't supposed to turn out like this. A terrible mistake was made, and I was forced to live a life I wasn't born to live.'

'What was the life you were supposed to have?' Danny asks.

'I'm not sure,' I reply. 'But I do know it was supposed to have been easier than how it was. It was supposed to be sweeter. There weren't supposed to be so many fights. There weren't supposed to be so many unexpected conflicts. I was supposed to sleep better at night. I wasn't supposed to be so scared all the time. It was supposed to be less cold. It was supposed to be less confusing. My muscles didn't ache in that life. I didn't wake at night in cold sweats. My underarms smelled nicer in that life. My stomach didn't shrink so often. I think I was supposed to have an in-ground swimming pool. I was supposed to have one of those fridges that has two doors that open outwards and a water fountain and ice cubes stored in one door. I was supposed to have a family.'

A tear slides down my left cheek. I shake my head. 'My name's not Vicki Peterson,' I say. 'I sometimes use the names of pop stars in place of my real name. I didn't think you'd know all the members of The Bangles. Most people only know Susanna Hoffs, but I'm starting to realise you're not like most people, Danny Collins.'

He shrugs, kicks a riverbank rock with the heel of his shoe.

'I'm sorry,' I say. 'I know I sound screwy. I understand completely if you would now like to shuffle quietly away from me and go about your business.'

He laughs. 'I'm all good, but thanks for the leave pass. So, what's your real name?'

'I don't know,' I say.

'Why don't you know?'

'Erica Finlay never told me my real name. She was supposed to tell me on my eighteenth birthday. That was the deal. But she jumped in the drink two months too early.'

I wipe my face with my palms. 'But all that won't matter after tomorrow.'

'What's happening tomorrow?'

'A policeman's gonna tell me who I am.'

I turn to Danny. 'You ever lived through a single moment in your life that gave meaning to every single tiny moment you lived through before it?'

Danny ponders this. 'Think I'm in one of those moments now,' he says. 'Why'd Erica Finlay never tell you your name?'

'She'd done somethin' terrible, Danny. Somethin' real bad. She told me she was my mum, but that was a big, fat, stinky lie. She told me that she stuck a paring knife in my father's throat. I asked her what a paring knife was and she told me it was a knife used to cut lemons.'

I look at Danny to gauge the impact of these words. He grimaces but still stands. Still listens. Danny Collins is an artist. Danny Collins is a listener. Danny Collins said he wants to share the night world with me.

'She always said that was the real bad thing she'd done. She told me she'd done that because my father was a monster. And I understood that because sometimes that's all some people feel like they have left to do when they wanna stop dancing with monsters. Do you know one Australian woman every week is murdered by a monster like that?'

'No,' Danny says, softly, 'I didn't know that.'

'Erica knew that,' I say. 'She said that was why we had to go on the run when I was a baby. She said that was why she couldn't tell me what my name was. But do you wanna know the truth about all that, Danny?'

'Sure,' he whispers, 'but only if you want to tell me.'

'I do wanna tell you the truth, Danny,' I say. 'I've been lying to people about Erica Finlay for too long now. I've been making up white lies for her. Lies that aren't supposed to hurt anyone. But I really need to stop telling those lies because I think they're starting to hurt me. They're making me angry. They're turning me into someone I don't wanna be.'

'Okay then,' Danny says, 'tell me the truth.'

'The truth is, Danny, that she'd done somethin' worse than stickin' that knife in my father's throat. She'd done somethin' so bad she knew I'd never be able to forgive her for it. And the moment I learned the truth about my name would also be the moment I'd learn the truth about what she'd done.'

I look across the nightscape. The Queensland Performing Arts Centre buildings are bathed in bright green lights. Whole walls of cream-coloured concrete buildings now looking like vibrant chunks of kryptonite.

'And tomorrow you're gonna learn the truth,' Danny says. He thinks on this for a moment, staring out at the water. 'But you're scared, because ... because ...' He thinks some more. Settles on his thoughts. 'Because you still love Erica Finlay.'

He leaves the words in the air.

I look into his eyes. Whisper, 'Who are you?'

*

One hour later. We're walking along the bikeway by the river. Heading for the lawns that roll towards the water from the box-shaped Gallery of Modern Art.

'So where do you live, Danny Collins?'

'I still live with my parents,' he says. 'Place on Hamilton Hill.'

'Hamilton Hill? Must be a nice place.'

Danny shrugs his shoulders. Hands in the pockets of his jeans. 'Well, you know that other life you were talking about?'

'Yeah.'

'You know that in-ground swimming pool you were talking about?'

'You got one?'

He nods. 'And you know the big fridge with two doors that makes ice?'

'Yeah,' I say. 'You got one of those, too?'

His big smile, curling at its left edge. Row of good teeth. He nods. 'Yeah, we're pretty fuckin' flash up on Hammo Hill.' He kicks a rock off the path into the river.

'You got any siblings?'

'I've got an older sister,' he says.

'What's her name?' I ask.

'Samara,' Danny says.

'What's it like?'

'What's what like?'

'Having an older sister.'

Danny shrugs. Looks up at the stars. 'It's like a baby-shit yellow jumper,' he says.

'How so?'

He shakes his head and laughs. 'When I was ten years old I went on this Scouts camp in a forest behind the Gold Coast,' he says. 'Mum checked my bag before I went and she said I hadn't packed a jumper and I said that was because all the jumpers I had were too small for me. So then Mum insisted I take this baby-shit yellow jumper that belonged to my sister.'

'Xanthous,' I say.

'Sorry?'

'Xanthous is the name of that baby-shit yellow colour.'

'Xanthous.' Danny nods. 'No way I'm gonna wear this xanthous monstrosity, right. It was unwashed and still stank of Impulse body spray. Then one night up in the cabins I can't sleep because some arsehole bully kid is giving me a hard time because I won the patrol sports tournament that day. I start missing home real bad and I'm stirring in my bunk and I'm cold and I decide my only option is to slip on Samara's baby-shit yellow jumper. Then, whaddya know, the smell of Impulse in the jumper reminds me of hugging my sister. And hugging my sister reminds me of home. And suddenly I don't miss home so much because a little bit of home is with me. Long story short, home for me is a baby-shit yellow jumper. Home is Samara. Samara is home.'

I smile at him. 'She still at home with you?'

'No,' he says, 'not right now.'

'Where is she?'

'She's in a mansion in the hills,' Danny says. 'Real flash place, this one. It's called The Plateau.'

'In-ground swimming pool?'

'Shit yeah,' Danny says. 'Got its own gym, too. Got its own cinema. Uninterrupted views across South East Queensland.'

'Your mum and dad own this place, too?'

'No.' He smiles. 'It's a rehab retreat.'

'I'm sorry to hear that.'

'S'all good.'

'What's she trying to kick?'

'Meth,' he says.

I shake my head. 'Fuck, why'd she jump that train?'

'I keep asking myself that,' he says. 'First thing I thought about was my part in it. Had I ever done something to her? Had I ever hurt her? Did I not support her? Did I not love her enough or somethin'?'

'Then you moved on to your folks,' I say.

'Yep,' Danny says, 'in a matter of minutes. And then I thought about some friends of Samara's who'd done some bad shit in the past just to get back at their parents because their parents were selfish pricks.'

'Are your parents selfish pricks?'

'No,' he says. 'That's the thing. My parents are fucking amazing. Rich as fuck, but if you met them you wouldn't necessarily know right away they were rich as fuck. They're not dicks about it. They're really kind. Total bohemian artist weirdos who are almost ashamed of the fact they've made a small fortune running a law firm. They fight and argue a bit, but nothing to call Dr Phil about and they love the shit out of Samara and me. They love Samara so much. And when I think about it all, the only thing I can come up with is the fact that she was bored. She was bored with her life. She was bored with the life she was born into. She was bored with the in-ground swimming pool. She was bored with the fridge with two front doors that makes its own ice. She was bored being Samara Collins.'

'Takes some serious privilege to get that fuckin' bored,' I say.

'Have I not told you how flash we are on Hamilton Hill?' Danny smiles.

We walk on. Come to the upside-down bronze elephant sculpture outside the Gallery of Modern Art, where I met Detective Topping.

'Meth's a hard kick,' I say. 'Not just the physical stuff. Hallucinations an' shit. Aggression. Watch out for the mental stuff when she comes home. They get a thing called anhedonia, an inability to feel any form of pleasure. There's no longer any joy in any experience. And no family can fix that. No friends. No baby-shit yellow jumpers. No TV, no food, no sex, no movies, not even the Timothée Chalamet ones. She'll go deep into the dark and the only thing that will pull her out is the sun. Not the way it shines, I mean, but the way it moves up and down. Just plain ol' time, Danny. And then one day you'll all be listening to "Ob-La-Di, Ob-La-Da" on the radio up on Hamilton Hill and it'll feel like a fuckin' miracle when she taps just one big toe to the beat.'

Danny stops walking. 'Fuck me,' he says, 'that's quite the insight.'

I shrug. 'I used to deliver meth hits to addicts across Brisbane.'

'What?'

'That was my old job,' I say.

'You delivered meth to addicts across Brisbane?'

'Not just meth. Cocaine sometimes. Heroin mostly.'

'Are you fuckin' serious? You were a fuckin' drug courier?'

'I told you I was going to tell you the truth.'

'You ever make any deliveries to Langside Road, Hamilton Hill?'

'No.'

'You do know you're part of the reason my sister is a mess,' Danny says.

'Nah,' I say. 'When someone wants to be a mess, it doesn't matter what faces pop up between that person and the mess.'

'Nah, I call bullshit,' Danny says. 'That's a shitty thing to do for a buck. I don't care how shrunk your stomach is or how small your rusted van home is. That's messed up, and I'm afraid you're more than likely going to hell for it.'

'Well, you'll be happy to know I'm leaving the illicit drug industry,' I say.

'What are you going to do now?'

'I'm gonna go to art school. Then I'm gonna go be a ground-breaking international artist. I'm gonna travel the world, sipping coffee at small green coffee tables and painting beautiful pictures.'

Danny laughs. 'Can I come with you?'

'Sure, but you gotta bring your own art supplies.' Too much about me. I switch the conversation back to Danny. 'Was Samara the reason you were crying on the bridge?'

'You saw me crying on the bridge?'

'Just before those scooter boys crossed your path,' I say. 'I saw you. Big heavy tears you had to wipe away with the back of your hand. Were those tears for Samara?'

Danny smiles. 'You want the truth?' he asks.

'That's all I want tonight.'

But Danny doesn't say any more on this. He moves closer to the elephant sculpture. The great bronze creature seems puzzled as to why it's been turned upside down by the universe. Ears like throw rugs. Curled trunk. Mighty tusks almost touching the ground. Up is down. Down is up.

'It's called *The World Turns*,' Danny says. 'Kiwi guy did this. Cost the government a million dollars. I reckon ten million would still have been a bargain. This is the best piece of public art in Brisbane.'

He moves close to the upside-down elephant's right eye. Moonlight and council lamplights illuminate the boy from Hamilton Hill as he does a handstand at the base of the sculpture, resting his raised legs against the elephant's great stomach. 'People always see the upside-down elephant when they look at this sculpture,' he says, blood rushing to his head. 'But they always miss what the elephant is staring at with that upside-down right eye. The best way to see it is by seeing the world the way the elephant sees it.'

He flips his legs back down, clearly fit and athletic. 'Come have a look,' he says. I move to the sculpture, feet by the elephant's right tusk. 'Do a handstand,' Danny says.

'I can't just do a handstand,' I say.

'Sure you can. You do the handstand and I'll hold your legs up against our elephant friend here.'

'You better hold me up,' I say.

'Trust me,' he says. 'You gotta look right from the spot where the elephant is looking. You gotta become the elephant.'

'Become the elephant?' I repeat.

'*Beeeee* the elephant,' Danny says, like he's a Tibetan monk.

I place my hands in the bark mulch surrounding the sculpture. Close my eyes, kick my legs into the air and let them fall into Danny's arms. He gently rests my feet against the elephant's large central body. I open my eyes and see the world upside-down, dizzy for a moment with the perspective shift. The starry sky is now where the river should be and the river is where the sky should be. And that means Erica is in the sky when I'm like this. Upside-down buildings and upside-down bridges. And then I focus on what the bronze elephant has been staring at all this time through its wide-open right eye.

'A rat,' I say. A bronze sculpture of a rat.

Too much blood's rushing to my head, so I swing my legs back down to earth, where my feet belong. Catch my breath. Dust away the bark mulch pieces pressed into my palms.

'So, why's the elephant staring at a rat?' I ask.

'Well, I've asked myself that very question many times,' Danny says. 'One reading might be that the mighty elephant has gone to great lengths to get close to the rat. That is, a powerful and mighty creature has chosen to appreciate what is meek and unseen. These are the lengths it's willing to go to in order to see the world from the poor little rat's perspective. But then we must remember that this land around us is a place of rats. I got this friend from uni, Tess. First Nations woman. Her grandmother grew up around here. She said the real caretakers of this land are the big fat water rats that live on the edge of the river. Round here, she said, the rat doesn't have to hide in the shadows. Round here, the whole world turns just to get a glimpse of the rat. Now look closer at that little rat.' Danny hunches down. 'See how it's turning away from the elephant. Thing couldn't give a fuck about the elephant. So, round here, in this world, it's the rat who is powerful and mighty and it's the elephant who is meek and unseen. And suddenly the biggest and most eye-catching creature on the planet somehow becomes ...' Danny thinks on the word he's looking for.

I find it first. 'Invisible,' I say.

And the artist stared at Danny Collins for a full minute in the moonlight because she had never met someone who spoke about the power dynamics between elephants and rats and she wondered how the world might look to her now if she saw the strange boy from Hamilton Hill more frequently in it. They talked for hours that night, their backs on the soft grass that slopes up from the bronze elephant and rat. The artist flipped through Danny Collins's sketchbook, asking him where his images came from. Asking him about the things he put inside his images. The things he drew. The things he inferred. The things he felt. They spoke about their favourite artists. They spoke about pencil widths and the nibs of pens. They spoke about their city. They spoke about the Olympic Games coming to Brisbane.

Danny Collins said he couldn't wait for the Olympics because he couldn't wait to see how the city of Brisbane was presented to the world in the opening ceremony. He described his vision for the ceremony. There were dancers with pineapples for heads. There was a whole army of dancing hairdressers from Stefan salons. There were tributes to the Pancake Manor on Charlotte Street and there was an interpretive dance scene that involved five teenagers sucking on vape pens outside the Hungry Jack's in Queen Street Mall. King Wally Lewis was to enter the stadium riding a giant inflatable ibis. Then, just when the audience least expected it, there was going to be a harsh-truth section: scenes of mid-1800s farming settlers around Ipswich giving biscuits laced with arsenic to local Aboriginal people, and of the early-1900s Indigenous massacre at Bentinck Island in the Gulf of Carpentaria, and a musical number charting the rise and fall of the 1970s and 1980s Queensland Government and police corruption and all of its accompanying rampant underworld murder and violence, set to the sound of 'Staying Alive' by Redcliffe's favourite sons, the Bee Gees.

The artist said she hoped the opening ceremony would devote a segment to Brisbane's housing crisis. She saw a musical piece that told the story of a Brisbane girl raised in a junkyard city of cars, all set to the sound of 'Dreamworld' by Midnight Oil. The artist said she worried about what the Olympics would mean for all the people she knew sleeping rough. She was concerned they'd be driven out of the city. She pointed out that the Olympics would start in winter and all the warm and safe spots to sleep in would be off limits.

The artist spoke of how the city of Brisbane was a source of despair and joy for her. Despair for the tiny little moments of cruelty she saw daily. Joy for the kindness. The takeaway shop owners who set food aside for Brisbane's homeless. A homeless community that looks out for its own. People leaving blankets for others in secret storage spots. People sharing entry codes to private toilet blocks. People sharing Netflix passwords and Wi-Fi passwords and Spotify passwords and library cards and gym access tokens.

Danny and the artist spoke about their dreams and their futures and then they spoke about dreaming when you're awake and everybody else is asleep. And then the artist turned her head to a council lamppost by the river and thought about the relationship between light and electricity and her own heart. The lamp was fixed to a black pole that kinked across the riverside walkway the way a bedside lamp hangs over a nighttime reader. She wondered if the light from the lamppost was brighter than it was when she'd ambled along that walkway only a week before. She wondered if the very presence of Danny Collins had a connection to her vision. Would things shine brighter in his orbit? Would the stars shimmer for her more regularly? Would the moon offer her more light each night than the sun allowed?

*

We look to the stars. Backs on the grass.

Danny rolls on his side. Props his head up with his left hand. 'Hey, you still wanna know why I was crying on the bridge?' he asks.

'Yeah.'

He sits up. He's breaking fragments of a twig between his fingers. 'It's a bit messed up.'

'It is?' I sit up now, too. 'Well, now I really wanna know.'

He tosses a bit of a twig over his feet.

'Sometimes I go to the middle of that bridge and I look over the edge and I think about jumping off,' he says.

'Right,' I say, wondering where he's going with this.

'But I'm not doing that in a sad, death way,' he says. 'I'm doing that in an alive way.'

'An alive way?' I nod, trying my best to keep up.

'I don't think I'd ever jump, but sometimes I really think hard about it, and it terrifies me,' he says. 'And then it makes me feel alive. It makes me feel grateful. Because in that instant I feel like I've saved myself from certain death. I don't know what part of me wants to jump, I can't explain where it comes from, but it's like some weird part of me always wants to die. I think that's why I'm scared of heights. Like, have you ever been on one of those balconies in one of those high-rise apartments on the Gold Coast?'

'No,' I say. 'I live in a van.'

'Right,' he says. 'Sorry. Entitled dick.'

'You're entitled to be.'

'Those Gold Coast apartments have balconies as high as the clouds, but the railings on the balconies don't even go up past your belly button. You could trip over and that'd be it. Splat. I think some people get scared on those balconies because they are scared of the part of themselves that wants to die. For most of us it's among the few times in our lives when we come so close to so easily being able to end it all, and we're terrified by that voice in our heads screaming, "Don't jump, arsehole," and it's like, what sort of crazy fuck has to even say that to themselves? So, sometimes when I'm on that bridge I think all that stuff, and then those thoughts are like reminders of how fucking beautiful it all is. The thought of dying reminds me why I love it all so much. I look at the river and the buildings and the lights and the moon and the stars and the people going past and I say these same words: "You're so fucking lucky." Same dumb words every time. I just say it over and over and over in my head. You're so fucking lucky. You're so fucking lucky. And then, suddenly, it's thrilling. I'm so fucking alive and here. So alive and here that it makes me cry. And then I just let those tears come and it's ridiculous and embarrassing but it's beautiful, too, because it's true. I'm alive. I'm here. I'm so fucking lucky.'

Danny throws his twig away and turns to me.

'That's true, isn't it?' he asks. 'It really is beautiful, isn't it?'

'What?'

'All of it,' he says. 'Am I wrong about that?'

I lie back on the grass and look at the moon. Clouds are covering half of it in a ghost-white veil. 'Sometimes,' I say.

'We still telling the truth?' he asks.

'Sure.'

'Have you ever wanted to die?' Danny asks.

'Yeah,' I say, 'once.'

'When?'

'When Erica Finlay died,' I say.

'Because you loved her very much,' Danny suggests.

'I did,' I say. 'But it's more than that. I loved the woman she was helping me become. She was helping me be brave. She showed me how to be artful. How to see art everywhere. How to see the wonder. The wonder hidden inside life and the wonder hidden in me. I liked who I was around her. I think we all have these versions of ourselves inside us. These dream versions of ourselves. Sometimes we see them so clearly that we could convince ourselves that these people inside us actually exist. But then the world comes along and kills these people inside us. The world piles up on us and suffocates these people. It transforms them, sometimes without us even knowing. The world chops these people up. Disintegrates them. Makes them vanish. Never to be seen again.'

I turn my face to Danny. 'We still telling the truth, Danny Collins?'

'Nothing but.'

'You were talking about us being mirrors before,' I say. 'Can I tell you somethin' screwy?'

He nods.

'It's a bit messed up.'

'Well, now you really have to tell me.'

I turn my eyes back to the stars. 'I have this special mirror that I found in a council pickup,' I say. 'Sometimes when I look into this mirror, I see a woman who talks to me. She tells me things about my life and what I'm gonna do when I'm older. Sometimes she's in a red dress and she's lying on the grass just like this, staring up at the stars in all these exotic places across the world. And sometimes there's this handsome man lying beside her. This guy always walks into these moments and starts kissing her and he's always wearing this vintage brown suit—'

'Vintage brown suit?' Danny asks.

'Yeah, a vintage brown suit.'

Danny raises his eyebrows, nods his head.

'What?'

'Never mind,' he says. 'What's this woman's name?'

'Lola.'

'Lola,' Danny says, rolling the name around his mouth. 'What's she look like, this Lola?'

That's a good question.

'Well, she looks beautiful,' I say. 'She looks sophisticated. She looks tough and bright and strong. Most days. But then other days she looks hideous. Broken. Destroyed. Disintegrated.'

'I mean, what does her face look like?' Danny asks. 'Does she have a face like Sophia Loren's or Cate Blanchett's? Does she have a face like Beyoncé's or a face like a hatful of backsides?'

I think on this for a long moment. It's a good question. 'Well, I guess she has a face like mine more than anything else,' I say.

And those words are left to float in the summer air and then that air is filled with music. Danny turns his head towards the sound. The sound of piano keys drifting across Kurilpa Point.

'What is that?' he asks.

'That's Daisy,' I reply.

'Who's Daisy?'

'Daisy Gong. She's doing "My Heart Will Go On" again,' I say. 'Daisy only sings love songs. Preferably power ballads.'

We walk on to the Kurilpa Bridge, the steel and cable footbridge stretching across the river to Tank Street. It's lit up by blue lights and its structural masts rise up like pins in a pincushion, making the whole thing look like some alien spacecraft floating above our river. The bridge connects to a lofted walkway that bends around from the riverside path. Under the walkway is an upright piano that any member of the public is welcome to play. Nobody in Brisbane, however, plays this piano more frequently and with more gusto than Daisy Gong, who plays it almost every night when the city's gone to sleep, singing for an audience of possums, bats and water rats and the odd human pedestrian. Nobody knows how old Daisy is, but I think she's older than the piano she plays and the piano looks like it might still carry bloodstains caused by Billy the Kid in a Wild West saloon. Daisy was born in Shanghai and raised in Sydney and she lives today in the fourteen-storey Common Ground supportive housing complex on Hope Street, West End, a few minutes' walk from here. Rental prices for the apartments are based on a resident's income, which means people like Daisy Gong, who have about as much disposable income as the average Brisbane water rat, can actually afford to rent a place there.

Daisy spots us and smiles wide. 'Two moonstruck lovers,' she says between choruses. 'Strangers in the night.'

We laugh. I'm still carrying Danny's sketchbook and I rest it and my forearms on top of the piano. Danny's behind me, nodding his head to the unexpected music.

Daisy closes her eyes behind a pair of old reading glasses, her thin fingers floating across the keys. The song reaches its final notes and she tilts her head up to the moon as she plays. 'A full moon,' she says. 'That means lovers must dance.' And she deftly transitions from 'My Heart Will Go On' into 'Moon River', the one about drifters and dreams and fate and heading off to see the world.

The notes float around us.

'I think we have to dance,' Danny says.

'No, we really don't have to,' I say.

The notes soar all the way up to the summer moon.

'I think this is one of those occasions when you have to consider what people are gonna say about this moment,' Danny says, 'you know, a hundred years from now.'

'You waltz, my friends,' Daisy says, 'you waltz.'

'Workin' on it, Daisy,' Danny says. He turns back to me. 'C'mon, how bad is it gonna read a hundred years from now when they come to the bit where the sweet old woman is playing "Moon River" on the piano under the bridge and I ask you to dance with me and you turn me down?'

I consider that future as I stare at him, tapping my thumb on the top of the piano. The world is turning. Mistakes have been made. Mistakes will always be made. This cruel mistake of mine. This cruel mistake of me. And the brief correction of this night.

Danny holds out his right hand. 'Do you know how to waltz?' he asks, moonglow lighting his face.

But one day you will dance with a prince. She said that like she could see it.

His right hand out, left hand tucked behind his back, as though this is all formal, as though Daisy is playing in a grand ballroom in an English castle.

'No,' I say, 'never learned.'

He holds his hands up.

I reach out and hold them and his hands are soft and I hate that my hands could be cleaner – less dirt beneath the fingernails, fewer cracks from the summer sun.

'You mind if I lead?' he asks.

'No, I don't mind.'

'So, when you're ready, I'll start by stepping forward with my left foot and then you step back with your right foot,' he explains.

I nod.

'Then, from there, we're just a mirror,' he says.

'A mirror,' I say.

'Yeah,' he says. 'We're total opposites, but we're kind of exactly the same.'

'Opposites,' I say, 'but kinda the same.'

'You ready?'

'I'm ready.'

He steps forward with his left foot and I step back with my right, and he brings his right foot up to his left and I bring my left foot back to my right, and then he steps back with his right foot as I step forward with my left and he brings his left foot back to his right foot and I step forward with my right and now we're dancing. We're making box shapes beside Daisy Gong's piano and we're orbiting slowly towards the river's edge and I'm staring at his face as the world spins around me.

'Are you thinking about what happens when this waltz ends?' Danny asks.

'No, I'm just enjoying the moment,' I say. 'I just keep saying the same words inside my head.'

'What words?'

'He's so fucking lucky. He's so fucking lucky. He's so fucking lucky.'

He smiles. Left foot, right foot, turn. Right hand wrapped in his left hand. Daisy's perfect keys driving our steps.

'I think we should kiss when Daisy stops playing,' Danny says.

'Why do you think that?' I ask.

'It will be the perfect end to this part of your story,' he replies. 'People will love it, one hundred years from now. They'll talk about it for centuries. Imagine thinking back on this when you're eighty and knowing you did something as crazy as kissing me. How brave you were to do something so careless and romantic. Not caring about what happened next. Just caring about the moment. Just being alive and here.'

'You're so fucking lucky,' I whisper.

'I know,' Danny says.

'I haven't been so lucky,' I say.

'I know,' he says.

'I'll never be as lucky as you. That's just how it is.'

'I'm not so sure,' he says. 'What if your luck is about to change? What if you've had your share of shit? What if it's now time to collect your winnings? Right from this moment.'

'The world turns,' I whisper.

'What if every shit hand you were dealt was leading up to right here and now?'

'What if kissing you at the end of this dance is a spectacular mistake?' I ask.

'What if mistakes are meant to be made?' he replies. He gently raises his right arm to twirl me beneath it. Brings me back close to his chest. Close enough to know his breath and the beat of his heart. And then the music stops. Only a few notes short of a natural ending.

'Rain,' Daisy hollers, pointing at the sky. 'Heavy stuff.' She slaps the wooden lid of the piano down and the keys give one final low thrum. 'Sorry, show's over for now, moonlight lovers!' she announces. And she scampers into the dark beyond the Kurilpa Bridge, heading home.

The rain she warned us about takes no time to fall. Heavy and hard summer rain on our shoulders. But we stay in place. Our hands together, still in the formal waltz position. Bodies close. Bodies touching. Rain on his face. Rain wetting his hair. Rain wetting his lips. The lips he suggested I should kiss. One foolish kiss to end this part of the story. And I consider this possibility and I even see it happening in my head. I see him taking the lead. I see a kiss like a waltz. I see it as art. I see that kiss in a sketch in my head.

He leans forward and I lean back. I lean forward and he leans back. And we're a mirror. We are total opposites but exactly the same. I know he needs me to lead the kiss. Because that's what princes do. They let the girl lead. Girl leads, boy follows. But something stops me from leaning any further forward and I know it's my past. I know it's my mistake. We're not the same at all. We are opposites. And we always will be. I am not so fucking lucky. I am not so fucking lucky. I am not so fucking lucky. That's just how some of us are born. And the rain falls too hard upon us and I've let the moment go on too long, and he takes one step back that I do not follow.

His chest moves away from mine and he lets go of my hands. 'I really thought you were gonna do it for a minute there,' he says. 'Would've made a good story.' He smiles, wipes the rain from his face. 'I should go.'

'Yeah,' I say.

He has to talk louder in the rain. 'Which way you heading?' he asks.

I throw a thumb over my shoulder towards West End. 'I'm this way.'

He nods back to the city. 'I'm heading back over the bridge,' he says. Lifts his head to the sky. 'Hasn't rained this hard in months.'

I nod, wipe the rain from my face.

'I really like talking to you,' he says.

'I really like talkin' to you, Danny.'

'Do you wanna swap phone numbers or somethin'?' he asks. 'You know, in case we want to talk again.' He pulls an iPhone from the pocket of his jeans. 'What's your number?'

'I don't have a number.'

He slides the phone back into his pocket. 'Right,' he says. 'So how do I see you again?'

I shrug. 'I don't know,' I say. 'How did you see me that day on the corner?'

'I just looked up and you were there.'

'Well, maybe that's all you have to do,' I say. 'You can see me anytime, Danny. Just look up. And I'll be there.'

And the artist walked into the darkness beyond the Kurilpa Bridge. Legend has it that, in this very moment, the artist was struck by the vision of what would become one of her most iconic paintings, The Artist Embraced in a Passionate Kiss on a Bridge in the Rain, *famously featuring Danny Collins and the artist embraced in a passionate kiss, silver drops of rain splashing upon their shoulders. Thirty seconds later, she turned and saw Danny Collins pacing towards the Victoria Bridge.*

He, at that very moment, was asking himself what rare kind of dream he had wandered into when he'd walked through a sleeping city with the strange girl with no name. He wondered if there would be any taxis at the George Street cab rank because otherwise it was a long walk home to Hamilton Hill. Still, he thought, he was alive and here, and it was a walk he would welcome and a distance he might consider traversing on air. He was laughing to himself as he neared the very place where he'd said his first words to her and he couldn't believe he had been so brave. But he knew for certain that he'd said those words with a true heart, foolish and absurd as they seemed. He was so alive that he felt like sprinting through the hard rain. Felt like screaming to the sky that made the rain. And he was about to do both those things when he felt a finger tapping his right shoulder.

He stopped and turned to find the artist panting before him. She was spent and breathless from running in the rain. Confused, Danny Collins watched the artist take two deep breaths and gather her thoughts …

'Fuck it,' I say. 'I love you, too.' And I take two steps towards him and kiss his lips. And Danny Collins cups his hands around my ears and jumps from the bridge of reason – body and soul and lips – into a kiss with a girl with no name.

Never before have I felt so alive and here. He closes his eyes and I close mine and I see nothing but music. The notes of 'Moon River' popping in my head like exploding stars. And the only reason Danny opens his eyes again is because I've released him from this kiss.

'I'll be right here,' I say, rain smashing against my face now.

'When?' he asks.

'Tomorrow night,' I say. 'Every night. Any night you need me to be here.'

'Tomorrow night,' he says.

'Okay, tomorrow night,' I say. 'I'll be right here on the bridge.'

'What time?'

'This time. Right now. When the city has gone to sleep.'

'You'll be right here?' Danny Collins checks, pointing to the ground.

'I'll be right here, Danny,' I say. 'Just look up. I'll be right here.'

I turn away, start to walk back along the bridge. But walking's doing nothing to release the electricity trapped in my legs and in my heart and in my blood. So I do what I was born to do.

I run.

Things That
Go Bump
in the Night

Things That Go Bump in the Night

January 2024

Pen and ink on paper

There is often an overriding sense of distrust in the artist's work, especially when depicting her home city. Here, a simple road bridge extends into the all-seeing eye of the dead. She is, one suspects, speaking to the darkness inherent in any city, even one as bright as the capital of Australia's Sunshine State.

Soaking wet but I'm not cold. My blood's rushing too hard and fast through my arms and legs. I take the Riverside Drive walk home, the dark path that runs beneath Moreton Bay fig trees and sprawling gum trees, all the way to the back fence of Oz on Moon Street. Orange-tinted council park lights every thirty metres or so illuminating the summer rain driving hard in diagonal sheets. I pass the Parmalat milk factory with its giant milk vats and old steamy pipes and crates holding a thousand shrink-wrapped and empty two-litre milk containers. It's so good to be home. It's so good to be alive. I'm so fucking lucky to be here. What a glorious mistake I am.

I stand for a moment out of the rain beneath the Go Between Bridge, at the public exercise area where Brandon Box sometimes does his endless push-ups on an angled orange workout bar. A couple of floaters have set up two-person tents inside a sheltered garden belonging to Transurban Queensland, the folks who own and run the Go Between Bridge. They've tied a Woolworths trolley to a park bench with a yellow jockey strap and in the trolley is a blue heavy-duty hand trolley that floaters around here share when someone needs to load a heavy storage box into a car or wheel a carton of beer down to the barbecues at South Bank.

I walk on behind the Visy glass factory, with its rusting shipping containers coloured red, silver, blue and black. Two more small-tent, rough-sleeper homes beneath another Moreton

Bay fig, this one with a trunk the width of my van. Each tent has its own Woolworths trolley parked out front, and weather tarps stretching down diagonally from a rusting barbed-wire fence dotted with Wormald security signs to the leafy ground.

Another fifty or so metres along Riverside Drive I can see a body lying flat on the grass slope behind the rear wall of the Hanson concrete factory on Hockings Street, illuminated by a single orange council light. A few steps further on, I realise I'd recognise that mop of hair anywhere. Charlie. Big dumb drunk wanker has passed out in the rain again. Head and limbs at all the wrong angles for sleeping, like a crash test dummy that's just been shot through a car windshield. A silver wine bag by his side, its pouring corner sucked and twisted dry during the night. Charlie's regular weeknight bender blackout spot. The grass is soft and the breeze is usually cool here in summer. He wouldn't have been expecting it to rain.

I'm already quickening my pace when I see a man emerge from the darkness ahead. Black boots. Black pants. A grey hooded jumper, the hood pulled over his forehead. It looks like he's carrying a club in his hands. No, not a club, a cricket bat. As he walks slowly out of the night towards Charlie, something inside me makes me start to jog. Even though I feel like turning around and running back to the Victoria Bridge, back to the waltzing arms of Danny Collins, I also feel like running forward because there is something terrifying about this man. And there's not another person in sight. The city is asleep in the heavy rain.

Closer now, I see the hooded man kneel to inspect Charlie, his right arm propped on his cricket bat. I start to sprint and the man reaches a hand out to Charlie's face, gently slaps his cheek.

'Get away from him!' I scream through the slamming rain.

The man is startled and he turns to me and I'm close enough to see his face now. Can't see his eyes under the hood but can clock his big doorstop nose and his thin lips, closed tight.

'Get the fuck away from him, psycho!' I scream. And I stumble as I come to a rough stop and reach into my right boot for my filleting knife. Pull it out and raise it to the man in the hood, who still kneels over Charlie. 'You lay a finger on him, I swear I'll stick this in you,' I bark, bluffing my way through at least half of that declaration.

The man stands and looks at me for a moment. Chin like a garden spade. 'No, you won't,' he says. His voice is soft, barely audible in the rain.

'Yes, I will.'

'No, you won't. You're a good person.'

'Believe me. I'm not. I'm the worst person in the world.'

'I assure you, you're not the worst.'

My right hand shakes as I hold my knife in the air. A long moment of thinking in the rain. Then I summon the nerve to speak. 'Are you the man who clubbed Leon Rooney?'

One word from those lips beneath the hood. 'Yes.'

'Are you the man who clubbed Bill Moffitt?'

'Yes.'

'What the fuck is wrong with you? How could you just kill people like that?'

'I've been asking myself the same question,' he says. 'I think it's because I'm not human.'

'Not human? You look pretty human to me. What are you, then, if you're not human?'

'That's the thing,' he says. 'I'm not anything. I'm not anyone. I'm nothing. I don't feel a single human thing in this world. I'm not even sure I'm here right now.'

He turns his cricket bat in his hands. A Gray-Nicolls Twin Scoop. For a moment I see cricket-ball cherries across the bat's face, but then I realise those aren't cherries. They're bloodstains.

He looks back down at Charlie Mould, snoring heavily on the grass.

'You can't club him,' I shout. 'You hear me? Not him, all right. He's my best friend. You want to know how to be human, then you could do worse than learning from Charlie Mould. He's a good one. He's a real good one.'

He turns to me then turns back to Charlie. It's as though he's weighing up his options. Tightens his grip on the bat's handle.

'Hey, listen,' I say. 'Look at me. Look at me.'

He looks up as I place my knife back in my boot.

'You need to club someone tonight, then let it be me,' I say, raising my hands in the air. 'I deserve it more than him. I used to sell hard drugs to people who were broken and desperate. I'm currently ratting to police on the family of drug dealers who helped me survive my teens. Got no honour whatsoever. Got no loyalty. Got no manners. Got no family. Got nothin'.'

The man in the hood shifts his feet and takes one step towards me.

'But,' I say. 'But, but, but ... I'd really prefer that you didn't club me because something beautiful just happened to me tonight.'

'What happened to you?' the man in the hood asks. It sounds like everything he says is being said through a sock.

'I fell in love,' I reply.

'How'd you do that?' the hooded man asks.

'What? How do you fall in love?' I see his chin moving up and down beneath his hood. 'Well, I don't think falling in love is something that can be done,' I say. 'It's not like oilin' the deck or payin' the gas bill. Falling in love is more like a rainbow coming out after a big storm. It just happens. You look up one day, and it's just ... *there*.'

'What does it feel like?' the man in the hood asks.

I breathe. Wipe the rain off my face with my left hand. 'Well, it feels like floating down a river, except that river is on the moon. Yeah, that's what it feels like. Feels like moon-river swimming.'

'Moon-river swimming,' the man repeats.

And the rain falls hard on the man in the hood. He holds his right palm out and heavy raindrops pool in the centre of it.

'You feel that?' I ask, holding my right palm out too.

He says nothing, stares at the rain on his palm as though he's never seen the stuff before, never felt it. Then he turns from me under the lamplight and walks back into the night, disappearing beneath the dark canopy of a row of old fig trees.

I exhale. Let my shoulders collapse. Let my pulse rate drop. What a fraud I am. Like some frill-necked lizard hissing at a red-bellied black snake. All bluff.

I rush over to Charlie. Stand over him in the rain. Kick him in the ribs. Not hard enough to bruise. Just hard enough to wake him. 'Charlie,' I say.

His head wobbles momentarily. Red wine–coloured drool spills from his lips.

I kick him again. 'Time to go home, arsehole.'

*

Morning now. Rain still falls. Roslyn knew the rain was coming so she built a tarp shelter in the corner of the yard for the residents of Oz to sit beneath while we wait for the kettle to boil on the small gas stovetop we share when the communal firepit is out of action. Me, Roslyn, June, Sully and Charlie sitting in a circle there. Charlie wears the Rip Curl shirt and X-Men boxer shorts that I helped him change into when we got home last night. He spoons from a tin of Black & Gold baked beans.

'He kneeled over you and touched your face, Charlie,' I say.

'Fuck me,' Charlie says. 'I nearly got whacked by a serial killer.'

'You need to go tell that cop of yours about what you saw,' Ros says to me.

'I'm meeting him this morning,' I say.

'Shame he didn't club me,' Charlie says. 'I coulda been famous.'

'It scared the shit outta me, Charlie,' I bark. 'It wasn't fuckin' funny. Some sadistic psycho freak creepin' round our neighbourhood with a cricket bat. You catchin' your fuckin' ugly sleep by the river. You can't do that shit, Charlie. Ya can't be passing out in the street like that anymore.'

Charlie looks up at me. Clocks the fear in my voice. Not fear for some weirdo creep who thinks he ain't human. Fear that I might lose my friend. Fear that I am losing my friend.

'I'm sorry,' he says.

'When was the last day you spent dry?' I ask.

He shakes his head. Angered by the question. Digs the spoon harder into the tin. 'What do you care when I was dry?' he asks.

'I care a lot. And that's a lot more than you deserve.'

'You find your prince from Hamilton Hill last night?'

No use in me answering that. Keep quiet. Let it pass. Let Charlie steam.

'So you met him?' Charlie asks. 'You two gonna meet again?'

'We might. You got a problem with that?'

'Yes, I do, in fact,' Charlie says, stuffing his mouth with a spoonful of beans.

'What's your problem, Chucky? You all bummed that I don't wanna spend the rest of my life with a drunk waster who's gonna get himself killed sleeping out in the streets?'

'No, that's not my problem.'

'So, what's your problem, Charlie?'

'My problem is that you think I'm a mistake.'

'What are you talking about?'

Charlie points around the circle. 'You think we're all mistakes,' he says. 'You think this is the worst kind of hell here, just being here with us. You think this is the worst fate a girl could ever find herself living in. You say it all the time. You think your whole life is a mistake and you think we're mistakes, too. And you think you're some kind of princess not deserving of all this. That's why you're gonna latch on to the first ticket outta Oz you can get. Enter Richie Rich from Hamilton Hill.'

'Grow up, Charlie,' I say. 'You're a fuckin' child.'

'Yes, I am,' he says. 'Now watch me toss my food!' And he stands and throws his tin of beans at the corrugated-iron wall of the Tinman's panel-beating shed. A loud bang echoes through the rain.

'That was useful,' I say.

'Do you have to litter all the time, Charlie?' June asks.

'Sorry, June, you got guests coming over or somethin'?'

'We all gotta live here, Charlie,' June says.

'Well, good news, June,' he says. 'Looks like you won't have to no more. Spoke to Evelyn yesterday afternoon. The Tinman's sold the shed.'

'What?' I exclaim.

Charlie turns to me. 'Deal's been done,' he says. 'Tinman sold up. He fucked us. Turns out the Italian Olympic volleyball team need this place more than we do.'

I feel sick in my stomach and that's not just because I'm hungry and haven't had my beans yet. 'Is he for real?' I ask Ros. 'He finally sold up?'

Ros nods mournfully. 'I'm sorry, sweetheart. State government's buying up places right along the river. I didn't know how to tell you guys. It's not the Tinman doin' it. It's his kids. They're sorting out his shit before the cancer finally does him in. It was an offer too good to refuse.'

'When do they want us out?'

'We all got a week to find someplace else to live,' Ros says.

June drops her head. Sully rests a comforting hand on his mum's shoulder. Charlie storms out of the yard, leaving the gate unlocked.

Ros calls after him, 'Hey, come back and wash your plate, ya spoilt prick.'

*

An hour later.

'Thanks for coming in,' says Detective Topping, his hands resting on a large yellow envelope.

'Wouldn't miss it, Geoff,' I say.

I nod at a large, muscular man with a flattop haircut sitting next to Topping in a white business shirt and a diagonally striped tie in the colours of the French flag and the Sydney Roosters rugby league club that Esther Inthehole follows.

'How are you?' Topping asks.

'Not bad,' I say, 'considering I had a rainy encounter with that psycho killer who's been knockin' off homies in the street.'

'You saw him?'

'Yep. He was walking up Riverside Drive with his cricket bat. Bloke looked like Steve Smith going out to face. We spoke for five minutes.' I turn to the man with the striped tie. 'He was gonna club my friend, Charlie, but I talked him out of it.'

'How did you do that?' he asks.

'I told him how I'd just fallen in love,' I reply. 'I think he found it sweet.'

'You fell in love last night?' Topping asks.

I have to laugh about it myself. So hard to believe. 'Yeah,' I reply, shaking my head, 'fell straight into the big gooey stuff. Like a big ball of cheddar cheese. Plop!'

Topping grins. 'They're gonna need a statement downstairs.'

'Yeah, no dramas, Detective Geoff. You know how much I like to help the boys in blue.' I wink at the man with the flattop haircut. Turn my head to the photo of Felicia and Celine and their koalas on the corkboard.

'How are the girls?' I ask.

Topping smiles, warmly. 'They're good, thank you for asking.'

I'm wondering why his hands are resting on that yellow envelope.

He pulls his chair closer to his desk, squares up the envelope, clears his throat.

I study the eyes of the other man. Not as warm as Topping. In fact, he seems burdened by something. More than likely, I figure, whatever's in the envelope.

'This is Detective Sergeant Cameron Millar from the Western Australia Police Force,' Topping says. 'Cameron flew into Brisbane from Perth yesterday because he wanted to meet you in person.'

There's a thick manila folder of papers resting under Millar's right elbow.

'Bent nose,' I say.

'Excuse me?' Millar replies.

'Cameron means "bent nose".'

The officer chuckles. Grips his nose, self-consciously confirming its straightness. 'It's real nice to meet you in person, I gotta say. There's a whole lotta people back home who can't wait to meet you, too. We've been looking for you for a very long time now.'

'How long's a very long time?' I ask.

'About eighteen years,' Millar replies. 'You might not realise it yet, but you're a very special woman.'

'What makes me so special?' I ask.

Millar smiles. 'Your story,' he says.

Play it cool. One wily girl and two wily cops. No need to rush this.

'I hear you're quite the gifted artist,' Millar says.

This makes me smile at Topping. 'You told him I was a gifted artist, Geoff?'

He nods. 'I just told Officer Millar how privileged I felt when you showed me a few of your sketches after our last chat.'

'I did a drawing of you that same night,' I say. 'I gave you the head of a bear in the drawing.'

'Why a bear?'

'Because you're strong but kinda gentle and you scare me just a little bit.'

Brief laugh from Topping.

I look at the photo of Felicia and Celine. 'And because you'd do anything to protect your cubs,' I say.

He nods proudly. 'You think it will make the exhibition?' he asks.

'What exhibition?'

'Your exhibition in the New York Met?'

I smile again at this. He remembered.

Topping turns to Millar to explain. 'We were talking about how one day there is going to be an exhibition of her work in the Metropolitan Museum of Art in New York.'

'I see,' Millar says.

'There'll be tour groups in the gallery exploring her life and work,' Topping says.

Millar turns to me, a puzzled look upon his face.

'I find it motivating to consider what all those people are going to one day make of my life choices,' I say. 'It reminds me to apply a strong sense of significance to everything I do.'

Millar nods. 'I think this day might prove to be very significant for you,' he says.

I shrug. 'We'll see.'

A shadow falling across Millar's face now. Topping holds up the yellow envelope. There's a ball of fuzz inside my brain.

'Officer Millar here works closely with the Western Australian branch of the National Missing Persons Coordination Centre,' Topping says. 'We ran your bloodwork through DNA data systems of every state and territory. We found a match in the WA sample database.'

A ball of lead inside my belly. I'm not supposed to be here in this room.

'Officer Millar and his team have since put together significant documentation that I have seen and verified.'

Millar's fingers tapping on his thick folder of papers. I'm not supposed to be talking across this table to these serious men. This has all been a terrible mistake.

'Who am I?' I ask.

Topping nods, cups his hands together silently. Sits up in his chair. 'You told me when we first met that you were gonna be famous some day,' he says.

I laugh this off. Just my artsy-fartsy dreams. Say it out loud enough times then the universe might hear me and decide to make my dreams come true.

'Did you really mean that?' he asks.

'I guess so.'

'Do you really want that?'

'Want what?'

'To be famous?'

'I don't know,' I say. 'I mean I just want to make an impact on the world. Making an impact on the world sometimes means becoming famous, too.'

'What if I told you that you were already famous?' Topping says. 'What if I told you there was a brief time, about eighteen years ago, when you were the only person the people of Western Australia were talking about?'

Sickness. Bellyache. Black tar turning in the pit of my stomach. 'What the fuck are you talking about?'

'I'm talking about your name,' he says. 'I'm talking about who you are. Where you came from. Why Erica Finlay couldn't tell you who you are.'

I turn my head to the door of the office. It's only about four metres from my chair. I should run. I never should have stopped running.

'There are things you need to hear,' Topping says. 'But I'm not one hundred per cent certain that it is best for you to hear these things entirely from me.'

'Well, who else is gonna tell me these things?'

Topping hears the question, brings a closed fist to his lips, nods his understanding. 'Can I show you something?' he asks.

'That depends on what you want to show me,' I reply.

'I want to show you a photograph of someone we've located in Perth. This person is more than willing to fly here to meet you in the coming days. She wants to see you in person. In fact, she's been waiting all her life to meet you. And I'd really like you to meet her if you're up for it. I think you will understand everything when I show you the photograph. Can I show you the photograph?'

I look at the yellow envelope in Topping's hands. Look at his daughters holding those koalas with such care.

'Can I show you?' he asks again.

I nod twice. Pull my chair closer to the desk.

Topping slides an A4-size photograph across the table. It's a paper printout of a simple selfie. A girl with hair like mine. Smiling. Dimple in her left cheek. Older than me. Prettier than me. She wears a brown jacket over a white shirt, sleeves rolled up to her elbows. This is the information. This is the backstory, otherwise known as the truth.

'So, who's that?' I ask. But I don't really need to ask. The girl's face gives me all the answers I need. And I already want to dissolve. I already want to run. Run to the Victoria Bridge and dive into the Brisbane River and swim to the origins of that muddy brown snake. And live down there with Erica Finlay and her new best friends, the Queensland lungfish.

Topping, soft and tender and direct, bearer of truth and sleepy koalas. Bear of a man. Protective of his cubs. 'She's your sister,' he says. 'Would you like me to tell you her name?'

I stare deep into the image in my hands. Bring it close to my eyes, almost close enough for me to brush my eyelashes against the photograph.

'Yes, please.'

'Her name is Phoebe Gould,' Topping says. 'Phoebe is the woman who wants to tell you who you really are. She's asked to be the one who tells you everything. She's convinced the story will be easier to … *digest* … if it comes from her. We tend to agree,' he continues, 'but we're gonna play it how you wanna play it.'

'It's that bad, huh?' I ask.

Millar leans forward at the desk. 'It will be a difficult story for you to hear,' he says.

'I can handle difficult.'

'Maybe difficult isn't the right word,' Millar says.

'What's a better word for it, Cameron?' I ask. 'Traumatising? Brutal? Impossible? Unbelievable? If it's any of those, don't sweat it. I can swallow any of those.'

He nods. Tucks his right thumb inside his fist and squeezes it three times.

'Sad,' Topping says. 'Sad is the word for it.'

'You must see a bit of it.'

'What?'

'Sad.'

'Yeah,' he says. 'I see a bit of it. Too much.'

'I'm sorry to add to the pile.'

He shakes his head. 'I'm sorry you'll have to hear such a sad story.'

'How sad is it?'

'Might be the saddest story I've ever heard. That's why I'm not sure you should hear it from us.'

We sit in silence for a moment. Millar taps a pen against the desktop.

Then Topping leans forward. 'Listen, why don't you think about it for a moment,' he says. 'I'm happy to tell you more right now. Or, with your permission, we could facilitate this meeting for you both. You could work through the story together.'

I say nothing. Just stare at the image in the photograph. Stare at her eyes. Gould. Phoebe Gould. 'Phoebe is a beautiful name,' I say. 'Phoebe means "radiant". Phoebe means "light".'

I bring the image close to my eyes again. Observe how her ears stick out like mine. Note the way the fingers of her left hand grip the edge of her jacket. No speculation, just facts. The facts of her face. Like staring into a mirror.

Topping leans in close. 'Please understand, there will be no expectations of you whatsoever,' he says. 'She will ask nothing of you. You won't have to say a word to her if you don't feel comfortable.'

Dizzy now. Spinning ceiling. Sinking floor. And I can't see Phoebe's face anymore because I'm crying. I sit like that for thirty seconds, staring at the girl in the photograph. Then I slide the image back across the desk. 'It means "peace",' I say.

Topping puts his right hand to his chin. 'I'm sorry, what means "peace"?'

'Your name,' I say. 'Geoff. I like to look up the meanings behind names. I know the meaning for almost any half-popular name you could throw at me. But I didn't know yours, Geoff. Then I was on the computer at the State Library the other day. I looked it up. Your name means "peace".'

Topping raises his eyebrows, nods.

'I thought that was just right for a man like you, Geoff,' I say. 'You help people solve things. You find out who committed a crime and you bring them to justice and that comforts the victims. You deliver answers for people. You bring them peace.'

A brief smile from Topping. 'That's nice to know,' he says.

I take a moment to collect myself. Two deep breaths. Wipe my wet eyes with shaking fingers. One more deep breath. Phoebe means 'radiant'. Phoebe means 'light'.

'I want to hear it from her,' I say.

*

Two hours later and I'm standing in the doorway of a kitchen in an apartment in Quay Street, in the Brisbane CBD, backpack over my shoulders, thinking about the waltz I shared with Danny Collins, as Brandon Box sinks his right boot into the stomach of a handsome, muscle-bound Italian man named Julian Rossi. I hear the sweetness of 'Moon River' in my head, but all I can see is the violence of Brandon Box. Julian used to be a friend of Brandon's. Not no more.

'Ouch!' Brandon shouts as Julian brings his knees to his chest. 'Hey, Julian, you like Batman?'

Julian is too dazed and groggy to respond. He has immaculately groomed facial hair. Black lines running from his earlobes to his jaw, forming a glorious fountain of stubble that explodes across his chin and bottom lip.

White kitchen. White leather lounge. Red and blue vases and green ferns. Julian has a framed Picasso print on the wall of the living room that runs off the kitchen. *The Weeping Woman*. The woman in the painting wearing the hat with the blue flower and crying her eyes out might well represent all the grieving mothers of the bloody Spanish Civil War. She might also represent Julian's mum.

'You a fan of the Caped Crusader?' Brandon continues. 'I am.' He stands over Julian, elbows out in a superhero stance, fists pressed against his pelvic bones. 'I love anything to do with Batman. I've even been watchin' the old *Batman* TV series from the 1960s. You can stream every episode on Apple TV. Whenever Batman clobbers someone, all these funny words come flyin' out the screen.'

Brandon drives his closed right fist across Julian's left cheekbone. 'Ker-blam!' he hollers. Another boot to Julian's stomach. 'Kapow!' he screams. Then he locks Julian's head under his right armpit. I instinctively pat the pocket of my jeans, running my fingers over Topping's phone, as though somehow it might protect me from this violence, fourteen floors up in a city residential tower.

'I'm addicted to that fuckin' show now,' Brandon says. 'But the funny thing is, I'm not even watching it for Batman anymore. I'm watching it for the bad guys. The Joker. The Riddler. The Penguin. Total mad cunts. You should see the Penguin scrap in this show, Julian. He's a crafty fucker.'

Brandon drags Julian into the kitchen's marble-tiled cooking space. 'The Penguin will use anything to clobber Batman with.' He opens a cupboard door by the kitchen sink. Finds a stove pot and bangs it on the back of Julian's head. 'Donngggg!' he hollers. And his deranged belly laughs fill the kitchen.

Then he recklessly throws the stove pot across the room and it smashes into a stack of unwashed dinner plates. He opens three drawers next to the kitchen sink and finds a wooden rolling pin, which he cracks across Julian's shoulder blades. 'Snapppp!' he sings.

Brandon lifts Julian's head and talks into his ears. 'Tell me where it is, fuckface.'

'I can't,' Julian says. 'It's Barlow, man. Barrrrlow! *Pleeease*, bro. He'll fuckin' do me, Bran.'

'Well, that's what happens, Julian, when little kittens start rollin' around with lions,' Brandon says. 'You start fixin' deals behind my mum's back after everything she's done for you? You start makin' new friends when we're the best friends you ever had? You fuckin' hurt me, Jules. Worse than that, you went and hurt my mum.' He reaches across the kitchen benchtop and rips the toaster cable from the wall.

I close my eyes and think of Danny Collins standing in the middle of the Victoria Bridge. See him smiling. That's the future. 'Tomorrow night,' he said. Tomorrow night is tonight. I will see him again tonight in the flesh.

I keep thinking about the first words he ever said to me. Those words will seem preposterous to someone writing the story of my life a hundred years from now. *I love you*, he said. *Fuck it*, I said back to him, *I love you, too*. Because that's what an artist would have said. A great artist would have chosen romance like that. A great artist would have chosen danger. *I love you*. The most dangerous words in the world.

I open my eyes again. Brandon swings the toaster at Julian's bloodied face. 'Kaboom!' he screams in triumph. He staggers for a moment above Julian then grips him by his buttoned navy-blue silk shirt and pulls him off the ground.

'I'm not gonna ask again,' Brandon whispers.

Julian hangs limply in Brandon's grip. 'Pantry,' Julian says. Breathless and spent. Blood spilling from his mouth. 'The potato sack.'

Brandon drops Julian hard on the kitchen floor and goes to the pantry door in the corner of the kitchen. Kneels in the pantry. I see him tossing brushed potatoes over his shoulder. Three or four of them land on Julian.

'Pass me your backpack,' he says.

It takes me a moment to realise he's talking to me. I slip off my Adidas bag and toss it to Brandon. He stands up and hands the closed backpack to me as he rushes towards Julian's apartment door. 'Don't open that bag,' he says.

*

Driving through hard rain in the city now in Brandon's Nissan. I haven't said a word to him since we left Julian's house. He tears open an energy bar with his teeth, his right hand still on the wheel. Takes two large bites. Offers the half-eaten bar to me.

'No, thanks.'

He finishes the bar and takes a blast from a bottle of fluorescent blue Powerade. Burps twice.

'Who's Barlow?' I ask.

He flashes a look at me. Throws his Powerade onto the back seat. 'The fuck you care?'

I shrug. 'If I gotta spend so much time with you, I might as well learn a thing or two about what the fuck it is you do.'

Brandon shakes his head, rolls his eyes. 'You know Zeus?'

'Yes.'

'You know Shiva?'

'Yes.'

'Barlow's one rung above those motherfuckers,' Brandon says. 'Most motherfuckers suck Mum's dick. Aiden Barlow's the only motherfucker Mum kneels down for.'

I nod. 'Small but fiery,' I say.

'Huh?'

'Aiden. It means "small but fiery".'

Brandon laughs to himself. 'Well, he's one of those things.'

Then he slams the accelerator and we speed up St Paul's Terrace, towards Spring Hill. Take a right into Parish Street and stop outside an assisted-housing block called Ashton House. This is where my former Oz neighbours, Serge and Samantha, found a home. Finally, a room with a roof and electricity and running water. Because they were about to have a baby. Because they were about to raise a family.

'Why're we stopping here?' I ask.

'Why else would I be stopping here?' Brandon replies, then gets out and slams the door shut.

I catch up with him as he pads towards the pale green front door. The lawn hasn't been mowed for months. Grass up to our kneecaps.

'But nobody here is usin',' I say.

Brandon scoffs. 'How long's it been since you seen Serge?' he asks.

'Not Serge,' I say. 'No. He doesn't use.'

'When will you ever wake up and see the truth about the animals you call friends? He's in for three grand.'

'He's about to be a dad.'

'No, he's not.' Brandon seems almost gleeful to break the news to me. 'Them junkie ovens don't bake buns too good.'

I stop on the spot while Brandon enters the shared hallway, knocks aggressively on Serge's door.

I snap back to reality and run after him. 'You sold gear to Serge Martin? You're fucking sick.'

'Hey, who am I to turn away a needy customer?' Brandon asks. 'Poor guy's girl takes off to Sydney and then he comes to Uncle Brandon chasin' a taste.'

This man leaves me breathless. This man is not human. He belongs with that man in the hood holding the cricket bat.

'Please don't hurt him, Brandon,' I plead.

Brandon chuckles. Nobody coming to the door.

'He's gentle,' I say. 'He's a good man. He lived for nothin' in his life but Sammy.'

'He's not a good man,' Brandon says. 'Good men pay their debts.'

He knocks again, harder this time. Slow footsteps inside the room. A figure moving closer to the door. A soft and broken voice. 'Who is it?' Serge calls.

'It's Elvis Presley,' Brandon says. 'I been a so lonely, Serge. You ain't been round to see me.'

A long silence behind the door. 'I'm sorry, Brandon. I had a few emergencies come up.'

'Open the door, Serge,' Brandon says.

'Please go easy with him,' I whisper.

Serge keeps making excuses. 'I'll have that cash soon. I just—'

'Open the door, Serge,' Brandon repeats, taking a step back and stretching his thigh muscles by pulling his calves up towards his backside.

Serge rambles on. 'I never expected things to blow out like they—'

The door flies open, Brandon's powerful right leg breaking through the flimsy wood where the door latches on to its lock.

'Brandon!' I scream.

Serge lands on his backside and Brandon pushes the front door wide and invades his home like the tyrant lizard he is. No grace. All claws and teeth and an invisible tail that could crush a man's skull like a walnut.

'Brandon, wait!' I yell.

Serge starts pushing himself backwards across his unit's exposed and unvarnished timber floorboards, scrambling for safety.

'Now why didn't you open the door, Serge?' Brandon asks.

Serge reverses into a corner of his living room, between a cheap flat-screen TV and a bookshelf that holds only four books and a couple of vinyl records. He's so gaunt, so flimsy. Flimsy as this flophouse. Thinner than when I last saw him. Yellower in the face, too. Xanthous. He wears only a tee and old and frayed Stubbies shorts, and I can see pink and purple bruising on the insides of his arms. The place smells like sewage.

'Why you makin' things so hard on yourself?' Brandon asks, coming across like a concerned schoolteacher admonishing a schoolboy who's brought bubble gum into class. 'It's all very simple. You kindly hand me the three grand you owe Mum and I'll kindly refrain from stomping your face in.'

'I'm sorry, Brandon,' Serge says, 'I don't have it.'

'Wrong answer, Serge,' hollers Brandon. And he drives a large and heavy black steel-cap labourer's boot into Serge's shins.

Serge howls in pain and pulls his legs in, the same way I see huntsman spiders shrink into themselves when Ros is chasing them from the food-prep table in Oz. A ball of a man in the corner of the room. Broken and begging for understanding.

'I'm sorry,' he says. Looks to me. 'Hey, sis, you tell him I'm good for it. I just lost me hours at the butcher's shop, that's all. I'm gonna straighten up and get me job back.'

But shame fills Serge's face when he looks at me and that makes me look away and that's when he starts weeping hard. 'I'm sorry,' he says. And I know he's saying sorry to me more than to Brandon. And then he weeps more, head to the floor, squirming, aching, his left hand pressing on the floor, like he's doing a push-up. Like he wants to reach through the floor. Reach through and find the thing that he lost. The baby, maybe. The future. Sammy. The best version of himself, which he had a glimpse of. All too briefly. Or maybe for too long.

'Stop it, Brandon,' I shout. 'He's got nothin' to give you. You shouldn't have been sellin' to him in the first place. You knew he wasn't good for it.'

Brandon drives four more kicks into Serge's bare legs, timing his impact with his words.

'Where.' *Crack.* 'Is.' *Crack.* 'Our.' *Crack.* 'Money?' *Crack.*

Serge reels in pain and fear. 'Noooooooo,' he screams through tears.

Brandon steps back for a moment and slaps his cheeks with excitement. Waking himself up. A boxer in the corner with his trainer after the round-one bell. Bounces in a circle. 'Woooo,' he hollers. Thrilled by the tension. Buzzed by the power. Breathing air hard through his nose. Sharp sniffs. 'Woooo, woooo,' he repeats. 'Simple evolution, Serge. Survival of the fittest. You're weak. You give in to temptation. I give in to nothing. That makes me strong.'

Brandon stalks closer to Serge in the corner and his twitchy and busy right boot readies itself for another kick. And then I throw myself over Serge's shaking body, and now it's my shins that take the pain of the next blow. The impact sends a flash of white shock through my brain and I kick out in Brandon's direction. 'Fuckin' stop it, you monster,' I scream. There's spit coming from my bottom lip. I'm rabid. I'm a wolf. I'm a she-bear. 'That's enough!' I shelter Serge with my left arm and point at my chest with my right forefinger. 'I will square it,' I yell, so loud that my voice breaks. 'I'll square it, you hear me, you fuckin' lizard. Flo can take it out of my pay.'

Then Serge Martin, a weeping mess, wraps his arms around me like he's just a boy. A scared boy who doesn't know why the world turned so far upside down. He's shaking. I can feel his sweat. Can feel his fear. Tears running down the face nestled into my neck. 'I'm so sorry,' he rambles. 'So sorry. So sorry. So sorry.'

Brandon takes a step back, assesses the sight of me and Serge in this tragic corner of this tragic living room. 'Look at you,' he says. 'Still thinkin' these filthy animals deserve your love.'

Then I see a trickle of water running in a straight line along a wooden floorboard beneath my legs and realise my arse is wet with something. My nose tells me what it is. A pool of Serge's fear-sprung piss forms around us and I can't remember seeing something more bereft of hope.

Above me, Brandon begins to laugh. So hard that it hurts his ribs and he keels over with his elbows pressing his belly, and now all I see is the tyrannosaurus. He's not laughing. He's roaring. Just like I remember him roaring by the river when we were kids. *Roar.* The tyrant lizard. *Roar. Roar. Roar.*

Serge's voice in my ear. 'I'm sorry,' he says again, 'I'm sorry.' And I rest my hand on his arm that holds me tight, and it's only now I realise he's not wearing his magic green cardigan.

*

Sketch this moment in my mind. The artist and the monster, driving south down Hardgrave Road, West End. Pen and ink on paper in my head. Power lines hanging across the street. A blue corrugated-tin roof. White picket fences. A house with two red Chinese lanterns flanking the front door. A laser tattoo removal shop. Telstra phone box. Bus stop with a bench wide enough for four humans to sit on. Lefkas Taverna, the Greek food place at the end of the road. Caravanserai, the Turkish restaurant. Left into Dornoch Terrace.

'You smell like Serge's piss,' Brandon says.

I say nothing. Just stare out the side window.

A bay of cycles for hire. The old brick Highgate Hill estate called Toonarbin, with a front bay window like the ones I saw at Danny Collins's house on Hamilton Hill. A red postbox. A public park and a blue gazebo, where I could talk with Danny Collins about the merits of Barbecue Shapes and Pre-Raphaelite artistic discontent.

I look into the car's side mirror. Think I see Detective Geoff Topping's blue Honda CR-V, two cars behind us. Hope he's following me. Feel safer beside the monster when Geoff's following me. Tap my fingers on Geoff's iPhone in my pocket. Did he hear all that business with Julian? Did he hear all that carnage with Serge?

I sketch Brandon Box's Nissan in my head, pulling up at a parking space directly in front of the Torbreck apartment complex. Brandon switches the ignition off. I follow him into the foyer. Flo will meet us at his apartment. She says she wants me to wait there. She has my weekly wages.

We go up in the boxy lift. Down a hall and into Brandon's apartment. I drop my backpack on the carpet by the front door. Brandon takes a tall glass tumbler from a high kitchen cupboard. Fills the glass with tap water. Glugs it down without pausing for breath. 'Water?' he offers, holding out the glass.

I shake my head.

'You can use my shower if you want,' he says. 'I can find you a T-shirt or somethin' to change into.'

'I'll shower at The Well,' I say.

'You're just gonna stand there smellin' of piss?' he asks.

'When's Flo getting here?'

'She's on her way,' he says.

I go over to Brandon's dining table. Pull a chair out.

'You're not sitting there,' he says. 'Not with all that junkie piss on your arse.'

I push the chair back in and lean against the white living room wall. Brandon starts chopping bananas and pears on a red plastic cutting board with a small stainless steel Füri knife. Scrapes the chopped fruit into his blender. Spoons in a series of cream-coloured powders from his ice cream tubs. Tops the mixture up with a tumbler of water. The blender cranks into violent motion and Flo's only son lets the machine rattle on loudly for longer than he needs to. Then he switches it off and pours his muscle-building mixture into the tumbler and glugs the whole drink down in thirty unbroken seconds of zealous swallowing and gulping.

He burps loudly and looks at me like he's expecting me to pin a ribbon above his heart for selfless service to body sculpting. Burps again.

Then his mobile phone buzzes on the kitchen bench. He answers as he rinses the tumbler. 'Yeah, we're here. Yeah, she's with me.' Looks up at me. Listens intently. Eyes drilling into me now. 'I understand,' he says.

Something grave across his face. Something dark. Not shock. Think it might be hurt. Feels like someone's telling him about a loved one who just died. He drops his head. Turns round to face his oven. Leans a hand on its rail. Whispering. 'Yeah, I won't fuckin' do anything, all right.'

He taps the phone with his thumb and swings back round, slams it on the kitchen bench. Makes fists with his hands and presses them hard on the kitchen benchtop as he takes long, deliberate breaths, in and out.

At last, he looks up at me, still leaning against the wall.

'Take your shirt off,' he says.

'Excuse me?'

'Take your shirt off.'

He comes around the kitchen bench and into the living room.

'What did you say to me?' I ask as I move off the wall and seek refuge behind the glass-topped IKEA table.

'Take. Your. Fucking. Shirt. Off. Now,' Brandon spits.

'What the fuck are you talking about, Brandon?'

We start to circle the table, pushing dining chairs in to clear the way.

'You rat cunt,' he says. 'Take that fuckin' shirt off now or I'll fuckin' rip it from you.'

'Have you gone insane?' I ask.

He bangs his fist on the glass tabletop. 'Detective Sergeant Geoff Topping, you loopy fuckin' bitch,' he says. And he circles the table again as I circle it too. Monster and girl. Shark and goldfish. 'Husband to wife Kate Topping. Father to two daughters. Felicia Topping, aged eleven. Celine Topping, aged nine. You had a meeting in his office.'

Lead inside my heart now. Cement inside my legs. Flora's got big fat eyes everywhere in this dirty city.

'Why would you do that?' Brandon asks. That dead face. The dead eyes.

Speak quick. Speak now. 'He's helping me find out who I am,' I say. 'He's organising a meeting for me. He found the sister I never knew I had. He's organised a meeting for us, Brandon. Four days from now. She's coming over from Perth just to meet me.'

'Detective Topping did all that for you?' Brandon asks across the table. Blood-red face. Veins popping in his weightlifter's neck. He leans forward to hiss at me like a cobra. 'You mean the same Geoff Topping who has been heading up an investigation into my mum's business affairs for the past three years. The same cunt who's made my mum's life a living hell. I wonder what that sneaky blue fuck asked from you in return?'

And now Brandon flexes his arm muscles and raises his fists high and drops them like a gorilla on the tabletop and my world shatters around me just as the glass shatters. No more circling for the shark, for there's nothing left to circle. Just two metres of broken glass on the living room carpet between us.

I'm temporarily stunned and that's how he gets a head start on me. I've barely run a metre before he's scrambled across the glass and crash-tackled me hard onto the carpet. I try to wriggle from his grip but he's too strong. He crawls on me like the tyrant lizard he is, rolls me beneath his thighs, and I'm sure he's going to kill me, so I scream the only name that comes to mind.

'Geoff!' I scream. 'Geoff! He's going to kill me.'

'You fucking rat,' he says. And his closed right fist drives into my left cheek and my teeth mash the insides of my mouth and blood pools in my throat. 'Where is it?' Brandon barks. And he yanks my T-shirt up and his sweaty, grubby hands rub across my body, my breasts, my pelvis, over the sides of my belly and behind my back.

'Geoff!' I scream to the ceiling. 'Pleeeeeeasssse.'

Brandon pats my shorts and his hand finds something hard in the right pocket, and he digs in there aggressively and pulls out Geoff Topping's secret, stupid fucking covert was-always-gonna-get-me-knocked spy phone.

Brandon holds it up and he's clearly never seen such a strange-looking phone. 'Fuuuuuck!' he screams. Then he snaps the phone in two and furiously smashes those two pieces together so they shatter into smaller pieces.

'You fucking snake,' he yells. Then his big hands reach around my neck. And now is the time I die. All versions of me. The bad ones and the good ones and the one I always dreamed about. The monster tries to say something through his gritted teeth, but his furious words only exit his mouth as spit. I see his dark eyes and know his cold intention is only death. And he straddles my torso so tightly, every pound of his weight squashing my belly and arse into the floor. His big hands on my throat. His angry thumbs pressing down on my windpipe, and I can't breathe. 'Top—,' I say. 'Topping—'

I scratch and claw at his face. Blood across his cheeks. Skin beneath my fingernails. My palms pushing at his chin. I bring my hands to his fists to try to pull his grip from my throat. Suck for air and find only suffocation. Eyes closing to black.

He lifts my head and slams it into the carpet. 'Fucking animal,' he spits. 'Fucking worthless animal.'

I suck for air. Think. Knife. Think. Boot. Knife. Boot. Reach. I release my right arm from his steellike grip and stretch as far as I can along my side and raise my right leg and hook my calf back towards my hand. Fingers reaching now for the boot. Can feel the leather rim, my sock. I hook my leg around like a chicken wing. Sucking for air. Stay alive, I tell myself. *Stay here*, Erica Finlay whispers to me from the bottom of the river. Eye to eye with the monster. *Stay here, I love you.* Don't let him see where these fingers are going. Eyes closing now. No air inside me. Blacking out. Need to breathe.

My fingers find the handle of the filleting knife that the monster's mum, Flora Box, taught me to use when I was fourteen years old, working in the filleting and gutting room of the best seafood shop in Queensland. I pull it from the boot. Everything going black inside my head. Think I'm dying now. Think I'm not gonna stay here anymore. Just a circle of light. A circle of light. How wide is the circle of light? Wide as a can of Pasito. How do I sketch a circle of light on a blank white sheet of paper? The light is formed by the darkness we choose to place around it.

A full grip on the knife now. Bring my right hand to my side. Slowly. Don't let the monster see. Don't let the monster know. Bring my right hand slowly up to my belly. Now open my eyes and see the monster for who he is. Now drive my blade upwards and straight into the soft flesh below his Adam's apple.

Brandon coughs. A flood of blood bursts immediately from his mouth and it falls on my face and I turn my head to avoid this sickening shower. His face, the colour of toothpaste, the colour of ghosts, shows a mix of awe and terror and shock and slow muscle-man thinking. Then his own blood fills his windpipe. He gargles on it. Spits it all up on me then gargles again. He still has strength left and I know his final desire before his own eyes close to black will be to strangle out of me the little air, the little life, I have left in my body. And we will both die here. The monster named Brandon Box and the girl who never got to know her name. Light to black. Black to light. Light to black. Colour fading. Life is a black ink sketch on white paper now. Black ink everywhere. Only black.

But now the sound of Brandon's apartment door being kicked open. And a single bullet shot from a gun. And Brandon Box is perfectly still because that bullet has penetrated the back of his brain. His dead weight flops upon my chest and I can smell his sweat and I can smell his head flesh and I start to breathe and then I start to scream uncontrollably. Nothing but primal screaming. No words in it. No girl in it. No human in it. Only animal. Scream after wail after scream.

Detective Sergeant Geoff Topping rushes over and pulls Brandon's body off me. I look down my chest and see my body covered in Brandon's blood. And I'm shaking so hard that I can't speak.

'Sshhhhh,' Topping says. He pats my forehead. 'I'm here now. Everything's going to be okay.' He checks the pulse in my neck. 'Breathe. Just breathe. Slow down. You're safe now.'

He kneels at my side and his face is so welcome to me. His face is so good to see from down here with my head on the carpet. He holds me and I feel like a koala being held by one of his daughters.

'I'm gonna get you outta here,' he says. 'Breathe now. Breathe.'

I catch my breath. And I still my heart. And I have enough air in my lungs to speak and I turn my face to his. 'Quick as a flash,' I whisper.

He puts a gentle and calming hand on my right shoulder. 'Quick as a flash,' he repeats. And he grins at me just before another loud bang echoes from behind him. And, in the madness of this moment, I don't understand why this sweet blue meanie drops instantly and inexplicably to my side. And, here inside the horror of the great mistake that is my unfolding life, I don't understand why there's a hole in the back of Geoff Topping's head and why there are all those awful chunks of red-coloured matter around the edge of that hole.

'No!' I scream. And I lift my head to see Flora Box standing at the door of her son's apartment, a pistol still pointed at Topping.

And in my mind I see his daughters, Felicia and Celine. Lucky moon. They're holding koalas. Holding those koalas with such love and care. And I start to weep.

Flora turns to look at me. A lime-green fleece. A yellow polo-shirt collar poking out of the neck. Capri pants. Big clear spectacles scanning the room.

Think. Knife. Think. My fingers moving. Knife in my hand. The same knife that just killed Flora's son, the monster whose bloody body she zeroes in on now, adjusting her glasses, like she's staring at an abstract painting her brain's too small to understand.

She paces forward slowly. I pull myself awkwardly to my feet and move away from her across the living room as she approaches Brandon. She doesn't even look at me. Her gun hand falls to her side. 'Stay where you are, pet,' she says. Soft. So soft that voice. She's looking only at Brandon when she says this. And I catch my breath as I watch Flora lean down to inspect her son's body. He's lying facedown on the carpet. She studies the bullet hole in the back of her son's head. Can't see the knife wound in his throat. Turns her attention to Topping, lying on his side on the carpet. Her left shoe. An ASICS Gel-Quantum. The artist misses nothing. This shoe presses against Geoff's limp shoulder. Checking if he's dead, but it feels to me like she's wanting him to wake up. Willing him. Then she points her gun square at his head and doesn't move a single feature in her face as she fires two more bullets into Geoff's brain.

I turn away with my face in my hands, then make a dash for the front door.

But Flora's pistol is on me. 'I said stay where you are.'

I stop. Too stunned to speak. Too broken to form the directives in my mind that would tell my voice box to open and my tongue to bend to say the words I need to say to explain the sight before that terrifyingly plain woman's wide-open eyes.

No sound from her. No recognisable emotions on her face beyond curiosity, interest in inspecting the impossible. The curious and impossible sight of her only son with his belly pressed against the floor. A mother scanning the scene like some kind of emotionless robot. A cyborg. She's only half-human now. Because she's lost a human part of her. Her mother part. Her son part.

It's just Flo and me. Just the mother of a dead son and the scrapyard van girl with no name. 'He was ...' Just a whisper. A breathless sentence I cannot finish. Finally, I spit the words out. 'He was killing me, Flo.' I run my hand across my chest and find it covered in his blood.

Flo says nothing. Looks at my face for the first time now. And I follow her eyes behind the big lenses of her spectacles. Maybe five or six metres between us. Two or three metres between the front door and my feet. Those blank eyes of hers moving from my head down my torso to the fish-filleting knife in my right fist, its blade shaft painted red. My eyes moving down her right arm to the gun that just killed a good and decent man who was raising two girls named Felicia and Celine. Not a sound between us. But the artist misses nothing. Flora's fat right forefinger shifts ever so slightly across the trigger of her gun. And now her right elbow moves and I know in my heart and in my Monet blood that she is going to raise that right arm and fire at me.

But my right arm moves quicker than hers. I whip it back and throw my knife straight at her face. She turns her body, raising her left arm to shield her mug. The business end of my knife digs deeply into her left shoulder. And we're both temporarily stunned by the way it wobbles when she cranes her neck to inspect the wound.

Now Flo screams. Banshee screaming. Rabid and lost and inhuman. And she makes the mistake of pulling the knife out of her shoulder before she raises her gun at me, and I have enough time to duck my head, grab my backpack and dash out of this mirror-walled hellhole apartment. And now the gunshots. One passing behind me and lodging in the living room wall. Another whizzing over my hunched head and into Brandon's neighbour's front door across the hall.

I sprint to the big green door to the fire escape. Wheezy Flo will never take the stairs. One more gunshot behind me as I enter a concrete and steel stairwell winding between walls of old brick. I zigzag down fourteen floors of crisscrossing staircases, leaping two, three, even four steps at a time.

Shots coming from above me now and, glancing up the stairwell, I see Lady Flo leaning over a railing to meet my gaze.

She points her gun again and fires, but she's run out of bullets. 'I thought you wanted to stop running,' she screams.

I consider that statement for a moment as I catch my breath.

And then I run.

The Girl on the Lam

The Girl on the Lam

January 2024

Pen and ink on paper

Perhaps the artist's most celebrated image, sketched in darkness while she was on the run from Flora Box and a collection of dangerous men hell-bent on ending her life and, in turn, destroying a certain career as a world-famous artist. The creature from previous works has now grown. The creature has revealed itself. Monstrous and malevolent. Unavoidable and, as far as the viewer can tell, unbeatable.

Think. Run. Think. Run. Here's what I can't do. Go back to the scrapyard on Moon Street. Think. Who does Flora phone first about her dead son, the man whose bloody face I can't remove from my thoughts? She phones her best friend in all the world, Ephraim Wall. Then what happens? Ephraim Wall tells six of his closest thug friends how I killed Flora's beloved son, Brandon, the man whose face I see above me in my head, teeth clenched, spitting at me as he strangles me. The tyrant lizard, roaring. Ephraim then calls all those blokes with unsettling pasts who help pack the fish boxes in the cold back rooms of Ebb 'n' Flo. He calls lanky Nathan Rose with the dyed blond goatee. He calls The Priest. None of those brown-nosed suck-ups will say shit about the fact that Brandon is a psychopath who had it coming. About the fact that I was acting in self-defence. About the fact that I wanted to end the Tyrannosaurus Waltz.

Here's what I *can* do. Run to Roma Street Police Station. Ask for Detective Sergeant Cameron Millar. He knows my story. He even knows my name. I can tell him what Flora did to Topping. She shot my friend. She shot a good man who had just saved my life. Millar will protect me.

Wait. Don't run there just yet. My filleting knife. I threw it at Flora Box. It lodged in her arm like a tetanus shot. My fingerprints all over it. Inked in blood. The knife that I stuck in Brandon's throat. How do I not go down for that? How does

Millar protect me from that? No. Don't run there just yet. Flora's got a rat on the inside of the blue meanies HQ. Her thugs will be waiting for me there, flanking the marble entry steps to the station. Fuck.

In my head, I see a girl in the year 2100, dressed in a yellow peacoat, standing in front of my art inside the Metropolitan Museum in New York.

'I didn't think she was capable of such violence,' the girl says to her mum.

'A woman never knows exactly what she is capable of, sweetheart,' the mum says, 'until she knows exactly what she is capable of.'

I didn't think I could do it and now I wish with every drop of blood in my body that I hadn't. I did it in self-defence, but who's gonna care about that when I get up and plead my useless case in front of Justice Cavanagh in the Brisbane Mags Court?

Home. The scrapyard in Moon Street. I want to go home but that's another thing I can't do. Ephraim's boys will be waiting for me there. First place I'd look. They'll be there already, their faces getting all up close and personal to my neighbours. Thug meanies scaring June and Ros and Sully, and Charlie if he's home. Dark men with crew cuts, thugging about in our peaceful yard. The place we're being booted out of. The world turns. The world turns. But when does it right itself for me? Home. They're kicking us out of our home. So, where's home for me now anyway? Home is anywhere. Home is where the throbbing red blob is.

Here's what I *can* do. Run just like this. I sprint downhill along Gladstone Road, Highgate Hill. Big wide footpaths. Cars passing me now on their way into the city. Run past low-set cottages and white picket fences and well-kept front yards. Past the Highgate Hill TAB and the bottle shop next to the Golden King bakery. Two old ladies waiting at the traffic lights on Blakeney Street, staring at me as I run past them. They're looking at my clothes and wondering why I'm covered in blood. How the fuck did I get so much blood on me? Red splattered over me like the splattered blues and blacks and yellows in the Land of Jackson Pollock. I've got to get off these main roads. Run. Just keep running. Never stop running. Never should have stopped running. Never should have sat on our arses by the river selling drugs for Lady Flo. Stupid dumb-arse drug runners selling dumb-arse drugs. Never should have let her jump into the river after that miracle child in the pram. Never should have let her be brave. Stupid dumb-arse courage. Never should have let that woman be anything but mad.

Flora Box, the monster. My boss, the monster. She turned into someone else. She was something else. She was darkness. She was the darkness that artists use to build light on the page. Build light. Think light thoughts. Think happy thoughts. Lemon crêpes around the scrapyard fire. That turtle Erica and I saw once, swimming in the town of Seventeen Seventy. Riding Macaroni to the station from Ursula's house, riding at high speed along the Sandgate waterfront, saltwater winds blowing and tickling my eyelashes. That beautiful boy on the bridge. *Danny Collins*.

Run. Into the customer toilet at the side of the white, red and blue Liberty petrol station on Gladstone Road. I lock the door behind me. Pump a soap dispenser. Wet and wash my face, my blood-stained arms. Brandon Box's dark blood swirls down the drain. I'll run to Cairns from here, I tell myself. I'll run to Canberra, I tell myself. Don't need anything but a thumb to hold up on the highway. Could make it to South Australia on the strength of my raised thumbs. Could run to Alice Springs. Could hide out in the desert. Could run to Weipa and ask some of Erica's old friends to help me. What did they know me as back then? What did she say my name was? Claudia? Holly? What was it again? Who was I back then? Pamela? Donna? Maria? So many names over the years. So many and none at all.

I stare into the washroom mirror. Topping is gone. I see his girls in my head holding koalas. Felicia and Celine. Lucky moon. Who's gonna tell them their dad's not coming home? Geoff means 'peace'. Geoff means a lump in my throat that makes it hard to breathe. Water. I need water. Put my lips to a grubby faucet. Three gulps of water that tastes like metal.

I see my face in the mirror and see the girl in the photograph that Detective Topping pulled out of the yellow envelope. I see Phoebe. My older sister. My family. I have a family. I have a sister. I have a story. The saddest story Detective Sergeant Topping ever heard. The story Phoebe's flying all the way from Perth to tell me.

I slap my face with water. Only a matter of days. Monday, 3 p.m. Revelation hour. Illumination o'clock. Topping said I could choose the place and I said we should meet in the Starbucks coffee shop at the bottom of the Myer Centre. Erica's favourite spot. That's where my sister's gonna be waiting for me. I'm gonna walk in and sit down and she's gonna tell me who I am. So here's what I *can't* do. I can't run away from her. I need to meet her. I will not run away from her. And here's what I *can* do. Stay. Stay *here*. *Stay here, I love you*. And that's what the prince said, too. *Fuck it. I love you*. He was brave. He took the story to marvellous places. He took the story exactly where I wanted it to go. *You'll be right here?* he asked. *Just look up. I'll be right here*, I replied.

Danny. Soon the sun will fall and the moon will rise and Danny Collins will walk across the Victoria Bridge to meet me. He'll look up like I told him to and I won't be there. Because I can't be there. Because I know deep down that staying is impossible for me now. How can I stay? Flora's got men on the book right across this city. All of those men have eyes, and that means she's got her eyes everywhere. She sees everything. I walk onto that bridge tonight, Ephraim will be cutting me up like a mako shark an hour later. I cannot stay. I must not stay. All I must do is run.

I wipe my face with a paper towel then toss it in an overflowing bin. Random words graffitied above the washroom mirror: *You just can't afford to ignore the bells.*

Rain outside. Coming down hard. The kind of hard rain the universe turns on like a hose over South East Queensland in summer. The kind of hard rain that can flood this city in a matter of hours. A flood is always coming in this place. I need to get off the street. Hide from the rain. Hide. Yes. I need a place to hide. I need a place to wait. I need to think of a plan. I need to stay. I need help.

I stare into the mirror. 'Lola?' I whisper. 'Lola? Are you there?'

I take a deep breath. Put my face closer to the mirror. 'Lola. Please. I need you. I need you more than ever.'

I wait for Lola to appear, but this petrol station mirror has no magic. Nothing but me there. Me and my messy brown hair that now looks like a bird's nest blown sideways in a storm. I unzip my Adidas bag to look for my brush and see the hessian potato sack that Brandon found in Julian Rossi's pantry. I loosen the drawstring, pull it wide and find the reason Julian was beaten to a pulp. Three blocks of cash. All $100 notes. Maybe fifty k all up.

A loud banging on the washroom door. 'This toilet is for paying customers only,' a man barks.

I zip up the bag. Burst out of the washroom. A bearded man in a blue polo shirt and black trousers saying, 'I have to clean this thing. It's not your personal shithouse.'

Run now. Run again. Find a place to hide. Where do people hide in this city? Think. Where?

Of course. In holes.

Run.

And the artist felt the rain hitting her shoulders and arms and she felt safe inside it. She felt hidden. Invisible. If she was to have sketched this moment in her life, she would have sketched her boots splashing in puddles as she sprinted past the brown-brick classrooms of Brisbane State High School on Vulture Street. She would have sketched the tall palm trees and the short poincianas bending in a wind she saw turning a woman's umbrella inside out. She would have sketched the white plastic garden chair being blown from the deck of a yellow-brick unit on Browning Street. A row of ten wheelie bins with red lids turning and knocking against each other like restless soldiers on parade. People finding shelter under the awning of the Red Stone Pizzeria. Small hailstones rattling off the tin roof of the West End Uniting Church. A message to the public on the church's notice board: Life has no remote. Get up and change it yourself.

The artist ran across busy Boundary Street. Outside the Indian Kitchen takeaway shop on Vulture Street, she stopped to catch her breath. She bent over and rested her hands on her knees, sucking in air beside a woman with curly grey hair in a yellow raincoat who was talking to herself. The woman's words made no sense to the artist. 'Get out of my head,' the woman said, slapping her left temple with her palm. 'Get out of my ribboned head.'

The artist ran.

*

I turn left off Montague Road into Canoe Street. No floaters to be seen. No pedestrians at all. A whole world of people in their houses, staying out of the hard rain. The St Peter the Apostle Church is closed for spiritual business. I open the small red iron entry gate, run down the path to the left of the church, and scamper down a strip of grass to the secluded backyard. Catch my breath for thirty seconds then kneel and speak into the hole my friend Esther calls home.

'Are you there, Esther?' I enquire.

A voice snaps from within, 'Who's that?'

I realise I've woken her from a nap. Esther values naps like she values Cherry Ripe chocolate bars.

'It's me, Esther,' I say, between deep breaths. 'It's Liv Bytheriver.'

'Liv?' Esther replies. 'Why you out in the rain?'

'I'm in trouble, Esther. I got nowhere else to go.'

'What's goin' on, Liv?' Esther asks.

'I need a place to hide, Esther,' I reply. 'I need a hole. I need to come in there with you.'

'Not a chance, kid,' Esther says. 'Nobody comes in here.'

'Please, Esther,' I say. 'Just for a few days.'

'Why? What have you done, Liv?'

'Let me crawl in there with you and I'll tell you all about it,' I say. 'Please. Just this once. There's people after me, Esther. Dangerous people.' Tears falling from my eyes now. 'I'm scared, Esther. I'm really fuckin' scared.'

A long moment of silence. Can't see a thing in the hole.

'Don't swear like that,' Esther says. 'I'll have no swearin' in my home. Rule number one: Esther's hole, Esther's rules. You got that?'

'I got it,' I say. 'Esther's hole, Esther's rules.'

'Good,' Esther says. 'Now get in 'ere and get yourself dry. Didn't I tell you there was a flood comin'?'

The Hunter and the Prey

The Hunter and the Prey

January 2024

Pen and ink on paper

The closest the artist comes to a genuine self-portrait, and it's broken into the twelve pieces of a shattered mirror. The intention of the work might be found within its title, a clear nod to the philosophical notion that likens the act of looking into the mirror to a predatorial hunt, a search for self-knowledge in which the looker is both the hunter and the prey. The title may also refer to the time the artist was chased through Brisbane by a group of ruthless underworld criminals.

Alone in the hole. Must be almost midnight. Esther's home is wider than my van bedroom but half the height of it. Crawling space only. The hole stinks of Esther's sweat and body odour and a rose potpourri she found in a wheelie bin on Granville Street. Esther can tell you the wheelie bin nights and pickup mornings of almost any suburb across Brisbane.

There's a square of old, frayed carpet stretched across a slab of hard concrete beneath us. Decades ago, this space was used as a cellar and storage room by the church. Above us are wooden floorboards and a long-sealed hatch now covered on the other side by a modern kitchenette in Father Kikelomo's vestry.

Esther sleeps on a ratty mattress and she's given me a purple yoga mat to lie on and an old tartan blanket to throw over myself at night. My pillow is a Dollars and Sense shopping bag filled with Esther's rolled-up underpants.

This is my third night in the hole and it hasn't stopped raining outside since the afternoon I ran from Brandon Box's apartment. The kind of rain so relentless it feels like it's soaking your insides. I've spent the whole time staring out of the triangular hole in the wall thinking about my mistake of a life and what's left of it. Nothing to be seen out there but grass and a small segment of a jasmine vine climbing over the churchyard's rear fence. Yesterday I watched a grey-brown bird land on a patch of grass and bounce in a circle for me. Fluffy ball of a bird with a tiny red beak and a tall, narrow tail sticking straight up in the air. Think it was a superb fairywren. The bird that Danny spoke about. The bird that has a secret code in its birdsong that helps its babies find their way home in the dark. I whistled to the bird through the hole, and it looked into the blackness of this dank hideout and turned its head in puzzlement. Then it raised its little red beak to the sky and sang a love song as clear and true as any love song Taylor Swift ever wrote. And when it flew away, I wondered if it had left me with a secret code in that song that might help me make my way through the dark.

*

This hole is well stocked. Endless cans of tuna and beans and various fresh fruits that Esther scavenges on her regular hunter-gatherer odysseys into the night. I'm chewing on a chocolate and cranberry muesli bar. Esther has left me with a red and grey camping lantern that runs on rechargeable batteries. It has a built-in AM radio. I listen to news reports in the dark and wonder about the outside world I cannot see. Someone just shot five people in Jefferson City, Missouri. A 212-metre-deep sinkhole has opened up beneath a Chilean corn farmer's tool shed. There's a story on the news about Amsterdam's 'bicycle fishers', who are responsible for hauling fifteen thousand bicycles out of the city's canals each year. Apparently Amsterdammers take great satisfaction in watching a bicycle soar through the air, crash through the water and sink into what the reporter calls 'Europe's bicycle graveyards'. All this bike talk makes me think of Macaroni, currently chained to the scrapyard fence at home, and Macaroni makes me think of Charlie. I wish he was here with me in this hole. Charlie would make this fun. Charlie would make this an adventure, not a nightmare. Home is where the throbbing red blob is.

I turn the radio tuning knob and listen to old pop songs on 4KQ. 'Hey, St Peter' by Flash and The Pan. 'My Mistake' by Split Enz. 'Borderline' by Madonna. Brick walls around me. Some cups and bowls on an upturned cardboard box acting as a coffee table. Esther says her eyes have grown accustomed to the darkness in here. Says she has evolved down here into someone possessing the eyesight of an owl but the wisdom of an ox. Solitude makes you stupid, she says. Community makes you bright, she says, in mind and heart. If she wasn't so solitary and stupid, she says, she would be living in a two-bedroom flat with air-conditioning in Burleigh Heads on the Gold Coast and not in a hole in the back of a church in West End. Last night I asked Esther how she manages to cope with the constant darkness and she said it was hard at first but then she came to see the darkness as a kind of blanket that was as comforting as the tartan blanket I was hugging to my chest. Dark rooms are good for dreaming when you're awake, she said. She likened this room to one of the blank pieces of paper I'm always sketching on, to a canvas for dreaming on. The room was a theatre, she said, and she could project her daytime dreams across its black walls. Anything could be seen in this hole, Esther said. See it in your mind. See it in the hole.

'What's showing tonight?' I asked Esther last night.

'It's Patrick Swayze,' she replied. 'He's twenty-five years old and dressed in lederhosen and he's holding my hand as we climb the Swiss Alps.'

Nothing real to be seen in darkness, she said, and nothing real to see you. You can be invisible down here. When you're invisible, you're no one. When you're no one, you can be anyone. Esther said she's not really a recluse. Just doesn't like being seen. There are some people in this world, she said, who will do anything to be seen. They'll build great houses on hilltops and they'll make their cars and their muscles and their boobs and backsides stand out like lighthouses and they'll live their lives loudly because they measure success in handclaps and cheers and decibels. Esther likes being quiet. Esther likes being unseen. In the dark. In the hole.

Footsteps on the grass outside. I grip an axe handle by my side, the closest thing this home has to a security system. A hand pushes something through the hole and I switch on the lantern to see what it is. A bright yellow raincoat.

'Just me,' Esther says. 'Turn that light out.'

She's wearing a raincoat herself, with the hood fixed tight around her chin and cheeks. I just caught a brief flash of Esther's face. I've seen her face more times over the past three days than I have in the past three years. Strong jawline. Big smile when it gets going. Green eyes and silver hair with some strands of black still hanging in there. The hole's been good for her complexion: uncracked porcelain skin like the Goths I see milling around the Hungry Jack's in Queen Street Mall. Ain't nothing ugly about Esther Inthehole. Inside or out.

'Did you see him, Esther?'

Esther slips out of her soaking wet raincoat. Shakes it and spreads it out in a corner of the hole.

'Yeah, I saw him,' she says.

'What was he doing?'

'Same as last night,' she says. 'And same as the night before that. Just standing there in the middle of the bridge. But he was kinda dressed up tonight.'

'Whaddya mean "dressed up"?'

'He was in this nice brown suit.'

'A brown suit?' I say. 'In the rain?'

'Yeah. All vintage and classic it was. That boy's handsome as an old tree, ain't he?' She elbows my shoulder. 'But the poor bastard also looks like some kinda sad puppy dog standing there on that bridge. Standing in the rain, holding his umbrella. What sort of spell did you cast on him?'

Danny Collins waiting for me on the bridge in a vintage brown suit. There again tonight. The first night I was here, I asked Esther if she could go on a scouting mission for me. She walked right past him. Her head was down but her eyes were up. She got so close to him that she could see the sketchbook he had tucked under his left armpit as he sheltered beneath a large black umbrella in the middle of the bridge. In the middle of *our* bridge. Smack-bang on the spot where we first met. Just waiting there for me. The prince from the painting. And my heart bounced like a rabbit in a carrot patch when I heard Esther say these things.

Esther walked on to Fortitude Valley, where she wanted to sift through some bins behind the Calile Hotel on James Street. She crossed back over the bridge some two hours later and Danny was still there. That right there, I realised, might have been the sweetest thing anybody's ever done for me. I wanted to crawl out of the hole and sprint all the way to the bridge. I wanted to explain to Danny Collins why I hadn't turned up, why I wasn't there every time he looked up. And now it's three nights in a row he's waited for me. He keeps coming back. He keeps looking up. And I keep not being there.

'Why would he keep coming back like that, Esther?'

'Kid's clearly screwy in the head,' she says. 'But it's what's in his heart that's makin' him stand in the rain like that.'

'How many nights do you think he'll come back, Esther?'

'Well, judging by the hangdog look on his face, I'd say he's got either one more night in him or the rest of eternity. Honestly, I ain't ever seen a boy so spellbound. What the hell did you do to him?'

'Nothing,' I say. 'We just talked.'

'Must 'ave been more than a bit o' talkin' between yuz.'

'We danced a bit,' I say.

'And ...?'

'Then we talked a bit more.'

'And then …?'

Esther can't see my smile in the dark. Can't see me at all, but she knows how I feel. I feel alive. I feel … I feel … what was that word he used?

'Then the rain came and we said goodbye,' I continue. 'We went our separate ways and I was on my way home but then I thought about changing the story a bit. I thought about a more dramatic ending to the night. I chose danger, Esther. I cartwheeled instead of walking. I ran after him and I tapped him on the shoulder and he turned around.'

'What did he look like in that moment?' Esther asks, sinking back into her mattress.

'How do you mean?'

'Did he look confused?' she asks. 'Did he look happy to see you? Did he look relieved?'

'He just looked true,' I reply. 'Handsome and true. He looked like a prince, Esther. His hair was all drenched and his cheeks were all pale and clean in the wet and he had all these little streams of water running down his forehead and around his eyes and along the curves of his nose and over the hills of his lips.'

'Then you said something you probably shouldn't have said,' Esther guesses.

'How'd you know?' I ask.

'We always say things we shouldn't in those moments,' she replies.

'Yes. I told him I loved him.'

'Of course you did,' she says. 'Shit, that poor boy didn't stand a chance.'

More rabbits bouncing in my gut. I throw my tartan blanket off my folded legs. 'I've gotta go meet him, Esther,' I say, scrambling towards the hole.

But Esther grabs my shoulder. 'You can't,' she says. 'Ephraim's boys, kid. Flo's boys. They're still creeping around out there.

Darting their heads around like hyenas looking for a feed. I passed two of them standing outside the scrapyard fence. They were right in front of your van, Liv. Then I walked along the river and saw two more of them having a smoke down where the cruise boats leave, in front of the State Library. Saw another one walkin' up and down Queen Street Mall. He still had his Ebb 'n' Flo polo shirt on, covered in fish guts.'

I sit back down on my yoga mat. 'What am I gonna do, Esther?'

'You're gonna wait,' she says.

'Wait for what?'

I lie back. Rest my head on my host's bag of rolled undies.

'Wait for the flood,' Esther says. 'This hole will be flooded soon. This whole street will be flooded, too. Half of West End's about to go under. This rain's not gonna stop.'

I turn my body, prop my head on my right palm. 'You seein' the future again, Esther?'

'Just a bit of it,' she says. 'But that bit's all you're gonna need.'

'I don't wanna die drownin' in this hole,' I say.

'Don't worry, you'll be long gone by then,' she says.

'What am I gonna do, Esther?'

'You're gonna wait until that river rises twelve feet again and starts spilling over its banks,' she says. 'You're gonna wait until all that rainwater runs down from the mountains and they let those dams run free, and you're gonna wait for all that water to rise up again through the city's drainpipes and sewer pipes and carpark drainage holes and the city turns to chaos and Lady Flo calls all those thug watchmen back from their sinister pickets because she needs them to save her precious seafood market and everything inside it from certain flooding. That's when you'll be safe to move around. You'll be invisible in the chaos of the flood. Then you can go see if that boy is still waiting for you on the bridge, and if he's as stupid and beautiful as I think he is he'll still be there and you'll have to tell him that he's gonna have to wait some more because you're runnin' away. You'll have to meet your prince some other time, in some other place on the other side of fate. Some other life. And then you'll go meet your sister and you'll have your answers and your name. And then you will run.'

'What if I don't want to run anymore?' I ask. 'What if I want to stay with my sister?'

'Then you will die,' Esther says.

'Why?'

'Remember the dream I had.'

I remember. The monster sipping tea in Starbucks. The monster is Erica Finlay. The city is drowning and I want to get away, but the monster holds me down in the flood. I start swallowing water.

'Everybody has crazy dreams, Esther,' I say. 'Doesn't mean they mean anything.'

'I know that,' she says. 'But that happened to be a dream that meant something.'

'How do you know that?'

'That dream scared me,' Esther says, 'and the scary ones always mean something.'

'I haven't told you where I'm meeting Phoebe,' I say.

'Where are you meeting Phoebe?' Esther asks through the darkness.

'The Starbucks café at the bottom of the Myer Centre.'

'Of course you are,' Esther says.

'I think I suggested Starbucks only because it was on my mind after you told me about your dream,' I say. 'So it's probably your fault I even suggested it.'

'Of course it's my fault,' Esther says. 'That's why I don't like to talk to people. I'm better off staying inside this hole and keeping out of everybody's business.'

'Do you think I should stay away from Starbucks?' I ask.

'It doesn't matter what I think,' Esther replies.

'Why doesn't it matter?'

'Because nothing's gonna make you stay away from Starbucks. You need to meet your sister. You need to know your name.'

We lie back in silence. Rain falls hard outside.

'Where you gonna go when this hole floods, Esther?' I ask.

Esther takes a moment to answer. 'I'm gonna go climb the Swiss Alps with Patrick Swayze in lederhosen.'

*

The hours pass and the river rises. Maybe it's Erica Finlay down there with the lungfish requesting all this chaos across the city. She knows I need to make my great escape. Get out of this dreadful hole for a bit. I listen to scratchy ABC 612 Brisbane flood updates on Esther's red and grey radio lantern. Over one million square kilometres of Queensland is flooded, an area greater than the area of France and Germany combined. The Brisbane metropolitan area has received 484.8 millimetres of rain in the past month, three times the long-term average. A family of four has perished inside a Mitsubishi Lancer that was washed away when they attempted to traverse a flooded crossing in Pullenvale, western Brisbane. A nine-year-old boy named Harley Page has drowned in a flooded pedestrian tunnel in Tanah Merah, south of Brisbane. A bull shark swam into the dressing sheds beneath Suncorp Stadium. More than a thousand people in Ipswich have fled to high-ground evacuation centres in schools and halls and showgrounds. The supermarket shelves are empty. The SES has distributed 90,000 sandbags from emergency depots across the city. Men in tin boats are rescuing weeping and frantic people from their porches in Jindalee, Goodna and Rocklea.

*

And now it's Monday. Today's the day she tells me my name. My sister is flying over from Perth this morning. She'll land in a city in the grip of flood. A city in chaos.

'Thank you, Esther,' I say as I prepare to head out. I hug her tight in the darkness. I'm wearing the yellow PVC raincoat she found.

She pulls its hood tight so all that's showing of my face is my eyes and nose and mouth. 'Stay away from that river,' she says.

'I will. You should be leaving now, too.'

'You know me, I don't move so well in the daylight.'

I peer out of the hole at the pouring rain. 'Not a lot of daylight out there today,' I say. 'You gotta leave this place, Esther. You can't stay here no more.'

I turn on the lantern and hold it up to her eyes. To my surprise, she doesn't hide her face away like she normally does. She smiles at me and her smile is knowing and warm and right. I didn't know she had such beautiful green eyes. Her hair falls across her face and I see a vision of Esther on her wedding day, how pretty that face would have been behind a thin veil.

'You're beautiful, Esther,' I say. 'You're beautiful in the dark and you're even more beautiful in the light.'

She closes her eyes. 'Stay away from the river,' she says.

*

Hard rain on the shoulders of my raincoat. My boots splash through deep puddles that have formed in the grass outside Esther's hole. I have to undo the three black buttons on the raincoat to swing a leg over the fence between the church and The Well. I scurry across the centre's yard, trying not to crush fresh lettuces and capsicums in the organic community garden as I take the quickest route to the windows of the kitchen and cafeteria area. Kneel down to stay out of view. Duck my head up once because I'm stupid and can't resist stealing a look inside, where I see Evelyn Bragg lifting various industrial cooking tools and tables and chairs to high-ground benchtops with the help of a dozen houseless regulars. Then I sprint to the front of the centre. Hide behind the large square sign that carries words in the Yuggera language, welcoming visitors. The esteemed E.P. Buckle rambling English nonsense in my head.

The artist knew that if she was seen by anyone on Moon Street then word would soon get back to the monstrous Flora Box, who was desperate to exact bloody revenge upon the artist for the unfortunate but necessary killing of Brandon Box. Hiding out for days inside the hole beneath the St Peter the Apostle Church on Canoe Street, the artist had refined a simple and achievable plan, one that would keep her alive. One centred on her scheduled afternoon meeting with her sister, Phoebe, who was flying across the country to meet her.

As she hid behind the welcome sign to The Well, the artist was struck by a strong sense of destiny. It was almost as if every moment of her wild and complex and confusing childhood had been leading to this very day. She watched people running through the rain in Moon Street, carrying armchairs and television sets and boxes filled with family heirlooms. Tables and sofas being loaded into trucks. Homeless locals with bin bags of clothes over their shoulders, scrambling to find new homes. It felt to the artist like the end of the world. Or maybe it was just the end of a story.

I can see two delivery trucks parked in the street in front of the Ebb 'n' Flo shop. Young men in blue polo shirts – Flo's young men – are loading Styrofoam boxes and weight scales and cash registers and office equipment onto these trucks, normally filled with iced red emperor and flathead and fresh blue swimmer crab. I pull the raincoat hood tighter. Mustn't let those young men see my face.

I vault the low brick fence and run left down Moon Street towards the scrapyard we call Oz. Scurry down the left side of the Tinman's shed to a high silver gate – the way we enter Oz on the rare occasions when we come in via Moon Street rather than through the rear gate that opens onto the riverside walkway, which I use almost every day of my life. If Flo's goons are still waiting for me to come home, they'll be waiting there, by the river.

There are four rusting car-engine cylinder blocks at the side of the shed. Each has a row of holes on top shaped like cup holders in cinema seats. I kneel at the second last block, reach into the last hole and grip a plastic keychain in the shape of the Incredible Hulk's head. Unlock the long shackle padlock on the side gate, leave the gate open as I drop the Hulk back in the engine block hole, then close and lock the gate behind me again.

I turn to find two of Ros's potted chilli plants cracked, and soil spilled across the grass. Her firepit has been tossed upside down. All the windows in the cars have been smashed. The rear gate has been booted off its hinges. The place has been ransacked. Everything we value in our version of a home has been destroyed. Everybody's gone. My neighbours. My stitched-together family.

Some of June's and Sully's belongings are strewn across the yard outside their open campervan door. I step inside the van to find bags of sugar spread over the floor. Packets of oats have been flung across their dining table. Violence and intimidation. The strong muscling in on the weak. I think about how scared Sully must have been. I think about how loud he must have screamed. And they were looking for me. It's all my fault. I ruined Oz. Destroyed our home.

There's that lump in my throat again. A lump of shame this time. I step out of the campervan, and that's when I see my magic mirror lying flat on the ground by the Tinman's work shed.

I scurry to it. Fall to my knees, which sink deep into the sodden, muddy ground. The mirror has been smashed into a hundred pieces. There are cracks everywhere and glass dust where fragments have popped out of the matte-gold frame. It's an unfinished jigsaw puzzle of misshapen mirror pieces reflecting a horrific version of who I am: my right cheek falling off my face, my left ear severed from my head. A broken porcelain doll version of me. Left forearm detached at the elbow. Right hand missing two fingers.

'Lola?' I whisper. 'Lola. Are you there?'

Nothing. Nothing but this cracked me. This fractured me. Mutilated me. 'Mirror, mirror, all broken and cracked,' I whisper, 'please return to me, Lola, please come back.'

I look into the mirror and all I see is my tears. Welling in my eyes and falling on the cracked mirror pieces like the rain that falls on my back. I try to piece the mirror back together, but it's a waste of time I don't have today. I drop my head and close my eyes to stop the tears.

Then a voice rises from the mirror beneath me. 'Why are you crying?'

I open my eyes. 'Lola,' I whisper.

She's lying in a dirt hole. Rich brown soil. Colour of dark chocolate. Lola Intheearth. Lola Inthehole. But this is not like any image of her I've seen before. This one is made from a hundred different versions of Lola. Her right cheekbone occupies one solitary fragment of mirror glass and this fragment belongs to a twenty-five-year-old version of Lola with flawless skin, but the fragment containing her left cheekbone shows exposed and cracked dry bone from a skeleton version of Lola. Another piece of the mirror captures a pure green eye with mascara and flapping eyelashes, while another contains a deep black hole where her eye used to be. Same red dress as always, but in some mirror pieces the dress is torn and faded while in others the dress is new and vivid and fresh. Some fragmented parts of her arms belong to a ninety-five-year-old wrinkled version of Lola and some belong to a fifty-year-old suntanned version of Lola. Two pieces form her mouth and in one she smiles from a thirty-year-old face while in the other her lips sag because that version of Lola has been infected by a disease that has turned her lips the same hue of black that I use in my sketches. All the parts of her body in all the broken pieces of my magic mirror are moving out of sync with each other. Everything is distorted.

'I asked why you're crying,' Lola says.

'It's all falling apart, Lola,' I say.

'What is?'

'My life, Lola. Every part of it.'

'I know,' she says.

'What do I do?' I ask her.

'You find your answers,' she replies. 'You meet your sister. You hear the truth. You do not ignore your past.'

'Topping said it's the saddest story he's ever heard.'

'I told you,' Lola says, 'your past is an unimaginable horror show of tragedy and intrigue. But, please remember this, the past has nothing to do with who you are. And the past has nothing to do with who you will be.'

'Who I will be,' I say. 'Who I will be in the future? You said my future was a triumph, Lola.'

'It has been,' she says. 'And it will be.'

'What's triumphant about this?' I ask.

'You're still breathing, aren't you?' Lola replies. 'You still haven't jumped in that river, have you?'

'I thought it would be better than this,' I say.

'I said it would be bad, then good, then worse than ever before, then better than you could possibly imagine.'

'I don't believe you, Lola,' I say.

'You must believe me.'

'I can't see it. I can't believe anything you say. I think you're just telling me what I need to hear.'

'Please believe me.'

'I'm so sorry, Lola. I can't believe you. I don't believe you.'

My vision is captured by a fragment of the mirror showing Lola's disconnected left hand. The forefinger on this hand dissolves into the rich soil beneath it. Then her entire hand disappears into the dirt. Fades away into the brown earth beneath her.

'What is that hole you're lying in, Lola?' I ask.

Then all the parts of her left arm in mirror fragments dissolve into the earth.

'You need to get out of that hole, Lola,' I say.

But she doesn't move. Just lets other parts of her body dissolve the same way. Her waist now. Her pelvis.

'Lola, please, what are you doing?' I ask through tears.

'I gotta go away,' she replies.

'Why?' I ask.

'Because you want me to.'

'No, I don't. I really don't want you to, Lola. Stay here, Lola. Stay here, I love you.'

Her shoulders. Turning to dust. Her neck. Lola Inthepieces. Lola Intheground. Lola Inthegrave.

'No, Lola. Don't go. How will I ever see you again? They broke my magic mirror.'

'The mirror was never magic,' Lola says.

'It wasn't?'

'Of course it wasn't. Magic mirrors don't exist.'

'Then how come I can see you now?'

'Because *you* are magic,' Lola says. 'You've always been magic. You've never needed a mirror to see who you are.'

'But what if I can't do it again?' I ask. 'What if I can't make you appear again?'

'Do you remember that thing you said about love?' she asks.

'What thing? What did I say?'

'You said love is not something we can do. It's more like a rainbow after a storm. You just look up one day and it's there.'

She smiles as the diseased and infected side of her mouth crumbles into the dirt.

'Lola!' I scream.

Then the smiling side of her mouth disintegrates too.

'Lola, please,' I cry.

The last piece of Lola to disappear into the dirt is her right eye.

I collapse in tears above the fractured mirror. Nothing in the reflection now but a girl in a raincoat in the heavy rain with her knees pulled up to her chest, crying in despair.

Then a voice rings through the downpour. 'What the hell you doin', Princess?'

Charlie. And I sit up, wiping tears from my eyes. He's holding a box of canned goods with *Foodbank* on its side. He drops it as soon as he sees me. Runs at me, throws himself at me. Clamps his arms around my body, presses his head into my chest. Holds me for thirty seconds and we say nothing during the embrace. I remember hugging Erica like this. The kind of holding that's full of requests. *Please don't go. Please don't do that again. Please don't ever leave me.* I wrap my arms around my best friend.

Finally he says, 'I thought you'd run again,' his words muffled by my shoulder. 'I thought I was never gonna see you again.'

Two friends in the rain. Charlie lifts his head and rests his forehead against my forehead. 'You're the only family I got,' he says.

'I'll never leave you, Charlie,' I say. 'Even when I leave you, I'll never leave you.'

'What the fuck did you do?' he asks. 'Flo's lost her mind. She sent her boys to tear this place apart. They scared the shit out of us. Trashed everything in sight because they thought we were bullshitting when we said we didn't know where the hell you were.'

Then I see the cuts and bruising on Charlie's face. Rub my thumb along a purple bruise across his swollen upper right cheek.

'Who did this?' I ask.

'Ephraim,' Charlie replies. 'He went fuckin' psycho. Kept asking me where you ran to and I kept tellin' him I didn't know shit about where you ran to, but he wouldn't believe me. In the end I had to tell him how you met that pretty boy from Hamilton Hill on the bridge and maybe you ran away with him. Because that's what I actually thought.'

'Where's everybody now?'

'St Mary's Church is taking in all the West End floaters until the flood passes. They're sayin' everything's goin' under across Brisbane again.'

'Why haven't you left yet, Charlie?' I ask. 'This whole street will be under water soon.'

'I wasn't leaving without you. I knew you'd come back.'

He fetches his Foodbank box and pulls me towards his panel van. We clamber inside to shelter from the rain. Charlie finds a towel and runs it through my soaking wet hair, then sits back on his mattress. Something fragile in him. 'I thought you'd run off with him,' he says.

I shake my head. 'I was hiding with Esther Inthehole at St Peter the Apostle,' I say. 'Did you give Ephraim his name?'

'Who's name?'

'Danny's name,' I say. Visions in my head of Ephraim's men knocking on Danny's front door. 'Did Ephraim ask for the name of the boy on the bridge?'

'Of course he did,' Charlie says. 'But I said I didn't know his name. Then he kicked me in the ribs four times for good luck and then he fucked off. Ephraim's goons have been stalking around here ever since, waiting for you to come home.'

I shake my head. Run my hands over my face.

'What the fuck did you do?' Charlie asks again.

I undo the buttons on my raincoat, peel the wet yellow PVC off my skin. Sit back against the closed rear doors of the panel van. Knees up, hands clasped together. The memory makes me shudder. The blood in it. The monster in it.

'I stuck a knife in Brandon's throat,' I say.

Charlie drops his head, covers his eyes with his palms.

'It was Topping who killed him in the end,' I say. 'But I sure as shit helped. I did it, Charlie. I had to. I had to end the waltz. I didn't know I could do it. But I felt the monster blood in me. It was runnin' hard in me, Charlie. I couldn't stop it. And then Flo killed Topping … Poor Geoff … his girls.'

My friend shakes his head and that head-shake makes me weep because I know Charlie knows how screwed I am. Charlie knows that Flora Box will never stop searching for me until I'm dead. She will never let the murder of her son go unavenged. She will never swallow the imbalance.

'He was trying to kill me,' I reason. 'He was on top of me. Those big hands around my neck. I was going black. I was fuckin' dyin', Charlie. Then—'

'Stop,' Charlie says. 'You don't have to tell me shit about why that slimy fuck deserved to die. You just have to tell me you got a plan.'

I nod three times.

'What are you gonna do?' Charlie asks.

'I'm gonna meet my sister at three p.m. in the Starbucks coffee shop beneath the Myer Centre,' I reply. 'I'm gonna find out who I am. And then I'm gonna run.'

'Where you gonna run to?'

'As far north as I can go,' I say. 'Weipa, if I can make it that far. I know some people there who will help me.'

'What are you gonna live on?' he asks.

I unzip my backpack. Open the potato sack wide for Charlie. 'This will be a start,' I say.

Charlie's eyes filling with fire. 'Fuck me,' he says. 'What's that?'

'Our Christmas bonuses came early this year.'

'I'm comin' with you,' Charlie says.

'No, you're not,' I say. 'You're not jumpin' into my nightmare.'

'All right, I won't go with you,' he says. 'But please know that when you run away, I will be running away too. I might be a metre or two behind you. Maybe even beside you. But that will be pure coincidence. So feel free to ignore me.'

I give the skinny boy with the Beatles cut a half-smile. 'You really wanna come with me?'

Maybe the truest nod of his head that I've ever seen him give. Maybe the sincerest thing I've ever seen Charlie Mould do. 'There's nothin' for me here,' he says. 'Never has been.'

I lean over and wrap my arms around my friend. 'Colourful,' I whisper.

'Colourful,' he whispers back.

'I got some things to do before I go,' I say. 'Meet me at Starbucks at the bottom of the Myer Centre. I'll be there at three p.m.'

'So will I,' he says.

There's something fresh in Charlie's eyes. They look bluer than I've seen them in a while. I sit back and peer around the van. Paperback thriller books. Empty chip packets. A box of Goldenvale Corn Flakes. A banana skin.

'Fruit?' I say. Rare to see Charlie Mould eating solids, much less fresh fruit.

I scan the van again. 'No wine bags? No bottles? You're eating bananas. You feelin' all right, Charlie?'

He scoffs. 'Haven't had a drink for four days.' Shrugs his shoulders. The kid's comin' off all 'no big deal', but we both know it's a big fuckin' deal.

'What happened?'

'Found God in the bottom of my wine glass,' he says. 'We cut a deal. I give up the piss and you come back home. Looks like She held up her end of the deal.'

'She?'

'Yeah, by "God" I mean Jennifer Lopez.'

We laugh. I kick Charlie in the shins. 'I'm proud of you,' I say.

'Well, don't go gettin' your hopes up.'

'Don't worry, I won't.'

Charlie hangs the wet towel over the front passenger seat.

'I gotta keep movin',' I say.

'I'll see you at Starbucks at three o'clock,' he says.

'Starbucks,' I repeat, 'at three.' I move to the door, then remember what I came for, and turn back to Charlie.

'Hey, I need you to give me something before I go,' I say.

'What?'

'I need the key to Danny's house.'

Portrait of the Artist Lying Flat on Concrete, Apparently Stone-Cold Dead

Portrait of the Artist Lying Flat on Concrete, Apparently Stone-Cold Dead

Date unknown

Pen and ink on paper

A puzzling anomaly, a sketch almost out of place among the works included in our exhibition. Opinions have varied regarding the date of its creation, giving rise to likely apocryphal theories that this was, in fact, an act of presentiment and the artist was exploring intuitions of a future she could not possibly see. Note the clear evidence of blood gathering around the artist's abdomen. And, as always, the suffocating city stands above her, unmoved and uncaring, the Brisbane City Hall's towering clock face being the only witness to the artist's seemingly inevitable demise.

Start spreading the news. I'm leaving today. Leaving the river behind me. Leaving the dead, wet leaves beneath Macaroni's speeding wheels. Leaving the homes on flat tyres. Leaving the barbed-wire fence of my filthy scrapyard home. Leaving Oz. Goodbye, Moreton Bay fig. Goodbye, flood chaos city. If it's flooded, forget it, said all those ads on ABC radio inside Esther's hole. Forget it all. Forget the past. Forget Erica Finlay. Forget brave Christina. Forget all the names they gave you. Forget all the lies she told you.

Riding in my yellow raincoat. Brown boots on my feet. My backpack on my shoulders but protected under the raincoat so I look like the hunchback of Notre Dame on a joyride through the flooded streets of Brisbane. The backpack carries everything I own now.

Four pairs of underpants
Two pairs of shorts
Two T-shirts
One pack of Huggies Baby Wipes
Twenty-five of my favourite sketches
Three blocks of bona-fide drug money

I pedal hard through driving rain. Goodbye, Victoria Bridge. I see the river below. There are waves in it today and there are never waves in that river. The bitch is so cross that she's sending out waves of rage from her twisting and turning body. I watch half a house float swiftly down the river. Torn from its stumps somewhere upstream. Fire-coloured rust stains on the roof that bobs in the angry water. The house is chased by an upside-down yacht called *Miss Behavin'*. Following the yacht is a torn stretch of river pontoon with chains and locks and gates still attached to it, making madcap circles as it pushes on towards the Pacific.

I ride on through the city. Goodbye, Queen Street Mall. Goodbye, traffic controllers on George Street directing panicked drivers who never should have gone to work today. On through the rain down Elizabeth Street and on past the ominous Cathedral of St Stephen, where ibises and magpies and kookaburras are finding shelter from the rain under eaves and awnings and the church's arched stone entrance. An Amart furniture truck nearly hits me as I speed across the intersection of Elizabeth and Creek streets.

I ride on. Goodbye, Fortitude Valley. Goodbye, New Farm. Goodbye, Newstead. And on along the bike path that runs beside the angry and rising river. All the way to the house on Hamilton Hill.

*

The tall black gates to Danny Collins's home are open, and from there I can see a silver Mercedes-Benz parked in the gravel turning circle surrounding the fountain. I pedal hard down the driveway, staring up at the white curtains in Danny's top-floor bedroom window. When I'm close to the steps leading up to the front door, I pull hard on Macaroni's front brakes, the wheel skids and I nearly go flying over the handlebars.

I drop the bike hard to the ground. Rush to the front door. Finger on the doorbell. Finger on the doorbell. Finger on the doorbell. I stand back from the door, wiping rainwater off my yellow coat. Jump up and down to shake more water off me, and a pool of water forms by my feet. Heart about to burst. Stupid, dumb, unreliable pump. When will you ever play it cool for me?

The door opens. A woman in a grey cardigan that hangs over a peach-coloured shirt. Early fifties maybe. The mother from the oil painting I saw in Danny's dining room. But she's earthier in this doorway than she was in the painting. More real. Same brown hair, but it's hanging flat instead of flowing.

Her left hand stays on the door handle and her right thumbnail scratches nervously at the nail of her right forefinger. 'Hello,' she says. It sounds like a question: *Hellooo?*

I don't know what to say to her. Standing here frozen on a marble porch at a fairytale home on Hamilton Hill.

'Can I help you?' she asks.

Say something. A question. Start with a question. No questions come to mind. A name, then. Start with a name. Tell her your name. You don't know your name. You've never known your name. Just say something nice, then. Just say something that will make her feel nice, too.

'Danny,' I say.

'Danny?' she repeats. 'You've come to see Danny?'

'Yes,' I say.

'And who should I say has come to see him?' she asks.

'It's ... It's ...'

Who, indeed, has come to see him? Who? Who. The. Fuck. Are. You? Too much silence and space between the question and the answer I don't have. The woman smiles, opens the door wider.

'You're the girl from the bridge,' she says. 'You're the invisible girl.'

'He told you about me?'

'He can't shut up about you,' she says. And she laughs when she says that, and I laugh with her. She knows that's a nice thing to say to a girl. Nice thing for a girl to know, that there's a boy in her world who can't stop talking about her. Danny's mother wants to make me feel nice, too. 'He keeps telling me how miraculous it all seemed,' she says. 'The fact he ran into the very girl he'd been drawing so often in his sketchbook.'

I nod. Fingers fiddling nervously with the black buttons on my raincoat.

'Have to admit,' Danny's mother continues, 'I thought it was a pretty beautiful story, too.' She folds her arms across her chest now. Leans a shoulder against the doorway frame. 'Maybe it was even one of those meant-to-be-type stories,' she says. 'Danny certainly thinks it's one of those. That's why he keeps going down to that bridge every night in the rain, coming home soaking wet and going straight to his room to draw more pictures of the invisible girl who never seems to want to materialise on the bridge.'

'I wanted to be there every night,' I say.

'*I* wanted you to be there every night, too,' she says.

'Why did he keep going down there if I wasn't there?' I ask.

She shakes her head, smiles briefly. 'Well, I have a fair idea why,' she says. 'But that's a question you should probably ask my son.' She steps back, pushes the door towards me till it's almost closed but still ajar.

That's the space of my hope. The width of my missed opportunity. I turn around and see my yellow bicycle being showered by more rain under a still-grey sky. Dig the house key from my raincoat pocket and grip it in my right fist.

Then a voice behind my back. 'Mum says you want to ask me something?'

I turn around. He's wearing a black shirt and blue jeans. Looks like he's just got out of bed. Messy hair. Sad eyes. Bare feet. Hands in his pockets. He looks so handsome in the doorway that I wish I wasn't wearing this ridiculous raincoat. Here he is looking like James Dean, and here's me looking like Paddington Bear.

'What did you want to ask me?' he tries again.

I look down at my fist. Squeeze the key. 'Why did you wear the brown suit to the bridge?' I ask.

'You saw me?'

'I didn't see you. My friend Esther saw you. You were wearing a vintage brown suit? Why were you wearing that?'

He runs a hand across the stubble on his chin. 'Well, I thought it might be us you saw,' he says. 'You know, in the mirror. You're the girl in the red dress and I'm the guy in the brown suit who keeps coming into the frame to give you a kiss. I wanted to make that real for you.'

'Why do you keep going down to the bridge at night when I'm not there?' I ask.

He takes two steps towards me. I take one step back. He stops on the spot and holds his hands together at his waist like he's part of a church choir singing Latin songs about angels. Just staring at me now. Standing and staring.

'I kept thinking about that story they're gonna write about you,' he says. 'The one they're gonna put up alongside your paintings in the Met. I thought about how great it would be for people to read about how I never gave up, how I just kept seeing you in my head and how I just kept wishing I would look up and see you there in the middle of that bridge. I thought that would be a really beautiful part of your story.'

I keep my head down. Can't look at him when he talks so soft and tender like this. He thinks on his words. Delivers them slowly and carefully. I almost can't hear him in the heavy rain.

'Then when you kept not turning up, I thought I might become just a sad part of your story,' he says, 'just a line that everybody passes over.'

I sneak a look at him. His head's down, too. Then he lifts it up to look at me and I snap my head down again because I'm foolish and I'm also something else entirely.

'But then I realised that I didn't care what type of part I played in the story,' he continues. 'It doesn't matter to me. Sad. Mad. Tragic. Beautiful. Doesn't matter. I just wanna be in the story.'

I feel my lips trembling. Heart about to burst again. Want to run to him and throw my wet raincoat arms around him and kiss him in that doorway. Want to kiss him until the flood recedes and the sun comes out and the moon replaces it for the night.

Instead, I just look away. Turn my face to the grey sky that won't stop crying. 'I wish it worked like that, Danny,' I say. 'I wish we could write the stories exactly as we want. But now I know that's just my bullshit artsy-fartsy dreaming. We can't change shit about our stories because they're being written by someone else. They're being written by the powerful ones. The lucky ones. Like Flora Box.'

He moves closer to me. 'What happened to you?' he asks. 'I can help you. Let me help you.'

'You can't help me with what I need help with,' I reply.

Closer still. 'How did you know where I live?'

I turn back to him. Move two steps closer. Hold out the house key in my right hand. Tears welling in my eyes. Too embarrassed to say what I need to say. 'Take it. It's yours.'

He lifts the key from my hand.

'I didn't tell you the whole truth,' I say, 'because I was scared you'd stop talking to me. And I really liked talking to you.'

Pain and puzzlement across his face.

'Your sister owed a debt to my boss, Flora Box. Flora accepted that house key from your sister to square the debt. That house key was my Christmas bonus from Flora.'

Danny staring at the key. Filling holes in the story in his head.

Tears flowing now. 'Me and my best friend, Charlie ... we spent Christmas night inside this beautiful house,' I say. 'We looked after the place. We didn't take nothin'. Well, I think Charlie stole one of your mum's earrings.'

I shake my head. Eyes to the ground. Kick a heel into the marble beneath me. 'I saw you in the painting in the dining room,' I say. 'I thought you looked beautiful. Then I went to your bedroom and I saw all those photographs of you and all your friends on the corkboard. Then I lay down on your bed, Danny. I'd never laid down on a bed like that. I put my head on your pillow and I looked around the room and wondered what it would have been like to be raised in a family like yours.'

I rub a tear away with my finger. Unconsciously snort something wet up my nose. 'Then I put my hand under your pillow and found your sketchbook,' I continue. 'I opened it up, Danny, and for some strange and beautiful reason I saw myself. It felt like a Christmas miracle because I think it was. That's how Erica said it would happen. She said it would just be ordinary life, but it would feel designed. It would feel like art. Like something I'd sketch in my head. It would feel like everything suddenly had a reason to be. It would feel like everything made sense. It wouldn't matter what my name was or what my past was because it all had a reason to happen now that you were in my life. That's how it felt on the bridge the other night, too. And I went to sleep holding your sketchbook in my arms. It was the best sleep I've ever had in my life.'

I let my tears run down my face. I honour them. Honour the feeling in them. Let the feeling run, past my lips and over my chin. Let him see it. Let him see how it felt. How it feels. Then he might understand.

'I'm so sorry, Danny.'

He studies the key resting in his open palm. He shudders, like he's been prodded with a stun gun, like he's just waking up. I wait a moment for him to say something, but he keeps his head down. I think he's crying, too. Think he's keeping his head down because he can't bring himself to look at me.

I say his name. Say his beautiful name. 'Danny,' I whisper.

And I wait for him to look up, but he doesn't.

I turn around and slump heavily down the marble steps. Slip the hood of my raincoat over my head and hear the rain smack against it. Pick up my bike and hold the handlebars as I say one final sentence to the boy by the door with the key in his hand. 'Please stop going to the bridge.'

Only now does he lift his head up. He closes his hand around the key. Stares at me. 'No,' he says.

'What?' Maybe I didn't hear him right in the rain.

'No,' he repeats. Then takes two steps forward from the doorway. 'I'm not going to stop going to the bridge.'

I shake my head. Lift my right leg over Macaroni's crossbar, place my right foot on the pedal. Time to go. Time to leave this story here. 'I won't be there,' I say. 'I'll never be there, Danny. I'm running away. I can't stay in this city.'

He takes three more steps towards me. 'Let me help you,' he says.

I look at his face. The bones in his cheeks. His mouth open wide now. And I know his heart is beating as fast as mine. 'You can't help me, Danny,' I say. 'The story's been written. Someone else wrote it for us. I'm sorry, Danny. I'm sorry.'

I push down hard with my right foot. Pedal down. Pedal up. Ride. Don't turn back. Don't look back at the boy. Ride away from the prince and his mansion on the hill.

Rain smashing my face. The river will be rising higher. The river won't stop rising. I hope this flood drowns this whole fucking city. I hope it carries us all away to the Pacific. All the buildings. All the weatherboard homes on stumps with red tin roofs. All the pretty purple jacaranda trees. All the shops and all the cars with dead tyres that all them sorry floaters will sleep in when the world comes to watch us light Olympic torches. Wash it all away. All the hate. All the past. All the present. All the mums and all the dads. All the children. All the miracle babies in their prams. All the drawings. All the dreams of girls with foolish thoughts of taking flight. All the love stories across this godforsaken city. All the girls on yellow bicycles. All the boys running in the rain. All the bad timing. All the cops. All the killers. All the longing. All the love—

Sudden loud footsteps in the gravel. I look behind me. 'What are you doing?' I scream.

Danny Collins is running after me along the driveway. This beautiful boy named Danny.

'Stop,' he shouts through the rain. 'Let me help you.'

'Stop following me,' I shout back. 'You can't help me.' And I'm sobbing like a fool in the rain. 'Stop it,' I say, but I'm saying it to myself, too. Stop it. Stop feeling this moment. Stop caring. Stop weeping.

'I'm *not* gonna stop,' he yells. Breathless. Panting hard. 'I'll go to that bridge every night if I have to.'

I ride harder. So fast the rear wheel slips and slides in the gravel. I go out the tall black gates and take a hard left onto the street and the gap between Danny Collins and me lengthens, though he's still sprinting hard. I ride between expensive parked cars and clean white footpaths and giant fig trees with leaves that are shaking wildly in the storm. And then I'm riding too fast for him and he knows he's beat.

He stops in the middle of the street and he calls out to me once more. 'I see you,' he calls through the rain. 'I'll always see you.'

And then I'm gone. The girl on the yellow bike in the yellow raincoat. Weeping in the rain.

Pedal hard. So hard it turns your thin legs to iron. Don't ever stop pedalling. Don't stop to feel all of this. Ride from this. Run from this. Never stop running. It's what you were born to do.

River Monster

River Monster

January 2024

Pen and ink on paper

At once the most fantastical sketch in the artist's oeuvre and the most truthful. It's almost as if, at last, the artist has removed her rose-coloured glasses and seen her troubled world for exactly what it is. Deadly. Violent. Monstrous.

Standing with Macaroni on the corner of Adelaide and Albert streets, on the edge of King George Square, in the heart of the CBD. Waiting for the little green man to flash at the traffic crossing. Everybody reacting to the city-wide flooding in their own weird way. Some rush by frantically carrying Coles grocery bags filled with canned goods and toiletries. A man rushes past me clutching two sixteen-roll packs of Quilton toilet paper. Some people sit in cafés eating scones with jam and cream, as though a rising flood is business as usual in the city of Brisbane and if their heels aren't wet yet then there's no reason not to finish their English Breakfast tea.

Cars and buses gridlocked on Adelaide Street because everybody had the same idea of leaving work early and driving out of the city on roads they know will surely be roadblocked by the police in a matter of hours. A man in a white Toyota Prado slams his fist on his car horn because someone cut him off, and he leaves it blowing for almost thirty seconds, which makes him seem broken and damaged and flood-crazed. That's how some people turn in these rain events. The rising water electrifies them. It's like shock treatment. Some walk around the city wide-eyed and pale-faced, speaking of the end of days, or at least the end of Brisbane.

Further down Adelaide Street, I can see Ivan Salhus and his longtime street buddy, Pot, rolling up their sleeping bags. If they have any sense, they'll head to St Mary's Church, which sits on a rise on Merivale Street, South Brisbane, to wait out the rain event with a hundred other Brisbane floaters. I lift my eyes up to the Brisbane City Hall clocktower. It rises almost a hundred metres and to me looks like a great big sketching pencil pointing at the grey clouds, its apex a sharpened graphite tip. I feel like I could rip that pencil from the City Hall roof and draw a portrait of Danny Collins on that endless sky canvas, and I would give this sketch a name: *I'm Sorry I Rode Away from You in the Rain, Danny Collins, But I Had to Go and See My Sister.*

The tower's clock face is five metres wide and its black metal minute hand is three metres long and it makes a small movement that tells me the time is now 3.10. I'm ten minutes late for the meeting with my sister, the most important meeting of my life. How could I be late when she has flown across the entire country and no doubt had to ask a cab driver to take her into a city centre that most people are currently trying to escape from? My sister's name is Phoebe. Phoebe means 'radiant'. Phoebe means 'light'.

A wave of cars reluctantly slows at the crossing, the traffic light buzzes and the little green man flashes. I push Macaroni to the middle of the street. Rain still batters down on my raincoat hood, my ears now accustomed to the sound. My boots are soaking wet and I could no doubt wring my thick blue socks and fill two coffee mugs with dirty rainwater. My backpack is still under my raincoat, keeping my favourite sketches safe and dry. Those sketches of my life. My dreams. My future. Erica. There's even a sketch of Flora Box in there. My nightmare.

I've almost made it to the other side of the street when I hear a car horn beeping loudly and aggressively from the row of cars sputtering in the rain at the crossing. I trace the offensive sound to a green Volkswagen Golf not more than five metres from my left shoulder. At first I can't make out the driver's face through the fogged-up glass but then he rubs it with his fist and leans close to the glass.

It's Glenn Ash. The man they call 'The Priest'. The man who runs the wet floor at Ebb 'n' Flo. I like Glenn, so my first instinct is to smile at him, but then I see he's not smiling back at me. There's nothing but sin on his face and I suddenly realise that he's more than likely looking for me under strict orders from Flora. He shakes his head and there's menace and frustration and pity in that face. The traffic lights change and I'm still standing in the way of the traffic and Glenn's car is still stopped at the lights. Both of us frozen, like the two-day-old midweek prawns Glenn defrosts in saltwater brine and passes off as fresh.

The cars behind him honk their horns and I'm snapped back to my purpose. I rush Macaroni across the street, lift the front wheel onto the pavement then let its back tyre hit the kerb hard so it bounces up like a bucking bull trying to jettison a cowboy. Glenn's tyres spin and screech on the wet asphalt as his car takes off and speeds along Adelaide Street. I don't have to see him to know what he's doing right now. He's calling Ephraim Wall on his mobile phone and telling him he just saw the girl from Moon Street who stuck a knife in Brandon Box's throat.

Pushing Macaroni, I sprint up the Albert Street end of Queen Street Mall, zipping between office workers and supermarket shoppers and then a group of school students sucking on vape pens outside the 7-Eleven. Hundreds of people are sheltering under the mall's awnings.

Macaroni's right pedal clips the calf of a large man in a tracksuit outside the Telstra mobile phone shop. 'What the fuck?' he exclaims.

'Sorry,' I say, pushing on.

'Watch where yer goin', ya cunt,' the tracksuit man barks behind me.

I scurry across the centre of the mall and find Charlie waiting for me outside the Hungry Jack's on the corner of Queen and Albert streets. Arse on the ground, knees up, eyes darting between every person who passes him. He's got an old blue Mountain Designs backpack over his shoulders and, by his side, a large, bulging, red-white-and-blue-striped plastic storage bag with a busted zipper.

'I just saw Glenn Ash,' I say, urgently, while doing my best to swallow my instinct to scream and panic.

Charlie looks up at me. 'Did he see you?'

'Yes. But he was stuck in traffic. He couldn't get outta the car.'

'He'll be talkin' to Ephraim as we speak.'

I nod.

'We should get the hell outta here now,' Charlie says.

'Not until I've seen my sister.' I point at the storage bag beside Charlie. 'What's that?' I ask.

'That's my stuff,' he replies, looking up at me.

'What stuff?' I ask.

'My clothes. My books. My hair dryer. My snowdome collection.'

I shake my head. 'What the fuck, Charlie? That's too big to take on the road. We might have to go a long way north and you can't be carrying that fuckin' bag along highways an' shit.'

Charlie stands, grips the storage bag's flimsy plastic handles and hauls it over his shoulder, grimacing briefly. 'It's all good,' he says, bending his back. 'Like a snowflake on my shoulder.' Then he straightens up, takes two deep breaths. Smiles.

'You sure you wanna come with me?' I ask.

A sharp wink of his left eye.

'You're gonna miss that panel van,' I say. 'That thing was your home.'

'Bullshit,' Charlie says. 'Only place that's home to me is somewhere by your side.' He takes a step closer to me and places his hands on my shoulders. 'Now, you ready to meet this sister of yours?'

I nod, take a deep breath. Undo the buttons on my raincoat. Slip out of the wet yellow plastic and hang the coat over Macaroni's crossbar. Stand in front of the Hungry Jack's window and assess my reflection in the glass. Wet hair looks like a bowl of spaghetti. Still got my backpack over my shoulders. Black shorts and an old purple T-shirt. Wet socks. Wet brown boots. Shaking knees. Shaking fingers. 'I'm ready,' I whisper.

Wheeling Macaroni on past a Nike shoe shop and the House of Hoops store that sells the expensive basketball shoes Charlie is always dreaming about. On past the OPSM spectacles store, stopping to let a truck pull out of a driveway that runs down into the Myer department store. We're only ten metres from Starbucks. I feel sick. Realise I haven't eaten for hours and there's nothing but air in my stomach and that air is a cruel wind spinning little twisters in my belly.

'All right, you're up, kid,' Charlie says. 'I'll hang outside and keep an eye out for Flora's grunts.'

But I remain standing in front of the glass. I've lost all motor functions. Can't move my right leg to make it start walking.

A warm hand at the top of my back. The hand of my friend, Charlie. 'C'mon,' he says, softly. 'She's waiting for you.'

Right foot. Left foot. Right foot. Hands nervously gripping the straps of my backpack. I peer through the Starbucks shopfront. Normally this coffee shop would be filled with patrons sipping large lattes, pumpkin-spice frappuccinos and hibiscus tea lemonades, but this afternoon it's empty. Everybody's getting out of the city. Everybody except that woman with the brown hair that hangs just past her shoulders. I press my head to the glass and now I can see her clearly, sitting there alone at a table for two, her left hand holding a small white coffee cup. She's wearing a smart black cropped jacket over a plain white T-shirt and there's a bright red watch on her left wrist. I watch her scrolling through something on the phone on the table in front of her. And then I hear a word from the mouth of my friend Charlie Mould. 'Fuck.'

I jerk my head round to find Charlie pointing past my shoulder at something further along Albert Street. I follow his finger.

'It's the Priest!' Charlie says.

Glenn Ash is standing on the other side of the street at a crossing, bouncing on the spot and looking left as he waits for a break in the thick flow of traffic. Then he turns and, as though he can sense me even this far away, his eyes find mine. He shakes his head twice. Words in that movement: *Don't you dare run away from me again.*

I turn back to the coffee shop and press my forehead to the glass, so close my warm breath fogs the window. Need to see her one more time.

'We gotta get outta here,' Charlie urges.

But I can't leave without her seeing me. I want her to look up. Want her to know I'm not invisible. Want her to know I came to see her. It was just the story that made me run away again. I wanted to stay. I want to stay. *Phoebe, look up.*

I glance round and see Glenn Ash rushing across Elizabeth Street, narrowly avoiding being clipped by a speeding red Kia. Here he comes. *He's coming for me, Phoebe. I'm sorry, I have to run now.*

Then, as I prepare to go, my sister raises her head from her phone and meets my gaze. The light in her eyes. The sunshine in her smile. Phoebe is radiant. Phoebe is light. She makes me smile.

She stands up, arms by her side. I raise my hand and place my right palm flat on the glass. Contact. Connection. Hope in that smile of hers. Tears in it, too. A laugh from her now. Uncertainty in it, her joy shifting to confusion. Words in it:

What are you waiting for?
Come inside and meet me.
I have waited all my life to meet you.
What are you waiting for?

'Run,' Charlie says. 'Run!'

Glenn Ash is almost upon me. I give my sister one last look and step back from the glass, taking a deep and pained breath of thick air. This will be my last vision of her. Shaking her head. Her puzzlement. Her pain.

I run. Charlie is already sprinting back up towards the Hungry Jack's, lugging the heavy jumbo storage bag on his shoulder as he runs. I push Macaroni as hard as I can and shoppers and pedestrians sidestep awkwardly out of my unwavering path.

'Come on, run faster!' Charlie screams, turning to find me.

We take a sharp left and run along the tactile paving trail at the upper end of Queen Street Mall. I sneak a glance over my shoulder and see Glenn Ash pushing shoppers out of his way as he shortens the space between us.

We run past the Myer Centre and the mall's performance space. Past staircases that descend to underground bus stations.

Shouting from someone behind us. A large, burly man is pulling on Glenn Ash's arm, clearly not taking kindly to having been shoved aside.

Charlie uses the delay to slow down and wait for me to catch up. 'Ditch the fuckin' bike,' he says.

'No, you ditch that fuckin' bag and double me on the bike,' I say.

Charlie shakes his head but makes his decision an instant later. He drops his jumbo bag on the mall paving and grips Macaroni's handlebars. 'Get on,' he says.

I sit on the bike's crossbar as Charlie powers up through the mall, gaining more speed with every turn of the pedals. Soon we've extended the distance between us and our fish-gutter, oyster-shucker pursuer. We zip through a row of black safety bollards at the top of Queen Street Mall and Charlie stands up to pedal like a Tour de France rider powering uphill, panting and grunting as his thin legs push down hard on the pedals and the bike speeds towards a currently open and traffic-free George Street. I can see the Treasury Casino across the street and beyond the casino I can see the Victoria Bridge, where Danny Collins was waiting for me during those nights I spent in the hole. Just as we're about to speed across the empty street to a brief slice of freedom, a black BMW bursts through a red light and brakes right in front of Macaroni.

The bike's front tyre slams hard into the car's impervious black metal, launching Charlie and me onto the hood. My right shoulder strikes the car first and my head spins for a moment but soon clears enough for me to make out the person staring at me from the front passenger seat. My monster, Flora Box. Lips pressed together. Eyes of a tyrant lizard.

I dart my head to the driver's side. The cold blue eyes of Ephraim Wall stare back through the glass, his hands almost choke-holding the steering wheel.

Charlie rolls off the car and onto the asphalt. One of Flora's grunts – it's Nathan Rose, the guy with the dyed blond goatee – is already out of the car and marching towards him.

'Charlie!' I scream. But Charlie, dazed and groggy, looks up too late and the hands of Flo's thug are already around his throat.

'Run!' Charlie yells.

'Charlie,' I holler again.

'Fucking run!' he sings again.

And I follow my best friend's demands this time and roll off the hood and lift Macaroni up from the ground and grip the handlebars. And I'm ready to push the bike across George Street when I hear the roar of Ephraim Wall.

'Do not run away from me,' he barks.

I look back to find him standing outside the car. He briefly opens one flap of his jacket to show me the black pistol butt sticking out of the side of his pants. I see Nathan Rose drive a fist into Charlie's face, knocking him out, instantly. I lock eyes with Flo in the passenger seat. The mother of a dead son. Only death in her stare now.

I look again at Ephraim Wall. He shakes his head. 'Don't,' he says.

But I do.

The traffic lights turn green and some cars stay still to gawk at the scene while others accelerate through the crossing. These are the cars I run straight towards, weaving dangerously through the moving traffic. One or two vehicles screech to a halt; some maintain their speed and nearly crash into me as I scamper across the street, pushing Macaroni like a bobsled by my side.

I make it across the road and look over my shoulder to see Ephraim Wall reluctantly slipping back into the driver's seat. He can't leave Flora Box sitting in the middle of George Street traffic. Nathan Rose bundles Charlie into the back of the car and the BMW speeds away. I push Macaroni across the road and into Brisbane Square and on past the white stone steps of the Treasury Casino, then come to another traffic crossing at William Street. Just one street between me and the Victoria Bridge. I'll hop on Macaroni, cross this street and ride away. Ride like the wind. But where do I ride to and how can I leave without Charlie?

I swivel my head from side to side, searching for the black car. Ephraim will be circling the block. He can drive into William Street, but cars aren't allowed on the Victoria Bridge. Four cars zoom along William Street and there's a brief break in the traffic. I'm about to step onto the road when I feel a hand grab the back of my neck.

'You fuckin' idiot,' Glenn Ash says. 'What have you done?'

I instinctively pull my neck away, but Glenn only strengthens his grip, holding me the way I've seen him hold whole red-throat emperor fish when he's placing them in an ice box. I flail about, kick at his left calf with my boots.

'Calm the fuck down and stop making a scene,' he says. 'There's a knife up my left sleeve. I don't want to have to use it.'

'I'm glad you brought a knife, Glenn,' I say, wrenching my neck back. 'Maybe I'll get a chance to use it myself. Didn't you hear about what I did to Brandon? You really don't wanna bring out the monster in me.'

'Shut the fuck up and start walking,' he says.

He pushes me and Macaroni across the street and onto the left-side pedestrian walkway traversing the Victoria Bridge. He holds the side of my T-shirt discreetly, pretending we're two people who actually care about each other, a father and daughter maybe, taking a gentle stroll across a bridge during a major flood.

He pulls out a mobile phone, taps a number. 'I've got her,' he says. 'Yeah, go to the South Bank end of the Victoria Bridge.' He slips the phone back in his pocket.

We walk across the bridge, the rain not as heavy as it was before but still beating down and filling the wild brown river beneath us. The bridge is lined with flood watchers, who have come to take in the city's best view of a catastrophic flood that will ruin homes across the city, decimate suburbs, even wash loved ones away forever, taking them down into the darkness of the drink to spend eternity with the Queensland lungfish. The gawkers stand under umbrellas, gasping as upturned boats and savaged jetties and pontoons are tossed and turned in the water like they were made of foam rubber.

'You're working for monsters, Glenn,' I say.

'No shit, Sherlock,' he says. 'I always wondered when you'd realise that.'

A man in a grey business suit scurries towards us from the southern end of the bridge. Umbrella in one hand, briefcase in the other. Blond hair. Lean and fit. As we pass each other, he studies Macaroni closely. We move on, but then he calls out to us. 'Excuse me,' he says. An accent in that voice. American. Canadian, maybe.

I stop and turn to the man. Glenn rests a warning hand on my left shoulder.

'May I ask you where you got that bike from?' the man asks.

I nod and, without a second thought, reply, 'I stole it from Roma Street Parklands.'

'Excuse me?' the blond man says.

Glenn digs his fingers hard into my collarbone. Laughs and offers a cordial smile. 'She's just being silly,' he says. 'Don't mind her. It was a birthday present.' And he hurries me along the bridge.

But the man in the grey suit is confused. He starts following us. 'Wait, please stop,' he says.

Glenn quickens his pace.

The man in the suit catches up with us. 'That's a canary-yellow Bianchi road bike,' he says.

'It sure is,' I say and smile.

'My best friend had a canary-yellow Bianchi road bike stolen in Roma Street Parklands two years ago,' he says.

I nod enthusiastically. 'Well, that's funny,' I say, 'because I stole a canary-yellow Bianchi road bike from Roma Street Parklands two years ago.'

'Shut the fuck up,' Glenn spits.

'I'd call the police if I was you,' I continue.

Glenn stops and turns to the blond man in the suit. 'If you know what's good for you, you'll kindly fuck off now,' he says. Then he pushes me on, his hands back on my neck.

The blond man stays back a moment then approaches Glenn once more from behind, this time tapping his right shoulder with his briefcase. 'I'm sorry, I can't just let you walk away with that bike,' the man says.

I hear Glenn suck a breath of air through his teeth. He squeezes my neck tighter and I know now that the short-ex-prisoner-fuse inside Glenn Ash has dwindled to the length of a matchhead.

'*Excuuuuse me*,' the man with the briefcase bellows. 'I'm talking to you.'

And the blond man's briefcase connects again with Glenn's shoulder. Too hard this time.

And The Priest's fuse is lit.

Glenn releases his right hand from my neck, spins around and, in one fluid motion, drives his concealed blade into the left side of the blond man's ribs. The man drops immediately and silently to the rain-soaked asphalt walkway.

I need noise now. I need attention. So I scream as loud as I possibly can through the driving rain. Banshee wailing. Hysterical. And I drop my bike and take three stunned steps back from Glenn Ash and his concealed knife, and red rage fills his cheeks because he knows what I'm doing.

'He stabbed him,' I scream, pointing at Glenn. 'He stabbed him!'

And several flood gawkers holding umbrellas turn their attention from the caramel thickshake river to the blond man squirming in a pool of blood formed by another kind of river, one that begins in his ribcage.

I turn and run. 'Help me,' I scream. And Glenn Ash runs after me.

Must keep making noise. Must keep screaming. I sprint along the bridge, wailing, 'He's got a knife! He's trying to kill me.' And several people standing under umbrellas along the bridge rail turn to face me, looking startled as they assess the scene.

'Help meeeee!' I scream.

A handful of brave young men in raincoats and windcheaters who look like rugby players spread across the walkway behind me, blocking Glenn's path.

'Outta my fuckin' way,' Glenn demands, but the wall of young men does not break. Instead I see muscular bodies smothering Glenn Ash, and his legs and arms thrashing about as the young men wrestle him to the wet ground. It's a rugby scrum on a rainy bridge.

More people gather around the scrum and soon there's nowhere for Glenn Ash to go, except maybe to a police station and then back to prison, where he might want to try hanging himself again on a strip of razor wire.

But still I run.

*

All of my life's possessions bouncing inside the black bag still hanging from my shoulders. Never stop running. I sprint along the bridge, no time to even look down at the water that stole Erica Finlay from me when I was just a girl who liked to draw stuff. This life of mine. This story of mine. Imagine this part of the story, I think to myself. Imagine what all them artsy-fartsy people are gonna say when they hear E.P. Buckle recount this moment in the Met.

The artist ran, her heart thumping and her head spinning. She feared for her best friend, Charlie Mould. They'd taken him from the street. Kidnapped him in broad daylight. She wondered if he was still alive. She wondered if Flora Box had enough black ink inside her black-ink heart to kill a wild fuck-up as adorable as Charlie Mould. The city of Brisbane had gone mad. Gawkers on bridges popping their eyes at all the river carnage. Nowhere was safe for the artist. She kept glancing about as she ran, watching for faces she recognised. The faces of Flora Box's men. All the faces she saw packing boxes in the back of the seafood market. The faces of the men who wanted to kill her now.

The artist ran.

I reach the end of the bridge and follow the pedestrian footpath left into the Queensland Cultural Centre forecourt. Just as I make the turn, I hear the sound of tyres screeching on asphalt – Flora Box's black BMW swerving into the forecourt's U-shaped driveway, which wraps around a small garden topped by a tall white flagpole.

I take a shortcut across the garden then leap down a pebblecrete staircase towards the entrance to the art gallery carpark as the BMW accelerates around the driveway. But I'm too pumped, too panicked, and I leap too high and land too hard. I feel my left ankle roll inside my boot, bones twisting inside my skin, and pain shoots up my left shin.

The BMW screeches to a halt in front of me, blocking my path, and I almost hit the car headfirst. But I save myself by springing off my right foot and lifting my left leg high, like all them Olympic hurdlers will do when they come to my savage city in 2032. I leap onto Flora's shining hood and dent it with two heavy steps before jumping off the other side, almost breaking my already twisted ankle as I hit the ground. Behind me, I hear a door open and slam shut. Someone's coming after me.

Run. Down the thin white concrete footpath past the rook-shaped Victoria Bridge Abutment. Down to the place where I lost Erica. The place where little Christina's pram rolled over all that blue-grey cobblestone and dropped into the river. The police and SES have taped off the riverside walkway running along the State Library and the Gallery of Modern Art. I duck under chequered tape and sprint past an SES warning sign into floodwater that reaches up to my kneecaps.

I hear splashing behind me. Take a quick look over my shoulder. Nathan Rose, the thug who punched Charlie in the face, is panting as he runs. He's unfit, but his anger keeps him upright. I quicken my pace, sloshing through the water. Past the Gallery of Modern Art and the sculpture of the upside-down elephant and the brave and powerful water rat. *The world turns*, Erica said. *The world turns for all of us*, she said, and I want it to turn me now and dump the monster behind me on his thick metal skull. Then I want this world to toss him in the river, where Erica can spend the rest of her life sucking the flesh off his sunken bones.

Don't think. Just run. Past anchored cruise boats bobbing precariously in the river like rubber ducks under running bath taps. Past terraced gardens designed to look like the Hanging Gardens of Babylon. Under giant poincianas with flame-coloured canopies that hang over the riverside walkway and look so bright against the grey storm sky.

The thug is still behind me, but I'm increasing the gap between us. Even with a busted ankle I'm quicker than him. He needs to drink less beer and eat more Aldi sardines. Thug motherfucker. The casual way he punched my friend in the face. Cold-blooded tyrant lizard with no air in his ribs.

Run. Run. Just keep running, I tell myself. But I can't keep going like this. I need to get off this path. The walkway climbs left up the higher ground of Kurilpa Point. No floodwater slowing me down now. I duck under the Kurilpa Bridge, scamper past Daisy Gong's upright piano, now drenched with rain. There are normally at least ten floater tents under the shelter here. Today, they've moved on to escape the flood. The only things left are a few abandoned trolleys, a semi-circle of milk crates and a now-soggy boardgame. The Game of Life.

Just me and my monster on this path now. I run under the William Jolly Bridge, where Pablo Picasso likes to paint. Where the great artist said I had to weep to achieve my dreams. Well, if that's all it took, Mr Picasso, then consider my end of the deal upheld. Because I'm crying now in the rain. Crying with the pain. Crying for Charlie. Crying for the hurt I brought to Danny Collins, the boy in the mansion on the hill. Crying for my sister who flew across Australia to see me. Crying for Erica Finlay in the river. Crying because I'm running past the scrapyard behind the Tinman's shed and all I want to do is go inside that yard and open the sliding door to my van and fall asleep then wake up tomorrow morning with a circle of sunlight on my belly. A circle of sunshine made just for me.

'Stop,' Nathan Rose calls behind me. 'I'm not gonna hurt ya.'

What a fuckin' nimrod. He's getting desperate. I would break his spirit now if I kept running, but I can't do it. Got no spirit left myself. My head is heavy, full of rushing blood. My ankle feels busted, like it's swelling even as I run, turning to concrete, which seems somewhat appropriate as I pass the great river-facing side wall of the Hanson factory and turn left off the path at the lamppost where Charlie likes to pass out during his benders.

The concrete factory's closed for the day. The dawn shift premix trucks made their deliveries hours ago. I run along the front security fence to the gate, squeeze my right foot between two of the gate's vertical pickets, push myself up from the base rail and flip myself over in a cartwheel motion. I stifle a scream as I land hard on my left ankle, then scurry across the loading area, where Charlie used to ride his skateboard, Brandon Box used to write profanities in the asphalt with chalky rocks, and I used to draw things I could see in my head, like Brisbane River monsters.

A monster's still after me right now. A real-life monster with a blond goatee, in jeans and a blue fish-market polo shirt. I look up at the blue rocket-shaped silos at the back of the complex, the conveyor belt running down from the top of the factory on my left to the water tower on my right. The amusement park ride we thought would be so much fun.

I slip into one of the parking bays and hide behind a grey concrete wall then take five deep breaths, with my hands on my knees. This is the place where Brandon Box stuck his hands up my shirt when I was a girl. Where I first saw the monster.

Heart chuggin' like a coal train now, I slowly edge myself along the wall and look back towards the security fence. Nothing on the street. Just the sound of rain and wind.

Then I see the top of the thug monster's head in the rain. He's walking along the factory's security fence, peering up Hockings Street, looking for his nameless prey, the girl who seems to have vanished from the face of the earth. Abracadabra. Alakazam. Damn, damn, damn. The monster turns to his left and approaches the gate. I creep backwards silently, climb over a yellow gate and scurry into the heart of the mixing plant.

I look up and see an iron roof with skylights some twenty metres above me. Climbing almost to the roof is an intricate structure made of aquamarine-coloured steel frames, silver staircases and platforms, and grey mixing tanks and pouring shafts. There's no order to it, so it's like staring up at a game of snakes and ladders.

Above the skylights it's just grey sky and the rain hammering the glass. It's dark inside the plant and that's a good thing because it means I can hide from the monster. I get down low and scamper through a maze of machinery. Squeeze down the side of what looks like some kind of control panel. Then I hear something. The sound of metal on metal. The monster seems to have found a pole of some kind and he's banging it against machinery and dragging it along the concrete walls behind me, maybe pushing something along the ground. He's getting closer and I'm running out of space. He's armed and I've got nothing but my backpack filled with drawings. I sketch this moment in my mind. *Girl Out of Options. Girl with Nowhere to Go in the Concrete Plant.*

I turn sharp left around another mixing tank and come to four large containers in front of a dead-end concrete wall. Two are filled with small grey-black rocks, the other two with fine yellow sand. Again, the sound of the pole banging on metal behind me. The sound of the monster's voice. 'Don't make it harder on yourself,' Nathan Rose calls. 'Flo just wants to talk to ya.'

I spot a thin gap between the last tub and the concrete wall. Big enough for me to crawl into. I take my bag off my shoulders and duck down there, heart set to burst. Hold my breath as I unzip the bag, so slowly it makes no sound. Take out my sketches. Some twenty-five drawings. The best I could do. The ones I was going to put in a portfolio and show to the admissions officer at the Queensland College of Art. Another time. Another world. Another girl.

I scatter the sketches on the ground. The pole bangs louder now. 'You're pissing me off, you little cunt,' the monster shouts. 'I swear the next thing I'll be swinging this pole against will be your skull.'

I stand up, hold the bag open at my chest, start shovelling handfuls of the grey-black rocks into it.

'You got nowhere left to go,' the monster yells. 'You trapped yourself, ya little rat.'

The rocks fit around my belongings and the blocks of cash. Fistful after fistful after fistful. Soon the bag is heavy in my hands. I step softly to my right and top it up with handfuls of sand. Scoop after scoop after scoop. The damp sand mixes with the rocks until it feels like I'm carrying a bowling ball in my bag. I zip the bag then scoop up one more fistful of sand before I retreat between the tub and the concrete wall.

Crouching low. Out of sight. Stay here. Stay down. Don't make a sound. Gripping the sand so tight my fingers ache. Slow breaths, in through the nose and back out through the nose because I don't dare open my mouth. Then I hear the faintest sound of rubber shoes padding across the concrete floor, the pole in the monster's hand brushing against metal as he squeezes through a gap and into my dead-end space. I hear his shoes walking on my favourite sketches then I hear him pick one of those sketches up off the concrete floor.

I lean forward from my narrow hiding space and I see Nathan Rose with the pole tucked under his left arm and his head down, looking into the image. It's the sketch I called *The Tyrannosaurus Waltz*, the one I drew based on the stories Erica told me about the kitchen she danced in with my father. Nathan seems mesmerised by the sketch. So I must make my move. Do the brave thing. The reckless thing. I must choose danger. This moment will be an incredible story for E.P. Buckle to recount in the Met in the year 2100. It will be even more incredible if I survive it.

Now. Go now. The brave thing. Now.

I spring from my narrow space and run at the monster with the pole under his arm. I scream and the sound rattles him and he takes a moment to clock what's coming at him before he drops my sketch and reaches for the pole. But I'm all song and dance, all confusion and distraction. I keep screaming loudly then I throw the fistful of sand at his face and he drops the pole to shield his eyes because he doesn't know what I'm throwing at him and it's only when he wipes the sand out of his eyes that I swing my heavy bag of rocks and sand and cold, hard-drug cash at his face and it lands flush on his nose and blood is already pouring from his nostrils when he lands flat on his arse with his right hand touching a sketch of mine I like called *Girl with Cold Potato Scallop*.

Running now. I steal a glance behind me and see the thug unwittingly rubbing blood across his face then looking at his red right palm and howling with rage. I squeeze past a large mixing tank and a control panel then through a series of metal boxes and machines with prongs and scoops and funnels. Then I come to the passage that leads to the truck bays, but the tyrant lizard has blocked my course with a large metal electrical box the size of a refrigerator, tipped over on its side.

I push feebly against the box but couldn't move it even if I did have any strength whatsoever left in my arms and legs. I turn around in time to see the monster with the blood-red face enter the passage I just ran down. He looks like some kind of mad cannibal warrior from an ancient cult who cover themselves in blood when they hunt.

I look at the metal framework reaching to the roof of the building. The only way out now is up. I sprint back to the middle of the passage and pull myself up onto the edge of a mixing tank. There's a lip on the tank that's wide enough for me to balance on. Flo's thug grips the top of the tank and starts to pull himself up too, as I try my best to stay calm and balanced, arms out straight like a gymnast. If I slip, I'll fall into the wide hole in the centre of the cone-shaped tank, which drops to some dark place I can't see.

When I've rounded the lip, I lean over almost half a metre, grab one of the crossbeams of the metal framework then plant my right foot on one of its X-shaped cross-bracings. And now I climb. Carefully shimmying up and across, like a cat burglar climbing a garden trellis. Soon I'm five metres or so off the ground and about five metres across the framework, from where I'm close enough to hang a leg out over thin air and find a footing on the edge of a steel platform, part of a series of metal staircases that plant workers must use to access the conveyor belt, roughly another ten metres above me.

I look down to see Flo's thug coming up the framework beneath me. He's stronger than me, angrier than me, climbing faster than me. I reach my left hand out, grip the top of the platform's safety railing, pull myself over it awkwardly and fall flat on my back, sucking in short breaths. Above me, I see the entrance to the conveyor belt and I now see that as my only way out.

I pull myself up as I watch the thug shuffling across the framework. The staircases are so steep they feel more like ladders, and my legs burn as I raise my knees high enough to make it up each step. Three staircases in all to get to the conveyor belt, and when I reach it I realise the shaft is sealed off by a locked safety door.

Flo's thug has gained ground on me and is already on the second steel staircase and climbing fast. No more time to think. Only time to be brave and reckless. Time to tell the story how I want to tell it. Time to make it out of the story alive. There's a large open space in the wall of the building to accommodate the conveyor belt, so it's possible to climb onto its curved, corrugated-metal roof. The rain is still hammering down and I can see thin rivers of rainwater running down the corrugations. I picture Brandon Box standing on top of the tube all those years ago. Thought he was mad for doing it. Wrong in the brain. I must be wrong in the brain too, then, because I grip the top of the tube with my hands and pull my chest and then my belly and then my right leg up onto the roof. I bring my left foot up to the roofing and I'm crouching now, like a surfer searching desperately for balance, at the highest point of the tube, and I go all bubbleheaded and woozy when I glance down. Must be fifteen metres to the ground below me.

Right foot. One step down. Left foot. Another step down. One more step and then another after that. And then I feel a shiver in my toes, a tingling of knowing and dread, an electricity inside me that comes from a place beyond my understanding. It's a warning. A way of seeing the future, the kind of thing Esther Inthehole talks about. We can all see the future just a little bit.

And in this very moment I see myself slipping off the roof and I see my brains spilled across the asphalt.

But then I remember the way Brandon Box made it back down. So I plant my arse firmly on the rain-wet iron with my legs in front of me and start pulling myself forward with my feet. Slow and deliberate movements. No sudden jolts. Straddling the roof when I need to find my balance again, like I'm on a horse saddle. Soon I'm about a third of the way down and pleased to think I'd have to endure a drop of only ten metres to my certain death now.

Behind me the sound of boots on corrugated iron. Flo's blood-faced thug stepping out onto the tube. I grip the roof tight with my legs, slowly turn my head round to look over my shoulder and see him crouched low and turned to his side, shuffling down like he's moving along a surfboard. He's braver than I am. More willing to move quickly. And he's gaining on me. 'Ya didn't listen to me, rat,' he says between steps. 'Ya shoulda listened to me.'

I turn to face forward again and pull my sore arse hard and fast down the roof. But I hear the thug's steps getting closer. *Stomp. Stomp. Stomp.* 'That's the trouble with young people today,' he says. *Stomp. Stomp. Stomp.* Right behind me now. 'They never listen to their—'

Then all I hear is the sound of rubber slipping briefly on metal and then the kind of sound a watermelon would make if it was dropped from ten metres onto asphalt. I look down to the ground and the trauma of what I see is somehow immediately transformed into a work of art. A sketch in my mind. Pen and ink on paper. *Dead Thug with Crushed Watermelon Head.*

Shaking and nauseous, I drag myself slowly but surely to the bottom of the tube, then climb down and run across the loading bay to three old trucks that look like they haven't been driven in a decade. I fall to my belly and commando-crawl beneath the middle truck. Collapse on the ground, stretch my arms out and catch my breath. It's dry and safe here and all I want to do is sleep. All I want to do is dream. All I want to do is weep. I want to go painting with Pablo Picasso. I want to see my paintings in the Met. I put my cheek to the asphalt. It's sticky and warm. I breathe. I close my eyes. I dream.

*

Someone calling my name. It's my sister. She's in the Starbucks coffee shop at the bottom of the Myer Centre. She's screaming my name and I'm standing outside looking in at her and I can't hear the name that's coming from her lips. 'I can't hear you,' I say.

My sister says a word silently and I know what that word is through the glass because I can read her lips. 'Colourful,' she's saying.

And I say it back to her. 'Colourful.'

She taps her left ear. 'Can you hear me?' she asks. 'Can you hear me?'

Then the whole coffee shop is filled with a tsunami of floodwater. And there are fish swimming past my floating sister now and there are simple household items that don't belong in this dream. A vacuum cleaner. An orange bedside lamp. A child's toy piano. The old television set that Erica Finlay and I watched the Pablo Picasso documentary on when I was twelve years old.

My sister presses her face against the coffee shop window. She screams something at me, but only bubbles come out her mouth.

*

Then I open my eyes and night has fallen in the real world.

'Can you hear me?'

A man's voice. Deep and strong and loud and angry. From beneath the truck I see rain still falling on the loading yard. Drops of rain standing out in the orange light of the concrete plant's nighttime security lights.

Scenes from the day I've just had rush past me. A girl riding away from Danny Collins. A girl running away from the sister she's never met. A girl leaving her best friend in the hands of thugs. A girl escaping from the man who fell from the conveyor belt. This girl was born to run.

'Can you hear me?'

It's Ephraim Wall. He's shouting from the street, beyond the front gate of the concrete plant. 'Come out now and I'll leave him be,' he calls.

Silence for a moment. Only rain. Lighter than before. The flood might have peaked by now. But still the city feels abandoned. Something dead about it. Like every resident of West End has moved to high ground. Maybe they have. Maybe they got in their cars and motored to Hamilton Hill or Wavell Heights or Jamboree Heights or Wellers Hill. Maybe there's only me and Ephraim Wall left in all of West End. But then I hear Ephraim's fist meet flesh and bone and then I hear the wail of my best friend, Charlie Mould, and I know there's someone else who didn't leave without me.

'You hear that?' Ephraim shouts. 'I don't know how much more this kid can take.'

I slip the backpack off my shoulders and wedge it into a space above the truck's rusting and long-dormant drive shaft. Ephraim can have my life, but he's not having my drug money. Then I crawl out from underneath the truck, stay low and scramble to a stack of white masonry blocks resting on a wooden pallet beneath a wide, cream-coloured water tank. I creep around the edge of the masonry blocks and hide behind a large boulder bearing a bronze plaque commemorating the plant's redevelopment.

I can see Ephraim standing in the middle of Hockings Street beneath a streetlight, soaking wet. Beyond him, I can see that the Brisbane River has spilled its banks throughout the day and has swallowed up most of Riverside Drive. Where there used to be a road and parked cars owned by walkers and rowers and market sellers, there is now a lake of floodwater partially lit by the amber streetlight. Lying flat on his back at Ephraim's feet is Charlie. His face is puffed up with bruising. Old dry blood beneath his nose and across his mouth and chin.

'I'm losing my fucking patience,' Ephraim shouts as he drives his right boot into Charlie's ribs. My friend's wailing makes me weep and it makes me stand up from behind the commemorative boulder. 'Stop it,' I shout. 'Leave him alone.'

Ephraim whips his head to where my voice is coming from.

'I'm coming out. Just leave my friend alone.'

I walk across the loading yard and pull myself up and over the security fence. Wince when my left ankle drops into the mulched garden bed below.

Ephraim eyeballs me as I hobble into the middle of the empty street. Spent and broken and dirty and tired. I turn my head to look around. No people. No cars. Only the rain and Ephraim Wall and my friend with his back flat on the ground.

'You quite fucking done?' Ephraim asks, shaking his head.

I move quicker as I near Charlie and I'm already crying when I kneel by his side. 'I'm so sorry,' I say.

I use the rainwater on his forehead to attempt to rub the blood off his face, but I only spread it around his cheeks and chin. 'I'm so sorry,' I whisper again. I take his hand and bring it to my chest. Hold him tight. His body's shaking and I want to stop it from shaking. I can feel something pulsing through his body. See his eyes struggling to stay open.

'Let's go,' Ephraim says.

'We can't leave him here like this,' I say through my tears.

Ephraim takes a step back and parts his jacket to pull a black handgun from his waist. He cocks the pistol and points it at my head.

'Stand up and walk,' he says, 'or I'll leave you both lying here.'

My tears fall hard and I bring Charlie's hand to my forehead then rub it along my cheek. 'I've gotta go, Charlie,' I say. 'I'm sorry.'

Charlie can only make gestures with his hands in response.

I stand up slowly. I'm woozy with emotion and all the activity and my fear of this man with the handgun pointed at my face. When I finally summon up the courage to look at him, I'm briefly stunned to see a figure moving beyond his shoulder. A shape. A shadow. Becoming clearer now. A man dressed in a hooded jumper emerging from the bushes.

'Start walking,' Ephraim demands.

I stand still, pretending to be groggier than I am. More spent. More frozen. My eyes see, but pretend not to see, the man crossing the street. That strange and terrifying man with a hood pulled down over his eyes and a cricket bat in his right hand.

He raises his left forefinger to his lips. A message for me. *Be quiet. Don't say a word.* Just let the story go where it needs to go. Let them read all about this on the walls of the Metropolitan Museum of Art. The impossible journey that shaped the greatest artistic career the world has ever seen.

'Start walking!' Ephraim spits.

I shake my head at him. 'No,' I say.

And his face is stunned by that single perfect word and it's the last word Ephraim Wall hears before a Gray-Nicolls Twin Scoop cricket bat smashes across the right side of his skull. He's knocked out instantly and the gun falls from his hand as he drops face-first to the ground.

The man in the hood stands over his body. Blood running out of Ephraim's right ear.

The man in the hood turns to me. Tilts his head like he's studying me, wondering how I found myself in this situation. Light rain falling on us both.

Then the man in the hood slots the cricket bat into some kind of holster he has fitted to his back. He looks alien in the rain. Inhuman. Not of this place. He studies me and Charlie for a long moment. Then he holds his right hand open beneath the rain. Drops start filling his palm.

'I feel it,' he says. 'Do you feel it, too?'

I hold my palm out. 'Yeah, I feel it,' I say. 'I've always felt it.'

He nods as if this all makes perfect sense to him. Then he leans down, pockets the gun, grips Ephraim Wall by his ankles and drags him roughly, face to asphalt, across the street and into the endless darkness beyond the Moreton Bay figs.

I wait a minute or so in silence, expecting him to re-emerge, but he doesn't. Nothing but darkness and the sound of the restless river.

Just Charlie and me now in the middle of the street. I kneel back down beside him. His eyes have closed. They look like the fresh beetroot balls Ros used to grow in the scrapyard. The rest of his face looks like a sheet of red sandpaper that's been rubbed for two hours against rock. He's sleeping or unconscious.

I've done this too many times to count. Woken my friend Charlie up when he's been lying in the middle of some place he shouldn't be lying in the middle of. 'Oi, Charlie,' I say. Push him in the ribs with both hands. 'C'mon, wake up, Charlie, we gotta go.'

I slap his thighs. Push him again. Shout, 'Charlie, wake up! We gotta go.' One more push in the ribs and he opens his eyes and I can breathe again.

'Is this heaven?' he asks.

'Yeah, Charlie,' I sigh, breathless and spent. 'Fuckin' West End, Brisbane.' I take his hand. 'Now get up, ya runny egg. We gotta get outta sight.'

He almost topples over the first time I try to raise him up on my shoulder. But he's strong enough to get an arm around my neck.

'I can't see shit,' he says.

I lead Charlie towards the flooded river. Quickest way to get where we need to go. Easiest way to stay out of sight. We stagger like wounded battlefield soldiers. I've seen oil paintings in the Queensland Art Gallery of Australian prisoners of war helping each other up dreadful jungle hills, shirtless and bloodied, patches over wounds on their heads. That's how we're walking now. Wounded and tired and broken.

'Where we goin'?' Charlie whispers.

'Back to Oz,' I say.

I take the high ground along a grassy riverside slope that runs around the back of the concrete factory. River water laps at our feet, but there's enough dry land for us to make it all the way home.

'If this hill ain't flooded, then the scrapyard won't be flooded either,' I say. 'We can rest there tonight.'

'Then what?' Charlie mumbles.

'Then we run,' I say. 'First light. We head north.'

'How far north?' Charlie asks.

'As far north as you wanna go, Charlie,' I reply.

'We can go all the way to the top of Queensland,' Charlie says.

'We can go all the way to the top of the world, Charlie,' I say.

'Where is the top of the world?' Charlie asks.

'It's wherever we are, Charlie.'

All the council lights are out along Riverside Drive and I can't see a thing. The rain is easing further and the moon is trying to raise its pretty head over all that dark cloud, but I still can't see more than a metre in front of me. Charlie leans on my left side and my right arm is continually reaching out to touch the rusting rear wire fences of all the industrial sites along

Riverside Drive, which will guide us home. We trip on fig tree roots and slosh through low-lying areas. The faint outlines of the flooded riverside trees look like monsters with ferocious crooked arms and fearsome claws, while the mangrove treetops rising out of the river resemble the fins of great and terrifying sea monsters.

'Almost there, Charlie,' I say. 'You'll be home soon.'

Then, deep in the darkness in front of me, I see a circle of light coming from what I think is the fence of our scrapyard. A floating circle of light made just for me. A pure white dot bobbing haphazardly in the black.

'What is that?' Charlie asks.

'It's a flashlight,' I say.

The light grows bigger as it comes closer to us and we stagger towards it and a figure in black.

When it's about ten metres from us, the circle of light stops moving.

'Hello,' I say.

No reply.

'Hello,' I say again. 'Is that you, Ros?'

Still no sound at all but the lapping of the river water at our feet. And I still see only darkness and that circle of light. But then comes the night-cracking sound of a gunshot, and I feel Charlie's weight slump on my left shoulder and I feel his legs buckling beside me and I turn to see a ball of blood spilling red across his white shirt in the light.

'Charlie!' I scream.

And now I know who holds the flashlight. I know it from the shape of that monster in the dark behind the glowing flashlight. Darkness from the light I place around it.

'Charlie,' I whisper. And I fall to the ground with my friend. He curls up in a ball and I throw myself over his body to shield him from any more gunshots and he feels so warm and small in my embrace. 'Charlie,' I whisper through tears that spill over my eyelids, just like the water spilling over the banks of this muddy river. And I hold him so tight. Wrap my legs and arms around him and squeeze him because I want to keep all that blood inside him, all that blood that keeps running out of his chest. And then I feel his body shaking and I squeeze him tighter still and I press my cheek against his cheek and whisper to him, 'I'm sorry, Charlie, I'm sorry.'

His body stops moving but still I hold it tight. Weeping over him. Rocking his body back and forth. 'Charlie,' I say into his ear. 'Charlie. Charlie. Colourful, Charlie. Colourful.'

A voice from the darkness behind me. 'You killed my baby boy,' says Flora Box.

And now there is a rage in me. I pull myself away from my lifeless friend. Stand up. Look straight at the light. Stand strong and brave before the woman I still cannot see.

'Your baby boy was a monster,' I say, taking one step forward. 'You raised that monster. You made that monster.'

Another step forward. 'You raised him to believe he could do anything he wanted to do and get away with it, including strangling me to death.'

Another step forward. 'Your baby boy was trying to kill me.'

And another. 'Your baby boy deserved to die.'

A gunshot cracks through this moment. It makes me stop moving but it doesn't make me stop breathing. To my surprise, the shot doesn't even seem to have touched me.

I take another step and Flora Box fires her gun again. Once more, the gunshot makes me stop but does not make me stop thinking. Does not even touch me.

Another step. 'Don't you see, Flo,' I say, 'you can't hit me.'

And another. 'You can't hit me because you can't see me.'

She shoots again.

'I have the power of invisibility,' I say. Then I close my fists and let the rage in me move like electricity pulsing from my toes to my knees that lift my legs, to my heart that fuels my courage, to my memory that fuels my fate.

'I'm nobody,' I say, stepping forward again. 'I don't even exist.' One more step. 'I'm invisible.'

And I charge at the light. I hear the crack of another shot but don't stop running. A wild screaming is seeded in my belly and it blossoms in my throat and I roar at the light as I sprint towards it, spit and sweat and snot and tears and dirt across my animal face. Now I'm the monster. Now I'm the tyrant lizard. Now it's Lady Flora Box's turn to dance.

A final gunshot sounds as I leap like a rabid werewolf towards the light. I feel a stabbing pain in the side of my stomach. A pain I've never felt before. Something just passed through my flesh, but my brain doesn't tell me what it was because all I can think about is getting my hands on her flesh, my arms around her body. Driving my shoulders into her belly and raising her whole heavy body into the air. Driving, driving, driving her towards the high-tide river that's been waiting for me since the day I was born.

'Noooooo,' Flora wails. 'Nooooo.'

But I keep driving with my shoulders. Floodwater up to my ankles. Then floodwater up to my kneecaps and I feel the rocky border of the river's edge beneath my feet and I push us both into the welcoming embrace of the summer-warm river.

*

Total darkness down here in the drink. Unseen currents tossing us around. Flo gripping the neck of my shirt. Then her hands move to my throat and she wants to strangle me like her son wanted to strangle me. I swallow a mouthful of river water as I grab her wrists and try to pull her hands away. Kick at her shins and her ribs. But she doesn't let go.

I need to breathe. I need air because I want to live. I want to keep noticing things. I want to keep seeing things. I want to keep drawing things.

We bounce off what feels like the side of a boat or a mooring or a segment of a pier, destroyed in the flood and now snagged on the mangrove roots growing from the sides and bottom of the river, and Flo loses her grip. But now she clings desperately to the right sleeve of my T-shirt. I pull my head back hard, trying to rise to the surface, but she keeps pulling me down. And I see now that she's not moving in the water, because she's stuck on something. Wedged in. She can only hold on to me.

The river has her now. The river wants to keep her. And I realise it's only her that it wants. It doesn't want me. And soon she will run out of air. Soon I will be released. So I calm myself, save my breath. One Burpengary. Two Burpengary. Three Burpengary. The longest I've ever held my breath underwater is two minutes and sixteen seconds. I reckon I've got about another thirty seconds left in me, tops. I tell myself I am a Queensland lungfish, a thing of wonder, a lost piece of the evolutionary puzzle, the great missing link between amphibians and humans.

Flo's hand is still pulling me down, furiously gripping the bottom of my T-shirt. Then the water lightens. The rain must have stopped up there in the real world and the moon must have come out. A full moon, maybe. A full M&M chocolate moon for a werewolf monster like me. I look up and realise I'm not far at all from the surface, not far at all from air. The light moves across my shoulders and across my arm and across Flo's fist and then across her face. The light comes from the darkness we place around it.

Sketch this moment. Sketch this stunned and sorrowful face before me. The colour of it. Zombie green. The colour Picasso used when he painted his dead friend Casagemas. She looks like an oil painting in this light. Cracks in her face. Wrinkles and the realisation of failure. Flo lost this one. And I realise how old she is at the very moment I realise she's dead. Sketch her fingers falling away from my T-shirt. Sketch myself down here. Sketch the artist kicking her legs hard and rising to the surface of the water. Sketch all this life. Sketch this wondrous breathing. The artist will live for now. The artist will breathe. That's all that is certain at this point. Breath. Nothing beyond breath. And I burst through the surface of the water and open my mouth like I'm swallowing an orange but all I'm sucking in is air. Deep, desperate inhalations.

The current pushes me towards the central channel of the river. The rain has stopped but the water's still frenzied. Bitter and violent. Debris floating past me. Tree trunks and branches. Chunks of destroyed river craft. Great sheets of plasterboard torn from someone's home. Everything, including the artist destined for New York, funnelling towards the mouth of the river, past Portside Wharf and Luggage Point and the Port of Brisbane, with its unsinkable freight ships, to the mouth that wants to spit me into southern Bramble Bay and out into the Pacific Ocean.

I bob and rise and fall over waves. Try to swim towards the southern bank. Look up to find my bearings. That's the Merivale Bridge above me. White arches. Concrete and rusted iron. I see the black shapes of trees on the river's edge. Try to cut across the current with three, four then five freestyle strokes, but the force of the river keeps pushing me back to the middle.

There's a sharp pain in the side of my abdomen. Like there's a bee crawling through my stomach that keeps stabbing me with its flaming hot stinger. *Fuck.* I swallow a mouthful of water and it tastes like dirt. I feel I might pass out if I keep trying to swim across the current. Better to relax, I think. Like Erica Finlay told me to. Save my energy. Maybe someone will see me in all this black water. In all this violence.

I decide to put my faith in heroism. Not even heroism. Humanism. The kindness of strangers. People are good. People are miraculous. Was that what Erica Finlay was thinking? She was floating on her back just like this. Giving herself over to the whims of the river. *If you ever find yourself in that thing when it's really high and really movin', Santa, the only thing you can do is lie on your back and relax and float and pray to God you're not invisible.* My eyes close briefly and then adrenaline rushes back through my body when I'm caught in a current that spins me in a full circle. Eyes up. The sky whirls above me. Is that the world turning now or is it me turning? *The world turns for us all*, Erica Finlay said. The stars shine for us all, too. They're out again now. The grey clouds have slipped away to hover above the Pacific and the stars sketch shapes for me on that eternal black canvas. Stars have names. The brightest ones do, at least.

I drop my head back and spread my arms and legs out in a star shape. Float like this, I think. Save whatever strength you have left and give yourself over to fate. Oh, this beautiful mistake. I'm not scared of dying. I'm just scared of all the things I'll miss out on.

My starry-sky vision is broken for a moment as I float beneath a strip of concrete and steel, the underside of the William Jolly Bridge, where Picasso was painting his blood-coloured blob in my dream. Home is where the throbbing red blob is. I feel mine in my chest. A thudding secondhand charity-shop muscle. The bee sting burning in the side of my stomach is making that heart work harder. Work overtime.

Turning like a dry leaf on the water. Backwards now. Towards the mouth of the river. Bright blue lights above me. And I must be fevered because I think for a moment that these blue lights are low-hanging stars, but they're just the lights of the Kurilpa Bridge, where the river takes a hard right towards the Brisbane CBD. White steel beams on its underside, all covered in spikes to stop the pigeons from shitting on them.

Still floating. The river widens and the speed of its central current builds and I feel my body drop briefly then spin around again. Pain in my stomach and I think of that last gunshot. Then I think of Charlie. *Colourful, Charlie.* And I don't wanna be here anymore. Don't wanna be in a world without him. Don't wanna be in this water. And this grief hurts more than the side of my belly hurts. My tears flow as I drift downriver with the wreckage of the flood. I'm starting to feel cold. Body shivering. Teeth chattering. Soon I will sink. Soon I will be swallowed by the river and maybe I will meet Erica Finlay again, down among the reeds and the roots where the lungfish swim, and maybe then I can ask her why she did what she did.

Another bridge fills my vision now, the underside of my favourite bridge in Brisbane, the Victoria Bridge. Those wide, smooth structural supports running right across it. Count them. One, two, three. I turn my head to look at the river's edge. This is where Christina dropped into the drink. Water has flooded the T-junction of the three concrete pathways where Christina's parents argued before the pram rolled so dramatically into my personal history.

Eyes up now. Darkness under the bridge, then the stars in the sky. And also ... *a face.* The face of a man. Or maybe a boy. The impossible face of someone I know. High up on the pedestrian walkway, his head leaning over the bridge's railing. For the briefest moment, we lock eyes. He sees me. *He really sees me.* What could possibly be going through that boy's mind in this moment? He was staring down at the water and then my face appeared below him. Floating here like a water ghost. A spirit. A dream.

Nobody else on the bridge. No flood gawkers watching the carnage below. They've all had their fill. Only this man. Only this boy. I keep my eyes fixed on him and he's staring down at me as I float further away from him along this great brown serpent. I'm leaving him and there's nothing he nor I can do about it. Then, when I've drifted almost thirty metres from the underside of the bridge, my skull collides unexpectedly with the shell of a yellow marker buoy. My neck cracks on impact and the current pushes my body up against the plastic base. There's a yellow power box above the base and then a bright orange light, like a police emergency light, that's blinking on and off at me beneath a bright yellow metal 'X'.

I reach my arms instinctively and desperately around the base, which is about as wide and round as a roulette wheel, but I can't get a grip on it. I'm pulled round and just as I'm about to be dragged away again by the current, my left hand makes one final blind lunge and finds a metal loop on the base. I swallow more water as the current stretches my body until I look like Superman flying through the sky. I start pulling myself in closer to the buoy and manage to get my other hand onto the loop. Then I take two deep breaths and summon enough energy to reach out my left hand and find another loop about half a metre further round the base. I get both hands on this loop, and now the current is once again pushing me into the buoy rather than pulling me away from it.

Enough time to take a breath. Enough time to gather my thoughts as the manic river swirls around me. I hear a call from the boy high up on the bridge. Two hands at his mouth, screaming something I cannot hear. I'm too weak to hold my head up for longer than ten seconds. Too weak to keep holding on to this buoy. Too weak to hold on to living. My head drops groggily into the water and then I flip it back up again because I'm not quite ready to give up, and I look back at the bridge, where I see the boy on the pedestrian walkway bathed in the glow of a council lamppost. See him take a spray jacket off. See him climb over the safety rail.

He screams at me again, but I can't hear what he's saying. Now he's outside the safety rail, shuffling along the edge of the bridge. He stops, wraps an arm around a lamppost and leans out, looking straight down at the water, as though he's studying the patterns in the river. The currents. The flow. My head drops again and when I lift it up once more I see the boy jumping feet-first into the water. I nearly lose my grip on the buoy. Feel like I'm going to pass out. Feel sick and cold and weak and tired and something that might be close to death.

The boy disappears in the water. The brave diver who seems to be trying to rescue me. My eyelids close involuntarily. I force them open, one at a time. Something moves quickly towards me in the water. My eyes close again. For longer this time. The darkness. The sweet, comfortable darkness. Maybe I'll sleep now. Sink away into this beautiful, warm blackness behind my eyes. But the boy's voice wakes me again. A word. A scream. 'Nooooooo,' he wails, and my eyes open again to see arms moving through the water. A strong swimmer. Someone who must have won medals for that technique. Moving like a submarine and driven faster by the current.

My eyes close again. Black. Open again. And now I can see the face of the boy swimming towards me. The face of someone I know. The face of Danny Collins. The face of a prince. So close to me now. But still too far. My eyes close once more and my hands let go of the buoy. I feel my body being freed. I belong to the river now. Nothing more to do. Nothing more to think about. Nothing more to wish. Nothing more to dream. Nothing more to sketch. Nothing more to regret. Nothing more to hate. Nothing more to love.

But then a hand grips my loose left wrist. Firm and fierce and strong. And my body stops drifting. I hear his agonised wailing as he pulls me back towards the buoy. Feel his legs around my waist pulling me into him. His arm around my ribs. All of him. His warm breath and his embrace.

I have only enough strength left to open my eyes once. I see his powerful left hand clinging to the loop on the buoy. He pulls me into his body and I tuck my head into his neck and close my eyes. 'You saw me,' I whisper.

And then I sink again. Disappear completely into the warm darkness behind my closed eyelids.

*

There's daylight down here in my water sleep. Dreaming light. Bright dream light. Blinding light. Full sun by the river.

'What are you drawing?' Erica Finlay asks.

'You, Erica Finlay,' I say, adding three quick pen strokes to her jawline. 'Makin' a mess of it.'

We're sitting on the concrete garden edging at the base of the Victoria Bridge Abutment.

'Why can't I get your face right?'

'It's because you know the truth,' she says. 'It's because you've always known the truth.'

'What truth?'

'You know what I did to you.'

'Yeah, I know, Erica Finlay,' I say. My eyes on the lines I'm sketching in ink. 'I think I've always known. I just didn't wanna admit it. I needed to love you. And I loved you so much. I loved you more than anything on earth. I loved you more than all the ice in Antarctica. More than all the moons in the universe.

'You took me, didn't you?' I ask. 'You stole me from some place where I belonged. Nabbed me like a pack of bubblegum you never paid for. You took something precious that didn't belong to you. The most precious thing of all. You took a life.'

Erica Finlay looks away to the river, nodding her head. 'I was looking for something to love,' she says. 'Then I found you. I loved you from the moment I held you in my arms.'

'How could you do something so ... *monstrous*?'

'It wasn't me,' she says. 'I mean, I wasn't me then. I wasn't anyone. I wasn't even human. I wasn't even here.'

There's a splash in the river behind Erica Finlay's shoulder. She stands up. A new mother screams for her baby, but we carry on talking.

'Why do you keep calling me Erica Finlay?' she asks.

'That's your name, isn't it?'

'Not anymore,' she says.

'What's your name, then?'

'It's the most beautiful name in the world,' she says. 'It's Mum.' She wipes a tear from my eye that I didn't even know I was shedding.

'I wanna come with you,' I say.

'That would be a waste,' she says.

'Of what?'

'Of everything you're gonna do. Everything you're gonna be.' She stares into my eyes. 'Stay here,' she says, 'I love you.'

And then she runs to the river's edge. I hear a splash but I don't see what caused it. Because I'm staring only at my sketch. And I know now why I keep making a mess of it. It's because I haven't been drawing the face of Erica Finlay at all. I've been drawing the face of Lola.

Two
Lovers
sitting
on a
Branch..
watching a
Pterodactyl
Fly
across
a Full
Moon

Two Lovers Sitting on a Branch Watching a Pterodactyl Fly Across a Full Moon

January 2024

Pen and ink on paper

Reportedly sketched while the artist was recovering from a near-fatal bullet wound in hospital. An image of unashamed romance, deliberately sentimental. Two lovers – presumably the artist and her one true love, Danny Collins – perched on a branch overlooking a city that no longer seems so menacing. Little is known of why the artist chose to capture the pterodactyl flying across the face of the moon, but many believe this to be a representation of the artist's hard-won acceptance of the past.

Of course, it's always time that wakes us up. And I don't just mean alarm clocks and such. I'm talking about the movement of time that wakes up babies in wombs and tells them it's time to see the world. I'm talking about the kind of time that takes our loved ones away. The kind that says you're done seeing the world or the world is done seeing you. I guess I thought my time was up in that river. And I get a bit scared when I think about how willing I was to go down into the roots and reeds of that smelly brown reptile. But then time went on and it brought me a boy named Danny Collins. He lifted his head out of the water and splashed around me and I felt like I was dreaming. Was I?

It's correct to say that it's the beeping of a heart monitor that wakes me up this afternoon from my long sleep, but it's more correct to say that time wakes me up. My time is done sleeping. My time is done dying, too. Time to live now.

A white ceiling lined with holes the size of the pink rubber on the end of an HB pencil. The smell of ammonia and disinfectant. Daylight. Hospital staff talking outside my room. People in blue scrubs buzzing past the open door. A poster on the wall to my right warning of the dangers of melanoma. A drip fixed with a strip of yellow tape to the top of my left hand. A stiff white bedsheet over my legs. A dull ache in my abdomen. But I'm not in agony. Painkillers, maybe, in the drip bag on the portable stand on the left side of my bed.

And a man in a grey suit sitting on a chair. Blue tie. Right foot resting on his left knee. In his lap, a tube of papers wrapped in brown protective paper. Silver pen in his left hand.

'Welcome back,' says Detective Sergeant Cameron Millar.

I remember him. Cameron means 'bent nose'. He's the guy who flew from Perth to see me. He's the guy who knows my sister, Phoebe. Phoebe means 'light'.

'Where have I been?' I ask.

'From what we have ascertained ...' Millar says, letting the words hang in the still air, 'you've been to hell and back. I was getting worried about you. You've been out cold for five days. You had a bullet pass right through the left lower quadrant of your abdomen.'

I lift my white bedsheet and see the belly dressing fixed with strapping that wraps around my torso.

'Millimetre to the left and it coulda gone through your colon and that coulda put the lights out for good,' he says.

I rest my head back on the pillow. Look up at the ceiling. 'Invisible,' I whisper to myself.

'Sorry?'

'Nothin'.'

'Nurses said you only started stirring this morning,' Millar says. He points at a clear plastic cup with a toddler's drinking spout. 'You want some water?' he asks. 'They said you'd wake up thirsty.'

I look at the water and put my hand on my throbbing belly. 'I am thirsty, but I think I'd vomit it up,' I say.

'You take your time,' Millar says.

My dry lips. I roll my tongue over the deep cracks.

Millar pulls a rubber band down the tube, leans over and spreads the papers out on my bed. They are my sketches. And where I have been can be traced in those sketches. To hell and back in black ink on paper. Deliveries in the suburbs. Friends and foes. Monsters and princes.

'They found these in the Hanson concrete plant on Hockings Street,' he says.

I reach for the sketch on the top of the pile. Feel so weak. But I want to hold that sketch. It's a piece I called *The Artist and Her Best Friend Charlie Mould and a Seafood Shop Full of Sharks*. The sketch makes me cry.

'Did you find Charlie?' I ask.

Officer Millar nods. 'We found Ephraim Wall first,' he says. 'His body was dumped by the old gas stripping tower behind the Souths Leagues Club. Half his head caved in.'

'It was the man in the hood,' I say. 'He saved my life. I watched him drag Ephraim into the dark.'

'You see his face?'

'Bit of it.'

'Do you think you could draw the bit you saw for me?'

'I can draw anything.'

Millar pulls a small notebook from his shirt pocket. Scribbles a note with a pen. Pockets the notebook. 'I'm sorry you lost your friend,' he says.

I turn away from Millar. Find a poster someone has pinned on the wall to cheer up kids in hospital. A picture of a pterodactyl in flight beneath the words, *Always be yourself, but if you can be a pterodactyl, be a pterodactyl*. I want to be a pterodactyl.

'I'm sorry you lost yours,' I say.

Millar nods in silence. 'Geoff's service is tomorrow,' he says.

'How are his girls?' I ask.

'They keep saying they're all right—'

'But they're not.'

'No,' Millar says. 'They're not.'

Water filling my eyes. Felicia and Celine Topping. Two girls holding koalas. Unlucky moon.

'You must come across it a bit,' I say.

'What?' Millar asks.

'Loss,' I say.

Millar smiles. 'Yeah, I come across it a bit.'

'Was it worth it?' I ask.

'Worth what?'

'Was any of what they were doing worth Geoff dying?'

'Of course not,' Millar says. 'It's never worth it. But, because of you, they got hold of Julian Rossi, the gentleman Brandon Box roughed up. He leaked like a sieve. They couldn't shut him up. He went full disclosure on Aiden Barlow.'

'The Great White Shark,' I say.

Millar nods. 'Barlow's arrest could mean an estimated seventy-five million dollars' worth of illegal drugs not crossing Australian borders every year.' Millar shrugs his shoulders. 'That's gotta be worth somethin'?'

He pulls his chair closer to my bed. 'There were footprints in the mud around your friend Charlie's body,' he says. 'We found Flora Box in the water, wedged between a mangrove root and a concrete block, about fifteen metres from the river's edge.'

A flash of Flora's pale white face, dead in the water of my memory.

'Danny?' I ask.

'He's fine,' Millar says. 'Brave kid. We reckon he must have held you up in that water for at least fifteen minutes. Bunch of graffiti kids saw him hollering for help. Little rats shouldn't have even been near the river. That whole end of South Bank had been taped off by the police and SES.'

Millar nods at the strapping around my belly. 'The water rescue team did a good job stopping the bleeding, but they all thought you were done. So did the nurses.' Millar points at the sketches. 'But I kept telling them there was no way you weren't comin' back because you still had an exhibition to get to in New York.'

A tear spilling over my lower left eyelid. I give the detective a brief smile. Turn my eyes back to the pterodactyl. I want to be a pterodactyl.

'Where's Danny now?' I ask.

Millar nods to a brown vinyl chair on the opposite side of the bed. 'He was sitting right there ten minutes ago,' he says. 'He's been sitting right there the whole time. Hasn't left your side for five days. I'm hoping he's gone for a shower because he smells like shit.'

Danny Collins. The prince in the picture. *One day you will dance with a prince*, Erica Finlay said. And one day you will find a prince who will sit for five days beside your hospital bed. My heart is a balloon, warm air inside it, expanding beneath my breast bones.

Millar checks his watch. Stands. 'I gotta run,' he says. 'I'll tell the nurses you're back in the land of the living. But listen, I'm gonna need a full statement from you when you're up to it. So don't you go runnin' away on me.'

I nod and smile because that's a nice line for a girl who's been running all her life.

Millar moves towards the door.

'Detective Millar?' I say.

He turns round.

'My sister,' I say. 'Phoebe.'

'Yeah?'

'Is she still in Brisbane?'

He nods heartily. 'She's still here,' he says. 'You want me to set up another meeting?'

'Yes,' I say, 'I'd like that very much.'

Millar smiles and turns to walk out the door but a thought pulls him back into the room. 'Oh, by the way,' he says. 'Julian Rossi keeps talking about a big bunch of cash that Brandon Box stole from him. Three banded blocks of pineapples. Fifty-three thousand dollars in total. You don't know anything about that, do you?'

I think on this for a moment. 'No,' I say, 'haven't got a clue.'

Millar studies my eyes, a half-smile forming on his face. 'Just checking,' he says. Then he disappears.

A hospital orderly enters my room with a tray and a clear plastic cup of apple juice and leaves it on a high bed-table. I'm halfway through an egg and lettuce sandwich when I hear a gentle knock on the door. Put the sandwich down on my plate.

Danny Collins in the doorway. Danny Collins in my room. Danny Collins in my life.

'You saw me,' I say.

He smiles. Shrugs his shoulders.

'Of course I saw you,' he says. 'You're all I can see.'

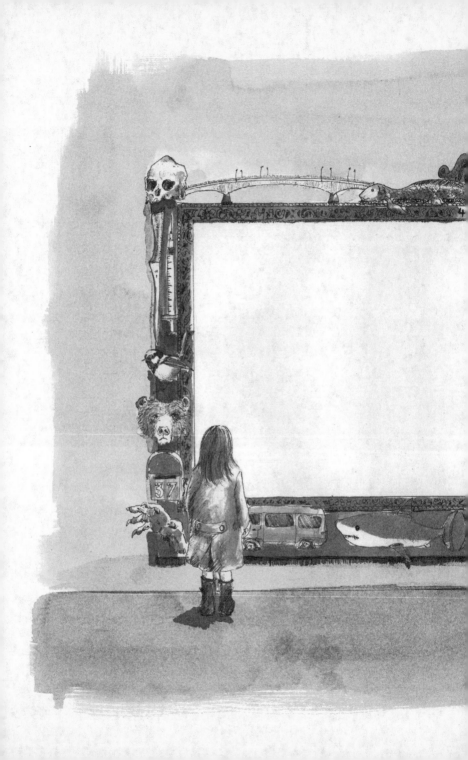

Girl in Yellow Peacoat

Girl in Yellow Peacoat

February 2024

Pen and ink on paper

Little is known about this work beyond the fact it was the artist's favourite of all her early ink sketches. A tribute to you, the viewer, the person who makes all art possible.

So I keep seeing this girl in a yellow peacoat in the year 2100 and this girl is looking at my artworks in an exhibition in New York's Metropolitan Museum of Art. And she's come to the last room of the exhibition, where E.P. Buckle is rambling all that stuff about that terrifying chase through the Hanson concrete factory and the brave actions of the love of my life, Danny Collins, who saved me from sinking to the bottom of the river. She's listening to E.P. Buckle describe this very moment that's unfolding in real-time right here at the end of Moon Street, West End, where I stand leaning on a broom beside my old neighbour Ros as we watch a bulldozer digging its toothy front blade deep into the earth of what once was our scrapyard home called Oz. The Tinman's old brick workshop has been flattened. And now the dozer turns the soil of Oz upside down and scoops great mounds of scrap and waste into a skip.

'They destroyed their home,' says the girl in the yellow peacoat, tapping her mum's side. 'Where did they all go to live?'

'Who knows?' the girl's mum replies.

Well, June and Sully have moved four hours north to Bundaberg. Barnie from the Bedrock Wrecking Yard came to their rescue and traded June an air-conditioned 2016 LDV G10 van for her Newlands caravan. Barnie knew he was being royally screwed, but he gets a kick out of being royally screwed by Brisbane's homeless and I hope God or someone equally influential like David Bowie or John Lennon is looking down on Barnie from above. June's found nursing work at Bundaberg Base Hospital, and she and Sully are currently parked on the Bundaberg Showgrounds next to a temporary flood recovery centre that people from all corners of Queensland's Wide Bay region have been flocking to. Ros still hasn't found a place. She's been roughin' it every night in Musgrave Park.

I watch the dozer pick up a huge load of earth containing my broken magic mirror. See the Amina frame snap in half and then into pieces as it's crushed inside the skip.

'But what did the artist do without her magic mirror?' the girl in the yellow peacoat gasps in the vision in my head.

Ros and I turn away from the yard and amble back along Moon Street towards The Well. Slosh through an inch of street silt and mud beneath our boots. Blazing heat today and the stink of sewage and city waste. Life after flood. Multiple floods. Another one struck Queensland six days after I got out of hospital. They call that a knockout punch. This one flooded the entire ground level of The Well – a day after Evelyn Bragg received the news that The Well would survive the Olympic refurbishment of Moon Street. Her great petition of names had worked. She found herself on page three of the *Courier-Mail*, talking about how much a place like The Well has never been more necessary, especially in a time of widespread flood recovery. The government's handing Evelyn a big bag of cash to renovate the centre. New kitchen equipment. New rec room. A new art room where floaters can go to paint, which Evelyn said she's gonna call 'Charlie's Place' in honour of my best friend. She's assured me the room will be colourful.

But before all that, Evelyn and six centre regulars, including me and Ros, have to sweep and mop and hose toxic mud and silt out of every corner and crack inside the building.

'So, who's winning, Ros?' I ask as we step carefully through the mud that slips and slides beneath our feet.

'Who's winning what?' Ros asks.

'Who's winning today in the Battle of Good 'n' Bad Shit?'

'Bad shit, of course,' Ros says. 'Bad shit always wins, kid.'

Just as she says that, three council buses drive into Moon Street and park outside The Well. A truck pulls up behind them and a man in the back of this truck starts handing brooms and mops and high-pressure hoses to the hundred or so volunteers who file out of the buses like soldiers in a well-drilled platoon. These volunteers all wear high-vis pink shirts that say *Mud Army* across the front. They march straight into The Well and take their instructions from Evelyn Bragg.

'All right,' Ros says, turning to me. 'Today I'm gonna call it a draw.'

*

'Did she ever meet her sister again?' the girl in the yellow peacoat asks.

'Of course she did,' the girl's mother says. 'She had to know the answers.'

A circle of dawn sunlight on my belly. A single ray of sunshine made for me, formed by a rust hole in the roof of the van. I put my thumb and forefinger to it. How wide is it this morning? Wide as a can of Fanta. I bring my left hand to the circle of light and let its yellow moon bounce across my open palm. Who am I?

'Amanda,' I whisper.

Amanda means 'beloved'.

'Diana,' I whisper.

Diana means 'divine'.

'Brenda,' I whisper.

Brenda means 'sword'.

'Anna,' I whisper.

Anna means 'grace'.

I take the hand of the shirtless man who sleeps beside me. Entwine my fingers with his and the circle of light splits into two half-moons where our palms meet.

'You sleep all right?' Danny mumbles into his pillow.

'I did,' I say. 'I had a Pablo dream.'

'Oh yeah? Where was he?'

'He was painting a great big bull in the most vivid red oil paint on the stone tiles of King George Square,' I say, running my finger along Danny's arm like my finger was a paintbrush. 'It took up the whole public space. Nobody could walk across the square. People were complaining because they had to take the long way round. They were all gonna be late for work. They started screaming at Picasso. Then people were spitting at him. Throwing to-go cups of coffee at him. Then people started walking across the painting. They were destroying this masterpiece with their footprints and I was shouting, "Stop, stop, it's the greatest work he's ever done and he's doing it just for us," but I couldn't stop all the people charging across it. They just kept charging.'

'Like bulls,' Danny whispers.

'Yeah, like bulls,' I whisper back.

*

An hour later, the side door of my orange 1987 Toyota HiAce van with four flat tyres slides open. Danny holds a tray carrying a plate of bacon and eggs and toast and a bowl of fruit salad and a glass of cranberry juice and a cup of coffee. Behind him I can see across the manicured lawn of the Collins family estate. Danny's mum and dad let me shift the van to their yard. They offered to pay for its relocation, but I told them that I had savings of my own to cover it.

'Big day,' Danny says.

'Real big day,' I say.

After breakfast, I'm sitting on the van's side doorstep tying my shoelaces when Danny wheels a mountain bike up to my feet. Dust and mud across the wheels and frame.

'It's not a Bianchi road bike,' he says, 'but it'll get you across town.'

I grip the handlebars, squeeze the front brakes, get a feel for the bike. 'It's perfect, Danny,' I say, slipping my leg over the crossbar.

Danny hands me a backpack. An old schoolbag of his. 'Bloody big day,' he says.

'Real bloody big day,' I say.

'You sure I can't come with you?' he asks.

'Yeah,' I reply, smiling. 'I'm sure.'

I put my right foot on the right pedal and I'm about to ride away and Danny turns to go back to the house. But then I grab the sleeve of his shirt and pull him in to my chest. 'Hey, you,' I say. And I bring his lips to mine and we kiss long enough for me to see this whole sunshine morning scene etched in ink on sketch paper.

The artist closed her eyes. She was struck in that moment by a profound sense of security, a knowing, a certainty that she would never again be homeless because the boy's lips were home to her. His soft lips were four walls and fireplaces and kids beneath Christmas trees. She finally opened her eyes again and saw his face like she was seeing it again for the first time.

'I see you,' the artist said.

'I see you,' said Danny Collins.

*

I'm in my friend Ursula Lang's bedroom in her house on the Sandgate beachfront. We're standing in front of the tall bedroom mirror.

'Now take a step back,' Ursula says.

One step back and I see the dress in full. A red cocktail dress. Cross-straps at the back that expose my shoulder blades. A hem that ends at my kneecaps and fans out like I'm permanently spinning.

Ursula inhales sharply, loud enough for me to hear. 'And Audrey Hepburn wept, for there were no more worlds to conquer,' she whispers. 'Spin around once for me.'

I make a full 360-degree spin on my bare feet.

She puts a knuckle in my spine. 'Back straight,' she says. 'How do you feel?'

I feel like smiling. I feel like Nicole Kidman. I remember what she said. 'You make me feel like a star, Ursula,' I say.

Ursula looks into the mirror and runs her hands through my hair. A thick and brown lost cause.

'What time are you meeting her?'

'Two o'clock,' I say.

'Good,' Ursula says. 'We still got time to fix this bird's nest.'

*

Eleven stops back to the city on the Cleveland line. I push the bike off the train at Central. Wheel it down the ramp that flows to the corner of Edward and Ann streets. People gathered at the traffic lights, waiting for the little green traffic man to make his appearance. Red and white Australia Post box. Smokers on the garden edging. Telstra phone box. This is where I used to stand and announce to the world that I was invisible. Screwy I must be. Cracked I must be.

I look across the road to where Danny sat with his sketchbook. I didn't see him that day, but somehow he saw me. The traffic lights buzz and the little green man guides pedestrians across the road. Maybe I'm wrong, but I could swear I see people looking at me when I walk. Just little glances. The occasional stare. Think it might be the dress. Or maybe it's the hair. Just keep walking.

I take Adelaide Street, where I pass the portable writing desk of a man in a brown hat who spends his days recording the real-life love stories of Brisbane strangers on an old sky-blue Olivetti typewriter. I want to stop and tell him my story, but it isn't finished yet.

Onwards, into Queen Street Mall. A busker in a straitjacket is balancing on a board and a rolling red can. 'I didn't think this through,' he says into a microphone taped to his ear. Busy workers snack on sushi and sip green smoothies on the mall's public benches next to the bike racks where I chain-lock Danny's mountain bike to a cross pole.

Nerves. Butterflies in my belly. I stop in front of Hungry Jack's and assess my reflection in the glass. I know this person. I've met her before. Her limbs are not bony and awkward and alien. Her limbs are strong and elegant and beautiful. The curls in her brown hair. That's Golden Age Hollywood stuff. The way she smiles and nods at me is thrilling. I know this woman so well. Because we have been through so much together. She got me through the saddest days of my life. She stopped me from jumping in the drink. She's the only reason I'm standing here today. She's so confident, this woman in the red dress. So international. So wanted. Not unwanted. She is so very valuable, this woman in the red dress.

Fingers through my hair. Adjust the straps on my dress. Time to walk. Down Albert Street in the direction of the botanic gardens. Past the Nike shoe shop and the House of Hoops store and the OPSM spectacles store and then I stop outside the Starbucks coffee shop at the bottom of the Myer Centre. Put my forehead against the thick shopfront glass. And now I can see my sister, Phoebe, sitting at a table with two chairs. She drinks from a tall iced tea through a straw, places it back on a coaster on the table. Checks the time on her watch and turns her head towards the door and I can tell she's done that more than a few times today.

Then, maybe because of instinct and maybe because of blood, she looks over at the shopfront. She's surprised to see me staring at her. And then she's delighted. She smiles like I smile. And she cries like I cry. Tears running immediately down her face. And I shake my head and run to the door and rush inside and step between a couple talking by the coffee pickup area then sidestep around a cluster of people blocking access to the dining section of the café. Take two steps up to the raised dining area and march to her table.

She's already standing when I reach her. I stop an arm's length away. And then I step forward and hug my sister.

And Phoebe told the artist who she was. She spoke for an hour without pause. She smiled at times and she cursed at times and she wept at times. For what was lost and for what had been found again. Her real mother's name, Phoebe said, was Anna Gould, née Parsons. A good woman. A kind woman. The kind of woman who kneeled when she spoke to kids so she could be on their level. The kind of woman who wrote Christmas cards to friends she hadn't spoken to in years. Anna Gould hadn't been an artist, though she'd had dozens of those mindfulness colouring books. She was a brilliant cook. She was an avid reader of spy novels. She loved the ocean and Phoebe once saw her swimming naked in it. She lived in the semi-rural suburb of Bedfordale, south-east Perth. She worked for twenty-five years as a Myer sales assistant. She specialised in women's shoes and sometimes women would complain to Anna Gould, long after the artist disappeared, about busted Sandler wedges and colour fading in the lining of their stilettos. Anna would wonder to herself how such women would fare if their entire world collapsed around them in the space of a single Saturday morning. Her grieving was unseen. Her irreparable heartbreak was invisible to all. She was the kind of woman who would weep for hours when she thought no one was home.

She was diagnosed with cancer of the pancreas when Phoebe was fourteen years old, and Phoebe didn't believe the doctors when they said cancer was an arbitrary selector. There was no reason and explanation for it, the doctors said. But for so long Phoebe felt that the cancer had been willed to her mum's body by grief. She felt that the cancer was brought about through sadness. And Phoebe asked the artist if she was familiar with the notion of true sorrow causing physical disintegration and the artist reached across the table and gripped her sister's hand tightly and said she was very familiar with such a notion.

Phoebe said Anna had married their father, John Gould, in June 1999. He was an oil and gas electrician with Western Gas. He and Anna had met in a karaoke bar in Northbridge. John bought Anna a vodka, lime and soda to congratulate her on a soaring and triumphant karaoke rendition of Madonna's 'Like a Prayer'. Phoebe Gould then told the artist the true date of her birth: 12 July 2005. The artist took a long moment to comprehend the fact she was almost three months younger than she thought she was. Then Phoebe Gould carried on.

Anna and John had divorced in 2012, she said, citing an inability to jointly overcome multiple traumas relating to the shocking and inexplicable disappearance of their youngest daughter in 2005. John Gould, Phoebe said, was currently unemployed and living alone on a property in Serpentine, fifty-five kilometres south-east of Perth.

'Is he all right?' I ask.

'Not really,' Phoebe says. 'He's a bit of a mess, the old man. Drinks a bit. Doesn't talk to no one. He doesn't even know I'm here talking to you.'

'You didn't tell him?'

'I wanted to see how it went first. If it went bad, I don't think he could take it. That might be the last straw, ya know what I mean? He blames himself for what happened.'

'This isn't going bad, is it?' I ask.

'No,' Phoebe replies. Her smile is pure light. Phoebe means 'light'. 'This is going good,' she says.

I lean across the table. 'Tell me what happened, Phoebe,' I say. 'Tell me what she did.'

Phoebe pulls a lock of brown hair behind her ear. Moves her chair closer to the table. 'Three days after Christmas 2005,' she says. 'It was the hottest day recorded that year. Mum and Dad took us to the Canning Vale Aqua Park, along with half the population of Perth. You were just a bub. Six months old. I was two and a half. You were sleeping in a baby capsule under a portable gazebo. They were about to take us home. But Dad fucked up ... and ... it was the easiest fuck-up in the world. Mum had taken me to the women's toilets to get changed. Place was packed with people. Dad saw some bloke he knew from high school. He got up and chased after him for a stretch, left you in the capsule under the shade. So fucking dumb and simple. He got talking longer than he should have. By the time he came back' – she scratches her head, like she still can't believe it – 'you ... were ... just ... *gone.*'

Gone. For eighteen years. Gone too soon. Gone too long. So that's it, then. It's all so sickeningly mundane and simple. Poor John Gould. Gone all messed-up and reclusive because of me and Erica Finlay. Gone. In the head. John Inthedark. John Intheguilt. *John Inthehole.* Bloke never leaves his house. Never got over fucking up like that. It destroyed his marriage, that one mistake. Erica destroyed my life and his life and my real mum's life. That stranger who claimed she was my mum. Can see her in my head now. Can draw the moment in my head. Ink and pen on paper. *Erica with the Baby in Her Arms.* Erica Finlay disappearing through a summer crowd of people in their swimmers. A sleeping baby tucked up tight in her shoulder.

'She always vowed to protect me from monsters,' I say.

I see her placing the baby in an infant's car seat. See her driving that baby on an endless highway, going nowhere and anywhere across Australia.

'But she was the monster, Phoebe,' I say. 'My mum was the monster.' And I feel like I'm going to vomit up the bacon and eggs and toast Danny made me for breakfast.

'Why would anyone do something so cruel?' Phoebe asks.

And I know the only answer to that. 'Love,' I say. 'She needed someone to love.'

And Phoebe tells me how for six months or more my name was in every newspaper and every television and radio news broadcast in Perth. Journalists were parked outside Anna and John Gould's house for months, waiting for fresh leads on the tragic and shocking story of the missing baby girl with the name that everybody knows except me. Phoebe speaks of the private sadness. No solutions. No completions. No endings.

'You haven't told me what my name is,' I say.

'I wasn't sure you wanted me to tell you,' Phoebe says.

Phoebe understands. Phoebe is thoughtful. Phoebe is light.

'I want you to tell me,' I say. 'But I also want you to know that I can't be the person you're about to say I am. Whatever that name is, it's not gonna be me, Phoebe. That name will have nothing to do with who I am and where I've been and where I'm going. I don't want to spend the rest of my life being the girl who was stolen. Some fuckin' trauma-baby people remember from a headline. Those cops in Perth will shout that name from the rooftops and they'll poke cameras and lights in my face and I'll have to spend the rest of my life talking about pain and hurt and sorrow that doesn't belong to me. They'll take the woman I wanna be and replace her with someone I am not. I swear there's someone great inside me, Phoebe, and I know for sure that they'll kill her if I let them. They'll dissolve her. They'll make her disappear. And I'll never get her back. Never see her again. Does that make any sense to you, Phoebe? Or is that just the screwiest thing you've ever heard in your life?'

Tears in Phoebe's eyes.

Tears in my eyes, too. 'I'm sorry, Phoebe,' I say. 'I'm so sorry for what happened. I'm so sorry for Anna's pain. I'm so sorry that John's a mess and I promise I'll do all I can to help make him better again, but I can't be that—'

'Stop,' Phoebe says. 'Stop.' She shakes her head.

I stop.

'You don't have to explain anything to me,' she says. And tears fall down Phoebe's face. She drops her head and wipes her eyes with the sleeve of her T-shirt. A deep breath. Reaches across the table with both hands, shelters my hands beneath hers.

'Listen to me,' she says. 'I'll call you whatever you need me to call you, as long as I can call you my sister.' And she makes me cry and laugh at the same time and I briefly choke on my joy. I'm so happy she just said that, because I've only known my sister for an hour and already I know I love her more than all the daisies in Denmark and all the lollipops in London.

She leans over and says a name softly. I see it before I hear it. I see the name fall from her lips. A given name. A simple name. Short. Four letters. One of those sweet, rolling-easy-off-the-tongue four-letter words like 'hope' and 'moon' and 'care' and 'snow' and 'home' and 'love'.

'Iris,' she says. 'That's the name you were born with. Iris Gould.'

And the name hangs in the invisible space between us.

I grip my sister's hands tighter. 'Iris,' I say, rolling the name around my mouth. No doubt about it. 'It's a beautiful name.'

My sister nods and smiles. Phoebe Gould, blinding me with her light.

'It means "rainbow",' she says.

I know. And my mind lights up temporarily with a cinema showreel of another whole life I might have lived as Iris Gould. Schoolyard Iris and wedding-aisle Iris and dinner-table Iris with mashed potato and bowls of vegetables and three perfect kids in the suburbs. Iris Gould makes me smile.

'It's beautiful, Phoebe,' I say. 'But it's not who I am.'

She takes a breath. Nods her head in understanding. Fingers playing nervously around the base of her drinking glass.

'So, who are you?'

And I think it's right that my sister should be the first to hear it. So I lean over the table and whisper a name in her ear.

Who Are You?

March 2024

Pen and ink on paper

The last great black and white sketch of the artist's early Girls on the Lam Period. She transitioned to oils on canvas soon after this image, moving into her blindingly colourful Rainbow Period. A magazine journalist once asked the artist about the origins of this sketch, suggesting it was a mirror image to the very sketch that opens this exhibition, *The Tyrannosaurus Waltz*.

'It's the same scene, but the monster is missing,' the journalist noted.

'That's right,' the artist said.

'You destroyed the monster?' the journalist asked.

'Yes, I did.'

'How did you do it?' the journalist probed.

'With a pen,' the artist replied.

Who am I? I'm the girl sitting at a desk in the South Brisbane office of Dr Rose Tanaka, senior lecturer at the Queensland College of Art. She's the woman with dyed blonde hair and a bright yellow jumpsuit. She's flipping through a plastic portfolio of my ink-on-paper sketches and she's laughing at my art. But laughing in a good way. Laughing the way I laugh when I see shooting stars or green ants carrying leaves that must be four times their body weight.

She stops on a sketch I entitled *Big Dumb Fuckin' Cocaine Meathead Boy Monster Idiot*. 'What's this one about?' she asks.

'I used to deliver drugs around the city for a woman named Flora Box,' I say. 'This was a cocaine drop for four university boys in the Marriott Hotel.'

'Why do they have faces like wolves?'

'Not wolves,' I say. 'Jackals. Death dogs. That's just how they seemed to me. Just boys trying to act like Egyptian gods.'

Rose flips to another image. *She's Got the Whole World in Her Hands*. My sketch of Roslyn holding the globe keyring.

'A key?' Rose asks.

I nod. 'I used to live in a scrapyard by the river,' I say. 'My neighbour Roslyn gave me that key because it opened the back of a yellow Holden Gemini that contained the answers I needed to unlock the truth of my past.'

'What did you find there?' Rose asks.

'An elephant,' I reply.

Rose thinks about asking another question but seems to reconsider and returns her attention to my portfolio. A portrait of Ursula. 'Where do you want to go with your work?' she asks.

'What do you mean?'

She turns to an image I called *I Don't Need You to Let Me*. 'What sort of artist would you like to be? What are your dreams?'

'I want to have a career so important and influential that when I die at the age of ninety-five they hold a posthumous exhibition of my work in New York's Metropolitan Museum of Art,' I say. 'A renowned art critic will lead tour groups through this exhibition, and he'll tell the stories of my life and work.'

I point at Rose Tanaka. 'He'll talk about you,' I say.

'He will?'

'Of course he will,' I say. 'He'll talk about you and people will learn about how inspiring you were to me in this very moment.'

'They will?'

'Of course they will. Because this is the moment when you changed everything for me.'

'I did?' Rose beams.

'You did.'

Rose laughs. 'Well, I'm glad I was able to do my bit.'

She flips to a pen and ink portrait of a woman. The older sister Kylie Minogue never had. Short hair, like some gutter kid from 1800s London.

'Mmmmm,' she says.

'What is it?' I ask.

She studies the image. 'This is a stunning portrait,' she says. 'It's truer than the rest. This one hurt, didn't it?'

I shrug.

Rose Tanaka looks at the bottom of the page. Reads the title I gave the sketch. *'Erica Finlay.'* Lifts her head and stares into my eyes.

'Who is she?' Rose asks.

I think on this for a moment before I give my answer.

'She was my mother,' I say.

Rose runs a finger along the name I've scribbled at the bottom of the artwork.

'Interesting name?' she says. 'Cool name for an artist.'

I nod.

'But that's not your real name, is it?' she asks.

I look at the name. 'It's real to me,' I say.

She smiles, stares at me with one raised eyebrow. Closes my portfolio. 'Well, you certainly show great potential. And it's very obvious to me that art has brought benefits to your somewhat … *unusual* … upbringing.'

As Rose talks, I reach into the black Adidas backpack at my feet.

'My only remaining concern is the question of how you plan to pay for the full three-year course,' Rose continues. 'We can certainly help with connecting you to various tertiary assistance prog—'

Before she can finish, I drop a closed potato sack on her desk. 'Do you guys take cash?' I ask.

*

Almost two hours later and I'm standing by the fence of a council park in Oxley, eleven stops from Central along the Ipswich train line. I'm watching Christina da Silva moving joyously back and forth on a playground rocker made to look like a yellow and black bumblebee. Brave Christina who survived the river, just like I did. Her mother, Bless da Silva, sits on a park bench by the playground, sipping a takeaway coffee as she thumb-scrolls the screen of her iPhone. Mostly young mums here today. And birds. Willie wagtails. Noisy miners. Scrub turkeys kicking up bark that's there to cushion noisy human minors when they fall from the monkey bars.

I stroll across the playground. Stop when I'm less than two metres from the park bench. Stand and stare at Bless da Silva, who hasn't noticed me yet. Wait ten long seconds for her to notice me, but she doesn't.

'Excuse me,' I say.

She looks up. There's a bright sun over my shoulders and it makes her squint. She puts a hand above her eyes to ease the glare.

'I'm sorry to bother you,' I say. 'But I need to tell you something about my mum.'

I take two steps closer to her so she can see me better. And in that moment she realises who I am. I can see that now on her face because what I see is fear.

'Do you remember me?' I ask.

She nods, smiles nervously.

'I remember everything about you,' I say. 'I think about you and Christina every day of my life.' I turn to Christina on the rocking bumblebee, her head hanging back over her shoulders, eyes to the blue sky. 'It was my mum who saved her,' I say.

'I know,' Bless says.

'I need to tell you something about her,' I say. 'Do you mind if I tell you something about her?'

I must look unhinged. Screwy as all get-out. Tears welling in my eyes. I must look damaged and broken, but I'm really not. I'm just trying to be true.

Bless studies my face for a moment then slides along the park bench. Nods to a spot beside her. 'Please,' she says, softly, 'sit down.'

I sit beside her. Hands by my side, fingers tapping nervously on the bench.

'I need to apologise to you,' I say.

'You've got nothing to apologise to me for,' Bless says.

My eyes on Christina. The girl howling joyously and wolf-like at something in the sky.

'Yes, I do,' I say. 'I hated you for what happened to my mum.' I nod at Christina on the rocker. 'I hated her, too. I was so angry. I hated the deal that was made. My mum for your daughter. I felt like I got the raw end of that deal.'

Then I cry because I see Christina's smile and that smile is life and that smile is art and love and future and beauty and more life again.

'But that's not true at all because that deal was fair and it was fair because your daughter is the most beautiful thing I've ever held in my arms,' I say.

And I'm weeping profusely now. And so is Bless. She's weeping in silence. No noise to her crying.

'And I think my mum wanted to go, anyway,' I say. 'Because she had done something terrible to me and I think she didn't want to stick around to watch me discover what that something was.'

I wipe my wet eyes with my forearm. Deep breaths. Don't stop talking now. 'She wasn't really my mother,' I say. 'My real mother's name was Anna Gould. Anna Gould was a very good woman and a deeply loving mum, though I never got to see her be one. She died of pancreatic cancer when I was twelve. She died in a Perth hospital room, and I was four thousand kilometres away in a van with four flat tyres beside the Brisbane River.'

I point to Christina. She's pulling herself out of the bumblebee rocker and running to a fort made of wooden planks and thick knotted ropes.

'The woman who saved Christina that day was named Erica Finlay,' I say. 'Erica is a beautiful name. It means "ever powerful". But she wasn't always powerful around this monster she was once married to. This monster really messed her up. He kinda turned her into a monster herself, and then she did something really messed up to me. And I've been trying to hate her for this thing she did. I've been really trying, Bless. But I can't. Because I still love her too much and I know that's fucked up, but I can't help it. We ran too far together. We spent too many nights side by side. And I've been thinking of ways that I can square it all in my head and be able to live with it and the best thing I can think of is … *her.*' My finger pointing at Bless's daughter. Christina. 'The best thing I can think of is how beautiful your daughter is.'

Bless nods. Slides closer to me across the bench.

'I came here a while ago and I saw you two together,' I continue. 'And you looked so beautiful that it made me feel better about it all. It made me feel like it was worth going through whatever I was going through if that girl there was that happy. If she remains that happy throughout her entire life, then I can live with whatever the fuck it is I have to live with.'

Bless puts a hand on my thigh and grips it tight. Sits up. 'Look at me,' she says. Puts her hands on my shoulders, stares into my eyes. 'I cannot promise you she will always be this happy,' she says. 'But you have my word that, for as long as I have breath, I will give her a life where she will have every chance to be every bit as happy as she is right now.'

And I close my eyes to stop my tears and Bless da Silva wraps her arms around me trying to stop those tears, too.

'And now I need to tell you something,' she says. 'I know what it's like.' She makes a rotating motion with her right hand. 'Being with the monster, I mean.'

Then she cries and covers her eyes with the palms of her hands.

'It wasn't my fault,' she eventually says. 'I'm so sorry for what happened to you. But I need you to know it wasn't my fault.' She wipes her eyes and closes her fist. 'He pushed it. He pushed the pram. I don't think he meant to push it into that river. I don't think he realised we were on such a steep slope. Just another one of his schoolboy tantrums. That stupid, angry man. But I had to tell all those cops it was my fault. I told 'em I forgot to put the brake down.' She grits her teeth and makes a fist with her right hand. Bangs her fist on her thigh two times. 'Like I was some spacey fuckin' ditz who let her kid roll into the water.'

She drops her head and weeps freely. Lifts her gaze briefly to make sure her daughter can't see her crying, then turns her head away. 'And I knew they all knew that was bullshit, and it made me so sick inside because we were all letting him off the hook. His mother thinks he's a hero. She didn't question it for a second. She thinks he died trying to save his baby girl and that's that. Nothing more to say. And sometimes I want to scream in her face and tell her how a woman died because of him.'

Then she wraps her arms around me. Hugs me so tight I can feel her tears on my neck.

'Your mum saved my daughter's life,' Bless says. 'And she saved *me* by doing what she did.'

I weep into her shoulder. Then our embrace is broken by the sound of Christina da Silva running wildly towards her mother. She crashes into Bless's kneecaps and climbs onto her lap with the same enthusiasm with which she climbed the playground fort.

'Awww, Mummy's crying,' Christina says. Pats her mum's head. 'Don't cryyyyyyyy, Mummy.'

Bless smiles, wipes her eyes. 'Mummy's not crying anymore, Christina,' she says, wrapping her arms around her daughter. Then she turns Christina's body to face mine. 'Now, Christina, can you introduce yourself to my friend here?'

Christina waves a chubby right hand at me. Giggles and jumps up and down on the spot for no reason and then climbs over her mum's thighs to stand between Bless and me. She runs a hand through my hair. Her gentle palm and her soft little fingers rest inexplicably on my cheek. 'You're pretty,' she says. And then for no reason at all she rests her forehead against my forehead and stares into my eyes with her bottom lip turned down. The kid must be cracked. Screwy as all get-out. I know a loop when I see one. This perfect little loop.

She's concentrating on something. Something in my eyes. 'I can see me in your eyes,' she says.

She sees her reflection. She's looking into a mirror. She pulls her head back a couple of centimetres but still stares. And I nearly cry when I stare back into her eyes because I can see in them a hundred possible versions of who Christina da Silva is going to be. I see her graduating from high school. I see her climbing mountains. I see her crossing oceans and deserts. I see her in a labour ward, holding a newborn baby. I see her in Paris beneath the Eiffel Tower. I see her dancing. I see her building a snowman with her son. I see her beneath a Christmas tree with her daughter. I see her at eighteen when she's young and beautiful and at ninety-five when she's old and wise. I see her. The pure and uncut meaning of her life. Hitting me in waves. The meaning of life through the eyes of a child, beginning to middle to end in thirty seconds.

'I'm Christina Tadhana da Silva,' she says. 'Who are you?'

Who am I? I am love. I am forgiveness. I am memory. I am misfortune. I am pain. I am art. I am friendship. I am family. I am sorrow. I am hate. I am rage. I am beauty. I am wonder. I am ink. I am blood. I am learning. I am longing. I am action. I am courage. I am laughter. I am joy. I am gratitude. I am fire. I am water. I am dirt. I am past. I am future. I am fate. I am taken. I am lost. I am returned. I am found. I am heard. I am seen. I am home. I am here.

'I'm Lola,' I say. 'Lola Inthemirror.'

Acknowledgements

The river is a metaphor, of course. The river is whatever stuff you carry inside that turns and stirs beneath your skin. Not trying to be all clever-like, just trying to say something about the people who pull us out of the river. You, dear reader, pull me out of the river. Thank you. Catherine Milne, you pull me out of the river. Scott Forbes, Pam Dunne, Madeleine James, Darren Holt, Alice Wood, Laura Benson, you pull me out, too. Every word, every cut, every fix, every save, every idea, every dazzling cover now feels to me like another act of friendship. Thank you, beloved teammates.

Paul Heppell, your love and care for Lola is evident in every glorious black-ink line you have threaded through this book. You wrote a story of your own with your profoundly beautiful images. Pen and ink *and love* on paper. Thank you from me, dear friend, and thank you from Lola.

Thank you to the tireless staff and clients of 3rd Space, Brisbane – formerly the 139 Club – for so generously allowing me to document the work of your extraordinary drop-in centre across a five-year period between 2013 and 2018. Parts of every humbling and heartening encounter I have had beneath your sheltering and utterly essential roof can be found inside this book.

Thank you, Mandy McAlister. You said something extraordinary to me beside the Brisbane river many years ago, and it inspired my favourite passages of this book.

Fiona, Beth and Sylvie, you pull me out and you push me up. It all feels elemental to me now. Not trying to be all clever-like, just recognising earth and air and fire when I see it. Colourful, with all my heart.

A Note from the Illustrator, Paul Heppell

It was Eli and Slim that got to me. The two of them meeting for the last time, sitting side by side, facing outwards, fishing, saying everything there is to be said. All the best conversations are had that way – in a car, at a table drawing or doing Lego, on a lounge playing video games – side by side, facing outwards.

I first read that perfect scene at a kid's birthday party. To avoid awkward social interactions, I'd taken a book, a pen and a sketchbook. The book that day, *Boy Swallows Universe*, had me openly weeping, and I immediately felt the need to draw that moment, with those two characters on the bridge in the rain. The writing was so perfect and there was nothing that needed to be added, no flourishes, no weird creatures – just two people sharing their hearts.

After I put the drawing up on Instagram, my wife, who had insisted I read *Boy Swallows Universe*, made me edit the post and tag the author. That's how I first came into the orbit of the creative star that is Trent Dalton. Gracious as always, he messaged me, and I promised to give him the drawing.

During lockdown, Trent rang me to talk about making prints of the drawing to give to the cast of the Queensland Theatre stage production of *Boy Swallows Universe*. Being an idiot, I tried in vain to wind up the conversation so that I could get back to a work meeting. Luckily, Trent is not the sort of bloke who is easily put off his stride, and he eventually brought the conversation round to the idea of collaborating one day, on a short story or a magazine piece. I swear I heard a physical pop in his head when he said, 'I mean it, let's do something.'

For me, the experience of working on *Lola in the Mirror* has been a fairytale, or like one of those Dickens novels where an orphan is rescued from obscurity. How else to describe getting a text from your favourite author out of the blue to say, 'Hey, interested in doing some illustrations for my new novel?' How else to explain the magic of being told the plot over the phone by Trent the master storyteller and instantly feeling you knew the character as soon as he said, 'And she draws.'

I feel so honoured to have played a small part in this amazing work. I will forever be grateful for the leap of faith you took, Trent, by giving me a go. Your constant enthusiasm, encouragement and amazing creativity have been so inspiring, and I am so fortunate to have experienced a never-to-be-repeated creative endeavour like this one.

I am also thankful to everyone who has ever bought, liked on socials, or said a kind word about my art. Special thanks to 'The Three' for being my trusted critics and biggest cheer squad, and to my three beautiful children, Will, Ollie and Noosh – 'You'll do things I only ever dreamed about.' And thanks most of all to my wife, Nerida. These drawings would not exist without you. I love you with all my heart.

'I'm so fucking lucky.'

www.birdsinsuits.com
Instagram: @pheppell

About the Author

TRENT DALTON is a two-time Walkley Award–winning journalist and the international bestselling author of *Boy Swallows Universe* and *All Our Shimmering Skies*. His books have sold more than 1.2 million copies in Australia alone.

ALSO BY **TRENT DALTON**

THE INTERNATIONAL BESTSELLER HERALDED AS
"THE BEST BOOK I READ THIS DECADE"
BY SHARON VAN ETTEN IN *ROLLING STONE*

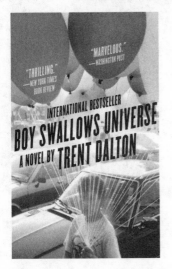

"Hypnotizes you with wonder, and then hammers you with heartbreak. . . . Eli's remarkably poetic voice and his astonishingly open heart take the day. They enable him to carve out the best of what's possible from the worst of what is, which is the miracle that makes this novel marvelous."
—*WASHINGTON POST*

"Achingly beautiful and poetic in its melancholy, *All Our Shimmering Skies* is a majestic and riveting tale of curses and the true meaning of treasure."
—*BOOKLIST* (starred review)

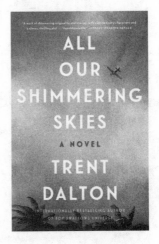